Night Vision

ALSO BY ELLEN HART

The Iron Girl

An Intimate Ghost

Immaculate Midnight

No Reservations Required

Death on a Silver Platter

The Merchant of Venus

Slice and Dice

Hunting the Witch

Wicked Games

Murder in the Air

Robber's Wine

The Oldest Sin

Faint Praise

A Small Sacrifice

For Every Evil

The Little Piggy Went to Murder

A Killing Cure

Stage Fright

Vital Lies

Hallowed Murder

Night Vision

A JANE LAWLESS MYSTERY

ELLEN HART

 ST. MARTIN'S MINOTAUR ✠ NEW YORK

NIGHT VISION. Copyright © 2006 by Ellen Hart. All rights reserved. Printed in the United States of America. No part of this book may be used or reproduced in any manner whatsoever without written permission except in the case of brief quotations embodied in critical articles or reviews. For information, address St. Martin's Press, 175 Fifth Avenue, New York, N.Y. 10010.

www.minotaurbooks.com

Library of Congress Cataloging-in-Publication Data

Hart, Ellen.
    Night vision : a Jane Lawless mystery / Ellen Hart.
        p. cm.
    ISBN-13: 978-0-312-37443-3
    ISBN-10: 0-312-37443-7
    1. Lawless, Jane (Fictitious character)—Fiction. 2. Women detectives—Minnesota—Minneapolis—Fiction. 3. Lesbians—Fiction. 4. Stalkers—Fiction. 5. Minneapolis (Minn.)—Fiction. I. Title

PS3558.A6775 N4 2006
8138.54—dc22

                                                        2006048348

First St. Martin's Minotaur Paperback Edition: December 2007

10 9 8 7 6 5 4 3 2 1

For Kathy,
my heart, my life

Cast of Characters

Jane Lawless: Owner of the Lyme House restaurant and the Xanadu Club in Minneapolis.

Cordelia Thorn: Creative Director for the Allen Grimby Repertory Theater in St. Paul.

Hattie Thorn Lester: Cordelia's three-and-a-half-year-old niece.

Joanna Kasimir: David's sister. Actress. Old friend of Cordelia's.

David Carlson: Joanna's brother. Interior designer in Atlanta. Old friend of Jane's.

Faye O'Halleron: Retired hairdresser. Resides at Linden Lofts.

Milan Mestrovik: Wine merchant. Resides at Linden Lofts.

Hillary Schinn: Aspiring journalist.

Freddy Kasimir: Joanna's ex-husband.

Gordon Luberman: Joanna's ex-boyfriend.

Kenzie Mullroy: Professor of cultural anthropology at Chadwick State, in Chadwick, Nebraska. Jane's girlfriend.

A. J. Nolan: Ex-cop. Private investigator. Good friend of Jane's.

Brandy Becker: IHOP waitress. Gordon's girlfriend.

What lies behind us and what lies before us
are tiny matters compared to what lies
within us.

—Ralph Waldo Emerson

Night Vision

1

When it came to leaving, Joanna always had to work her way through alternating layers of anxiety and fear and an ever-present hungry itch, one that whispered in her ear that it was time to go back out into the world again and prove she was a survivor. In the past fourteen years, her house overlooking Lake Pend Oreille had become not just a home but a safe haven. She'd never felt comfortable on display in Hollywood. She'd always looked upon her life there as a necessary evil.

Sandpoint was a town of some seven thousand people, situated at the tip of the Idaho Panhandle, just fifty miles from the Canadian border. When Joanna had first come here after the trial, it had seemed like the middle of nowhere, and that's just where she wanted to be.

Even before the trial, Joanna had been looking to get out of L.A. She hated the phoniness, the professional promises so easily made and broken, the casual lies, and the ignorant arrogance that came with power and privilege. Every morning she'd wake in her home in Bel Air with the same sense that something was breaking inside her. She was surrounded by friends, fans, business associates, and an adoring public, and yet she was hugely—cavernously—lonely.

For a time, she toyed with the idea of moving back to the Twin

Cities, back to her hometown of St. Paul, but that felt too much like failure. She wasn't the young, eager, innocent Jo Carlson any longer—theater major at the U of M, aspiring actress, starry-eyed wannabe. She was Joanna Kasimir, an internationally known film star with dozens of movie credits—and an Academy Award and two Golden Globes resting on her mantel. She could still remember the dreams she'd had as a young woman. She'd lived on little else for years. How could she have known what the flip side of those dreams would be? When she finally left L.A., she knew without a doubt that she was running for her life.

But life had a habit of never traveling in straight lines. It turned out that she wasn't running away so much as she was running toward something better. She'd found her mountain hideaway near Sandpoint two months after leaving L.A., bought it on the spot. She was as much seduced by the cathedral feeling of the big log house as by the tall timbers surrounding it, the view of the lake below, the fresh air, and the sense of peace all around her. She could make a stand here. She would dig in and see what life was really about. Amazing as it seemed, she'd come to love this place with the same passion she felt for acting. She'd never felt lonely here, not even for a day.

Afternoon sunlight flooded the living room as Joanna turned from the deck and walked back inside. She stroked her blond hair behind her ears, glancing down at her grubby jeans and T-shirt. She'd have to get used to wearing presentable clothing again while she was in Minnesota. The limo was scheduled for ten tomorrow morning. It would take her to the airfield where she'd board a private jet. She was pretty much packed, although she wanted to look through her closet one more time.

Heading up to her bedroom, she cringed when she saw the four extralarge suitcases spread open on her bed. Joanna Kasimir, the actress, adored beautiful clothing. It was all part of the split personality thing Joanna had been living with ever since she'd moved to Sandpoint. She was part small-town resident and general recluse, and part actress, a woman who could still command an audience and who still had the fire in her gut to act.

Cordelia Thorn, an old friend and the current creative director at the Allen Grimby Repertory Theater in St. Paul, had offered her a part she'd been wanting to play for years—Martha in Edward Albee's *Who's Afraid of Virginia Woolf?* The AGRT was one of the finest regional theaters in the nation, so it was an honor to be asked to join the company for a limited engagement. Joanna relished the challenge of bringing something new and definitive to the role. If nothing else, shrews were fabulous characters to play. At forty-seven, Joanna had long ago faced the fact that the film scripts she was being offered were, to put it bluntly, crap. The legitimate stage had become the refuge of the aging actress.

As she started to close the suitcases, the phone rang. Stepping over to the nightstand, she picked up the receiver. "Hello?" she said, standing with a hand on her hip.

"Joanna? It's Diego Veras."

Diego was her brother's boyfriend. She hadn't heard from either of them in more than a year. She felt a pang of guilt for not keeping in better touch but pushed it away. "Hi," she said. Her first instinct was to assume that something was wrong, but she felt it was best to go with a neutral question. "How are you?"

"Fine. Well, not so fine, actually." Diego had a heavy Spanish accent. He and his family had moved to California from Buenos Aires when Diego was fifteen. Diego and Joanna's brother, David, had met when David was in L.A. visiting her—must have been back in the early eighties. Diego was Joanna's age, a few years older than David, already an established architect at the time. "What's going on?"

"Have you heard from David?"

"No. Why? Is he okay?"

"To be honest, Joanna, I don't know. He . . . well, he left me. I thought he'd go off for a few days, think about it, and come back. He's done it before. But he's been gone a long time and I'm worried."

"How long?"

"Almost a month."

Joanna sat down on the edge of the bed. "Are you saying you have *no* idea where he is?"

"Yeah. No idea."

"Was he angry when he left?"

"Not exactly. *I* was. I told him things had to change or . . ." His voice trailed off.

"Or what? Tell me!"

"Or I was leaving him. Look, I blame myself, okay? I shouldn't have lost it like I did, but you don't know what it's been like living with him this last year. You haven't exactly been the world's greatest sister, Jo, so I don't think you're entitled to a lecture."

If he wanted to make her feel like a total shit, he'd succeeded. "He didn't say anything about where he was headed?"

"After I left for work one morning, he just took off. When I got home that night, his car was gone, and so were a bunch of his clothes. He took maybe five thousand from the wall safe. I had a guy run a check of his credit cards. He's not using them. He obviously doesn't want me to know where he is. I've talked to our friends all over the country, but nobody's seen him. I'm scared, Joanna. In the shape he was in, anything could've happened."

"What's that mean?"

"He's not well. Don't ask me what's wrong, because I don't know. I'm not even sure David knows."

"That doesn't make any sense."

"Welcome to my life."

She pressed her fingers to the bridge of her nose, closed her eyes. "Call the police, Diego."

"I did. He's officially listed as a missing person, but so what? It's not like they go looking for him."

"Then hire someone private."

He sighed. "I thought about that. But I keep hoping he'll come back."

"If *you* don't hire someone—and I mean *today*—I will."

"Okay, okay. You're right. But I wanted to check with you first, just in case he headed your way. I didn't really think he had."

Score another point for Joanna. She was a lousy sister.

"Can you think of anyone he might contact?" asked Diego. "I've called all our friends. Nobody's seen or heard from him."

Downstairs, the doorbell rang.

Joanna put her hand over the mouthpiece and shouted, "Annie, will you get that?" Annie Thompson was her live-in housekeeper and cook. Returning to Diego, she said, "I don't know. I'll have to think about it."

"Well, think fast, okay? I'm going crazy here. If you hear from him, you'll call me, yes?"

"Of course I will. You do the same." She explained that she was leaving for Minneapolis in the morning. She gave him the phone number of the loft where she would be staying. He already had her cell.

As she hung up, Annie sailed through the bedroom door carrying a large package wrapped in bright pink paper.

"Flowers, Joanna. I can smell them right through the wrapping." Annie was an energetic, sentimental, soft-bodied woman. Her mother was from Mexico, an illegal until her father, a rancher from Utah, had married her. She set the package on the dresser and stood back, waiting for Joanna to open it.

Joanna's stomach still contracted with dread at the sight of a flower delivery.

Ripping off the paper, her breath caught in her throat. It wasn't precisely like the flowers Gordon used to send, but it was close enough.

"Something wrong?" asked Annie. "Here, you should read the card." She removed a small pink envelope from the center of the arrangement.

With shaking hands, Joanna opened it and read:

> *Roses are the flowers of love.*
> *Can't wait to see you!*
> *Did you miss me?*

There was no signature, but then, it wasn't necessary.

"Who brought these?" demanded Joanna.

Annie seemed startled. "A delivery guy."

"What did he look like?"

"Tall, I think. Yes, tall. White. Middle-aged."

"Was it a delivery truck or a private car?"

"I didn't notice."

Joanna rushed to a window overlooking the front of the house. In the distance, she could see an SUV kicking up dust as it sped away down the hill.

"Did I do something wrong, Joanna? Please tell me! Are you upset?"

Panicked was more like it. Joanna grabbed the cordless phone off the bed and punched in the number of her lawyer in L.A. She was amazed to realize she still knew it by heart.

When the secretary answered, Joanna announced who she was and demanded to talk to Gershen Blumenthal.

"He's in a meeting. If you give me your number—"

"Get him out of the goddamn meeting! This is an emergency!"

While she waited, she glanced at the flowers. "I'm okay, Annie. But get those out of here. Dump them in the garbage."

"But—"

"Do what I tell you!"

A moment later, Blumenthal came on the line, his voice as booming and hardy as ever. "Joanna, what a nice surprise—"

She cut him off. "You've got to *do* something!"

"I do?"

"It's happening again."

"Joanna, if you'd just calm down and—"

"For God's sake, don't patronize me, Gersh! You've got to help me. I can't take this again!"

The lawyer was silent. Then, "What are you saying? *Be specific.*"

"Gordon." She swallowed hard and closed her eyes. "He's back."

2

Jane Lawless stood in her tiny upstairs office/dressing room at the Xanadu Club, gazing at a full-length mirror on the wall, straightening her black bow tie.

Back in the days when the club had been a movie theater, her office had been the projection room. She'd asked the architect who'd redesigned the interior to enlarge the projection window so that she could view the dining room and the dance floor. He'd not only enlarged it but also turned the small square window into a four-foot-wide circle. Viewed from the floor, it looked like part of a large starburst design. From the office, Jane could look down on a glittering subterranean world. The only public area she couldn't see was the long bar at the front of the house.

Jane had been a restaurateur in the Twin Cities for almost eighteen years. Her second venture, the Xanadu Club, had been open for just seven months, but already it had become Uptown's premiere nightclub. For the six months prior to its opening, Jane had been putting in nine-thousand-hour workweeks. She'd spent only a few hours a week at the Lyme House, her other restaurant. With so much to do, she could easily have gone tilt without the occasional afternoon off. If she'd had a brain in her head, she probably would have gone home and slept, but she'd been nursing two compelling new interests that could easily have captured all her attention if she hadn't kept a tight rein on herself.

Jane's father, who was a semiretired criminal defense attorney in St. Paul, had surprised the entire family last fall by going out and buying a Cessna Turbo Skylane. Years ago, he'd owned a Piper Archer, which he used mainly for business. But at the urging of his girlfriend, Marilyn, he'd sold it in 1989. Jane's dad had gone on to marry Marilyn, but when they'd divorced last summer, her father couldn't wait to get inside his own plane again. On Jane's forty-fourth birthday, he'd driven her out to Flying Cloud field, ushered her into one of the hangars, and showed her the plane. As she sat inside the cockpit with him, he'd presented her with the gift of flying lessons.

Jane was both stunned and thrilled. This was a windfall she'd never expected but one she saw the benefits of immediately. A year or so ago, she'd begun dating a woman who taught cultural anthropology at Chadwick State College in Chadwick, Nebraska. Long-distance romances sucked big-time. Jane and Kenzie lived too far apart to get together very often. But with the introduction of a small plane, the distance problem was no longer such a huge issue. Jane could fly down in a couple of hours, even come home the same day. That is, if she ever got enough time off. She was starting to see the light of day at the new club. The worst kinks had been worked out. She planned to take a much-needed vacation in the next couple of weeks, and part, if not all, of that time would be spent with Kenzie.

Jane had finished ground school last October and begun flight training in November. During the winter and early spring, she'd managed to log sixty-seven hours in the air and had earned her private license in June. Right now she was in the process of getting her instrument pilot rating. She had access to the plane whenever her father wasn't using it.

And then there was that second new interest that kept tugging at her.

About a year and a half ago, Jane had met a retired cop who'd become a friend. A. J. Nolan owned a private investigation company in the Twin Cities, which he ran out of his house. Nolan didn't do it entirely for the money, which meant that, most of the time, he took only cases that interested him. He'd helped Jane out once during a very intense time in her life.

Nolan kept insisting that Jane was a natural at investigation. Every time they got together for dinner or coffee, which was fairly often, he'd press his point home. He told her that her restaurants were great, but if she didn't agree to work with him, train under him, her true calling in life would pass her by. If she'd been less busy she might have taken him up on it.

Jane stood for a moment longer in front of the mirror, checking the look of her chestnut hair pulled back into a French braid, her diamond stud earrings, the blush lipstick, the hint of eye shadow, and then she left her office and walked down the curving art deco stairs to the dining room. It was just after nine and the house was jumping. All around her she could feel the pulse of the restaurant—strong, deep, rhythmic. Her own heart beat to the same rhythm.

The live Xanadu orchestra played only one thing—twenties- and thirties-era jazz. To enter the club, patrons had to be dressed formally, either in clothes they owned themselves, or by renting inexpensive formal wear from a shop next door. Everything from top hats and canes to twenties- and thirties-era gowns and shoes was available. The crowd dancing the fox-trot on the dance floor looked astonishingly authentic. The dress code had been *the* major risk Jane and her partner, Judah Johanson, had taken. Minnesotans liked casual, virtually demanded it. But the risk had paid off. People seemed to relish dressing up for a night out on the town.

Drifting through the crowd in her white tux jacket, Jane felt like Humphrey Bogart at Rick's Café in the movie *Casablanca*. Both her white and black tuxes had been hand-fitted by a downtown shop specializing in handmade men's clothing. The jackets were specially contoured to highlight her slim figure. She was in the best shape of her life and didn't mind showing it off.

As she was about to run down to the kitchen, the head waiter caught her eye and motioned her over to one of the wait stations. "What's up?"

"There's a guy in the bar that's been asking about you. Last I looked, he was still there, sitting by himself nursing a beer. He seems kind of lost."

"Did you get a name?"

"Sorry."

"Okay. I'll take care of it."

Jane greeted a couple of returning customers, then headed for the front of the house. Pausing at the entrance to the bar, she scanned the long, narrow room to see if she recognized anyone. A man was seated at the far end, his back to her. He was wearing jeans and a dirty-looking yellow T-shirt. An empty beer glass rested next to his hand. His hair was short, sandy-blond, and uncombed. Since the back of him didn't ring any bells, she decided to see if the front did.

Snaking her way through the crowd, Jane approached the bar. She stepped up next to him and said, "I understand you were asking about me."

The man swiveled around. He glanced at the tux, then looked up at her face.

Jane's pulse quickened. "David?"

"Jane? God, you look fabulous!"

She wished she could say the same about him. "What are you doing here?"

"I—" He ran a hand over his mouth, then over the stubble on his cheeks. "I needed to get away from Atlanta for a while. Thought a road trip might be just what the doctor ordered."

He stood up a bit awkwardly, rubbed the flat of his hands against his thighs. They stared at each other for a couple seconds, then, spontaneously, they both broke out in silly grins.

David threw his arms around her.

"I don't believe it," she said, hugging him tight.

Lifting her off the floor, David spun her around. They were both laughing when he set her back down and looked her square in the eyes. "Janey, I don't know how's it's possible, but you're even more beautiful than you were in college."

If there was a man on this earth whom Jane had ever truly loved, it was David Carlson. They'd become friends in high school, when they were both juniors. Years later, when Jane began developing the Lyme House, her first restaurant, she'd asked David to design the interior. It was a tricky look. The two-story log structure sat on the southern edge of Lake Harriet. Jane wanted the interior to be both rustic and elegant. David had done an amazing job, so good that it had led to other jobs in the Twin Cities. His business was starting to pick up when, on a trip out to L.A. to visit his sister in the early eighties, he met Diego Veras, the man who would become his life partner. The next year, David and Diego moved to Atlanta, where they'd been living ever since.

Back in high school, they both knew they were gay, but since they spent so much time together, people figured they were a couple. They didn't see any reason to disabuse their friends of that notion because it worked for them. Cordelia, Jane's best friend, was the only one who knew the truth. They'd been each other's dates to their junior and senior proms. David had been her "steady" at sorority events in college. The fact was, David was a flat-out great guy. He was smart and funny, and a fabulous dancer. Any chance Jane got to dance with him, she took. On a deeper level, it was the truth about their lives, their shared concern for what their futures might hold, that had brought them together and kept them close.

"Where are you staying?" asked Jane.

"Well," he said, looking a little sheepish, "that's the thing. I was hoping I could bunk with you for a few days. You still have that great house in Linden Hills?"

"Sure."

"Mind if I sleep on your couch?"

"David, there are four bedrooms in that place. I think I can offer you a bed, unless you prefer couches."

"No. A bed would be good."

She couldn't believe he was here. "We've got so much to talk about, to catch up on."

"I know." The silly grin returned.

"Let me run up to my office and change out of these clothes. Have another beer on the house. I'll be back in a flash."

"I'll be here," said David, his smile disappearing as he sat back down on the stool and turned away from her.

3

Jane was getting some lemonade out of the refrigerator when David entered the kitchen. He'd stowed his duffel bag in one of the upstairs bedrooms and had returned downstairs after cleaning up in the bathroom. Mouse, Jane's chocolate Lab, sniffed his clothes thoroughly, ending with his nose pressed against the back of David's right hand.

"Boy, this dog loves the way I smell."

"He likes men's cologne. What are you wearing?"

"Royal Copenhagen."

"Well," said Jane, getting down two glasses from the cupboard, "what can I say? He's got good taste." As she poured the lemonade into one of the glasses, she glanced at David. He looked better, cleaner, but his eyes seemed glazed, off center. "How's Diego?"

He gave her a tight smile but didn't answer. "Hey, Janey, instead of that lemonade, I don't suppose you've got an extra beer around here."

"Sure," she said. She wondered if he really wanted the beer, or if he just wanted to change the subject. "Diego still thinking about building you guys that dream house in the country?" As she uncapped the bottle, she noticed David's jaw clench. She had a feeling that what he said next wouldn't be the full story.

"Yeah. He's still tinkering with the plans." He sat down on one of the kitchen chairs.

"How's his blood pressure? I know he was having some problems with it."

"It's good. Well, as good as possible under the circumstances. You know that old saying? Don't let your babies grow up to be architects."

Jane half smiled, half laughed.

"We're both busy—too busy. But I suppose I shouldn't complain." He tipped the bottle back and took several hefty swallows.

Jane sat down at the table across from him. She was tired but still so excited by his sudden appearance that she didn't want to let him go for fear he'd disappear on her. She had no idea why she felt that way, she just did.

David typically looked a good ten years younger than his actual age. He just had one of those faces. Dick Clark. Leonardo DiCaprio. Dorian Gray. He also played tennis regularly, which kept him fit, and he watched his diet. Tonight, however, he appeared much older than his forty-four years. His sandy blond hair was as gorgeous and thick as ever, but the stubble on his face didn't look trendy, just unkempt. Jane had never noticed any wrinkles around his eyes before, but tonight they were not only there, they were deep. He seemed physically exhausted and emotionally down. She hoped that he'd get around to telling her what was really going on sooner rather than later.

Holding the cold bottle to his cheek, David sighed. "I'm beat. I drove twelve hours today."

"You can sleep in tomorrow morning. I have to spend a few hours at the Lyme House, so I'll be out of here by eight. Cordelia and I are driving to Flying Cloud airport to pick up Joanna around three."

His head snapped up. "Joanna? My *sister,* Joanna? She's coming *here?*"

"Sure. You mean you didn't know?"

He shook his head slowly.

"Cordelia talked her into doing a play at the Allen Grimby. She'll be in town until the end of January."

He groaned. "My timing, as usual, is impeccable."

"Why do you say that?"

"Joanna and I haven't spoken in the past year. We seem to have a problem with snits. We're in the middle of one right now. She drives me crazy sometimes." He took another swig of beer. "I'd explain it to you, but my brain's fried. Besides, it's all stupid, like it usually is."

"How long do you plan to stay?"

"Haven't thought about it. But long enough so that we get a chance to talk. Where's Joanna staying?"

"At Linden Lofts, where Cordelia lives. Believe it or not, Cordelia is the current president of the tenants' association. One of the other tenants is in Europe right now. She's been looking to sublet her loft. Cordelia thought it would be great to have Joanna under the same roof, so she arranged everything."

He scratched the stubble on his cheek. "Look, Janey, if Joanna's coming, there's a chance she may insist I bunk with her. It's not that she'd want me to, it's just that she'd feel obliged. I'd rather stay with you."

"Not a problem. You can stay here as long as you like."

He smiled, took hold of her hand. "Do you believe in reincarnation?"

"No. Do you?"

He shook his head. "But if it's true, maybe in an earlier life we were straight and you and me, we were married. Even after all these years, our connection's still there, strong as ever. Kind of amazing, don't you think?"

"I do," she said, squeezing his hand.

"We'll talk more tomorrow. I'll tell you why I came."

"Deal," she said.

As they both stood, David pulled her into his arms. "Promise me that you'll listen—that you won't judge."

"Of course."

"It won't be easy, Jane. In some important ways, I'm not the man I used to be."

She backed up and took his head in her hands. "I don't know what's wrong, David. But together, you and me, we'll figure a way through it."

He scrutinized her face for a long moment, then smiled. "Okay. I knew coming here was the right thing to do."

During the night, Jane heard David get up and pass her bedroom door on his way downstairs. The radio burst on in the kitchen. Mouse growled at the clamor of pots and pans mixed with rock music. Jane was a little surprised that David didn't try harder to keep it down, but she told Mouse that everything was fine. David was probably hungry. She should have thought to offer him some food with that beer. She fell back asleep to the smell of frying bacon.

The next morning, Jane showered and dressed while David slept. It was supposed to be a cool fall day, so she slipped into a pair of jeans, a red flannel shirt, and the cowboy boots Kenzie had bought for her the first time Jane had gone down to Nebraska for a visit. After rummaging through her jewelry case, she settled on a pair of gold hoop earrings. She wound her long hair into a bun.

Mouse was itching to get outside, so she trotted down the stairs with him, telling him what he was about to have for breakfast. Even before she reached the bottom step, she saw that something was wrong. The slate floor in the foyer was covered by a thin film of water.

"Lord," she said, glancing to her right and seeing that the wood floor in the living room was also wet. Following the sound of a running faucet, she entered the kitchen. Not only was the sink overflowing, but it looked like a bomb had gone off. Most of the cupboards and drawers were open. The counter was covered with flour, eggshells, dirty bowls, and soiled towels. The stove was covered with dirty frying pans. It looked like David had made himself pancakes, eggs, and bacon, but in the process he'd trashed not only her kitchen but her entire house.

She turned off the faucet and stood looking at the mess, trying to absorb the shock. Mouse started to whine. "It's okay, boy," she said, absently patting his head. Except, it wasn't okay. What the hell had David been thinking?

Walking back out to the dining room, she bent down to examine the Oriental rug. It was soaked through. And the wood flooring was swelling at the edges. She didn't know the exact amount, but she guessed it would take thousands to repair the damage. As she stood up, trying to figure out what to do next, David trotted down the stairs, rubbing the sleep out of his eyes.

"Morning, Janey," he said, stepping into the water in his stocking feet. "Eeewh," he said, his face puckering. "What the hell happened?"

Jane's hands rose to her hips. "You left the faucet running."

He stared at her. "I *what?*"

"When you came down in the middle of the night to fix yourself something to eat."

His eyes opened wide. Pushing past her into the kitchen, he gasped when he saw the mess. "Oh, my God," he said, sucking in his breath.

Jane felt instantly sorry for him. He'd been so tired last night. If she'd just asked him if he was hungry, none of this would have happened.

"It was an accident, David. It's partly my fault."

"How do you figure that?" He looked at her with twitchy, embarrassed eyes. "I . . . I don't know what to say. God, Jane, I'm so sorry. I can't believe I did this. I'll pay to have it cleaned up. It won't cost you a penny. Don't worry about that for a second." He looked around him. "I shouldn't have come. I should never——"

"David, stop it." She put her hands on his shoulders, forced him to look at her. "It was an accident. It could have happened to anyone."

"No," he said, shaking his head. He moved away from her, looking like a man trying to fight his way out of a thick fog. "Let me take care of it. I know what needs to be done. I'll handle it all, okay? Let me do that much."

"David——"

"No arguments. This was my fault. You go to work and I'll stay here. Except——" He turned to face her. "The problem is, the flooring will need to be torn up, taken out before they can lay a new one. Maybe even the subfloor. That will take some time, and I doubt you'll want to stay here while it's happening." He stepped past her into the dining room, then walked into the living room. "Your Orientals should be fine, but I need to get someone in here right away to remove them. If any of the furniture is water damaged, I'll have it replaced."

"I've got insurance, David."

"No. I did this, I'll pay for it. And I'll oversee the whole thing. It may take a while, but I'll make sure your house comes out of this as good as new. Better than new."

She still felt a little stunned, but mostly she felt awful for David.

"You'll have to move to a hotel, though. You can't stay here while the work is being done. I'll take care of that, too. Anywhere you want to go, it's on me."

"I can stay at the Lyme House. You designed my office. You know it's a great home away from home."

He sat down on the edge of the couch.

"Where will you stay?" she asked.

"Don't worry about that."

"I've done nothing but worry about you since you walked into the bar last night."

"I don't suppose we could agree that we'll probably laugh about this one day."

They turned at the sound of licking. Mouse was in the corner lapping up the water.

David shook his head. "That's what we need. Another ten dogs like him. The water would be gone in no time."

"You're crazy, you know that?"

His smile evaporated. "You know, Jane, you might be right."

4

Cordelia carried Hattie, her three-and-a-half-year-old niece, on her shoulders as she sauntered down the hallway to the loft where Joanna would be living during her stay in Minnesota. Since it was a sublet, and Cordelia had brokered the arrangement, she'd already been in the space and knew it was comfortable and clean, although the way Tammi Bonifay had it decorated was enough to make her gag. It was the same general space as her loft—sixty by eighty feet, with fourteen-foot-high ceilings, exposed brick, and floor-to-ceiling windows on one entire wall overlooking downtown Minneapolis.

Cordelia had kept her loft space open, with tall screens dividing off separate sections. Thus, she could change it at her whim. And Cordelia had lots of whims. She had a tendency to borrow pieces of old sets from the theater's storage garage. Since she was the creative director, nobody objected. Creative types were supposed to be eccentric, and on that score, it was Cordelia's mission in life never to disappoint.

But her visits to the storage garage had ended when IKEA came to town. All her gay boyfriends told her she simply *had* to go—if she didn't, they'd revoke her gay credentials. She was intrigued but not sold. At the time, she was in the midst of a languid, Deep South period. Thanks to many of the props and furnishings from the Allen Grimby's brilliant production of Tennessee Williams's *Summer and Smoke* last spring, so was her loft. With fake Spanish moss dripping from the screens, frayed Orientals covering the hardwood floors, old-fashioned couches and overstuffed chairs with frilly white doilies pinned to the backs and arms, and with the scent of magnolia potpourri in the air, the loft was a study in genteel disintegration. Cordelia had even ordered a bunch of potted palms from Bachman's. She was a bit annoyed to find that one of them was dying. But then it occurred to her that rotting vegetation was an essential part of Southern ambience. She nursed it along in its slow death and then allowed it a place of honor near the window when if finally bit the dust.

But all that changed the moment she entered IKEA. She was dazed. Mesmerized. So was Hattie. She loved playing in the children's area while Cordelia went hunting. Cordelia honestly couldn't remember the last time she'd been so surprised. Not only was the furniture cheap, but it was generally well designed—if you liked Swedish modern. Which she didn't.

But it grew on her. She was seduced by the weird names: The Hensvik bookcase, the Akurum/Lin/Jar kitchen island, the Fagelbo corner sofa, the Kvadrant panel curtain. Anno, Knopp, Lesvik, Ektorp, Hustad, Borgholm—presumably these were the designers, unless someone had an odd sense of humor. It sounded to Cordelia like a page out of the Minneapolis phone book, only on steroids. If you wanted Scandinavia in all its functionally boring glory—and who didn't like mass-produced sweet rolls, meatballs and gravy with lingonberry sauce, and cod?—it was right *here* in Bloomington, right across the street from that dreadful shrine to modern consumption, the Mall of America. Such a deal! Cordelia hated the Mall of America, but then she had to admit that she *consumed,* so she could hardly throw stones.

Thus Cordelia's Deep South period ended. When she found out she had to assemble all the new furnishings herself, she had a moment of misgiving. Not only did Cordelia Thorn not *haul,* she did not *as-*

semble. That's when she got the brilliant idea to invite all the guys who'd recommended IKEA to her over to her loft for dinner. After the pizza and pinot grigio were consumed, she told them to get busy. They did. In a matter of a few hours, Cordelia was swimming in a completely new ethos.

Thus began her IKEA period.

The loft Joanna would live in, one floor down from Cordelia's, was filled with both French provincial furnishings and tacky—though expensive—rustic country stuff. Captain's chairs. Velvet couches. Plaid upholstered chairs. Carved wooden trout on the walls. Hutches loaded with garish country-themed plates, all faceout. Lots of pictures of Jesus were scattered around, and knicknacks to the point of psychosis. There was even a Martin Luther bobblehead, but there were no blank spaces, not even in the bathrooms. Unlike her loft, with all its new, clean lines, this one was so covered in crap that Cordelia couldn't imagine finding another loft like it this side of the "country section" of lower hell—or east Texas.

The loft—again, unlike Cordelia's—was divided into rooms. Two bathrooms. Three bedrooms. A large living room. A large study. Big kitchen and formal dining room. Joanna was only one person and she wouldn't be spending that much time here. Cordelia liked the idea of having her under the same roof. It would make everything so much easier. And who knew? Maybe Joanna liked bucolic bric-a-brac, religious gewgaws, and quasi-patriotic plaster objets d'art. The only thing Joanna had seemed concerned with was the loft's security system. Cordelia had been president of the tenants' board for the past ten months, so she could attest to the fact that it was as good as, if not better than, any other downtown loft.

The Linden Building had originally been built as a two-story livery in the warehouse district of downtown Minneapolis. It had been constructed in the late eighteen hundreds and had housed horses and delivery wagons, which entered and left through oversized arched doorways. Cordelia thought the huge doorways were cool and should have been left the way they were. Because she herself was larger than

21

life—in every way—she was drawn to anything that was grand, dramatic, or excessive. But sometime in the early nineteen hundreds the doors had been bricked up and made smaller, and four more stories were added. Today, the six-story building was home to Athena's Garden, a Greek restaurant, on the first floor; a printing company on the next two levels; with the final three floors turned into lofts with glorious views of the city or the Mississippi River, depending on which side of the building you were on.

Cordelia bounced Hattie on her shoulders as she continued down the hallway to Joanna's loft. As she was about to slip the key in the lock, Hattie pointed to the door on the other side of the hall. "Yook," she said, growing excited.

Cordelia turned, squinting her disgust at Faye O'Halleron. Faye was the retired owner of a hair salon in Fort Dodge, Iowa. She'd grown up there, married and divorced there, and worked at the hair salon until she'd sold it and moved to Minneapolis six years ago. She'd been living at Linden Lofts for only about a year, but already she'd weaseled her way into Cordelia's infamous poker night. Faye was in her mid-seventies now, still a spunky old broad—a tall, flat-chested woman with short, dyed red hair and a face that looked like a road map of deep wrinkles. Faye liked to give advice, something she'd no doubt honed over decades of conversations with clients. Cordelia thought she was a hoot, but at the moment, she found her more frustrating than amusing. "Close the door, Faye. Joanna isn't here yet."

Faye took a drag off her cigarette. "Just checking." She had a deep, whiskey voice, a voice that a Mafia don would have envied.

"Yeah, well, Joanna needs some privacy. Remember? We had that little chat about leaving her alone, at least for the first few days."

"I'm not gonna *bother* her," muttered Faye, stepping farther out into the hall, a pissed-off look on her face. "Jeez, you must think everyone in this building is some pathetic star fucker. I've met my share of celebrities in my time, you know. I know how to act. Did I ever tell you about the time I gave Debra Winger a haircut?"

"Yes," said Cordelia, trying to sound patient. "Look, I just don't want people descending on Joanna as soon as she walks in the door. Who she chooses to make friends with is up to her. I'll be happy to introduce you, but give her a little space, okay? We clear on that?"

"I was just looking. A gal can *look*, can't she?"

"Hi, Faye," said Hattie with a shy little wave.

"Hi yourself," replied Faye. Her grin was lopsided. "You're as cute as a bug, you know that?"

Hattie's face puckered. "I'm not a bug!"

"It's an expression, Hatts," said Cordelia, patting her leg. "It just means you're sweet." She glanced at Faye. Out of the side of her mouth she whispered, "She's into a very *literal* idiom at the moment."

Hattie gave a big nod. "Yup. Sweet. Yike strawberries." Like all true Thorns, she wasn't plagued by self-doubt.

"Remember what I said. You ever need a babysitter—"

Cordelia held up a jewel-encrusted hand. "I've got you on the list. Between Hattie's live-in nanny and me, we can usually cover everything, but I'll keep you in mind."

"I love little girls. Don't forget." Faye fixed her eyes on the floor for a second, blowing smoke out of the side of her mouth, then turned her back to Cordelia. "Yeah. Well. Gotta go. *The Price Is Right* is on." She slipped back inside and shut the door.

Lifting Hattie off her shoulders, Cordelia entered the loft. She wanted to give the place one final look-see just to make sure everything was in order. Fresh linens. Fresh towels. Cordelia had already stocked the kitchen with the bare necessities—fresh-roasted coffee beans from Dunn Bros, a slice of double-cream Brie from Surdyk's, a loaf of Asiago pepper bread and two baguettes from Turtle Bakery, a dozen organic eggs and a large lump of brown sugar–smoked salmon from the Wedge, a quart of fresh OJ from Lunds, a pint of red pepper mascarpone and an antipasto salad from Broders, and for a treat, a dense, fudgy Finlandia Torte from Taste of Scandinavia. Cordelia figured these, and a few other essentials, were enough to tide Joanna over until morning.

"What *is* this pyace?" Hattie asked reverently. Today, Hattie was dressed in a long black velvet dress and bright pink slippers. At three-and-a-half, she was already a budding Goth—but with a few unresolved color issues.

"This is where Auntie Joanna is staying," said Cordelia.

"I *yuv* this pyace!" exclaimed Hattie, turbocharging over to a rack of cheap colored glass water goblets.

"No touching, okay?"

Before she could begin checking out the loft, the phone rang. Rushing into the kitchen, she picked up the receiver. It was a delivery guy downstairs wanting to come up with some flowers. Cordelia buzzed him in. At the same time, out of the corner of her eye, she saw Hattie climb up on one of the dining room chairs, pull her bubble gum out of her mouth, and plop it down on the wood tabletop.

"Hatts! Stop!" The interior wasn't exactly child-friendly.

Sprinting across the room, she reached the table just as Hattie squished the gum flat with the palm of her hand. "What did I tell you about gum? It belongs in your mouth."

"Or in my hair," added Hattie knowingly.

As Cordelia finished peeling the gum off, the doorbell rang.

"Coming," she called, depositing the sticky wad in a wastebasket.

When she opened the door, the delivery guy asked her to sign for the package. "You Joanna Kasimir?" he asked, cocking an eye at her.

"Yes," said Cordelia, scribbling her name.

"The actress?"

"What do you think?" she snarled.

"I think I'm leaving," he said, turning and walking away.

Cordelia glanced at the gray-and-orange paper the flowers came wrapped in and decided it was a tasteless florist. She looked around the room for someplace to set it. Hattie was now under the dining room table.

"It's *beau-ti-ful* down here!" She motioned for Cordelia to climb under with her.

"Hattie, do the math. Auntie Cordelia won't fit under there. Now come out this minute. I'm counting." She set the package on an end table, then changed her mind and moved it to the floor behind one of the hideous chain-saw sculptures.

5

You goin' out?" called Hillary Schinn's dad. Fred Schinn was a retired stonemason, a man with cottony white hair, a red face, and rough hands. And he was diabetic. He was lying on the couch in the living room of his Richfield home, cup of coffee resting on his stomach, his swollen legs propped up on a pillow.

Hillary was standing by the entrance to the kitchen, looking at herself in a full-length mirror that was hung on the back of the door. "Yeah," she said, standing sideways and pressing a hand to her stomach. She'd been on a diet for the past three weeks, ever since she found out that Joanna Kasimir was coming to town, but she hadn't lost more than two pounds. It was depressing beyond belief. Her boyfriend always said she looked great, but guys lied to get laid. It was a simple fact. She was a good thirty pounds over the number on the weight chart at her doctor's office, and that meant she was a frumpy butterball, one who still lived with her dad. How pathetic was that?

During her twenties, Hillary simply assumed that by the time she was thirty, she'd have kids, a great job, a reasonably handsome husband, a home, a yard, and a fat bank account—not a fat body. Nothing had worked out the way she'd planned. She'd gone to the U of M, got her degree in journalism, but the year she graduated the job market was in the toilet. Maybe she didn't always interview well. She was often immobilized by a bad case of nerves—just like right now. Her hands were clammy and her stomach was in knots.

To get by, Hillary had worked various dead-end jobs over the years—Burger King, the Nicollet Car Wash, the Town Talk Cleaners, and Blockbuster video. She'd finally taken a position at a local hospital. For the past two years she'd been selling flowers and balloons to the families of the sick and dying. It was too depressing for words, which only made it seem even more important that she find a job as a freelance journalist. All she needed was one measly break. If things worked out as she hoped, Joanna Kasimir would be that break.

"Where you goin'?" asked her dad, flipping channels on the TV.

"Out."

"Out where?"

"Don't pressure me, okay? I feel like my brain is about to explode."

He sighed loudly. "Always so dramatic. You got that from your mom. Hey, will you make me a sandwich before you go? My legs are really bad today."

The deal was that Hillary could live at home free of charge as long as she helped her dad with the upkeep of the house and also did the cooking and grocery shopping. Sure, her dad was ill, but he also used his illness as an excuse to get out of doing his part. "Can't you make yourself a peanut butter sandwich or something?"

"That's what I had for dinner last night—and the night before."

"Well, I'm crazed, can't you see that? I can't deal with anything else." She charged up the stairs to her room. She saw now that the dress she'd picked was all wrong. She needed a more professional look. Her closet was crammed with clothes—all the way from size ten up to size sixteen. She was a fourteen at the moment. And that thought made her remember the dark blue suit she'd bought last fall for a funeral.

"Here," she whispered, pulling it free. She shimmied out of the dress, dug through a drawer until she found a white silk blouse that wasn't too wrinkled, then slipped it on. Next came the pants. They were a little tight, which was just about the last straw, but she was able to get them zipped. The suit coat fit her perfectly. This, finally, was the right image. Professional but approachable. Friendly. Young. Hungry but definitely not desperate.

On the way to the airport, Hillary experienced everything from dry mouth to vertigo to shakes to nausea. She was a mess—both exhilarated and scared to death. She'd never met a celebrity before. Every off-ramp she passed was an opportunity to turn back, but she refused to look at them. She had to keep going. The alternative was just too horrible to contemplate.

Hillary had been lucky, which was another reason she thought this meeting with Joanna Kasimir was meant to be. She knew a guy—Noel Dearborn—who was an intern at the Allen Grimby Repertory Theater. He'd been itching to date her forever. She kept putting him off but never totally shut him down. The day he overheard the top brass at the theater talking about Joanna's plane coming in on September 24, three-ten P.M. at Flying Cloud, he called Hillary and told her the news. That was three weeks ago. Noel knew that Joanna Kasimir was Hillary's film idol. Hillary talked about her all the time. Hillary asked him once if he thought she looked like Joanna Kasimir. He said yeah, definitely. Which just confirmed what she'd already believed.

Forty-five minutes after she'd left her dad's house, Hillary parked her white Toyota Tercel next to a gray minivan. She'd never been to Flying Cloud airport before. The MapQuest directions had confused her, but amazingly, she'd made good time. So good, in fact, that she had almost an hour to wait until the plane landed. In an effort to get her mind off her anxiety, she decided to make a mental list of the things she wanted to say.

Except, instead of concentrating on the task at hand, Hillary was immediately overwhelmed by all the negative voices in her head—the ones that told her she was a failure; a rotten writer. A liar. A sham. She had no business thinking she could be a professional journalist. She was just setting herself up for a fall. Joanna Kasimir wouldn't give her the time of day because she'd see Hillary for the fraud she really was. The smart thing to do would be to leave right now, not waste everyone's time. But if she did leave, if this didn't work out, Hillary wasn't sure what she'd have left. If her life didn't change, she was beginning to think it wasn't worth living.

Leaning her forehead against the steering wheel, Hillary felt the weight of her own negativity squeeze the air out of her lungs. She'd been so upbeat, so thrilled when she'd first learned Joanna would be coming. She and Joanna were kindred spirits. They'd both suffered and survived. They were destined to be not just friends but sisters of the heart. Confidantes. Family. Joanna would take Hillary's hand in hers and smile that wonderful smile. "Sure," she'd say. "I'll give you an exclusive interview." And then she'd promise that they'd get together soon.

It had to work out that way. *It just had to.*

6

Ah, the toxic smell of ozone," said Cordelia, stopping for a moment and taking a deep breath. "I love airports." She adjusted her sunglasses, then resumed her pacing.

Jane figured they'd have some time to wait before the plane came in, so she'd saved her big news until now. Besides, she always felt apprehensive in Cordelia's Hummer, as if it might launch a missile at any moment. "You'll never guess who walked into the bar at the Xanadu Club last night." She leaned against the front of the truck, the runway directly in front of her. It was a beautiful autumn afternoon, cool and breezy. In Jane's opinion, the ozone didn't add much.

Cordelia stopped again. She was the only one Jane knew who could pace in three-inch heels over cracked pavement and not break both her ankles. "Who?"

"David Carlson."

She deadpanned. "You're kidding me."

"Odd synergy, wouldn't you say?"

"You mean . . . are you saying he didn't know his sister was coming to town?"

"Had no idea."

"Freaky."

Today, Cordelia wore a bright red, yellow, and blue sundress. She looked like a human beach ball. This was one of Cordelia's more restrained outfits. While on their way to the airport, she'd said she wanted to tone herself down so that Joanna could take the spotlight. Jane complimented her on her sensitivity.

"Why's he here?"

"I'm not sure," said Jane, looking up at the thin, wispy clouds spreading across the sky.

"He didn't say?"

"He said he needed a break, thought a road trip would be fun."

"Sounds like you don't believe him." She leaned back against the hood next to Jane.

"I'm not sure what to think. But something's not right."

"And you know this how?"

"He looks terrible—like he hasn't slept in weeks."

"You think he's ill?"

"I hope not."

"Maybe there's trouble in paradise."

"You mean Diego? He didn't mention that. On the other hand, he did kind of skirt the subject when Diego's name came up." Jane pushed her hands deep into the pockets of her pants. "I'm worried about him, Cordelia."

"Where's he staying?"

"Well, he was going to stay with me, but, see—"

Cordelia pushed off the hood and pointed at an approaching blip in the distance. Checking her watch, she shouted, "That's Joanna!" She began to wave frantically with both arms.

Jane wondered what Cordelia must look like to the pilot as the plane approached the runway. "Follow the bouncing ball," she whispered.

"What?" said Cordelia.

"Nothing."

As the small jet slowed and then taxied to the gate, Jane said, "We can't get past security without a ticket, so I guess we wait here. I figured there would be a swarm of reporters."

"No paparazzi," said Cordelia. "All information about Joanna has been stamped strictly Top Secret."

A moment later the hatch opened. The stairs came down and Joanna descended. She had on dark glasses and was wearing beige linen slacks and a matching long, belted cardigan. Her blond hair was tied back in a ponytail. She looked glamorous, tanned, and healthy—but years older than the last time Jane had seen her. Jane tried to remember when that had been and decided it was probably close to eight years ago, when Joanna had invited Cordelia and Jane to Sandpoint for the big Fourth of July celebration. They'd stayed for a long weekend.

For the moment, all they could do was cool their heels. A few minutes later, Joanna came out of the doorway, followed by a man pulling a luggage cart. Cordelia charged up to her and gave her the official "Thorn bear hug." Jane followed with one that was equally welcoming though less bone crushing. Joanna seemed happy to see them, but distracted. As they walked to the Hummer, she kept looking around, like she expected someone to leap out at her.

"There're no paparazzi," said Cordelia, reassuring her. "You can relax. Only a few people at the theater know your schedule."

"How was the flight?" asked Jane.

"Is *that* what you're driving these days?" Joanna asked as they approached the Hummer. She lifted up her dark glasses to get a better look.

"Sure is." Cordelia beamed and patted the rear end. "Ain't she a beaut?"

"What's it get? Twenty feet to the gallon?"

"How come everyone wants to slam my car?"

"Ever think about the larger ramifications of the gas crisis, Cordelia? Our dependency on foreign oil?"

"I drive a Mini," said Jane. "I figure that evens things out."

The burly guy pulling the cart loaded the luggage into the back of the Hummer.

As they were about to get in, something fluttered at them from between the parked cars.

They all turned as a woman rushed up to the right rear bumper. "Hi," she said, her eyes cast down. She seemed out of breath. "Can I talk to you for a second, Ms. Kasimir?"

Jane stepped in front of Joanna. "Can I ask what this is about?"

"I, ah . . . I was hoping that I could, you know . . . like . . . like, see, I'm a freelance journalist."

"You want to interview me?" asked Joanna.

The woman smiled shyly, finally lifting her eyes. "I'm such a huge fan of yours. Maybe even your biggest fan. I realize I'm nobody in the scheme of things, and you're, like, this amazingly successful celebrity. I'm sure you get asked for interviews all the time by really important people. Maybe this seems ridiculous to you. I wouldn't blame you if it did. But if you could just give me, like, even fifteen minutes, it would be such an incredible honor."

"Do you write for a particular paper or magazine?" asked Joanna.

"Well, like I said, I'm freelance." She tucked one side of her chin-length brown hair behind her ear. "But I've had pieces in *The Rake. Minnesota Monthly. City Pages.* I don't make a living at it yet, but it's my dream that someday I will. Everyone should have a dream, don't you think?"

Jane noticed Joanna's eyes flicker. Something the woman said had touched her.

"Yes, actually, I do."

"I'm a good writer. A really good writer, but sometimes I don't come across well in, like, interviews. I mean, like, sometimes I seem too aggressive, and at other times I'm not aggressive enough. I never get it right. But I know I could produce a piece on you we'd both be proud of. I don't want to bother you. I mean, just tell me to go away and I will. I'm used to being turned down."

"What's your name?" asked Joanna.

"Hillary. Hillary Schinn. I live in Richfield with my dad. He's ill and I help take care of him. And then I also have a job. But I've got plenty of time to write. I wouldn't disappoint you, I promise."

She was so eager, so earnest, thought Jane. She was attractive enough but didn't seem like she had much confidence.

"Do you have a card?" asked Joanna.

"No, but I wrote my information down for you." Hillary opened her purse and took out a folded piece of paper. "It's my home number. I have a cell phone, too, which I included. Look, I know I'm asking a lot—that you're very busy. But if you've got a few minutes someday and you want to get together, well, I mean, I'd be so blown away. If you want, I could send you some of my articles."

"Let me think about it." Joanna took the paper and slipped it into the pocket of her cardigan.

"Okay, sure. Gee, it was so great to meet you. I hope you have a wonderful time here. Thanks. I guess . . . I mean, I suppose I should get going." She backed away, smiling, her eyes locked on Joanna. "Thanks again. Really, this was so cool. Like, just meeting you, talking to you." She disappeared behind a dark maroon minivan.

"Uff," said Cordelia after she'd gone. "The price of fame, I guess. The weird ones are always out there waiting to pounce. I wonder how she knew when your plane would land."

Jane thought it was a good question, but Joanna didn't say anything. She gazed after the young woman for a long moment, then climbed into the backseat of the Hummer.

On the way back to Minneapolis, Cordelia brought up the subject of David. "He's in town, you know."

Joanna leaned forward, put her hand on the front seat. "You've actually seen him?"

"I have," said Jane. "He came to my restaurant last night."

"God, you don't know how glad I am to hear that. I've got to call Diego right away."

"Why?" asked Cordelia, glancing at Jane with one eyebrow discreetly raised.

"Because David's been missing for weeks. Diego is out of his mind

34

with worry." Joanna explained everything she knew, which confirmed Jane's initial impression that something was terribly wrong.

"Where's he staying?" asked Joanna.

"Well, he was planning to stay with me," said Jane. "But there was an accident in the middle of the night. David went down to make himself something to eat. He must have left the faucet on in the kitchen because when I got up this morning, there was water all over the house. It caused some significant damage. David said he'd take care of it. He was really embarrassed. Said I would probably need to move out for a few weeks while the work is being done."

"Where will you stay?" asked Joanna.

"At the Lyme House. My office has a big couch and a bathroom."

"No you won't," said Cordelia indignantly. "I won't hear of it. You'll move in with me."

"No, really—"

"The matter is settled. If you stay at the restaurant you'll be working twenty-four/seven."

"You're exaggerating."

She held up her hand. "The issue is closed. Hattie and I will take good care of you and Mouse until you can return home."

"And David can stay with me," said Joanna.

Jane closed her eyes. She recalled what David had said. She was glad Joanna was in the backseat and couldn't see her expression.

"Actually," continued Joanna, "this couldn't come at a better time. To be honest, I could use the company."

"Any particular reason?" asked Cordelia. Her nose twitched the way it always did when she sensed a secret.

Joanna was silent for a few seconds. Glancing out the side window, she finally said, "Something happened before I left Sandpoint. I almost called you and canceled the trip."

"What?" Cordelia nearly drove off the road.

"I didn't, so don't have a coronary. Look, I really don't want to get into it right now, but it . . . unsettled me."

"But," said Cordelia, staring at the road ahead, "you *will* talk about it eventually, right?"

Joanna turned to look at her. "You haven't changed a bit, have you."

"Prurient to the core," said Jane.

A slow grin broke over Cordelia's face. "I'm one of life's immovable objects, dearhearts. I am the sphinx. Always there, waiting and watching."

Bel Air, California
Spring 1989

If Joanna had learned anything in her many years in Hollywood, it was that physical beauty existed in a very small pond, but that ugliness was an ocean. She had to admit to a certain shallowness when it came to the opposite sex. She liked male beauty. She'd been married twice since she arrived in Hollywood in the fall of 1981. Both marriages had been lust at first sight. Marriage number one had slowly given way to disinterest and finally outright disgust. Marriage number two never even got off the ground.

The famous director Freddy Kasimir had been the first to catch Joanna's eye. She must have caught his, too, because it wasn't long before they were a hot item in the tabloids, then engaged to be married. Somewhere along the way she was cast as the ingenue in his next movie. The marriage had given her the professional break she'd been praying for. Once the door was open, she walked through and never looked back. She hated to think that Freddy was simply a means to an end, but in the final analysis—in the biography somebody was bound to write one day—that's the way it would look. Freddy had been a clever man. When the sex got boring, as it always did, he was capable of decent conversation. Maybe she should have hung on to him. At the very least, he made her laugh, and that was saying something with the caliber of narcissistic bad boys she was currently dating. To a man, they'd all fallen in love with their beauty and had a hard time wresting their attention away from the mirror.

Joanna's second husband, Cyril Connor, the Irish actor, had been another golden boy, but one who'd checked his brains at his cocaine dealer's front door. That marriage had lasted less than fifteen minutes. They were both paging their divorce lawyers when the limo hit the Pasadena freeway, five miles from the church. It was probably some sort of record. Joanna was deeply embarrassed, but she was capable of learning. After the second disaster, she nixed the marriage license thing and just slept with the Adonises.

And so, on this ordinary spring morning as she awoke from her usual fitful night's sleep, Joanna would have been surprised to learn that her life was about to take a major right turn onto a dead-end street. Living in Hollywood, Bel Air to be exact, was like a carboholic living in a bakery. The most beautiful people on earth swarmed to Hollywood like sugar ants to sweet poison. They were everywhere. Waiters. Mechanics. Department store clerks. As hard as she tried, Joanna found it impossible to maintain a "hands-off " policy. With her career in high gear, she could have just about anyone she wanted. Her sexual appetites didn't rise to the level of obsession, but clearly they weren't healthy. She knew, deep in her unanalyzed soul, that her lifestyle probably spoke loudly about spiritual emptiness. But how could her life be empty when she'd attained everything she'd ever wanted? That wasn't the way the American dream was supposed to work.

Today was a Thursday, eight days before her birthday. She had appointments in the afternoon but nothing pressing until then. Her brother, David, and his partner, Diego, had arrived earlier in the week with bags of opulently wrapped birthday gifts they'd brought for her from their home in Atlanta. They planned to stay for two weeks. They both liked to vacation in L.A. because, like Joanna, they enjoyed the view. But unlike her, David and Diego were monogamous. They seemed to be truly in love.

Joanna was happy for her brother, but seeing him with Diego always left her feeling vaguely on edge. Another red flag she scrupulously ignored. She did wonder why true love had somehow escaped her. She lived in a cocoon of constant affirmation and praise. She knew the mirror that everyone was so quick to hold up in front of her face lied, but she didn't think she was fundamentally flawed. "Redemption" was a word that occasionally flitted through her mind, though she never gave it any serious thought.

David and Diego were staying in the small bungalow next to the cabana. It was private and yet it had most of the comforts of the main house. Joanna had picked this place after looking at only six houses. It was everything she'd ever dreamed of times twelve. It was actually way too much for one person, so because of her working-class guilt, she adopted four cats in an effort to justify her existence. It made no sense, of course. Her reality—the manicured lawns and mansions, the movie industry filled with manicured people—was surrounded by another, darker reality: a teaming, chaotic mix of L.A. ethnicity, a pot that simply refused to melt. Joanna wasn't blind. She knew there was something deeply wrong with the excess she was surrounded by, and yet she dismissed her need to examine it. Plato be damned. The excess, as some called it, was her freakin' life! The problem was, when she ignored something fundamental, it had a tendency to scream at her until she turned and faced it. And that's why, in the end, she became a sitting duck, just waiting for the right hunter to come along and pick her off.

David entered the kitchen as Joanna was making herself a pot of coffee. He looked tousled and still rosy from sleep. He had the same sapphire eyes as she did, the same sandy blond hair. His was cropped short, while hers flowed down past her shoulders and was dyed platinum.

"It's official," said David, getting two mugs from the cupboard. He was dressed in a rumpled gray T-shirt and white running shorts. "I'm staying here. Never leaving. I'm hiring myself on as your pool boy."

"And what will Diego do?"

"He'll sit by the pool with a cold beer and build an amazing house of cards."

"Always the architect."

David hopped up on the counter, waiting as Joanna poured coffee into his mug. "That's smells fabulous. What are you up to today?"

Before answering, she stepped up to the window overlooking the side garden. The old gardener, a middle-aged Japanese man, had recently been replaced by a new fellow. She hadn't really taken much notice of him, but with his shirt off and his muscles gleaming with sweat in the bright morning sunlight, she noticed him now.

"Earth to Joanna?"

"Hmm?"

"What are you looking at?"

"Flowers."

"No, you're not." He jumped down off the counter and moved up behind her, gazing over her shoulder. "Nice. Who is he?"

"I think his name is Gordon. He's the new man the service sent out."

"What happened to the old one?"

Joanna turned, grinned, and poked him in the stomach. "You ask too many questions, bro. How should I know?" She picked up her mug and sauntered toward the door.

"And where would you be going?"

She threw him an innocent smile. "It's impolite not to personally welcome a new member of the staff. Don't leave, Davey. I'll be back in five."

He snorted. "Like hell you will."

Joanna hid behind a large chamise bush and watched the new gardener clean out weeds growing between the flagstones that ran along the north side of the yard. She was five foot five in her stocking feet and this guy wasn't more than a few inches taller. But he was built. His body looked like it had been chiseled from a block of cedar. His blond hair was wiry, waving slightly at the nape of his neck and falling in heavy coils over his forehead. He had a square head and a prominent cleft in his chin. Joanna wondered what he'd look like naked.

"I was curious what you'd think about my putting in some creeping thyme as ground cover between the flagstones."

His deep voice startled her. She had no idea he'd seen her standing there. Now she was embarrassed. Stepping out from behind the bush, she said, "That sounds like it might be nice."

"It's very fragrant. I love fragrance, don't you? 'Course, nothing beats a rose, in my opinion, but if you'd like, I could show you some landscaping ideas I have for this place. There's lots of ways to go, depending on what your personal preferences are." He'd been crouching, but now he stood. A shaft of sunlight caught the glistening sweat on his pecs.

Joanna found herself staring at the light feathering of hair just above his waist. "What did you say?"

40

"Well, I mean, do you enjoy butterflies? Birds? Or, like I said, we can do plantings for fragrance. Every garden should be special, should reflect the owner's tastes. But like I said, we can talk about it."

"Okay."

He smiled at her. "You're Joanna Kasimir?"

"That's me."

"I wasn't positive it was you. I mean, I knew this was your house and all, but I thought maybe you were a relative. You look better without all the makeup."

She wasn't sure if it was a compliment or a slam. "Thanks."

"Well, better get back to work. I wouldn't want my boss to think I was malingering."

She realized she was grinning. "Nothing to worry about there." She didn't want to leave just yet. "Are you from around here?"

"Me, no." He wiped the sweat off his forehead with his forearm. "From the Midwest."

"Me too," said Joanna. "How come you ended up in California?"

He gazed up at the sky. "I don't know. Wanderlust, maybe. I got my degree in forestry a few years back. I was offered a good job, but I wanted to travel."

"You mean you're not trying to break into acting?"

"Hello, no," he said, his smile fading. "That's the last thing on earth I'd want to get mixed up in."

"Not a moviegoer?"

"Nope. I like to read. And I like the outdoors. Movies and TV never interested me. Too fake."

Joanna should have been insulted, but instead she felt her pulse quicken. This guy was for real, not some Mel Gibson wannabe. Not only was he gorgeous, but he seemed entirely content with and absorbed by his work. She could tell by his demeanor that he wasn't the least bit impressed that she was a famous actress.

Joanna didn't realize it, but she was already hooked. "I'd like to hear your landscaping ideas. What time do you usually finish up?"

"Five, or thereabouts."

"Come up to the house when you're done. Maybe we can sit on the terrace above the pool and talk. I'll open a bottle of wine."

41

He scratched his head, then stuck his hand in the back pocket of his jeans. "I, ah . . . I don't drink. But a Coke would be great. Or water."

"I think I can manage a Coke," said Joanna. She wasn't sure what she was getting herself into, but the train had already left the station. She'd just have to wait and see where it took her.

7

Cordelia stood in the parking lot behind the Linden Building, hands on her hips, glaring at the luggage in the back of her Hummer. "How the hell are we going to get all this upstairs?"

Jane and Joanna looked at each other and burst out laughing. In unison they responded, "Cordelia Thorn does not *haul*."

"That's right, children. You know me well."

"Well, let's see what we can do," said Jane, pulling out a couple of the smaller pieces. Right about now she could have used two or three of her beefiest busboys.

As they were dithering about who would carry what, Milan Mestrovik popped his head out of the security door. "Need some help, ladies?"

Under her breath, Cordelia muttered, "Drat. He must have been watching for us from one of his back windows."

"Who is he?" asked Joanna, her face turned away.

"A pest," said Cordelia. Turning to Milan with a bright, cheery smile, she said, "We can handle it, thanks."

"No, no, I wouldn't hear of it," he said, rushing down the back steps. He wove his way through the parked cars and made straight for Joanna with his hand outstretched. "I'm glad your flight made it here safely. Milan Mestrovik. I live across the hall from Cordelia."

"Nice to meet you," said Joanna, allowing her hand to be pumped aggressively.

"I'm your biggest fan," said Milan, shading his eyes from the afternoon sun with his free hand.

"That's . . . nice to hear," said Joanna.

"You probably get that all the time, but in my case, it's true."

Everyone smiled awkwardly.

"We met once before," continued Milan, apparently oblivious to everything but his single-minded desire to talk to Joanna.

"We did? I'm sorry, I meet so many people——"

"That's okay. It was in L.A. At a political benefit."

"Right," said Joanna. "Right."

Still holding on to her hand, Milan said, "I first saw you in *Cry of the Nightingale*. You were stunning. But my favorite movie of yours is *All the Kings of the Earth*. You were beyond breathtaking in that one. You should have won the Academy Award."

"Thanks. I thought so, too."

Jane had the distinct impression that the man was pulsating—vibrating like a tuning fork. In his double-breasted business suit, he looked like an Eastern European opera impresario. Barrel-chested. Dark bushy eyebrows. Heavy Slavic features. Dark goatee. Flamboyantly styled longish black hair that puffed over his ears like wings.

"You're very kind to offer to help us with the luggage," said Joanna.

"I'll take care of it all," said Milan, finally releasing her hand. "Just head on upstairs. Don't give it another thought."

Fifteen minutes later, true to his word—and thanks to the dolly he'd borrowed from Athena's Garden—Joanna was all moved in.

"I'd offer you something to drink but——" She smiled wistfully. She spread her arms to what she assumed was an empty kitchen. "Some water?"

"Another time," said Milan, staring hard at her. He couldn't seem to take his eyes off her. "I'm single," he blurted out, "not that that means anything, I suppose. I'm sure you have someone special waiting for you back in Idaho—or Hollywood. But if you'd allow me——"

44

He took one of her small hands in his big, meaty ones. "You are . . . so lovely."

Joanna blushed. Laughing, she said, "I'll call you when I'm having a bad day."

"You do that. Promise?"

"Yes," she said. "I promise."

"I know you like wine. I read that in an interview you did with *Redbook*. Music to my ears." He kissed his fingers. "Actually, I'm a wine wholesaler. I don't mean to blow my own horn, but I'm an expert of some renown. If you'll allow me, I'd like to send up a case of my finest, including some rare cognacs."

"I don't know what to say," said Joanna.

"Just say yes," said Milan, beaming at her.

"Well, sure. I'd love it."

"Done. Expect the delivery this evening. Now, I know flying is tiring. I'll leave you to rest. But I expect a full report on the wines— what you like, what you don't like."

"Of course."

He kissed her hand. "And please," he said, looking up at her with his puppy-dog eyes. "You're always welcome to come upstairs to my loft."

"Thanks."

With one last rapturous look, he swept from the room.

Cordelia took a deep, cleansing breath and sank down on the couch. "I'm sorry about that, Jo."

"No," she said. "He's charming. A little starstruck, but charming."

"Everybody in the building can't wait to meet you."

"I suppose you get used to it," said Jane, perching on the edge of one of the velvet couches. When she'd visited Joanna over the fourth way back when, nobody around Sandpoint had acted like she was a goddess. They seemed to take her presence in stride, respect her need for privacy.

Joanna sat down next to Cordelia. "All this hoopla is one reason I love my place in Idaho. It's hard to leave."

"Oh, come on. You love all the attention," said Cordelia, kicking off her shoes. "Who doesn't love being adored?"

"It's not that simple for me," said Joanna, her expression losing some of its usual buoyancy.

Apparently realizing she'd stumbled into sensitive territory, Cordelia slipped her arm around Joanna's shoulders. "You okay?"

"I'm not sure how to answer that. A week ago I would have said I was fine, but——" She hesitated. "I don't suppose either one of you might know a good private investigator."

Jane and Cordelia exchanged glances.

"Actually, I do," said Jane. "He's an ex-cop. A good friend."

"How come you need an investigator?" asked Cordelia, moving in a little closer.

Something on the floor behind Jane caught Joanna's attention. She sat forward. "What's that?" She pointed.

"What?" said Jane.

"That package behind your chair."

Jane turned to look.

"Oh, that," said Cordelia. "It came for you this morning. A gift from one of your zillions of fans."

Joanna stood. "Jane, would you open it?"

"Me? Okay." She picked it up and stripped off the paper. Underneath was a bouquet of pink roses. "How beautiful."

Joanna recoiled. "Is there a card?"

"What's wrong?" asked Jane. Her eyes strayed to Cordelia, who looked every bit as thunderstruck as Joanna.

"Please," said Joanna. "Just read the card."

Jane pulled it free. "It says:

> 'Welcome home to Minnesota, land
> of ten thousand lakes and a hundred
> thousand lunatics. Hope you're
> laughing because I sure am. Can't
> wait to see you!' "

Jane turned the card over. "That's all it says."

"Who's it from?" asked Cordelia. "What's the name?"

"There isn't one."

Walking unsteadily over to the wall of windows facing downtown Minneapolis, Joanna said, "Get rid of them."

"Excuse me?" said Jane.

"What didn't you understand? The flowers! I said get rid of them! Burn them. Crush them. I want them annihilated!" She whirled around. "Call that ex-cop friend of yours, Jane. I want to talk to him. *Now.*"

Jane reached Nolan right away, but he couldn't make it over to the loft for at least an hour. During that time, Joanna retreated to her bedroom. Cordelia was just this side of frantic because of Joanna's reaction to the flowers and the note. She offered to make her something to eat. Food, in Cordelia's universe, could solve a multitude of problems, but Joanna said she didn't want anything. Just the PI.

While Joanna was resting, Jane and Cordelia stood in the kitchen and talked softly.

"You know Joanna better than I do," said Jane. "I'm guessing, but I think you know something about those flowers—why they set her off. Who are they from?"

Cordelia had already taken out the slice of double-cream Brie and was in the process of cutting the baguette into chunks. Food might not make Joanna feel better, but for Cordelia, it was a cure-all. "I can't talk about it."

"Why?"

"Because Joanna swore me to secrecy. I think you should call David. She needs him."

"I'm not sure that's such a good idea. Apparently they haven't been in touch for a while."

"What's going on with that woman?" demanded Cordelia. "Joanna never said anything to me about it."

Before Jane could respond, the phone rang.

"Will you get that?" asked Cordelia. Her fingers were covered with the creamy cheese.

Jane grabbed the cordless off the kitchen counter. "Hello?"

"Hiya, Babycakes! Did you miss me?"

Jane didn't recognize the voice. "Who's calling, please?"

"Joanna?"

"No, this is Jane Lawless. I'm a friend."

"Oh, hell," he said, laughing. "Sorry. This is Fred Kasimir. Joanna's ex. Is she there yet? I know her plane was due in around three."

"Mr. Kasimir, hi," said Jane. She'd never spoken with him before. "Yes, that's right, but she's resting now. Can I take your number and have her call you back?"

"Do you know if she got the package?"

Jane felt suddenly wary. "Package?" Just because this man identified himself as Fred Kasimir didn't mean it was actually him.

"The screenplay," he said impatiently. "I put it in the mail four days ago."

"I don't know. She hasn't checked her mail yet."

"Well, tell her to get on the stick! A project like this doesn't come along every day."

"Do you want to leave a number?"

"She's got my cell, but I have to turn it off. I'm just about to board a plane. Tell her I'll be in touch."

"I'll do that," said Jane. "Bye."

"Freddy Kasimir, huh?" said Cordelia, licking her fingers.

"That's what he said. He sent Joanna a screenplay."

"Really? Fascinating." She handed Jane a piece of the baguette with a thick smear of Brie on top.

"What if it wasn't Freddy Kasimir? I mean, it could have been anybody."

Cordelia stopped midchew. "Boy," she said, swallowing quickly, "it doesn't take your paranoia long to move into high gear."

Shortly after six, Joanna drifted into the kitchen. She'd changed into white jeans and a light blue silk shirt. She didn't look like she'd rested at all.

"Do we have any scotch?" she asked.

"Actually, we do," said Cordelia.

"Good woman," she said, lowering herself onto a ladder-backed kitchen chair.

This time, Cordelia didn't ask about food, she simply set a plate of olives, cheese, and smoked salmon in the center of the table.

Jane decided not to mention the call from her ex right now, just in case it turned out to be bogus.

A few minutes before six-thirty, the buzzer sounded.

"That's got to be Nolan," said Jane, rising and moving over to the phone attached to the kitchen wall. "Yes?" she said.

"Jane? It's me. I'm downstairs."

She buzzed him in.

When he reached the loft's front door, she hugged him briefly, then stepped back so he could enter. Nolan was wearing a brown polo shirt, dress pants, and, as usual, mirrored sunglasses. The color of the shirt almost matched the color of his skin. Jane was always struck by how much his presence still screamed "cop." He'd worked homicide with the MPD for sixteen years before retiring.

Joanna came out of the kitchen to shake his hand. "Thanks for coming."

They all sat down around the dining room table.

Nolan removed a small notebook from his back pocket, then folded his hands on top of the table. "What can I do for you, Ms. Kasimir?"

Joanna rubbed the back of her neck. "How much do you know about the legal problems I had back in 1989?"

"Nothing at all."

She gave a resigned nod. "That's good—it's the way it should be. What happened to me was pre-O.J., so in that respect, I suppose I got lucky. After the Simpson trial, celebrity trials became everybody's favorite pastime." She swirled the ice in her glass. "The fact is, I was stalked by a man for a number of months. After he attacked me in a motel room in Beverly Hills, he was arrested. It's a long story and I won't bore you with the details. The case went to court early in 1990. The man's name was Gordon Luberman.

"We were about a week into the trial when his lawyer came to mine with an offer. Gordon said he'd plead guilty to one count of felony assault and two counts of sexual battery, and he'd serve the sentences consecutively and also submit to anger management therapy if I'd consent to two things. First, he wanted the carrying a concealed weapon charge dropped. Second, he wanted the details of the case sealed. If I agreed, he'd said he'd plead guilty and serve the full eight years. I was desperate to get the trial over. I had no assurance that I'd win. Back then, there was no stalking law in California. Gordon had never committed a crime before—at least, not one that he was ever charged with. The ADA in charge of my case said there was a less than fifty-fifty chance we'd get a conviction, but with a jury you never knew for sure until the verdict came down. He said that he'd continue to try the case if that's what I wanted, but that this was a good deal and I should think about taking it. I just wanted Gordon gone, Mr. Nolan, so I agreed."

"I assume," said Nolan, flipping the notebook to a clean page, "that he's out by now."

"He was released in 1998. I hired a man to do surveillance on him for a couple of years. The last I heard he'd moved back to Winneconne, Wisconsin, was living with his mother, and leading a basically normal life. Before I left my home in Idaho to come here, I called directory assistance for Winneconne, then asked for 'Luberman.' He's not there anymore, Mr. Nolan." She took several sips of scotch to fortify herself. "That means he could be anywhere."

"Do you have some reason to think he's targeting you again?" asked Nolan.

She pressed her lips together to stop them from trembling. "He used to send me flowers all the time—a dozen red roses. Not the big American beauties, but small tea roses. The day before I left to come here, I received a bouquet of roses. They were pink, but I know they were from him."

"And you know this how?"

"I just *feel* it, okay? I can't explain it any other way. But the sense is very strong. I received another dozen pink roses here at the loft today. It's his calling card, Mr. Nolan. Both notes talked about how much he loved me. They even had the same tone as the old notes. Mocking. Menacing.

"I want you to find him and follow him. If he thinks he can start up a relationship with me again—if he's stalking me—I need to know. I need something firm—some proof—that I can take to the police. I absolutely refuse to let him define my life again. I spent months afraid to leave my house. It got so bad that, at one point, I even considered suicide. After the trial, I swore I'd never let that happen to me again. That's why you've got to get on this right away. We have to stop him. He's cunning, Mr. Nolan. And he's dangerous."

Jane had heard bits and pieces of this before, but most of it was new. Joanna never seemed to want to revisit that time in her life. She'd talked to Cordelia about it in much greater detail. Jane had already concluded that Luberman was the main reason Joanna had left L.A. and become a recluse, but she'd known few of the details.

Nolan made a couple of notes on his pad. "Okay, I'd be happy to look into this for you. I charge—"

"I don't care what it costs," said Joanna. "Just bring me something I can use to put him back behind bars."

"I'll do what I can. I can't promise anything."

"I understand that."

"I'm sorry I don't have a lot of time tonight, but we do need to find a couple of hours to sit down together in the next few days. You need to make notes. Write down anything and everything that's important about Luberman, about his methods, about his personality. Oh, and I need the names of your gatekeepers—the people who handle your PR and keep records of the potential nutcases in your fan base who regularly contact you."

"Of course. I don't have any of that information with me, but I'll get it."

Joanna dug through the trunk she'd brought and found a brown manila folder held together with rubber bands. She gave it to Nolan, telling him that it was all the written documentation she had on Gordon—on the trial, and all the info from the PI she'd hired in 1998.

After saying good-bye and that he'd be in touch, Nolan motioned for Jane to walk out with him.

On the way to the elevator, Jane said, "So what do you think?"

"I think," said Nolan, pressing the Down button and then turning to face her, "that your friend has a very serious problem. How well do you know her?"

"I've known her for years, but we're not close."

"She kept looking at Cordelia, like she needed her approval. Are they pretty tight?"

Jane nodded. "Joanna's brother, David, and I are the same age. We went to high school together, stayed friends through college and beyond. I'm much closer to him."

"So this is a family you care about."

"Absolutely."

"Okay, then I got a proposal."

The huge old freight elevator rumbled to a stop.

Nolan pulled back the wooden gate and opened the door. "Come downstairs with me."

"Why?"

"Aren't you the one who's been telling me for the last two months how she needs to take a few weeks off, get a little R and R? After the last year you put in, I think you deserve it. And if you want to change gears—and help your friend—I suggest you work with me on this."

Jane hesitated. "What would you want me to do?"

"For starters, you could look through this file." He handed it to her.

On their way down to the first floor, Nolan said he was on another case that would probably wind up tonight, but he wouldn't be home until well after midnight. He wanted her to go through the information, pull out the most salient points, and then he'd pick her up in the morning and they'd drive to Winneconne to begin their search. It was Luberman's last known residence, so it was the best place to start.

Jane thought about it as she walked Nolan to his car. "I'm not sure Joanna would want me to get involved."

"Only one way to find out. Ask her. Look, I'm going to leave the file with you. Put it in your car. If she doesn't want you on board, call

52

my cell and leave a message. I'll pick up the file in the morning. But if she does agree to it, burn the midnight oil and go over the information. I'll want a full report."

Jane wasn't sure if this was smart move or a stupid one. All she knew was that he'd made her an offer she couldn't refuse. "You got yourself a deal. I'll talk to Joanna and let you know."

8

Just before eight that evening, David pulled up to the front of the Linden Building. He sat in his red BMW with the motor running, drumming his fingers on the steering wheel. Jane had called him about Joanna. Maybe it was pure selfishness, but everything that had happened since coming to Minnesota felt so thwarting.

When Jane mentioned that Diego had called Joanna yesterday, sounding frantic, David felt something crack apart inside. He'd left Atlanta in order to protect Diego, but in the process, he'd hurt him badly. He'd acted impulsively, damaging, perhaps destroying, the one thing on earth he valued more than any other. He prayed Diego would forgive him, not that he deserved it. Maybe it was better if Diego blew up and called it quits. More than anything else, David didn't want to cause him any more pain, and if they stayed together, that's all he could promise.

Flipping open his cell phone, David saw that his mailbox was full. He'd turned it off when he left Atlanta. Scrolling through the messages, he noted that some were from his business partner, but most were from Diego. David had recharged the battery last night but hadn't switched it back on until this moment.

Tapping in Diego's number, he waited. He had no idea what he would say. Maybe he'd just let Diego scream at him. That would be easy enough. The prospect of being screamed at by someone other than himself was oddly appealing.

Diego's voice came across the line midway through the third ring. "David?"

"Yeah, it's me."

Silence.

"Hi," said David, telling himself to breathe.

"Where are you? Why didn't you return any of my phone calls?" Diego's voice cracked on the last word.

David pressed his fingers to his eyes. "I'm in Minneapolis."

"Minneapolis? What on earth are you doing there?" He let fly with a burst of Spanish invective. "I've been out of my mind with worry!"

"I know. I'm sorry."

"You're *sorry*?" Again, he swore in Spanish. "You damn sure better have more to say than *I'm sorry*. Tell me what is going on!"

"You know what it was like for me before I left. I thought I was losing it."

"Insomnia happens, David. It can be a really bad problem for some. But you could have gone to a doctor. Got a prescription. They have stuff to help you, that's what they're there for! A few good nights' rest and you would be okay."

"It's not that simple."

"Okay, maybe I'm oversimplifying. But to leave without telling me—"

"I was afraid."

"Of me? Because of the argument we had?"

David leaned his head back. "God, no, not you. Never you."

"Do you know what you put me through? Do you have any idea how worried I was?"

"Diego, listen to me. I promise I'll be home soon. Just give me a couple more weeks."

"*Weeks?*" More swearing. "Why should I? Maybe I should change all the locks, toss your clothes out on the street. Would you like that? You deserve no better!"

"I know. I'm not arguing with you."

"You get on a plane and come home. Now. Tonight!"

"I can't. Joanna's in trouble."

"What trouble?"

"Remember Gordon Luberman? She thinks he may be stalking her again. She's in terrible shape."

"I just talked to her yesterday. She was fine."

"Well, she isn't today. She asked me to stay with her until this gets sorted out. I couldn't say no." It was an excuse, and not exactly the truth, but it was all he had.

"You are acting so crazy, David, I don't know what to say, what to believe."

Diego's words felt like darts hitting his skin. "Call Joanna. She'll tell you it's the truth. Look, just give me a little more time. I owe it to my sister to stand by her."

"Will you call me? Will you come home as soon as you can?"

"I promise."

"You *swear*?"

"I swear, Diego."

"You will answer your phone if I call?"

"Absolutely. If I can't for some reason, leave a message and I'll call you back. I mean it. I won't disappear again. I love you more than I ever thought possible. If I've learned anything in the past month, it's that."

Long sigh. "God, I shouldn't say this, but it's so good to hear your voice. Are you well? Are you eating? Have you been in Minnesota this whole time?"

"I'll tell you more tomorrow, okay?"

"Ah," he groaned. "All right. I give you the time you need. Just stay in touch. Godspeed to you, *mi amor*. I will pray for you."

David felt tears burn his eyes. When he said good-bye, he choked on the word.

The smell of garlic and lemon, and the sound of waiters calling "Oompah!" assaulted David as he trudged through the first floor carrying his duffel bag. Jane told him that the service elevator in the Linden Building was right next to the mailboxes in the rear hallway, behind Athena's Garden. Earlier in the day, he'd spent a couple of uneventful hours sleeping in his car, but he was so sleep deprived that it hadn't even made a dent in his exhaustion. He walked through the lobby like a zombie, weighed down by a seemingly bottomless sadness.

Setting down the duffel, David read through the names on the register next to a phone. Tammi Bonifay was the name of the woman Joanna was subletting the loft from.

"Four oh one," he whispered, picking up the receiver and pressing the extension. Joanna would need to buzz him in. He wished he still had a few of those uppers left, but he'd used them all on the drive here. Joanna's voice startled him when she finally answered.

"Yes?"

"Joanna? It's David."

"I'll buzz. When you get off, walk straight to the end of the hallway. My door's on the right."

"Okay." It was an old building with a limited security system, but any security system was worth its weight in gold in a big city.

Up on four, David picked up his gear and headed down the hall. He liked old, banged-up, drafty lofts. Diego had renovated four or five in downtown Atlanta in the last few years. Gentrification of the seedier sections of town would only serve to push the rougher element somewhere else. "Like the burbs," muttered David, a wicked smile on his face. He may not have been an inner-city denizen in his youth, but he'd become one—and was damn proud of it. "But I digress," he whispered, pounding on Joanna's door.

When the door swung back, Joanna was shouting, "Stop that racket!"

"Hi," said David, forcing a smile.

"You look awful."

"You don't look so hot yourself."

He walked in, gave the place a quick look. "God," he said, his mouth dropping open, "I've just walked into a country-western wet dream." He dropped his bag, turned around, and hugged his sister. He was surprised by how fiercely she hugged him back.

"You okay?" he asked.

"No," she said. "Since you asked, I'm just this side of a nervous breakdown. How about you?"

"A nervous breakdown sounds good. If nothing else, the decorating in this place should push us over the edge. I feel like breaking knicknacks with a hammer. How about you?"

"Be serious."

"I am. When we're done, we can get drunk and sit in the bathtub singing 'Happy Trails to You.' "

She gave him a long, disgusted look. "Did you call Diego?"

"Yes, Mother."

She cracked a smile. "God, but it's good to see you."

"I thought you were mad at me."

"I was."

"And now you're not?"

"Actually, I can't remember exactly why I was mad. But it will come to me."

"Probably my generally obtuse behavior."

"Probably," she said, dropping down on the couch in the living room. She picked up a stuffed bear and hugged it to her chest.

"Maybe I was mad at *you*," said David, finding his own stuffed animal to hug—a fluffy white sheep.

"I seem to detect a pattern here," said Joanna.

"Are you saying we're predictable?"

"Boringly adolescent is more like it."

"Then maybe we should turn over a new leaf. No more yearlong snits."

"What's life without a little drama?"

He shrugged. Walking over to the windows, he looked out at the lights of downtown Minneapolis. "Great view. You really think Luberman's after you again? I mean, those flowers you got weren't precisely the same."

"I know in my gut that it's him."

In David's opinion, Joanna's "gut" wasn't famous for its accuracy. Even so, he felt deeply sorry for her. He wanted to help. "Are you scared?"

"Hell, yes!"

He noticed now that she was drinking. Normally, the hardest thing she ever touched was an occasional beer. Turning to the dining room, he spied two wooden cases of wine on the table. "You planning to drink yourself to death?"

"The wine? It's a gift from one of the tenants. He's a wine importer."

"Lucky you. You're already making friends."

"Yeah, lucky me."

He sat down on the couch next to her. "Just tell me what you want me to do. If I can help, I will."

"Thanks. Let me think about it."

"Have you unpacked yet?"

She took a sip of the scotch, held the glass to her cheek. "Yeah. Nothing else to do. Cordelia left a couple of hours ago. She had to get over to the theater. Jane left, too. She had to work tonight at that new restaurant of hers."

"Wanna go check it out?"

"The Xanadu Club? Right now?"

"Sure. Why not?"

She covered his hand with hers. "I do want to see it, but . . . I just don't feel up to it tonight. Besides, if Gordon is out there somewhere—"

"Don't do that, Joanna. Don't let him force you to live in a cave. I mean, look. It may not even be him. There may be some other explanation. Getting out would do you a world of good."

She listened but shook her head. "I know you're right, but the flight here was tiring. I just don't have the steam tonight. Another night, okay?"

"Okay." He glanced at his duffel bag. "Where do I bunk?"

"You're gonna just love this, Davey. Every room in this loft has a theme. I'm staying in the rooster bedroom right off the kitchen."

"Rooster bedroom? You dare talk about a 'rooster bedroom' to a professional interior designer?"

"You'll love it. Roosters everywhere. Resin rooster hooks. Rooster plates. A rooster braided rug. Even rooster sheets and pillowcases."

"Are there any rooster barf bags?"

She socked him in the arm. "And then there's another room that's sort of retro-Americana—photographs of old gas stations from the fifties, art deco malt shops, old cars, and stacks and stacks of old postcards. Oh, and there's a *Father Knows Best* poster over the bed."

"That's where I want to die, Joanna. It's too perfect for words."

"And the bathroom off that bedroom is decorated all in apple decor."

"Apple decor," he repeated, smiling with absolutely no warmth.

"The other bedroom is pigs and chickens. The Americana bedroom shares the apple bathroom with the pigs and chickens bedroom."

He put his hand over his stomach. "I may need to use that rooster barf bag sooner rather than later." He glanced at her out of the corner of his eye and saw her looking back at him. "What?"

"Why'd you take off from Atlanta? Diego was beside himself with worry."

"It's personal. Between Diego and me."

"Don't tell me you two are having problems?"

"Would that surprise you?"

"Yes! You guys have the best relationship I know. To stay with the retro theme, you're like Ozzie and Harriet. Lucy and Desi."

"Desi was a bastard. He and Lucy split because he couldn't keep his pants zipped."

"You mean . . . is *that* your problem?" Joanna set her drink down and stared at him full in the face. "Tell me, David. Has Diego been unfaithful?"

David figured he might as well let her believe what she wanted. It was as good as anything. "Our problems are between us. I can't talk about it."

"Oh, you poor boy. I can't imagine, after being together for so many years."

He didn't say anything, just tried to look tragic. "I think I'll stow my stuff."

"Sure, hon. Whatever you want. There's food in the fridge. I could fix you something, but—"

He laughed, probably too loudly. "You're such a great cook. Remember that chicken tartare you made once?"

"That's what *you* called it."

"That's what it was."

"So I undercooked it a little."

"It could have put an entire cruise ship in the emergency room."

She leaned her head back and smiled. "It's so great to see you. It's been too long. Sometimes I think the best part of my life was years ago, when we were kids. When everybody I loved was still alive."

"You mean Mom and Dad."

"I miss them. You and me, we're all that's left. No kids to pass on the line. Sometimes that makes me feel incredibly depressed."

David had never seen his sister actually high before, but he suspected she was pretty tight at the moment. Not slurring drunk, but not far from it. Maybe staying here wouldn't be so bad after all. But first things first. Joanna might not be a drunk, but she did like pills. And that's when he got an idea.

"I gotta pee," he said, rising from the couch.

"Use the apple bathroom. I'm using the sailboat one."

Exactly the information he needed. "Thanks. Be back in a sec." If he could just find himself a little plastic bottle of speed, he might survive the next few days just fine.

9

The IHOP on Reindeer Lake was always pretty dead by eleven P.M. A few customers straggled in, but mostly Brandy Becker spent her time standing behind the counter, refilling salt and pepper shakers. Normally, she worked seven A.M. to three-thirty, but last week she'd asked for a schedule change. She didn't want to be home in the evenings right now. It was just temporary, she'd told her boss. She'd be back working days in no time.

Brandy had been a waitress for most of her forty-three years. She was the mother of one son, Todd, who'd just begun his second year of college at UW-Madison. She'd gone straight from her mother and father's home to a marriage with her high school sweetheart. When her husband died less than a year ago, she was on her own for the first time in her life—on her own and scared to death. She had a little house not far from the restaurant, so she could walk to work. She had an old Dodge sitting in the garage, but she didn't drive. She'd never learned. There was no need, since her husband could drive her anywhere she wanted to go. She had a couple of good friends, but mostly she worked because, when she was by herself, all she did was cry. But then she met Gordon.

Last May—she couldn't remember the exact date—she'd noticed

a man come into the IHOP for the first time. She knew most of the regulars, and he wasn't one of them. She hadn't waited on him that morning, but she did see him looking at her. He never smiled, so he wasn't flirting. He just watched. A few days later he came in again. This time he sat in her section. She brought him a glass of water and asked what he wanted. He seemed so glum that she decided then and there she'd try to cheer him up. Everyone always told her that her kind heart would get her in trouble one day, but she never believed it.

"Why so sad, hon?" she'd asked as she poured him coffee.

"Do I seem sad to you?" he'd asked.

"Yeah, hon, you do. I know what it feels like myself, but it always passes. You just gotta remember that."

And then he'd smiled. He wasn't good-looking. Some people might call him "big," but that would've been a charitable way to put it. Then again, there was something in that smile that warmed her clear down to her toes.

"You're very sweet," he'd said.

"You keep smilin', you hear me?" she'd told him before he left.

The next day he'd come in again. They'd talked a little more. She found out his name was Gordon and that he was a landscape designer, had his own business. He impressed her then as a man of substance and integrity. He'd never been married and didn't have any kids. And he *was* a deeply sad soul, she could see it even more clearly. They were both sad and lonely, both recently devastated by the loss of a loved one.

And then one day, out of the blue, he'd brought her a dozen red roses, the little ones she loved so much. She was so touched that she agreed to go on a date with him. He took her to his home on Whitefish Lake and asked if she'd like to take a ride on one of his boats. It was a beautiful early summer evening and he seemed so nice, so interested in what she had to say, that she said yes. After they came off the water, he fixed her dinner—fried fish he'd caught himself, a green salad, and garlic bread. She remembered it with great detail. She'd never had a man cook for her before. And when he brought out the apple pie he'd made especially for her, she fell in love, right then and there over the plate of pie and ice cream. She felt guilty for moving on with her life so quickly, but Gordon was too wonderful to pass up.

As Brandy reached under the counter for another container of salt, a man she'd known pretty much all her life came in. Larry McColm owned the filling station across the street from the Laundromat. He was married with four grown kids. Sitting down right in front of her, he grabbed the menu but didn't open it. There was no reason to since he probably knew it by heart.

"What are you doin' here so late?" he asked, pointing at the coffeepot behind her.

"Gus changed my hours. It's just temporary. Hey, how's that new grandson of yours doing?"

He grinned while she poured him a cup. "He's amazing. Smart as a whip. He's crawling now, so he's into everything. Pulls out the pots and pans and bangs on them. But you know, the kid's actually got rhythm. Think maybe he's going to be a drummer."

Brandy laughed, leaning into the counter. "Bet your daughter would love that."

"Yeah, she'd probably insist that he practice over at our house." He sipped his coffee. "Did I tell you we got another one on the way?"

"No," said Brandy.

"Yup. Cindy's pregnant." He leaned closer to her, put a finger to his lips. "I did the math. Just between you and me, I think there was some hanky-panky before the marriage ceremony."

They both giggled.

"Yeah, well, young love," said Brandy. Out of the corner of her eye, she saw Gordon standing in the doorway. She had no idea how long he'd been there, but the look on his face told her he was still angry.

"Will you excuse me a second?" she said to Larry. By the time she came around the end of the counter, Gordon had taken a seat at a table by the windows. They'd had a bad fight last week. Gordon had scared her. He hadn't hit her, but he'd come pretty close. He'd left her house in a rage, slamming the door behind him. She hadn't seen him since that night. She was sorry for what she'd said and knew without a doubt that it was only a matter of time before they talked about it and she could apologize. But he needed to apologize, too.

As she stepped up to the table, he said, "Who's that guy you're flirting with?"

"Flirting?" She was taken off guard. "I've known Larry since I was in third grade. He's happily married, Gordon. We were talking about his grandkids."

"Yeah, right." He scowled down at a newspaper he'd brought with him.

She sat down. "Look, I'm sorry about the other night. I shouldn't have raised my voice at you the way I did. But you had no right to open my mail."

"That son of yours has it in for me. He's trying to break us up. I deserve to know what he's saying to you behind my back."

It was true that Todd didn't like Gordon. He'd called him a lying SOB, said that he was trying to control her life. Maybe Gordon was a bit controlling, but Todd never saw the other sides of him. The tenderness. The generosity. Without being asked, Gordon had begun taking care of her lawn. He'd even planted some new bushes in front of the house and created a beautiful wildflower garden for her in the backyard. He told her he wasn't always good with words, but hoped that his gifts would show her how much he loved her. She hated the fact that they'd been arguing about Todd. They had to get past it, back to where they started.

"All right," said Brandy. "I'll admit that Todd has his own opinions. But he doesn't know you the way I do. He can't break us up, sweetheart. You've got to believe that."

"You swear it? Because—remember what I told you the first night we were together? I'm nobody's one-night stand. You're my woman now and I expect certain things from you, just as you do from me. I love you, Brandy. I want us to be together forever."

"I know that. And I love you for it."

"Then tell your son to back off. If he can't treat me with respect, he has no right to be in your life."

Statements like that took her breath away. Maybe it was because he didn't have children of his own. She knew he was a good man, she'd just have to trust that he'd come to understand how important Todd was in her life. In time, Todd would become central to Gordon's life, too.

"I'll talk to him," said Brandy.

Gordon glanced over at the man sitting at the counter. "He's just a friend, huh?"

"Not even that," said Brandy. "Just a guy I've known a long time."

Staring at her hard, he finally seemed to relent. "I believe you. I've missed you." He reached for her hand.

She wanted to say she felt the same way, but something odd happened. She opened her mouth, but the words wouldn't form.

Gordon smiled, then opened the newspaper and began looking it over. "Thought maybe we'd take a little drive this weekend, spend some time in the Twin Cities."

"I work on Sunday."

"Can't you get it off?"

"Let me talk to Millie." She watched him flip through the pages. "You want something to eat?"

"Yeah, bring me the stuffed French toast and a couple of eggs over easy."

She took the order back to the kitchen, clipped it up on the check wheel, then hit the order bell. When she returned to the dining room to get him a cup of coffee, she glanced over at his table. He was reading the paper with a look of such intensity in his eyes that it stopped her. An instant later, a wave of anger passed over his face.

"Gordon, what's wrong?"

Before she could get to him, he was out the door.

Walking over to the table, she glanced down at the section of the paper he'd been reading. It was a story about Joanna Kasimir, the actress. There was a big picture of her next to a smaller picture of a theater in St. Paul.

Brandy sank down on the chair to study the photo a little more closely. Secretly, she'd always thought she looked a bit like Joanna Kasimir. Blond hair. Pretty. Well, pretty years ago. But Brandy was a little heavier and not at all glamorous. The story was about a play a Twin Cities theater was doing later this fall, with Joanna Kasimir in the lead role. Nothing particularly upsetting in any of that. Beneath it were a bunch of adds. One for a shoe store, another for a new tooth-whitening treatment. She couldn't imagine why Gordon had flown out of the restaurant with such a black look on his face.

As Brandy sat staring at the empty doorway, it suddenly occurred to her that she may have been a little too trusting. As quickly as the thought crossed her mind, she tried to bury it, but it popped right back up. Okay, she thought. Maybe she should take stock.

She'd been with Gordon for four months. With the exception of the last couple of weeks, they'd been incredibly happy together. She told herself—and everyone else in her life who would listen—that she was head over heels in love. And yet, against her will she was beginning to see cracks forming around the edges of that love.

"Be honest," she whispered to herself. "You don't have a clue who this man really is."

Bel Air, California
Spring 1989

Joanna returned home from her meeting at Paramount around four-thirty. Thankfully, she'd remembered the six-pack of Coke for Gordon. After stuffing it in the refrigerator, she took a quick shower, changed into a pair of tight jeans and a beaded bright coral camisole, and then headed down to the guesthouse to tell her brother to stay away from the main house for the next few hours. She was on the walkway above the cabana when she looked down and saw that Gordon was in the pool, taking a swim. The sight of him stopped her dead in her tracks. None of the men who'd worked on her property over the years had ever had the audacity to take a dip in her pool. Good looks be damned. This guy had crossed a line.

Storming down the stairs, ready to give him his walking papers, she hesitated behind a deck chair when she realized he was naked.

"Oh, hi," he called, stroking over to the side of the pool. He rested his arms on the edge and smiled. His teeth looked like extralarge Chicklets, the gum her father always chewed, but they seemed to fit his big, square face. "Thought I better clean up a little before I met with my employer."

"Well, yes, about that——"

"I cleaned your pool filter while I was at it. The guy who does the maintenance is lazy. And this is just a guess, but I don't think he's got the chemicals balanced right. I think you'll find that the alkalinity is low. That's

not good for your skin——or the pumps. I've got a bottle of test strips in my truck. I can check it for you later if you want."

"Well, actually——"

"You better look away while I get out. I'll get dressed and meet you back at the house." He hoisted himself halfway out of the water and just rested there, flexing his muscles and grinning at her.

"Um, okay."

Joanna looked over and saw that David and Diego's rental car was gone. With that situation handled, she headed back to her house. On the way up the flagstone walk, she tried to define what she was feeling. She was still angry that he felt he could just take a swim without even asking, but on the other hand, it was apparent he hadn't done it out of arrogance. He was confusing, and when it came to men, Joanna wasn't easily confused.

She was sitting on the terrace in one of the wicker chairs, drinking a beer when he trotted up the stairs. His hair was still wet. He'd tried to dry it, but it spiked in pretty much every direction. The fact that he didn't seem to care intrigued her. She'd set out a glass of ice on the glass table and placed the unopened Coke can next to it.

"Hey, thanks," he said, lowering himself onto the wicker chair across from her. "This is great." He held the cold can to his forehead for a moment, then poured the liquid over the ice. "Oh, crap."

"What?" Joanna was studying him over the rim of her beer glass.

"I forgot to bring the drawings and the notes I made."

"You made drawings?"

"When I broke for lunch, I got out my pad and pencil and walked around the property. This is a terrific setting, up on the hill like this."

For the next few minutes he went through the property, from the front to the back. He detailed the kinds of native California plants he wanted to use. He asked her a few questions, then said he thought she should plant for color and fragrance. He thought that the hill should be terraced, and that one section should be turned into a wildflower garden. "It would be a retreat for you, a place to center yourself and reflect."

"And . . . what would I reflect on?" she asked.

"How to stay sane in the midst of chaos."

"You think this is chaos?"

"Hollywood is—the lifestyle you're forced to live out here."

"Maybe I like chaos."

"Sure, I wouldn't doubt it. Chaos is freedom. Total freedom, in fact, but no meaning."

She set her beer down and leaned forward. "Who the hell are you?"

"Your gardener."

"You talk to me about flowers and meaning all at the same time. Hey, are you some kind of Jesus freak? Or a fundamentalist who's about to tell me I'm headed for hellfire?"

"No," he said, laughing. "I'm not even sure you could call me a Christian. See, I don't want to just believe in something because some minister says it's true from a pulpit, I want it to really be true."

"And what do you believe in?"

He sipped his drink, thought a few seconds, then said, "Redemption. Love. Second chances."

"You think you need a second chance?"

"No, I think you do."

Nobody had ever talked to her like that before. She had the odd sense that he could see inside her, down deep where she really lived. It was a place she rarely visited these days.

"So what do you think?" he asked.

Everything he said seemed to catch her off guard. "About what?"

"My landscape ideas."

"Oh," she said, picking the beer up again. When she'd invited him to come up to the house after he was done working, she'd imagined that the conversation would eventually lead to the bedroom. Apparently, she'd been wrong. He wasn't putting any moves on her at all, and again, that confused her. He didn't act like a normal guy. And then it struck her. Sure, he had to be gay.

She nodded, setting down her glass and pushing it away.

"You look amused. Did I say something funny?"

"No, I just figured you out."

"You did?" He grinned at her like the Cheshire cat. This particular look did have more than a hint of arrogance in it. "Okay, let's hear it."

She toyed with the beads on her camisole. "You're gay."

The smile evaporated. "I'm what? What the hell gave you that idea?"

"You're not gay?" she said weakly.

He crossed his arms over his chest and stared at her hard with those eerie light blue eyes. After a minute, he said, "Ah, I get it. You're worried because I haven't made a pass at you."

"I'm not worried," she countered. She wished she hadn't sounded quite so defensive.

"Does every man you meet have to be attracted to you?"

"No, of course not."

"But most are. They're not only attracted to your beauty but to your fame."

"Well, yeah, something like that."

"You've talked to me for a while, maybe got to know me a little. You think I'm just like every other guy?"

She blinked. "No, actually, I don't."

"You know, Joanna, I hope you don't take this the wrong way. I know on the outside your life looks pretty incredible——American dream–type great. A lot of women probably wish they were you and a lot of men no doubt wish they could make love to you. I'm just guessing here, but I'll bet it doesn't look quite so rosy from the inside. Any woman who thinks I'm going to sleep with her before I even know who the hell she is has a very low opinion of herself—— and of me. You might want to take a hard look at your values, Joanna, unless you checked them next to some casting couch. I'm sure you had lots of dreams growing up. Is this the life you really wanted?"

"How dare you talk to me like that. You don't even know me!"

He finished his Coke and stood. "If I'm not fired, I'll be back on Thursday. I can show you my drawings then, if you still want to see them." With that, he nodded and headed back down the terrace steps.

Dazed, Joanna sat and stared after him. She had no idea what had just happened.

Two nights later, Joanna stood on the deck overlooking her back garden and stared up at the immense vault of blue Pacific sky. She loved standing exactly in this spot, her hands curled around the wrought-iron railing, the soft evening breeze ruffling her hair. But she felt lonely tonight. David and

Diego had driven up to Santa Barbara earlier in the day to visit friends. They wouldn't be back for several days.

The irony of her situation wasn't lost on her. Millions of people around the world would kill to spend an evening with the famous, the talented, the gorgeous—drumroll—Joanna Kasimir, and yet here she was, alone and miserable. She was a Goliath who could be felled with a single stone.

Around ten, after soaking in the tub for an hour, she drifted back out to the balcony. She didn't feel like watching any more TV. She wasn't interested in the book she'd started. She'd called a couple of ex-boyfriends, but neither of them was home. That's when she got the idea to take a swim.

As she glanced down to see if she needed to turn on the spa lights around the pool, she was surprised to see someone doing laps.

"What the—" She squinted into the darkness. "Good Lord," she said under her breath. "It's him."

Feeling furious beyond belief, she raced back through the house and down the stairs. As far as she was concerned, she never wanted to see Gordon again. She'd thought about calling her local garden center to ask—no, demand—that they remove him and send someone new to care for her property, but she'd never gotten around to it.

Crossing the patio, Joanna's fury ramped up several more notches. Who the hell did this guy think he was? Using her pool like he owned the place! Maybe he was a psychopath and she should be afraid of him. But he seemed so normal that she discarded that idea almost as quickly as it entered her mind.

"What the hell do you think you're doing?" she yelled from the flagstone path. She flipped on the light switch. Soft lights illuminated the pool area. "Oh, God," she groaned. He was naked again. And he was smiling at her, treading water near the diving board. "Get the hell out of there now or I'll call the police."

He swam over to the edge, propped his arms on the ledge. "I'm sorry if I scared you."

"You don't scare me, you infuriate me."

He waited until she'd stormed through the gate before he said, "I know this may seem a little forward."

"Forward doesn't begin to cover it, pal."

"But I thought if I came up to the house, rang the front bell, that you wouldn't talk to me."

72

"You got that right."

He ran a hand over his wet hair. "I brought the drawings I made. Actually, I've done a bunch more since we talked."

"And I should care why?"

"Don't be like that, Joanna. I've never been anything but straight with you. If you don't like me, that's fine. I can live with it. But at least give the drawings a look. My work is very important to me. I'd like to make this place something you can be proud of—a home where you can relax and rejuvenate. If you don't like my ideas, I'll leave. You'll never see me again, I promise."

Light glinted off the muscles in his arms. She was appalled that she found him attractive, but apparently her hormones were on autopilot. She stared at him for a long moment, then said, "I'm bored." It was the truth.

"You're what?" He broke into a grin, then disappeared beneath the water. A moment later, he roared up, laughing.

"What's so funny about being bored?"

"Nothing, Jo. Nothing at all."

Nobody called her Jo except family and friends. He was neither. But for some reason, she didn't mind. "Oh, all right. Get dressed and bring you drawings up to the house."

"You got any of that Coke left?"

"Let's look at the drawings first."

"You're a hard taskmaster."

"And you're full of shit."

The smile faded. "I'm not, Jo. I'm the real thing."

She had no idea what he meant by that, and had no desire to find out. Turning away quickly because he was already halfway out of the water, she walked back up to the house. The entire way she repeated to herself, "Understanding Gordon Luberman is not necessary. Keep it simple." She'd take a look at his stuff. If it was any good, she might agree to it. If not, he'd be long gone before Saturday Night Live came on.

They sat together on the couch in the living room for the next twenty minutes with his drawings spread out on the coffee table. He had on a clean white Oxford shirt and jeans. His feet were bare. He smelled like the outdoors, clean and fresh, though mixed with a light scent of chlorine. When he talked about flowers and shrubs, about the trees he wanted to plant, and especially when he described the wildflower garden he wanted to create for her, his eyes glowed and his brow furrowed in concentration. He seemed completely unaware of how handsome he was, how graceful his movements were. She'd never met anyone quite like him before.

"So what do you think?" he asked, standing and gathering the drawings together.

"I like it."

"Which idea specifically?"

"All of them."

He rolled up the drawings, then slipped a rubber band around them. "You're serious?"

"Why wouldn't I be?"

Sitting down next to her, he turned to face her, looking deep into her eyes.

She felt uncomfortable by the searching nature of his gaze, but not so uncomfortable that she looked away.

"You're amazing, Joanna. You're like a jewel in a junkyard."

"Gee, what a flattering image."

"It hurts me to see you so unhappy."

"What the hell gave you that impression?"

"Come with me." He took her hand and pulled her out to the patio. Standing behind her, he said, "Look up at the sky. What do you see?"

She decided to play along. "Darkness. A few stars."

"Right. There are only a few we can see when we're in the city—the really bright ones."

"And you're about to compare me to a bright star. Not very original."

"No. I'm telling you that that's what you need. Something really bright to navigate your life by. Sailors used the stars for centuries to travel the open seas. On a clear night, they could be anywhere in the world and know where they were simply by looking up."

As usual, he'd confused her. She thought he was headed in one direction, but he took another. She wasn't sure what he was getting at, but she liked the feel of his hands on her bare shoulders.

"We need something really bright to navigate this dark jungle of a world by, Jo. Especially here in Hollywood. We need, like, some overwhelmingly important central value to keep us on the right course."

"And that value would be . . . ?"

He slid his hands to her hips and turned her to face him. "Love."

She blurted out the first thing to come into her head. "Love is for suckers, Gordon."

"But it's not. It's everything. It's the whole world." He ran his hand lightly across her face, brushed a wisp of hair off her forehead.

"What is this? Two days ago you didn't like me and now you love me?"

"I don't love you, Jo."

His words hurt, but she refused to let him see it. "Then . . . this is just a seduction scene? I'm supposed to fall into your arms. If that's it, Gordo, you can forget it. I've played that part too many times. I know where it leads."

"Good God, woman, you are so jaded. Why is that? What's eating at you that you won't face?"

"Why do you always assume there's something wrong with me? I hate that. I don't need your armchair psychology. Besides, I thought we were talking about love. My guiding star."

"We were."

"But you don't love me."

"No." He hesitated. "But I'm beginning to see that I could."

"Oh, goody. News flash, Gordo. I'm not suffering for male companionship."

"Yes you are."

She cocked her head at him. "Why do you keep correcting everything I say?"

He grinned. "Not everything."

"Feels like it to me. I mean, one minute you don't like me at all—"

"I never said I didn't like you, I just said I didn't want to sleep with someone I didn't know."

"So you've had an epiphany and now you know me?"

His expression sobered. "I realize it sounds strange, but I think I have had an epiphany, as you put it."

"Here comes the seduction scene."

He brought his face close to hers. His breath smelled both sweet and salty at the same time. "Would that be so bad?"

Joanna was trembling. She was sure he could feel it through her light cotton clothes. She wanted him so badly it scared her. "You're an excruciatingly principled man," she said, struggling to tuck her emotions back inside. "I, on the other hand, am not a particularly principled woman."

"I've noticed."

Their lips were just millimeters apart.

"Joanna, if we become lovers, it will mean something to me. I'm nobody's one-night stand. You have to know that up-front."

She was intoxicated by everything about him. "I do."

"Because, what it comes down to . . . is . . . I'd like to be that bright light in the sky for you, a star you could navigate by in the darkness."

"You are one strange dude."

He kissed her tenderly at first, his hands caressing her bare back, but when he began to undress her, his kisses grew hungrier, more intense. Joanna matched his passion with her own. It was at that moment, with her last consciously analytical thought, that she wondered if she was lost once again on another dead-end street, or if this time, she'd finally been found.

10

Jane sat cross-legged in the center of an oversized upholstered chaise, going through the file on Gordon Luberman. Joanna had not only consented to allow Jane to help Nolan on the case, she was actually enthusiastic about it. She was impressed by Nolan's credentials but said she didn't know him from Adam. She did know and trust Jane, and that went a long way toward easing her mind.

"Knock knock," came Cordelia's voice from outside the mahogany velvet theater curtain.

Cordelia had suggested that Jane commandeer the raised stage at the back of the loft for the duration of her stay. In the past, Cordelia had used it for impromptu performances, generally when she'd invited her theater friends over for dinner. At the moment, it was being used for storage—everything Cordelia couldn't bring herself to toss but that didn't fit with the new Swedish modern look of her place. Even with all the storage boxes and furniture, there was still plenty of room for Jane to stretch out, lots of lamps to choose from, and an exceptionally comfortable oversized corduroy-covered chaise to sleep on. The stage was maybe thirty feet long by ten feet wide. And it afforded more privacy than any other section of the loft. Mouse was nestled into a quilt next to the chaise. Like Jane, he was adaptable.

"Come in," she whispered. It was just after eleven. Hattie and her nanny, Cecily Finch, had already gone to bed. Jane had left the club earlier than normal because she wanted to get to work on the file.

Cordelia poked her head through the curtain, looked around briefly to make sure nothing would fall on her, then pushed her way through. "Yuck," she said, brushing off her black velvet evening gown. "It's dusty in here."

"Good thing I can live with dust."

"That's exactly the pioneering spirit I've come to know and love about you, Janey." She batted at a cobweb. Her gown had the requisite deep, plunging neckline, but this one was new. It had a thick row of silver sequins starting at the top and swirling all the way around the dress several times until it reached the bottom hem. Cordelia might have said bye-bye to her size-eighteen clothes when she was in her teens, but she was still a voluptuous beauty by anyone's standards.

"From the way you're dressed, I take it you're getting back from the Laundromat," said Jane, glancing at the gown.

"How nice that you find yourself so amusing."

"Mouse thinks I'm funny, too."

"Splendid. I always take my humor cues from Labrador retrievers." Cordelia fluffed her long auburn curls as she lowered herself into a rickety director's chair. She nodded to the file. "I thought you might need some help. As a deeply compassionate friend, it pains me to see Joanna in such turmoil."

Jane flipped through a bunch of photos, pausing to look at one.

Cordelia was off the director's chair in a flash. Plunking down next to her, she said, "Let me see those."

Jane handed her the one she was looking at.

"Wow, he *was* good-looking, if you like blonds with big muscles and equally big teeth."

"You've never seen a picture of him before?"

"Never."

That surprised her. "Well, this particular photo was taken a few days after Joanna met him. There's a date on the back of the picture. Now look at this one." She pulled another one out of the pile.

"He's older here," said Cordelia. "Leaner, but he looks even more pumped. When was this taken?"

"Shortly after he got out of prison in July of 1998. Most of the photos were shot by the PI Joanna hired to keep tabs on him. His name was Petrosik. He lived in Appleton, which was close to where Luberman headed when he got out. Luberman moved in with his mother. Apparently, this Petrosik kept tabs on him until his mother died in 2002. Right after the funeral, he turned in his last report."

"Did Luberman, like, do anything criminal during that time?"

"Petrosik said he was living a quiet life."

"Define quiet."

"No arrests. No documented run-ins with the law."

"What else?"

"Well, according to what I read, he liked to fish. Bought himself a used houseboat a few weeks after he returned home. Petrosik said he would take it out on Lake Winneconne around dusk and spend the night on the water."

"Did this investigator watch him *all* the time?"

"I doubt it. But he did spend a few evenings sitting by the shore, watching to see if Luberman came back. He didn't."

"What if he anchored the boat, then swam back to another spot? That would give him the entire evening to himself—free as a bird to do whatever he wanted."

"But without wheels. His mother's car was back at the boat landing."

"Maybe he had a girlfriend. She picked him up."

"That's an interesting point. There was a note here that a woman in a nearby town—" Jane paged through the file. "Yeah, here it is. Her name was Mandy Kiskanen. She lived in Poygan, another small town close to Winneconne. She was single, in her early thirties. She worked at a restaurant in Winneconne. Her friends all said she never dated, although one of them insisted that she'd been over to Mandy's place one night and a man was in the bedroom. She could smell aftershave, and there was a man's red-and-black hunting jacket on the couch. Apparently, Mandy hustled her out almost immediately. And then, seven months later, Mandy's body was found washed ashore on Lake Poygan. She'd been strangled. The murderer was never found."

"You think Luberman did it?"

"I think it's possible, not that he'd ever murdered anyone before."

"Did Petrosik make that connection?"

"He said that Luberman often wore a red-and-black hunting jacket. But then, lots of men do. Nobody had ever seen them together. According to Petrosik, he spent a lot of time turning his mother's front and back yards into a garden masterpiece. There was even a feature article on it in the local paper."

"Oh, joy," said Cordelia. "Every neighborhood needs a psychopathic gardener." She tapped a finger against her cheek. "So, we don't have any info on the last two years?"

"Not in this file. And there's basically nothing on the trial. If you recall, part of the plea bargain was that the details would be sealed. In one of Petrosik's early reports, he mentions that he's sure Luberman spotted him. If Luberman knew he was being tailed, he'd be on his best behavior—as long as he was being watched."

"Thus the houseboat. A way to leave prying eyes behind."

"Maybe. I just wish I knew more about what happened all those years ago." Jane let her words hang in the air, waiting to see if she could get Cordelia to break her silence.

Cordelia sat still for a few seconds, then pressed her hands to the sides of her face and groaned. "Lord, if I wasn't the poster child for moral integrity, the tales I could tell you."

"You can't tell me anything?"

"Janey, she's embarrassed and appalled by what she did. Can you blame her?"

"Okay, but can you just tell me this? I know Luberman stalked her, but . . . were they ever lovers?"

Cordelia shook her head. "I promised. I mean, I'm dying here. I'd like to tell you the whole megillah, but . . . I can't."

"It's just . . . if it wasn't Luberman, I wonder if someone else sent her the roses innocently. You know, just a fan. Or, on the other hand, maybe they *were* sent to rattle her. A copycat crime?"

"Not possible. The rose thing was never made public. Joanna made sure it was kept a secret."

Jane finished off her brandy and soda.

"Well," said Cordelia, slapping her thighs and getting up, "better go check on Hattie. You wanna come with me?"

"To do what?"

"Watch her sleep."

Jane wanted another drink, and Hattie's room was on the way. "Sure. Why not."

As Cordelia edged into the room, she motioned for Jane to follow. "Look," she whispered, standing over Hattie's bed. The little girl was lying on her side amid a sea of pink covers, her right arm circling a scruffy gray puppet, her left hand curled softly under her chin. "Isn't that the most staggeringly beautiful sight you've ever seen?"

Jane smiled, slipping a hand over Cordelia's shoulder.

"I've finally found the love of my life. Who knew it would be a kid?"

"Have you heard from Octavia recently?"

Octavia Thorn Lester was Cordelia's younger sister—Hattie's mother.

"She's in London."

"Doing what?"

"Being important."

After acting on Broadway for many years, Octavia was now off pursuing a career in film. She had brought Hattie to a location shoot in Switzerland last year, but when it was over, she sent Hattie back to stay with Cordelia. It was all supposed to be temporary—nothing formal had been worked out—but Cordelia assumed that Hattie would spend the rest of her childhood in Minnesota, which was fine with her. Octavia was always fluttering off to do something glitzy and important for her career. Or she was between houses. Or she was jetting off somewhere with the current man in her life and felt that Hattie would just be bored. The excuses were endless and obvious: Octavia had no time in her life for her daughter.

As Jane edged out of the room, she saw Cordelia bend down, pull the covers up over Hattie's shoulder, and then kiss her lightly on the forehead. Who would have ever guessed that a child-loathing, curmudgeonly old theater director, one who regularly fumed about ankle biters and rug rats, a person whose life had been focused on a single theme since she was old enough to recognize a stage, would become the living embodiment of Auntie Mame? Well, thought Jane, maybe, in the final analysis, it would turn out to be the part Cordelia was born to play.

Bel Air, California
Six days later

Joanna wasn't awake, but she wasn't asleep. She was somewhere in that in between state where her mind drifted. She could feel Gordon's strong arms around her, holding her against him, his soft breathing matching the rise and fall of her own breaths. In this fuzzy state, she slipped back easily to the last few days, walking along the beach together, laughing at the most silly, inane things, eating at strange new restaurants along the coast highway. It was all a jumble and a blur, but even in her altered state, she knew she was happy. Happier than she'd ever been.

Opening her eyes, the bedroom slowly came into focus. The bright morning light slanted in through the shades, throwing a pattern of lines across the bouquet of red roses on the dresser. Gordon had bought them for her after their first night together. Joanna still marveled at the way he treated her. There was none of the typical deference or desire to impress that usually attended her sexual encounters. At first, Gordon's behavior had intrigued her, but now it felt more like drinking a cold glass of water on a hot summer day. It had been a long time since she'd met a man who wasn't impressed by her name, who saw her for what she was—flaws and all.

Turning on his back, Gordon stretched and flexed his leg muscles. Without opening his eyes, he drew her hand to his lips and kissed it. "Happy birthday, Jo."

"You remembered."

"Of course, I remembered. What time is the party?"

"Two. It'll just be the four of us."

David and Diego had arrived home late last night, obviously amused to find Gordon and Joanna in the pool together. David raised his eyebrows as Joanna introduced Gordon. Diego just smirked. She knew what they were thinking: Gordon was simply one more boy toy in an endless stream of boy toys. They didn't stick around the pool for more than a couple of minutes. They probably figured Joanna wanted some privacy.

"Your brother and that guy——"

"Diego."

"Yeah. Is he a buddy? A business partner?"

"They're lovers. Or . . . partners, I guess. They've been together for five years."

"They're gay?" Gordon turned on his side to look at her. "Your brother's a homosexual?"

"That surprises you?"

He stared at her for a long moment, then shrugged. "No. I suppose not."

"David's hired a caterer. We're having all my favorite food. Shrimp. Pasta primavera. Chocolate cake. I'm sure as hell not about to watch my diet on my thirty-second birthday."

"Don't swear, Jo. It's crude."

"You swear all the time."

"I try not to."

She kissed his nose. "For you, I'll make the effort. But I can't promise total compliance."

His arms encircled her. "Can I tell you something?"

"Sure. Anything."

His expression grew serious. "I've never said this to a woman before, but . . . I think . . . I think I'm falling in love with you. Falling hard. Does that worry you?"

Hell no, she thought. But she said, "Why would it? I feel exactly the same way."

"You do?"

"Can't you tell?"

"This isn't a casual thing for me."

"For me either."

He brushed his fingertips across her face. "I want to be with you forever, Jo. For eternity. I want us to make a life together, to always be there for each other, no matter what happens. And there will be bad patches. Always are. But we'll get through them because of our love and our commitment."

"You beautiful man," she said, kissing him softly.

"I'll never say that in front of a priest or a judge," he whispered. "It's just between you and me. That's all we'll ever need."

"Okay," she whispered back.

"Because, I don't want to get married," he continued, pulling away from her. "Is that a problem?"

She laughed. "None whatsoever."

Gordon was gone for a few hours, but he returned right before the party, his arms full of fresh red roses. He kissed Joanna, then went to find a vase to put them in.

They walked down to the bungalow together. As they came through the front door, they found David and Diego sitting in the living room. Both got up and gave them a stiff greeting. The food was all laid out on the table. Balloons and crepe paper decorated both the living and dining rooms. Everything looked festive—except for David and Diego.

"Something wrong?" asked Joanna, linking her arm through her brother's.

"What could be wrong?" asked David.

His curt tone made her want to say "ouch." She put it down to a lovers' quarrel. David and Diego occasionally got into it. But then, after a few days, they always got over it—whatever "it" was. The fact that they were pissed at each other on her birthday was bad timing, but she shrugged it off. Nothing was going to ruin this day for her.

By four the presents had all been opened and the food was pretty much gone. They sat around the dining room table, drinking the last of the champagne and picking at the dregs of the cake. Both David and Diego had consumed more than their share of champagne. Joanna could tell that Gordon, who didn't drink, was pretty disgusted by them.

"Let's toast," said David, raising his glass.

"I can't toast," said Diego.

"Why the hell not?"

He tipped his glass over. "Empty."

"Not a problem." David pushed away from the table and disappeared into the kitchen, returning a moment later with an already open bottle of chenin blanc. "Here," he said, filling up Diego's glass. "Joanna?"

"She's had enough," said Gordon.

David shrugged and filled his own glass to the brim. Raising it high he said, "To Jo and Gordo. May they ride off into the red, white, and blue sunset together."

"Not a rainbow sunset?" asked Diego.

"No way," said David. "That's only for perverts like us."

"David?" said Joanna, her eyes searching his. "Look, if you guys are in the middle of a snit, that's between you, but could you do it later? This is supposed to be a celebration."

"Oh, we're celebrating," said Diego.

"Absolutely," said David.

"You could have fooled me," said Gordon.

David leaned over and draped his arm around Joanna's shoulders. "You're a real piece of work, you know that?"

She tried to pull away, but he wouldn't let go.

"My sister. The great actress. Too bad she isn't a better human being."

"That's it," said Gordon, standing up. "Joanna, let's go."

Joanna's head was spinning. Gordon was right. She'd had too much to drink. But that didn't explain what her brother had just said. "David, what's wrong with you?"

"Everything, Sis. Absolutely everything."

"Joanna, come on," said Gordon, yanking at her arm. "Let them drink themselves into a stupor. We've got better things to do."

Still glaring at her brother, Joanna got up. "We'll talk about this later."

"Bye," said Diego, waving at her like a prom queen.

"Yeah, ba' bye," said David, doing his stewardess imitation.

David's eyes looked so red that for a moment Joanna wondered if he was about to cry. She didn't want to leave him if he was truly in pain—if he and

Diego were about to break up or something—but he was being so abusive, leaving was probably for the best.

Joanna turned away and let Gordon lead her out, which, as it turned out, was one of the worst mistakes of her life.

11

The next morning, as Jane stood waiting for Nolan in the parking lot, her thoughts drifted to how serendipitous it had been that she'd met him, and how much her friendship with him meant to her. She'd spent her entire working life as a restaurateur, and yet during those eighteen years, she'd often been drawn to matters of crime and crime solving. For a time she decided that it was because her father was a defense attorney. As a child, she remembered sitting at the top of the stairs, listening to her mother and father talk in the living room. Her dad used her mother as a sounding board, taking cases apart, searching for a way to prove his client's innocence. The justice system wasn't supposed to work like that. People were innocent until proven guilty. But a lawyer was a storyteller, her father always said, and the best storyteller usually won.

Jane had grown up in a world peopled with criminals and victims. She knew that reality was often brutal, ugly, and final. She understood ambiguity, and yet she craved reassurance that she lived in a comprehensible moral universe. It was that need, she'd come to believe, that was at the heart of what always seemed to pull her toward issues of crime and punishment.

What Nolan offered her was something new: a legitimate entree into the world of the criminal. Jane wasn't a professional, nor was it likely she'd ever become one, but working with Nolan on a periodic basis would satisfy what she now saw was a fundamental need in her life and at the same time would allow her to keep one foot firmly planted in her everyday world—the world of restaurants that she loved so much. Jane felt certain that she could separate the two and still manage both of them successfully.

Nolan drove up in his black Toyota Highlander about ten after nine.

Getting settled in the front seat, Jane noticed that he'd bought them each a large cup of coffee.

"All the comforts of home," he said, backing out of the lot.

"Thanks. This is great. How far is it to Winneconne?" she asked, rolling her window down.

"Change of plans. After I left the loft yesterday, I stopped by the BCA in St. Paul to look Luberman up on the NCIC."

"You still have access to that?" The NCIC was the FBI's criminal information system. It was a computerized index of criminal justice information—records, criminal history, stolen property, missing persons. Jane was under the impression that it was available only to federal, state, and local law enforcement agencies. When Nolan was a cop, he no doubt used it daily. But as a civilian?

"Anyone can do a simple criminal background check at the BCA. All you need is the person's name and date of birth. Costs four bucks. A real deal, if you ask me."

"What did you find out?"

"Looks like a year or so after Joanna's PI stopped tailing him, he sold the family home and moved to Eagle Ridge, where he got a job at a lumberyard. He wasn't working while he was living with his mother."

"Yeah, I learned that from reading the file."

"Good. You can fill me in on that in a second. Here's what you didn't learn: Two years ago, he moved to Chamberlain—that's about ten miles south of Eagle Ridge. He started his own landscape company. Bought a cabin on Whitefish Lake. With all the new construction around Eagle Ridge, he's probably making a mint."

The Eagle Ridge section of Wisconsin was a popular tourist area.

The circle of seven lakes was covered with fishing lodges, old cabins, and an increasing array of vacation resorts. In the last dozen or so years, the land around the lakes had also become prime property for building new summer homes.

"What about his criminal history?" asked Jane, taking a sip of coffee.

"He's clean. Although, knowing what we know, a guy like that could easily operate under the radar."

"You think he's still stalking?"

"I wouldn't bet against it. Stalking is generally considered a serial crime."

As they merged onto I-94, Nolan adjusted the rearview mirror. "Stalkers are fairly predictable. I mean, psychologically, they follow a pattern."

"I've never read much about them."

"You should." He grabbed for his coffee. "Stalking is legally defined as willful, malicious, and repeated following and harassment combined with a credible threat intended to make the victim fear death or serious injury. Believe it or not, there weren't any stalking laws on the books until 1990. That seems incredible to me. One in twenty women will become a target of stalking at some point in her life. It's a devastating crime, with huge ramifications for the victim."

"Go on," said Jane, looking down at the river as they crossed over the Mississippi.

"Most victims know their stalkers. If they've slept with them, violence is significantly more likely to occur. These guys aren't typically psychotic, but if they're sociopaths, watch out. The motivation for stalking isn't primarily sexual. It develops more out of anger and hostility, usually because of a perceived or all too real rejection. These guys want control, and when they don't get it, they slowly begin to exchange reality for an imaginary world that's more empowering. It usually works like this. The guy thinks if he can just prove to her—whoever she is—that he loves her, then everything will be okay. They'll ride off into the sunset. When that doesn't work out, he moves on to, 'I can *make* her love me.' And when that fails, which it always does, he moves on to, 'If I can't have her, nobody can.' That's when things often get violent. We may not like to hear this, but a high percentage of stalkers who threaten their victims eventually act on their stated intentions."

Jane had not only never read much about stalkers, she'd never thought much about them—or their victims. Joanna always skirted the subject when it was brought up, though she never made light of it.

"Your turn," said Nolan. "What did you learn from that file?"

"Not as much as I'd hoped." She spent the next fifteen minutes going over every piece of information she thought might be significant. In the end, Nolan agreed that the most important fact had to do with the woman who'd been murdered not far from where Luberman had been living. But because there was no record of the 1990 trial, no psych evaluation from the prison doctors, and no information from the PI past 2002, there were too many holes to begin to form a clear picture.

"A little piece of luck did drop into our laps," said Nolan.

"Give."

"Happens that I know the sheriff of Eagle Ridge County. He's the first stop on our morning agenda."

Just after eleven-thirty, Nolan pulled into the parking lot of a two-story brick building in downtown Eagle Ridge. He gave his name to the deputy at the front desk. The man pointed them to an office just off the main reception area.

"Believe it or not, the sheriff's name is Al Hitchcock," said Nolan, as they walked down a short hallway. "Great guy. I used to play poker with his dad."

"His dad must have had a bizarre sense of humor."

"Yeah. That about covers it."

Nolan knocked on the open door.

The man inside, a thirty-something with thinning brown hair and a heavy mustache, looked up from a stack of papers. "Hey." He stood. "Great to see you."

They shook hands across the desk.

"How's that old man of yours?" asked Nolan, nodding for Jane to sit down in one of two empty chairs.

91

"Terrific. He's in Florida at the moment, but he said to say hi. Says he wants in on a game the next time he's in the Twin Cities."

"You tell him I'm always happy to take his money."

Hitchcock laughed.

Nolan introduced Jane as his assistant.

"Lawless," repeated Hitchcock, mulling it over as he sat back down. "Don't suppose you're any relation to—"

"He's my father," said Jane. Law enforcement people often recognized her last name. Raymond Lawless was well-known in the Midwest.

"How'd you hook up with this character?" he asked, grinning at Nolan.

"Long story," said Nolan. Again, he was all business. "So what do you know about Gordon Luberman?"

"Lots. Most of it unofficial. Before we get started, I want to thank you for giving me that information about Joanna Kasimir. That was totally off our radar screen. We knew he'd served time in prison but didn't have any of the details."

"My pleasure," said Nolan. He pulled out his pad, ready to take notes.

"Okay, Luberman lived up north in Winneconne for several years before moving down here. I assume you already know that. But what you don't know is that he'd been stalking a woman up there—"

"Mandy Kiskanen," said Jane.

"Who?"

Nolan filled him in as Hitchcock took notes.

"I'll check it out. If it was our boy, it may be just the break we need."

"So he was stalking someone else?" asked Jane.

"A woman who did the weather on a local TV channel in Appleton. They met when Luberman 'accidentally' scraped the side of her car with his truck. She said he was very charming, offered to pay for the entire thing himself so that neither of them would have to file with their insurance companies."

"Did he follow through with that promise?" asked Jane.

"Yes, and in the process, they began dating. She said she was on the rebound from a recent breakup. When she worked things out with the old boyfriend, she dumped Luberman—but he wasn't about to be dumped. At first she thought it was just stubbornness. But when he started following her, sending her red roses, calling her at all hours of the day and night, she got scared. Talked to a police officer. He told her to get a restraining order and start documenting the harassment."

"Obviously he was never arrested," said Jane.

"No. Seems his mother died right around then and he moved away. She hasn't heard from him since."

"She got lucky," said Nolan. "What else?"

Hitchcock leaned back in his chair, threaded his fingers over his stomach. "Well, as you can imagine, we don't have many people go missing around here. But a year ago, a woman who lived on Kenabig Lake disappeared."

"You think Luberman had something to do with it?"

"That's exactly what we think. Problem is, we can't prove it. We know he dated her, and we know from friends and relatives that she was scared to death of him."

"Anybody able to give details?" asked Nolan.

"Her cousin told us that Darlene—Darlene Schultz, that's her name—tried to break it off with Luberman, but that he kept showing up at her work. Or she'd go to the grocery store and he'd be waiting for her when she came out. He'd been calling her for weeks late at night, telling her she had to give him another chance. Professing his undying devotion."

"Sounds like his MO," said Nolan.

"Her dad said he was about ready to take a shotgun over to Luberman's place and have a little Come-to-Jesus meeting with him. But then she disappeared. The dad's positive Luberman's behind it. A female friend of hers told the father that, before she went missing, Luberman had phoned her, saying that if she didn't take him back, she'd be sorry."

Nolan shook his head. "That's a threat."

"Yeah, but the woman's scared and won't go on the record, so we can't get a warrant to search his property. And because it's hearsay, it's nothing we can arrest him on. You find anything I can use, you let me know."

"Sure," said Nolan.

"You got his address?"

Nolan flipped a few pages back in his notebook. "Fourteen Little Turtle Road."

"Follow Main Street out of town until you hit the turnoff for Chamberlain. Take a left at Fittman Road and follow it around the lake about a three miles. When you come to Mortonson Trail, turn left. Go about three-quarters of a mile until you see Little Turtle Road. It veers off to the right. You'll see a fourteen on his mailbox but no name. The cabin sits on a hill above the lake. Real pretty spot. But if you drive in, there's no real good place to park to surveil. If you want to brave the mosquitoes and the ticks in the woods above the property, you can do that."

"Where's his landscape company located?" asked Jane.

"In Chamberlain."

"I've got the address," said Nolan.

Jane felt like someone had just dumped a pail of raw sewage all over her. "I guess our guy isn't living the quiet life that it looked like on paper."

"Anything but," said Hitchcock.

"He dating anybody right now?" asked Nolan.

"Unfortunately, yes. Name's Brandy Becker. She's a waitress at the IHOP on Reindeer Lake. She's in her early forties. Husband died less than a year ago."

"Have you talked to her?" asked Nolan.

"Legally, I can't. You know the drill. I had someone approach her unofficially, but she's very timid and skittish. She wouldn't even talk to him. Luberman's aware that we're watching him, though. Sometimes, that can make a guy think twice."

"But Luberman's lost his fear," said Nolan. "If he ever had any to begin with."

"If he's after Joanna," said Jane, "maybe he'll leave this new woman alone."

"Don't count on it," said Hitchcock. "I've met some cold SOBs in my time, but he's by far the coldest."

"You've talked to him?" said Nolan.

"Sure. I've had him in here at least half a dozen times. He never gives up a thing. The arrogant prick doesn't even ask for a lawyer. He thinks he's smarter than everybody else. It's like a game to him."

"I have to say," said Nolan, "that I expected he might still be stalking." Standing, he reached to shake Hitchcock's hand again.

"I hope we can help each other," said Hitchcock. "This is one dude I intend to put away for good."

12

Hillary was on all fours in the bathroom, searching for a tiny garnet stud earring. If she didn't find it soon, she'd be late for work, which did nothing for her usual cranky morning mood.

"Hillary, will you hurry up," called her father. "Jesus, you'd think you were about to be interviewed on *Good Morning America*."

"Oh, hold your friggin' horses," she shouted. He was such a baby. The stud had fallen off just as she was about to slip the back on. She simply had to wear these earrings this morning because she'd seen Joanna Kasimir wearing a pair very much like them yesterday at the airport. Of course, Joanna's had been rubies.

Hillary's dad banged on the door. "Open up or I'm going to break it down!"

"Go ahead," she called back. "I'd like to see him try," she muttered, moving closer to the toilet. "Probably give him a coronary." That thought brought a smile to her lips. "There it is," she cried.

"There what is?" came his muffled voice.

She grabbed the stud, which had lodged itself in a groove in the floor tile grout. She inserted the stud and clamped the back on, then took a long appraising look at her makeup to make sure it was as understated as Joanna's, sprayed herself with a knockoff of Jean Patou's perfume Joy, and opened the door.

"Get out of my way," said her father, barreling in before she could even leave the room. "God, it smells like a cheap whore in here."

"You'd be the expert on that."

"What's that supposed to mean? Hillary, I've never gone to a whore in my entire life."

Maybe he should have, thought Hillary as she slammed the front door behind her. She drove to work listening to Rufus Wainwright, her newest musical passion. She had no idea what kind of music Joanna listened to, but in her mind she decided that Joanna would like Rufus.

Entering the hospital, Hillary took the elevator to the basement level. She stowed her purse in her locker, put on her pink smock, and unlocked the door to the flower shop. After switching on the lights and opening up the cash register, she stuck a sign in the door that read BACK IN TEN MINUTES, locked the room back up, and walked down the long hall to the cafeteria, which was already buzzing with people.

Stepping up to the pastry counter, Hillary ordered a chocolate doughnut and black coffee. The woman behind the counter, Carolyn Hanson, a gray-haired old shrew who thought she knew everything and was better than everybody else, gave her a lopsided grin. "So, did you see Joanna Kasimir yesterday like you said you would?"

Hillary could tell that Carolyn thought it was a big fat lie. Pulling a couple of ones out of her smock pocket, she said—as nonchalantly as she could manage—"Not only did I see her, we had dinner together."

"Right." The woman gave a phlegmatic nod. "Look, it's none of my business, Hill, but I don't understand why you spread this kind of ridiculous story around. A couple of the other servers told me you fed them the same line. You think by making stuff up, people are gonna like you better? 'Cause, it doesn't work like that. People just think you're bragging. Either that or you've got a screw loose."

"Believe what you want," said Hillary with a shrug. "I'll have pictures to show you in a few days. You can decide then if I'm telling the truth or not."

The woman stopped pouring coffee. "You're bullshitting me, right? Why would a famous person like Joanna Kasimir even *be* in Minnesota?"

"She's from here, you know. Grew up in St. Paul."

"I know that. *Everybody* knows that."

"She's in town to do a play at the Allen Grimby. It was announced in the paper ages ago." Hillary took a sip from the Styrofoam cup Carolyn handed her. "She said she'd get me front-row seats for opening night."

Carolyn looked at her skeptically.

"My doughnut?"

"Huh?"

"You didn't give me my doughnut. And hey, Carolyn, if you play your cards right, maybe I can get you one of those front-row seats."

Carolyn's hand hesitated just inside the pastry counter. "What about my husband?"

"Yeah, I suppose he should go, too." Hillary was loving this. Carolyn didn't know what to believe. On the off chance that Hillary might be telling the truth, she knew she'd better act a little more respectfully, not give Hillary the worst-looking doughnut in the counter, like she usually did. "I'll take the one way on the left."

"Sure. Right." She covered it with the waxed paper, then dropped it into a white paper sack. Reflecting on it another second, she reached for another doughnut, this time a raised glazed. "On the house," she said, giving Hillary a conspiratorial wink.

"See ya around," said Hillary, grabbing some napkins on her way to an empty booth. She was on top of the world today. She'd have to send Joanna a special thank-you note.

Hillary was midway through the second doughnut when she spied her boyfriend, Cody Felton. Cody was a psych assistant up on five west. She thought he was working an evening shift tonight, but apparently not. As far as looks went, Cody was a total conundrum. Sometimes Hillary thought he was good-looking enough to be a model. Not a *GQ* model. Something more funky. More edgy. Calvin Klein, maybe. Other times, he could look a lot like the dad on *The Munsters*. This morning, with his spiky brown hair standing straight up—for God knew what reason—he leaned more toward the Frankenstein look.

"Hey, babe," he said, striding up to the table. Psych PAs didn't have to wear uniforms, so he had on his usual khakis and a brown cotton sweater. "What's up? I called you last night, but your dad said you were out."

"I was."

He slid into the booth seat across from her. "At a movie?"

"No. You'll never guess."

"I give." He took a sip of her coffee.

"Remember I told you Joanna Kasimir was coming to town. Well, I met her at the airport. We ended up having dinner together."

"Shit, Hill. Will you back off with that crap?"

"It's not crap! I did see her."

"Uh-huh."

"I told her about you, what an incredible lover you are."

"Oh, Christ."

"No, it's true. I showed her your picture, the one of you on your motorcycle. She said you had an arresting profile. Exact words. Asked if you'd ever taken any acting classes."

He grunted, but she could tell it was an interested grunt. "Where'd you eat?"

"The Lyme House. It's on Lake Harriet."

"Cool, but kind of pricey."

"She paid."

"And . . . tell me again how you know her?"

"My mom was a distant cousin, but they kept in touch. I've known Joanna since I was a kid."

"Huh. Just kind of blows my mind."

"It shouldn't. I'll introduce you if you want."

"When?"

"Well, she's kind of busy at the moment. She's starting rehearsals today for a play she's doing at a theater in St. Paul. But she'll make time for us. That is, if you really do want to meet her."

"Hell, sure. She's, like, one of the most beautiful women in the world. Although, she's kind of old."

"Forties isn't so old." She glanced up at the clock on the wall.

"Jeez, look at the time. I gotta get back to work." Having said that, she made no move to go. Instead, she propped her head on one hand.

"How long's your break?" asked Cody.

"I'm not actually on break. I opened up and then left."

"God, Hill, I don't know how you expect to keep that job."

"Don't be such a worrywart. My boss never comes in until after ten."

"You should go. You've already had two warnings."

"Oh, all right." But she still didn't move.

"You know, sometimes, Hill . . . I don't know if you're telling me the truth. It bothers me."

"You think I'd lie to you?"

"You lie all the time."

She sat up straight. "Like what? Tell me one important thing I've ever lied about."

"For starters, your journalism degree."

"What about it?"

"You don't have one. You quit school your junior year."

Now she was pissed. "Who told you that?"

"Your dad."

"How the hell would he know?"

"Hillary, he was paying the bills. He knows when they stopped."

"That's crap, Cody. Don't you believe it." She stuffed the rest of the raised glazed in her mouth and chewed resentfully.

"You don't have to lie, you know."

"Like you never lie."

He groaned. "And what do I lie about?"

She sat back, folded her ams over her chest. "All this lovey-dovey crap. You just do it to get me in bed."

"Oh, Hillary."

"Admit it."

He reached across the table with an open hand. "Why do you have such a hard time believing I love you?"

"Because," she said, launching out of the booth, "if you loved me, you'd believe me, no questions asked. Besides, nobody ever really loves anybody. It's all self-interest."

"Sometimes you scare me, Hill. You really do."

"Yeah, well, live with it. Or dump me. It's up to you." She turned to go but remembered her coffee. Scooping it off the table, she stomped out.

13

Joanna and David sat on opposite sides of the kitchen table, staring blankly at each other. David was wearing a yellow-and-green tie-dyed T-shirt and faded jeans, and Joanna had on a blue chenille bathrobe.

"We must look like two people with bad hangovers," Joanna muttered.

"I wonder why. What time is it?"

"Almost noon." Her head was propped against her hand. If she didn't move, the banging wasn't quite as brutal. "Wish I had a cigarette."

"I thought you quit smoking during your health-food period."

"I did."

He leaned sideways and pulled a pack of Lucky Strikes out of his back pocket. He shook two out, then dug in his front pocket for matches. "Desperate times call for desperate measures."

They both lit up.

Blowing smoke out of the side of her mouth, Joanna said, "You didn't drink as much as I did last night."

"No."

"So why do you look so awful?"

"I slept on my face wrong."

She glanced at the refrigerator. "Want some orange juice?"

"Not if I have to get up and get it." He flicked his eyes to her, then tapped ash in a saucer.

"I thought I heard you roaming around out here in the middle of the night. And then again this morning."

"Needed a glass of water."

"No, it sounded like you went out the door."

He shrugged. "What are your plans for the day?"

She hated to admit it, but with Gordon lurking around again, she felt trapped just like she had all those years ago. She wasn't sure what she'd do once rehearsals began. "Relax, I suppose. Sleep. Wait to hear from that PI I hired." She took a quick puff off the cigarette, then leaned forward and looked David straight in the eyes. "I probably should have a heart-to-heart with my baby brother. Try to find out what's going on with him. If Diego cheated on you, babe, I'll help you kill him."

"Don't get so worked up. It's nothing several dozen Valium and a fifth of whiskey can't solve."

"Do you honestly believe that?"

He blew smoke circles into the air. "Nah. But it's a good line, don't you think? Russell Crowe could deliver it with a straight face, God knows how."

Sometimes Joanna didn't know how to read her brother. He had a habit of using humor to push away all the stuff that bothered him. As a teenager, he wore his heart on his sleeve and got it pretty badly mangled, so as an adult he sometimes adopted this frustratingly perfunctory view of life. Poses drove Joanna crazy. "I suppose you could help me run my lines."

"Hell, if I know you, you had them all memorized three weeks ago."

She dropped her head back on her hand. "Do you?"

"Do I what?"

"Do you know me? Do either of us really know each other?"

"Uh-oh. I think we're moving into dangerous territory for this early in the day."

"Be serious."

"Why?" He pushed back from the table. "I've got stuff I need to do. But first, I have to make myself look pretty."

"Like what stuff?"

"Weeeell, I don't suppose Jane told you what happened at her house."

"No." Before David could explain, there was a knock on the door. Joanna nearly jumped out of her chair.

"Take it easy, Sis. I'm big and strong. I'll protect you."

"This is a security building!"

He kissed her forehead on his way out of the room. "Then it has to be someone who lives in the building. Relax."

Joanna followed him into the living room, watching as he turned around and moved backward toward the door.

"Hey, remember what Mom used to say to us at night when we were little? She didn't allow monsters in our house. I actually be-lieved her, always felt safe. Well, you can believe *me* now, Sis. I won't allow any monsters in this loft. Okay?" He squinted through the peephole.

"Who is it?"

"Yikes!" He ducked down and cringed. "A monster!"

"You're nuts, you know that?"

He opened the door.

Joanna stood about ten feet behind him, feeling her stomach knot into a ball.

"Hi," said David. "Can I help you?"

The elderly woman standing out in the hall held a plate with a small loaf of bread in the center. "I'm your neighbor. Faye O'Halleron? I live across the hall."

"Nice to meet you, Ms. O'Halleron."

"Call me Faye."

"Faye. I'm David Carlson."

She peered over her bifocals. "Is Ms. Kasimir here?"

"That would be my eminent sister." He turned to Joanna, asking with a lift of his eyebrows if he should let her in.

Joanna nodded.

"She sure is, in all her dazzling morning glory." He swept his hand toward her.

"Oh my," said Faye. Her hands began to shake. "Is it really you?"

"She's real," said David, stifling a grin. "I agree, she's a little scary in the morning, but she's not dangerous."

Joanna shot him a nasty look.

"I, ah, baked some pumpkin bread for you, Ms. Kasimir. Oh, and for your brother, too." She smiled at him. "It's right out of the oven. Still warm."

"That's so kind of you," said Joanna. "David, will you take the bread in the kitchen?"

He bowed. "Yes, your grace."

"Bag it," she snarled.

"I hope you like it," said Faye. "It's best with butter, if you can stand the extra calories, which you can. You're much thinner in person."

"Would you like to sit down in the living room for a few minutes?"

"Sure! Thanks."

"David, bring Faye a cup of coffee."

"Of course, your grace."

"My brother's in an odd mood this morning."

"Yeah," said Faye. "I can see that." She sat down on the edge of the velvet couch. "I'm one of your biggest fans."

"That's always nice to hear," said Joanna, sinking down on a spindle rocking chair next to a chain-saw-carved bear sculpture.

"I've followed your career from the very beginning. When one of your movies is on TV, I always watch it."

People didn't realize how difficult it was to have a conversation with someone who just wanted to tell you how great you were. What could you say in response? *Yes, I know I'm fabulous. I'm sure you're fabulous too.* "That's . . . nice. Have you lived here long?"

"Not long, no. I'm retired. Have been for a couple of years."

"What did you do for a living?"

"I had my own beauty salon. Did hair. Nails. Facials. I employed four women and one man. When I decided to close up shop for good, two of the women offered to buy it, so I took them up on it." She accepted the cup of coffee David handed her. "If you don't mind my saying so, your hair could use some conditioning."

"Do you think so?"

She raised a hand. "May I?"

"Sure."

She rose from the couch and stepped over to the rocking chair, rubbing Joanna's hair between her fingers. "Good texture but dry. And you have a lot of split ends. Is it dyed?"

"Yes."

"Who's been looking after it?"

"I live in Idaho now. When I need something done, I go to a man in Sandpoint, that's the nearest town."

"Well, I hope you don't pay him much. He's not very good."

This time Joanna's cell phone interrupted them. "I better get that," she said, afraid that if she asked her brother to do it, she'd get another smart reply. Flipping it open, she said hello.

"Babycakes, it's me! I'm here!"

"My God. Freddy?"

"Just flew in last night. I'm staying at the Hyatt Regency. Did you read the screenplay yet?"

"What screenplay?"

"Didn't that woman I talked to last night tell you?"

"What woman? Tell me what?"

"Listen, babe, I mailed you a screenplay a few days ago. It's the best thing I've seen in years and it has an incredible part for you. No character piece, either. I'm talking the female lead! The shoot is in São Paulo, Brazil. Everybody's on board except you. I'm directing, of course. We got Tim Robbins. Chris Cooper. God, I love that guy. He could play a toilet and he'd be great. And get this. Here's your leading man."

106

"Who?"

"Kevin fucking Spacey!"

"You've got these people signed?"

"Signed, sealed, and delivered—if, and this is the if that concerns you—*if* I can get you for the female lead. The backers are ready with their checkbooks. Ron Sherry is producing."

"Comedy or drama?"

"A little of both. Think *Titanic* meets *American Beauty*."

"Is it a period piece?"

"Nineteen twenties."

Joanna liked the twenties. Women weren't just furniture in men's lives in the twenties.

"It's quirky, funny, tragic. It's got everything—and the writing is phenomenal."

"This is too fast, Fred. I mean . . . I can't commit right away. You know me. I need some time to think."

"All right. Think all you like, as long as I get your signature on the contract by the middle of next week. Here's the deal. You gotta pull out of that play. Get your lawyer to look at the contract. Tell the theater . . . hell, tell them whatever you want. You're sick. Your back hurts. Your hemorrhoids are acting up."

"Freddy, don't be gross."

"I'm just giving you some ideas. We start shooting late November, give or take. Now, I sent the screenplay to the place you're staying. I got the address from Marybeth."

Marybeth Flagg was her agent in L.A.

"Read it. If you read it and you don't like it, I swear I'll jump out of my hotel room window."

"Okay, okay." She laughed at his enthusiasm. Freddy always did that to her. Made her laugh. He was a complete creature of the movie industry, and yet she found him refreshing.

"When can I see you?"

"Give me a day to look at the script."

"Call me, Babycakes. Room seven twelve, Hyatt Regency. I'm ready to fly on this one. I love you."

"You do?"

"Hell, babe, I never stopped. Later."

Joanna hung up the receiver, feeling utterly speechless.

"I take it that was your ex," said David, sipping from a glass of orange juice. "He always has the same effect on you."

"What effect?"

"You look like a deer in the headlights."

She rolled her eyes. "He's shooting a film and wants me to be in it."

"How terrible!" said Faye, setting down her coffee. "You're talking about your first husband, right? Fred Kasimir? You can't seriously think of working with him. He hurt you terribly."

Joanna and David exchanged glances.

"It's okay, really," said Joanna. "Our breakup wasn't all his fault." She was a bit taken aback by the intensity of Faye's response.

"Oh, but you gotta be careful. I've followed him in the news. He's a womanizer. He'll only hurt you again if you get mixed up with him."

"This would be a business deal," said Joanna. It occurred to her now that if she left the country, it was unlikely that Gordon would follow her all the way to Brazil.

"But . . . you're not going to do it, are you?" asked Faye.

"I'll read the script. I owe him that much."

"If you don't mind my saying so," said Faye, looking like a woman who was used to giving her opinion and having it listened to, "you don't owe him a thing."

"No, but if the script's good—"

"Stay away from him," said Faye, her voice firm. "He's nothing but poison."

"I always kinda liked him," said David, standing next to the bear sculpture, his arm propped on the head.

"Davey?" said Joanna, chewing on her lower lip, her mind spinning in a million different directions.

"Hum?"

"If I ask you to run downstairs and get my mail for me, will you do it without acting like I'm the queen of England?"

"I'd be happy to." As walked over to the door, he added under his breath, "Boss."

Bel Air, California
Spring 1989

After the disastrous birthday party at the bungalow, Gordon took Joanna to a garden store, where they looked at bedding plants for several hours. Joanna tried hard to get her mind off David's behavior, but nothing she did seemed to work. She couldn't believe how selfish he'd been to ruin her perfect day. He knew how much her birthday meant to her. Maybe she was still a greedy child at heart, wanting everything to go her way, but for one freakin' day of the year, was that so much to ask?

Joanna had been a serious little girl, full of quirks and given to fits of temper. As a teenager, she never felt like part of the crowd, which only cut her off further. She saw her friends as shallow, interested only in the next date, the next keg party. She was much better than that. Joanna had set her sights on making something of herself. She wanted to achieve grand things. But after she'd won the golden prize, she came to the conclusion that shallowness was highly underrated. Shallowness was what allowed her to live in the world and not go stark raving mad. As far as Joanna was concerned, that was true for everyone—whether they admitted it or not. It was probably shallowness that allowed Joanna to ignore David and Diego for the rest of the day. They were selfish bastards and she was mad at them. End of story.

After a quiet, romantic dinner at a restaurant overlooking the Portofino Marina in Redondo Beach, Joanna and Gordon returned to her home in Bel

Air. They spent the rest of the evening making love. By the time she fell asleep in Gordon's arms, she'd forgiven David. Eventually, she always did.

The following day dawned in mist. Joanna walked out on the veranda overlooking the pool and the bungalow, where the world was washed in grays, everything indistinct, muted, softened. She regretted the way she'd handled herself yesterday and was eager to get down to the bungalow to set things right.

Gordon was lying in bed, watching TV when Joanna opened up her bureau drawer and removed a pair of clean sweatpants and a T-shirt.

"I'm famished," he said, stretching his arms high above his head. "When you get a chance, I'd like some scrambled eggs, toast, and coffee. Jam or jelly if you have it."

It was the first time he'd ever assumed that she would cook for him. They'd been together only a week, during which he'd always prepared the meals, if they ate in. He wasn't ordering her to do it, but he seemed to expect it, and that sense of entitlement annoyed her. She gave him an appraising look.

"What?"

"You really really *don't* want me to cook for you."

"Why?"

"First, because I'm lousy at it. Second, because I'm not your servant."

He surfed the channels, a disgruntled look on his face. "Come back to bed, then."

"No."

"Why not? Where are you going?"

"To talk to David. Not that it's any of your business." Her eyes were drawn to the crumpled sheet draped across his lower abdomen. His body was so tanned, so beautiful, so relaxed and at ease. It was like having Michelangelo's statue of David in her bed. Sitting down next to him, she trailed her fingers across his chest. "I'm sorry. Guess I'm not in a very good mood."

He glanced at her, then looked back at the TV. "What the hell bit your ass?"

"I treated David badly yesterday. It's bothering me."

"I'd say it was the other way around."

She shrugged, rising from the bed.

"We should hire a housekeeper, one who cooks."

And there it was: the first "we." She'd been waiting for it, but now that it was here, it didn't sit very well with her. "Let's talk about it later." She started for the door.

"I ordered a wood chipper, a backhoe, and a tractor grader. They should be delivered this afternoon. You need to sign for them."

"I what? Doesn't your landscape company deal with that?"

"It's not coming from the landscape company. I quit yesterday."

She stopped and turned around. Walking back to the bed, she said, "You did?"

"Jo," he said with exaggerated patience, "if I'm going to turn that hill of yours into a terraced garden, it's going to require a lot of time. I assumed you wanted it done before next year, so I didn't have a choice. I want to give this to you, babe. My gift." He took hold of her hand.

"How do you intend to support yourself if you don't have a job?"

Now he looked wounded. "I thought I'd move in here. Isn't that what you want? I mean, we're together now, Jo. I'm committed to you in every way. I want to make your life richer, more beautiful. I'm devoted to that."

"And in the meantime, I'm devoted to supporting both of us."

He dropped her hand. "What the hell's going on? I thought this was what you wanted. Why is everything about money? You're just like every other Hollywood whore. Money's your God."

"That's not true."

"You sure could have fooled me. I thought you were better than that. I thought you wanted something more."

"I do."

"You're pitiful, you know that? I offer you my love, my whole life, and you—with all your money—all you're concerned about is who's going to pay the light bill? Buy the Kleenex?"

She felt like a total shit. "Of course not. I didn't mean—"

"I'll never be like that, Jo, and I refuse to be sucked down to your level."

"Gordon, stop. Please." She sat down, moved closer to him. She believed him when he said he'd never hurt her. She believed he wanted what was best for her. She believed even in the face of her growing doubt. She had to trust someone, sometime, didn't she? If she couldn't, her life would be reduced to an emotional wasteland. When she put her hand on his chest, she

could feel his heart beating wildly. "I'm sorry. Really. I didn't mean to upset you."

He pulled her to him, kissed her fiercely. He'd never been rough with her before, but he was now, ripping the T-shirt off, breaking the clasp on the back of her bra. She felt helpless in his arms, breathless by the depth of his passion, by the sheer weight and power of his body. She wanted him. She bit his neck and tasted the salt and the sweat. "I love you," she whispered, sensing that she had to prove it. And she wanted to prove it more than she'd ever wanted anything before in her life.

With one thing or another preventing Joanna from leaving the house, she didn't make it down to the bungalow until two in the afternoon. Before she even knocked on the door, she noticed that David and Diego's rental car was gone. She had no idea what their plans were for the day, but if they didn't connect in any other way, David usually left a note for her on the kitchen table.

Joanna dreaded talking to them about what had prompted their obnoxious behavior at the birthday party yesterday. She remembered most of it through the haze of too many glasses of champagne. In the cold light of day, she figured it was probably partially her fault. After the party, it became pretty clear that Gordon didn't think much of either her brother or Diego. That pained her, and yet she couldn't blame him. His only real opportunity to get to know them had been at the party. If Joanna's experience with David and Diego had been limited to that, she wouldn't have a very good impression of them either.

Unlocking the front door, Joanna walked into a perfectly cleaned bungalow. She expected to see some leftover balloons or crepe-paper streamers, a few dirty dishes or filled ashtrays, but the interior was spotless, just the way it had been before they arrived. Stepping into the bedroom, she was surprised to find all the suitcases gone. She opened the closet doors and found them empty.

Surely they wouldn't have left without talking to her, would they? The question echoed through the silent rooms as Joanna reached the kitchen. There was no note on the kitchen table. In fact, the refrigerator had been cleaned out, the garbage emptied, the dishes all washed and put away. She stood amid the smell of pine cleaner and lemon wax, totally stumped. Surely her brother couldn't have been that mad at her. If he was, she didn't have a clue why.

Joanna sat down at the kitchen table to think. It made a certain sense that, if her brother and Diego really were having personal problems, they'd leave early, and without telling her. David tended to get very tight-lipped about personal issues, while encouraging her to tell all about hers. She forgave him that little double standard. But if he and Diego weren't having relationship problems—she'd seen no real evidence of that yesterday—then why did they go?

It struck her that perhaps David and Diego didn't like Gordon. Or maybe they felt they were third wheels now that Joanna had a new boyfriend. If they were just being kind, giving Joanna and Gordon some time alone, it wasn't necessary. If they'd only asked her, that's what she would have told them.

Joanna looked up as Gordon came through the back door.

"Hey, Jo, what are you doing down here?"

"Looking for my brother."

"They left right after lunch."

"You saw them? Did you talk to them?"

He shrugged, sat down at the table across from her. "I was taking a swim. I called good-bye, but they ignored me. It's no skin off my nose if they don't like me."

"Why wouldn't they like you? That's crazy, Gordon."

Another shrug. "Who knows what's up with them. Just forget about it."

Joanna had no intention of forgetting about it. As soon as she figured they were back home in Atlanta, she intended to call, read them the riot act. They never should have left like that. If she'd done something to upset them, they should have stayed and talked it out.

"I'm driving over to Stottlemeyers to get a sandwich. You want one?"

"Sure."

"Beef? Turkey?"

"Whatever you get is fine with me."

"You're easy to shop for." He grinned. "Or maybe you're just plain easy."

"Stop it." She knew he was teasing her about this morning. They'd stayed in bed until after eleven. She had a meeting in Century City this afternoon but had canceled it. Gordon had some things to buy for the slope renovation, so he wasn't going to be around, and someone had to be at the house to sign for all the heavy equipment he'd ordered.

"Let's drive up to Sausalito tomorrow," said Gordon. "I know that area really well. It'd give me a real kick to show my new lady around one of my old stomping grounds."

"I've got a meeting with my agent tomorrow."

"Cancel it."

"It's not that simple, Gordon. I canceled a meeting today so I could wait around here and sign that form. I'm working, honey. I have commitments."

"Sure. I get it." As he stood, he cracked his knuckles, then his neck.

Joanna had begun to notice that he did this almost ritualized cracking when he felt uncomfortable or threatened. He also had a tendency to yawn when he felt stressed. He probably was unaware of the signals he sent, but Joanna, like most women, was good at reading her man. "Don't be angry. Maybe we can do it next week."

"Sure. Next week. Except, by then, I'll be into the reconstruction of your hill. I can't just walk away and leave it."

"No, of course not. Maybe we can do it this weekend."

"Whatever." He stepped over to the sink, took down a glass, and filled it with water. "I know what you're doing, you know."

"And that would be?"

"You're punishing me because I quit my job. You're making a big deal out of the fact that you're working and I'm not."

"That's not fair."

"Jo, do you realize how quickly I could get another job in landscaping? They're a dime a dozen. What I have in mind for this place will double its value. I'm not going to be sitting around on my thumbs, doing nothing."

"I know that. I'm not punishing you. That never even entered my mind."

He turned to face her. "You know, on second thought, maybe I won't come back here with sandwiches. It would save me a bunch of time if I just ate at the restaurant, then took off for the valley."

She could tell he was angry. "Whatever you want. What time will you be back?"

"Late," he said. "Don't wait up."

"Gordon?"

He drank his water, set the glass in the sink, then left through the back door without another word.

The equipment arrived just before three. Joanna signed all the necessary paper-work, then hopped in her car and drove into Beverly Hills. She wanted the works—facial, nails, full-body massage, a new haircut, anything and every-thing that would make her feel beautiful and desirable. When Gordon got home tonight, however late it was, she'd be there waiting for him, ready to show him how much she really did love him. All relationships were a negotiation. They'd jumped into this thing pretty fast, before they'd had a chance to really get to know each other. She expected their first few months together would be rocky. But tonight, when they slipped between the silk sheets, they could forget about what they did together badly and concentrate on what they did together well.

By eleven, Joanna was sick of waiting. Gordon still wasn't home and she was losing patience. On a whim, she grabbed the phone and dialed David's number in Atlanta. She didn't expect them to be there. They had another whole week of vacation, so she assumed they'd decided to spend it somewhere else.

But Diego picked up after the third ring. "Hello?"

"Diego, it's Joanna."

Silence. Then Diego shouted, "David, it's your sister. You wanna talk to her?"

Joanna heard the response. It was a no. "Tell him I have to talk to him. If you hang up, I'll just call right back. And I'll keep calling."

"David," yelled Diego. "I think you better take this."

While she waited for her brother to come to the phone, she said, "Why did you and David leave like that? You never even said good-bye."

"We don't stay where we're not wanted," said Diego.

"What's that supposed to mean?"

Before he could answer, David came on the line. "What? Make it fast."

"How come you left without saying good-bye?"

"Gee, did I hurt your feelings? I'll say good-bye now. Good-bye."

"David, don't hang up!"

"Look, this hasn't been a stellar couple days in my life. You're entitled to your opinions and I'm entitled to tell you to go to hell."

"Stop! You need to explain. What opinions?"

"Oh, come on. Don't play ignorant. You're too big a coward to tell Diego and me how you really feel, so you send your pool boy."

"David, listen to me. I have no idea what you're talking about. None."

"I'm talking about Luberman."

"What about him?"

"You are so goddamn manipulative. Are you trying to tell me you didn't send him down to the bungalow before the birthday party with that lovely message?"

She was exhausted trying to drag this out of him. "No, I didn't send Gordon to talk to you."

"You're saying it was all his idea?"

"That's what I'm saying, yes."

A long pause. "This is the truth, Jo? He wasn't your messenger boy?"

"How many times do I have to repeat it. No!"

"Okay, but that still makes sense. He did it on his own, but you wanted him to do it. Just because you didn't actually order him to talk to us—"

"About what?" she shouted.

"He said you two had talked about how uneasy you were with our 'lifestyle.' That you never really wanted us to visit but couldn't bring yourself to say no."

"That's ridiculous!"

"Is it?"

"Yes!"

"Then where did Gordon get it?"

Joanna sat down on the floor in front of the couch. "David, this is very important. I want to know exactly—word for word—what he told you."

She could hear him light up a cigarette.

"Well, okay," he said, his voice losing some of its stiffness. "I'll play along. In fact I'd love to tell you. Maybe then you'll understand why this will probably be our last conversation this side of the grave."

"Just say it."

"All right. Gordo came down to the bungalow around eleven yesterday morning. He asked us to sit down in the living room, said he had something he needed to talk to us about. And then he let fly. Said that you were not only disgusted by faggots, as he was, but that it was all you could do to look me in the face. He said that you were a great actor, and that's why we didn't already know. He assured me that you loved me, but you'd never wanted me and Diego

117

to come visit. It just happened before you had the guts to tell us the truth. You were too kindhearted and blah blah blah. He said he believed in cosmic retribution and that if we didn't stop what we were doing, we'd be punished. He said you agreed, in principle, but in your case, you felt sorry for me, for the trashy way I'd chosen to live my life. He explained that he'd never believed that being gay or straight wasn't a choice, that Diego and I could be straight if we wanted—and that you basically agreed. He also said that our parents asked you if I was gay and you told them I was. That it nearly killed Dad, and that Mom was inconsolable." David's voice had grown husky, as if he was forcing himself not to cry. "Is that true? Did you tell Mom and Dad?"

Joanna was so shocked that it took her a moment to catch her breath. "Never, David. You asked me not to and I promised I wouldn't. I'd never go back on a promise. You know me better than that, or at least I thought you did. I figured you'd tell them at some point, but then the car accident happened right before you and Diego got together, so it wasn't possible. No, I never told them a thing."

"Let me get this straight," said David. "You're telling me that everything Gordon said to us was a lie?"

"Yes—except for his personal comments about how he sees being gay. That was probably true."

"He told us that we should leave and never come stay at the bungalow again. That that's what you wanted. If we decided to call or send cards or letters, that was one thing. But staying at your place was like rubbing your nose in our deviant behavior. Before he left, he said that it was your wish that we continue with the birthday celebration. That if we loved you, we wouldn't let any of this sour your big day. By then, I didn't give a rip about your big day. But Diego and I talked about it. Just because you behaved like a hateful shit didn't mean we had to. We tried our best to get through it. Our best, I guess, was to get drunk. And then, as Gordon suggested, we left this afternoon."

She shook her head and kept shaking it. "David, I'm dumbfounded. I never said any of that. We've never even talked about you." She stopped. "No, that's wrong. Gordon asked me yesterday morning if you guys were friends. I told him you were gay. That was it. That was all I said."

"So you don't—"

"David, I don't give a rat's ass if you're gay, straight, bi, pink, blue, or purple. You're my brother and I love you. Do you think I'm so intolerant, so narrow-minded and stupid that I don't see being gay for what it is—a variation. Like left-handedness. Like color blindness. It's no freaking big deal to me and it never has been!"

David didn't speak for almost a minute. Finally, he said, "Joanna, you gotta get rid of that guy. Do it now. Change your locks. Tell him you never want to see him again. He's poison."

She could feel a deep fury building inside her. "Don't worry. When Gordon gets home tonight, he's in for one big surprise."

14

Jane returned with Nolan from Eagle Ridge around five. After he dropped her back at the Linden Building, she hopped in her Mini and drove straight to her office at the Xanadu Club. She wanted to get all her business ducks in a row so she could feel comfortable taking the next two weeks off.

It was the peak of dinner madness when she finally headed down to the kitchen about an hour later. She noticed immediately that there was an edge, an urgency to the bedlam tonight. She found her executive chef walking around shouting orders. He stopped long enough to inform her that one of the line cooks had just taken off because her daughter had been brought to the emergency room with a broken arm. He and the sous-chef were in the process of trying to figure out how to cover it.

Thursday was one of the busiest nights of the week at the Xanadu, so this was bad news. Jane ran back up to her office and changed into her chef's whites, pulled her hair up into a bun, grabbed her hat, and returned to the kitchen, where she spent the next two and a half hours working the grill. Everything there was to know about how the food should be cooked, seasoned, and plated was already in her head.

By ten, orders had slacked off enough for Jane to call it a night. As she returned upstairs to the dining room, she felt her cell phone vibrate inside her pants pocket. She'd felt it several times earlier in the evening but couldn't stop to answer. Checking the number, she saw that it was David.

"Hey, kiddo," she said, trekking up the stairs to her second-floor office. He'd never returned the message she'd left him earlier in the day.

"Where are you?" he asked.

She could hear traffic in the background. "The club," she said, unlocking her office door and flipping on the light.

"Stay there. I'll be over in a few minutes. I was hoping we could talk."

"Great. When you get here, have one of the bartenders point you to my office."

Since she had only a few minutes, she decided not to change her clothes. She wanted to call Kenzie but didn't want the conversation to be rushed. Instead, she turned on her computer. She brought up Google and tapped in the word "stalker." In an instant, the search engine delivered twenty-two million Web sites. She still had questions, even after Nolan's brief tutorial.

Scrolling through the sites, she came across one that talked about women stalkers—the main question Jane had that Nolan hadn't touched on. On Pshcho-MED, she read:

> Female stalkers are classified as intimacy seek-
> ers. Their stalking generally arises from a desire
> to form a close relationship with the victim.
> Contrary to popular opinion, female stalkers
> are no less likely than males to threaten their
> victims or use violence. They feel they have a
> right to be part of their victim's life.

"Just peachy," Jane muttered, clicking on the next site. The woman journalist they'd run into at the airport yesterday leaped to mind. She was so clearly gaga over Joanna, although Joanna probably got reactions like that all the time. Seeing fame from this angle made it seem far less appealing. Roses truly did have thorns.

Next, Jane found a site that talked about celebrity stalking.

> Dr. Edwin R. Sontag, a psychologist at North-western's School of Medicine, has done extensive research on celebrity staking. In a recent article in the <u>North American Journal of Psychology</u>, he states that interest in celebrities runs the gamut, from <u>Tonight Show</u> junkies all the way to John Hinckley. On the innocuous side of the equation are people who join fan clubs or web groups, or those who buy lousy records out of loyalty.

Jane was surprised to note that Dr. Sontag included one in five people in this category.

> The next rung of the ladder is characterized by stronger, and perhaps stranger, feelings. These are the celebrity worshippers, people who see a specific celebrity as their soul mate. These highly intense fans are often men and women whose lives have gone off the rails for one reason or another. Personal trauma. The death of a significant loved one. The loss of a job. The celebrity worshippers are drawn to celebrity out of loneliness or emptiness in their own lives. Very often these people develop the delusion that they are having a love affair with the celebrity.

Jane kept moving through the Web sites. She was so interested in what she was reading that when she finally looked at her watch and saw that it was eleven-fifteen, she was surprised. And worried. David had said he'd be right over. So where was he? She picked up the phone and tapped in his cell number, but after his voice mail answered, she dropped the phone back on the hook.

By twelve-thirty, she was sitting at the bar, nursing a vodka martini, still waiting. She'd left four messages for him. She didn't know what to think, although her mood was growing less charitable by the minute. The club closed its doors at two. If he wasn't here by then, she figured she'd start calling emergency rooms.

Swiveling on the bar stool so she could focus her attention on the front door, she felt like she was waiting for water to boil. She watched an endless stream of customers come and go. At five to one, she was about to give up when David pushed through into the bar. Wearing new jeans, a brown suede jacket, and a clean white T-shirt, he looked much better than he had two nights ago. He nodded at her, motioning for her to follow him into the darkened dining room.

"What happened?" she demanded, hot on his heels. "I left you a bunch of messages. It's almost one in the morning. Do you realize you called me three hours ago?"

He seemed a little unsteady as he approached one of the tables, drew out a chair, and dropped down on it.

"Have you been drinking?"

He rested both elbows on the table and rubbed his face with the palms of his hands.

"David?"

"Needed a little Irish courage before I spilled my guts to Hurricane Jane." It was a name he used to call her when he was mad at her.

"What's going on?"

He sat there, face hidden by his hands, for almost a minute. When he finally removed his hands, he slumped back and sighed. "I'm hungry. You got anything to eat around this joint?"

"You make me wait all this time and all you can say is you're *hungry*?"

"Yeah. I even amaze myself sometimes."

She dragged him down to the kitchen and ordered him to sit at one of the prep tables. "What do you want?"

"I don't know. Whaddaya got?"

"Don't be fatuous. This is a commercial kitchen."

"Okay, then." He gave her a sunny smile. "I'll have two eggs over easy, three slices of bacon, and a couple pieces of wheat toast."

She glared at him.

"Fry the eggs in butter, please." He put his head down on the table and closed his eyes.

Jane was glad she wasn't standing near a chef's knife. While David slept, or rested, or whatever the hell he was doing, she prepared the meal. It smelled so good that she doubled the amount. She figured she might as well join him.

When she finally set the food on the prep table a few minutes later, he opened his eyes and sat up. Rubbing his hands together, he said, "This looks fabulous."

"Jam?"

"What kind?"

"We don't do breakfasts, so it will have to be lingonberry. We use that for the pork roast."

He turned up his nose.

Like, at this moment, she cared? "You'll love it."

She'd also made some coffee. She brought two steaming mugs to the table and pulled up a stool. "So talk," she said, taking a bite of bacon.

"Not now. Not yet. Let's just sit here the way we used to, just kinda let things flow."

She stared deep into his bloodshot eyes, trying to figure out what was going on. She decided it was best not to push. "Okay."

"For instance, how's everything going with that new woman in your life—can't remember her name."

"Kenzie."

"Right. The professor. You always went for the brainy type."

"I did?"

"She pretty?"

"I think she's gorgeous. She isn't Hollywood beautiful, but she has a quality. I'm not sure how to describe it."

"Try sexy."

"Well there's that, yes." She couldn't help but grin. "It's partly in the way she moves. She's athletic but not in the team sports way. She doesn't go to the gym. She rides horses. She's very lean and has long, incredible legs. But also, and I know this may sound hokey, but I love the way she thinks. Just wait, you'll meet her and then you'll get it."

"You dykes and your mind loving. Hot sex is what it's all about. Take it from a fag who knows."

Laughing, she said, "Right. That's why you've been with Diego all these years. It's just a sex thing."

He wiped a napkin across his mouth. "Okay, okay. So I know what you mean about the mind stuff. But, you know, it's more than that. Diego . . . he has a beautiful soul." He looked suddenly sad. "God, but I miss him."

"Then why are you here? Why don't you fly back to Atlanta?"

"Because," he said, pulling a leather flask out of his back pocket and setting it down next to his plate, "I've got to make sure your house is repaired properly. Can't leave in the middle of a mess I created now can I?"

They both knew he'd just skirted the question.

As David tucked back into his food, he added, "In case you're wondering, the floors in the kitchen, dining room, living room, and part of the back hallway all need to be replaced. I've sent your Orientals out to be washed. None of the furniture was damaged, except in the basement. Most of the water ended up down there. The carpeting in the rec room was removed today. I'd like to send the furniture to Goodwill and buy you something new."

"You don't like my taste?"

He cocked an eyebrow. "You call that *taste*? It looks like leftovers from a flophouse yard sale."

"Gee, thanks."

"If you'll let me, I'd like to redesign that entire section of the basement. The laundry room is fine, and so is the storage and furnace room, but, in my humble opinion, the rec room was a disaster before I came along and trashed it."

125

"I really don't know what to say, David. I could have contacted my insurance company."

"It's on me, babe. The least I can do."

"How long will it take?"

"A week to ten days, give or take."

"Seriously? That's all?"

"If I stay, I can ride herd on the contractors I've hired. That way, I know it will get done quickly and right."

"Okay, then think about this." Since they'd been discussing Kenzie, and because Jane was officially supposed to be on vacation and was dying to see her, an idea struck her. "Let's fly down to Nebraska on Saturday."

"Are you kidding?"

She quickly explained about the small plane her father had bought last fall.

"And you can fly it?" said David, taking a sip of coffee.

"Got my pilot's license months ago."

He seemed to hesitate. "What about Joanna? We can't just leave her in the lurch."

"Nolan's got it covered. I know I said I'd help, and I will, but how often do you make it up here? We'd only be gone one night."

Screwing off the flask's cap, he took a couple of swallows. "I don't know."

"Come on, David. Don't you want to meet her?"

"Well, sure. But—"

"Then let's do it. I'll make all the arrangements."

He still hesitated. "What if she doesn't like me?"

"Impossible."

"Yeah, I *am* pretty wonderful."

She balled up her napkin and threw it at him.

"Oh, all right. As long as you outfit me with a good parachute and lots of Dramamine."

"Believe it or not, I'm a good pilot."

"Sounds like you. You don't do things halfway." He tipped the flask back and took another couple of hits. "You want some?"

"No. And I think you should slow down."

He picked up his fork, then put it back down. "Jane, I just . . . I can't do it."

"Go to Nebraska?"

"No. I can't . . . I mean I don't—" His food was only half eaten, but he pushed the plate away. Pressing a fist against his mouth, he gave himself a couple of seconds, then said, "Look, I got a lot of stuff going on in my head right now, you know?"

"No, I don't know."

"I came here because I needed to find solid ground, a place to regroup, to think things through. And . . . because of you. I thought you could help."

"I want to help, David."

"I know." He smiled, reached for her hand. "But it's not that simple. If I talk about it, if I tell you what's going on, it will make it *real*. I'd have to stare it square in the face. I'm terrified it would kill me."

That stopped her. "What will? I'm in the dark here, David. Can't you at least give me some idea?"

"God," he said, wiping a hand across his eyes. He tried to change gears. He gave her smile that never quite made it. "I'm a mess. So what else is new?" He laughed, tried to make a joke out of it.

She wasn't buying. "Anything I can do, David. *Anything*. Just name it."

"Thanks. I love you, babe. Always have. Always will." He fidgeted with his ring, then began to pull against his gold watchband. He finally took off the watch, rubbed his wrist.

Jane couldn't help but notice. "David? What happened there?" His wrist was bright red, with narrow raw welts.

"Nothing," he said, quickly slipping the watch back on. "The band's too tight."

"No, it's not."

"Okay, but it has some sharp points on it. It's a piece of designer crap, never should have bought it, but it's the only one I have."

He finished the booze in the flask, then slipped it into his jacket pocket. "Look, I better get home. Joanna called me hours ago. Wanted to know where I was and when I was getting back." He smirked. "Get this. My sister's started smoking again. Ever since I left this morning, she's been in the midst of a flat-out nicotine fit. She didn't want to leave the apartment, so she went across the hall and knocked on her neighbor's door. Faye something or other. Nice old lady. Anyway, Joanna invited her back because the woman smokes. They've been sitting in her living room, puffing away most of the day. I guess I'm glad she found a friend in the building. Takes some of the pressure off me." He got up, but he was so unsteady, he nearly fell back down on the stool.

"I'll drive you home."

"No, you won't."

"You're way past the legal limit, David. Don't make me get rough with you." She put up her fists.

He laughed. "You think you can take me?"

"No, but I've got a couple of bartenders upstairs who do whatever I tell them."

He cringed. "The Gym Boys. I saw them on my way in."

"Give me your car keys."

"Jane, I *need* my car."

"Fine. I'll drive you back here in the morning. You can get it then."

"But I need it tonight."

"No way, David. The keys." She held out her hand.

After unsuccessfully trying to stare her down, he finally gave in. Fishing in his pocket, he pulled them out and pushed them across the table. "There."

As they walked out of the kitchen, he said, "Hey, you know, it might be okay if those Gym Boys mauled me just a little."

"Bag it," said Jane. "You're going home to bed."

15

When it came to the dark, Joanna was a coward. She couldn't sleep in a room without a night-light. As she lay on the uncomfortably hard mattress in the rooster bedroom, the red seven-watt bulb inside an opaque plastic likeness of Rocky the Rooster from the movie *Chicken Run* gave off barely enough light for her to see her hand in front of her face. She had the odd sense that she and Rocky were part of an old Victorian seance. Any minute she would begin to hear faint knocking sounds, tables would jump and move all on their own. Right then and there she decided that in the morning, she would look around for a different night-light, one that was brighter and didn't suffuse the room with such a sense of eerie otherworldliness.

Tucking the covers up under her chin, she tried to remember a time when she'd slept without a light in the room, when darkness felt restful and gentle. It was certainly before she'd met Gordon. She should have trusted her instincts all those years ago. God help her if she didn't trust them now.

Joanna had spent the afternoon reading the script Freddy had sent her. He was right. It was pure gold. She would kill to play the part. She couldn't believe he'd come through for her like this, offering her a part at a point in her life when she was literally scared to death to refuse. The timing seemed almost too incredible, but as usual, Joanna didn't want to exert the effort to analyze it.

After her evening of nonstop smoking, her lungs ached, but she'd been too keyed up to stop. She liked Faye, enjoyed her company, and was thinking that she'd take her up on her offer to let her work on her hair tomorrow. Maybe even have her nails done. Cordelia was expecting her at the theater, but with Gordon out there lurking in every shadow, she figured she could beg off one more day without the roof caving in. That would give her the weekend to make a firm decision about the movie.

For the first time today, Joanna closed her eyes but flipped them back up when she heard a rustling sound near the door. She felt momentarily suspended, searching the darkness for the cause of the noise.

An indistinct form moved into the doorway.

She sat up, held her breath. "David?"

"Hi-ho."

"Are you trying to give me a coronary?" She wasn't sure, but it looked like he was in his underwear and a T-shirt. "I can hardly see you."

"Really? Bad night vision. I can see you perfectly. Comes from eating your carrots."

"Haven't you gone to bed yet? It's after three."

"I'm cold."

"There are a couple extra blankets in my closet." She pointed.

"Thanks." But he didn't move.

"Aren't you going to get one?"

"Yes." He walked over to the empty side of the king-size bed and sat down on the edge.

"What the hell are you doing?"

"It's not clear to me."

"You're drunk."

"Probably." He stretched out, snapping a pillow behind his head.

When Joanna looked over at him, she saw that he was gripping a gun in his right hand. The hand was resting on his stomach.

Edging away from him, she said, "Maybe I'll go sleep in the living room."

"Whatever."

She hesitated. "David?"

"Hmm?"

"You're scaring me."

"Am I?"

"Yeah." She wasn't sure she should bring up the gun. She'd never seen him like this before.

"Maybe I should fix us some food," he said, turning on his side to face her. The gun dangled from his hand.

"No. Really. I'm not hungry."

"Okay." He closed his eyes.

"Are you planning to stay here?"

"Yup. Kinda tired."

She was at a total loss. She waited until his breath evened out and she was pretty sure he was asleep, then gently lifted the gun from his hand. He stirred but didn't wake. She eased off the bed and took the gun into the kitchen, where she flipped on the light under the microwave so that she could examine it. It felt too light to be real. That's when she realized she'd seen it before in the Americana bedroom. She pulled the trigger. An American flag flew out.

Joanna sat down at the table, tapped a cigarette out of the pack of Chesterfields lying amid the dirty dishes, and snapped a match to the tip. The question was: Did David know it wasn't a real gun? He was so sleepy, she couldn't be sure. But if he thought it was real, what was he doing with it? Why had he come into her room with it in his hand? It didn't seem likely that she'd get much sleep tonight with a potential lunatic in the loft.

Taking a deep hit off the cigarette, she wondered why she always had such stellar luck when it came to men. Boyfriend, business associate, brother. It didn't matter. "Maybe it's time for the convent," she whispered, leaning back in her chair and blowing smoke into the darkness. She imagined that there were worse fates. Not that she could think of any.

16

How come you were up and out so early?" asked Cordelia. She was standing in the kitchen, her generous hip resting against the granite countertop, waiting for her Toaster Strudel to pop up. Hattie was already at preschool, and Cecily was off having breakfast with her mom.

Jane sat at the kitchen table, watching Cordelia's morning nutritional ritual with a jaundiced eye. "I can't believe you still eat that crap."

"If *I* eat it, it's got to be the breakfast of champions, yes? And in case you didn't notice, I traded up. I'm no longer eating Pop-Tarts. These are much better."

Cordelia's eating habits ran from childish to avant-garde gourmet. Jane admired the culinary adventurer part of her nature but couldn't believe some of the choices she made. Shrugging, she went back to her oatmeal. "To answer your question, I was out renting a car. I'm driving back to Eagle Ridge this morning."

Cordelia's eyebrows shot upward just as the strudel did. "Why the rental car?"

"Because Nolan thinks my Mini would be too conspicuous. I need to do a little more checking around today." She leaned down and gave Mouse's head a scratch, then glanced at his dog bowl and saw that one of the cats was finishing up the last of the kibble.

"Didn't you do enough yesterday?" asked Cordelia. "You sure got an earful from that cop."

After returning to the loft last night, Cordelia had insisted on hearing every last detail that Jane and Nolan had unearthed.

"The thing is, we never actually saw Luberman. He wasn't in his office. We drove out to his cabin. His truck was there, but he must have been inside. I want to get a look at him, Cordelia. Meet him, if I can."

Cordelia drummed her long red nails on the countertop. "I suppose my Hummer would be too conspicuous, too, huh?"

"Well, *yeah*. Might as well drive a tank down the center of town."

She bit off one of the tips of the Toaster Strudel. "I have to admit, Janey, you've wounded me to the core."

"I have?"

"Now that you've got Nolan in your life, I'm no longer needed. And after *all* the years I've put in, the skills I've honed! The car chases. The breaking and entering. Hiding in bushes. Assuming alternate identities. I've been your decoy, your deal maker, and your sitting duck. Not to mention the time I saved your life by driving my Hummer through—"

Jane held up her hand. "I hear you."

Cordelia sniffed, trying to look tragic and racked by suffering. Then she took a big bite of the pastry.

"You're my best friend, Cordelia."

"Your partner in crime?"

"Absolutely. You can come with me anytime you want. I didn't ask you yesterday because I knew you're busy with the new play. I thought you couldn't get away."

Cordelia sighed dramatically, which was hard to do while chewing. "Joanna called a few minutes ago when you were in the shower, said she'd had a horrible night's sleep. She begged off, said she couldn't possibly make it to the theater today. So, as it happens, I'm free as a bird." She flicked Jane a plaintive glance, then looked away.

"Do you want to come along?"

"I thought you'd never ask." Stuffing the rest of the pastry in her mouth, she said, "Give me a couple minutes to get dressed." She picked up Hattie's PediaSure off the kitchen table and took a couple of swigs, then headed for the stairway up to her raised bedroom.

"Can you make it quick?"

She turned around. "Not if you expect me to dazzle."

"I can live with imperfection."

"That's obvious." She eyed Jane's cowboy boots, jeans, jeans jacket, and black turtleneck.

"Hey. It's a good look."

"For a cowpoke, maybe. But I'll take my cues from you—stay with the bucolic theme."

"What's that supposed to mean?"

"Wait and see, dearheart. Wait and see."

No matter how hard Cordelia tried, she simply couldn't get herself together in less than an hour. Jane sat in the living room and played with Mouse for a while. She'd already stuffed his leash in her back pocket. She looked through a couple of magazines, clipped her nails, watered some plants, watched a little CNN until she couldn't stand it another second. Finally, she hollered at Cordelia to hurry up. "If we don't get going soon, we'll be doing this surveillance with night-vision goggles."

"As it happens, I have a pair," said Cordelia, sweeping down the stairs in a red fox-hunting jacket, tan breeches, tall black riding boots, black leather gloves, and a velveteen helmet. A riding crop was pressed under one arm. "Really, Jane, it's a tangle. I've never seen anything in *InStyle* on how to dress to surveil. There are so many *unknowns*."

Jane stood and faced her. Apparently her comments about needing to be inconspicuous had not sunk in. Then again, things could be worse. Cordelia could have worn her matador outfit. Jane considered asking her to change but figured that would mean another hour before they got on the road.

Two hours later, after a stop for lunch—or, as Cordelia put it, "the ritualized sharing of nutritional goodness in the period of high sun"—

at the Norske Nook in Osseo, Wisconsin, Jane stopped the Chrysler Sebring in front of a storefront on Chamberlain's main drag. The building directly to their right was narrow, two stories, with the word MCCORMICK and 1902 carved in the cocoa brown sandstone just under the oversized arched window. The black-and-white metal sign above the doorway said LUBERMAN LANDSCAPE DESIGN.

"This must be the place," said Cordelia. Glancing around, she added, "These streets don't look very mean to me. But then, every town has a seedy underbelly, right?"

"That must be Luberman," said Jane, taking off her sunglasses and pointing at the man sitting in the window working at a drafting table.

"Him? No way."

He fit the general description. Blond. Late forties. But that's where the similarities ended.

"Must be an employee," said Cordelia.

"I don't think so."

"Listen, that guy in there is the human embodiment of the Michelin Man. It can't be him."

Luberman still looked strong, but the lean man who'd been released from prison in 1998 was now covered in a good seventy-five pounds of extra flesh. His arms reminded Jane of thick sausages and his face looked like stretched rubber, permanently reddened.

"That a hat on his head?" asked Cordelia, squinting.

"You need glasses. It's a bald spot." Jane slipped her sunglasses back on. "Let's go in. See what he charges for landscape work. If you do the talking, then I can stand back and study him. Just say you're in the area looking to buy a summer home."

Mouse, who'd been sleeping in the backseat most of the way, sat up and gave the building his full attention.

"You stay here, buddy," said Jane, turning around and giving his ear a friendly pull.

On the way in, Cordelia whispered, "I'm Lady Gladys and you're Rachael."

"No no . . ."

"Shhh."

They approached the front counter. Luberman worked another couple of seconds at the drafting board, then stood up. "Can I help you?"

"Are you Mr. Luberman?" asked Cordelia with an upper-crust English accent.

"Yes?" he said, a puzzled look on his face.

"My name is Lady Gladys Night . . . ah . . . bridge."

Jane cringed.

"Nightabridge?" repeated Luberman.

"That's correct. And this is my cousin Rachael."

"Nice to meet you both," said Luberman, gazing skeptically at Cordelia's clothes.

"We were wondering what you charged for your landscape services."

He rested a heavy forearm covered in blond hair on the counter. "Depends on what you want. You two live around here?" His gaze switched to Jane. She could tell he didn't like the fact that her eyes were hidden behind the dark glasses. It made reading her more difficult. And he *was* trying hard to get a read on both of them.

"My husband's family hails from Madison. We're on holiday at the moment, be here another fortnight. We live in London, but we're thinking of spending summers here. My mission is to seek out a home on one of these lovely lakes. Something upmarket. I need to find a bloke who can take care of the property when we're not around. Whatever needs to be done."

"What places have you looked at?"

"Actually, I'm just beginning my search. Haven't even hired an estate agent yet."

Jane got the sense that he wasn't sure whether to believe her or not but was leaning toward giving her the benefit of the doubt. He probably didn't want to turn away a potential customer.

"My American cousin and I were just driving down your high street when we saw your sign. I'm thinking that most of these properties around here will no doubt need landscaping work as well."

"What sort of place are you looking for? What price range?"

"Four, maybe five hundred thousand—American. Whatever it takes to get something suitable."

He raised his eyebrows. "Sure, I could handle that." He slipped a card out of the pocket of his blue polo shirt and handed it to her. "What does Mr. Nightabridge do?"

"He's in . . . plastics. Heavy-duty. Silly things, really. But lucrative. Very lucrative."

He nodded, chewing the inside of his cheek. "Like I said, I'd be happy to take care of whatever you end up buying."

"Wonderful. By the way, do you do the work yourself?"

"Most of it, yeah. I like being outdoors."

"Do you have . . . references?"

He reached under the counter and brought up a white packet. "There's a brochure in there with my price list and the names of the people I've worked for in the area. And, of course, I can customize my services pretty much any way you want."

Except for the whiff of paranoia, which probably wasn't obvious to anyone who wasn't looking for it, he seemed so normal that it was hard to picture him as a stalker, or worse, a murderer. Evil might be real, it just wasn't visible to the naked eye.

"Thank you," said Cordelia, moving the riding crop from one arm to the other. "I'll be sure to have my secretary look it over."

Luberman glanced down at her boots. "Do you always dress like that?"

"Like what?"

"I mean, are you a horse woman?"

"*Horses?* Heavens, no. What gave you that impression?"

Jane gently tugged Cordelia toward the door.

"Ta ta," she called, waving with her fingers.

Once they were safely back in the car, Jane said, "The point behind surveillance is not to arouse suspicions."

"Yes, I know. But I did a fine job—no need to thank me, Jane. My accent was impeccable, didn't you think? Even threw in a few Britishisms. And I gave you plenty of time to study him at close range. To be quite honest, I'm sure those teeth of his *must* be false. But that's just my opinion. I point this out because I'm not sure you noticed."

Jane's eyes rose to the roof of the car. "Let's get out of here."

"Ten-four. Mission accomplished. Where to now?"

"Let's drive out to Whitefish Lake."

"Didn't you do that yesterday?"

"Yes, but we only viewed the cabin from the road. We know he's at work today. That means it's safe to walk in and take a closer look."

Fifteen minutes later, they parked the car about half a mile from the entrance to the property, just in case somebody drove by and wondered what a strange vehicle was doing so close to Luberman's cabin.

Jane let Mouse out to run around the woods for a few minutes. "Not a very interesting day for you, buddy. We'll go for a run around Lake Harriet when we get home." She scratched his head and gave him a kiss. "We won't be long." She locked him back in the car, making sure to leave the windows open a crack. It was a beautiful fall day, with temperatures in the high fifties, but a car's interior could heat up quickly.

"You really love that dog, don't you," said Cordelia as they walked along the side of the dirt road toward the entrance to Luberman's land.

"I don't know what I'd do without him."

"He's really taken to Hattie."

"I know. Dogs and kids belong together."

"Speaking of Hattie." She reached into her pocket and removed her cell phone. "She should be home from preschool by now. She usually calls me." Flipping it open, she said, "Well, lookey here. Seems that while we were in Luberman's place of business, I got a call from my dear sister." She pressed a few buttons and then listened to the message. When she was done, she flipped the phone closed. "Huh."

"What?"

"She's coming to town."

"Really? When?"

"She just said soon. She wants to introduce me—and you, by the way—to the new love of her life."

"Goodie. Can't wait. If she marries the guy, this will make it an even half dozen, right?"

"She won't marry him."

"Why do you say that?"

"It might interfere with her movie career. That, Janey, comes first, last, and in between. She needs to be free to charm her way into the bedrooms of the powers that be."

"Boy, you really don't think much of her."

"She'd use anything necessary to climb her way to the top. And since she's growing older by the day, the quickest way to cut through all the red tape is with, shall we say, the *personal* touch."

It all sounded so sordid. Jane understood that Cordelia often painted Octavia with a blacker brush than was strictly necessary. Octavia was already rich, having inherited Hattie's father's legendary wealth. So this wasn't a money grab. It was Octavia's professional ambition that drove her. And her ambition, her need for success—as everyone around her knew—was immense.

"I'm sure the new boy's beautiful and crazy about her," said Cordelia as they rounded the turn onto Little Turtle Road. "They always are."

The house sat on a small bluff overlooking the lake. Woods circled around behind the property and thinned out as they reached the service drive. A deep-green lawn spread out in front of the house all the way down to the beach. A wide wooden dock jutted out into the bay, with two boats tied to the end. The large white one looked new, part fishing boat, part pleasure craft. The word PRO-LINE was printed on the side. Jane judged that it was probably a good twenty feet long. The other boat appeared to be a handmade houseboat. It was much smaller, maybe twelve feet in length if you counted the pontoons it rested on from end to end. The house part of it didn't look much bigger than eight by eight. And the motor itself was smaller, possibly quieter. It looked beat up, like it had been used hard for a long time.

"Come on," said Jane. "Let's check the place out."

The grass around the cabin had been recently cut. Up the hill, a section of woods was in the process of being cleared. Luberman had cut and neatly stacked logs from the trees he'd removed. He must have had a recent fire because the smell of wood smoke lingered in the air.

"Nice place," said Cordelia.

"Secluded," said Jane.

The cabin was two stories high with a steep gable facing the water. Windows covered the front, from the ground all the way to the tip of the gable, allowing for a panoramic view of the lake.

Jane climbed the steps to the deck that ran across the front of the cabin. Luberman had spent some bucks, not only on the boats but also on some expensive outdoor furniture. A new stainless steel gas grill sat next to what had probably once been used as a potting shed table but was now part of his outdoor kitchen. Wildflowers were tied together in bunches, hanging upside down on metal hooks jutting out from the house, drying in the afternoon sun. Clay pots had been lined up along the edge of the deck. A few contained the usual hothouse flowers—New Guinea impatiens, dahlias, begonias. But on the whole, Luberman seemed to favor succulents and cacti.

Jane stepped up to the window, cupped her hands around her eyes, and looked through the glass. All the furniture had a north-woods feel to it. The walls were covered in knotty pine. A Native American blanket rested on the back of the leather couch. Next to the wall-mounted plasma TV was a rifle rack. Next to that hung an assortment of old, rusted tools. The place seemed comfortable enough. Nothing was out of order. If Jane hadn't known *what* Gordon Luberman was, the cabin and the surrounding grounds would have made her think the man who lived here might be an interesting person to get to know. She shivered at the thought.

"Down here!" called Cordelia.

Jane turned and saw that Cordelia was standing on the aft section of the houseboat. "What is it?"

"Just come here." She was leaning over, examining something on the floor.

Jane jumped off the deck. As she did so, a flash of sunlight glinted off something up near the top of the service drive. She paused, her heart racing as she visually inspected the area. Nothing was moving. She couldn't see a car or a truck. She hadn't heard one, either. She stood a minute longer, watching the trees. Whatever it was that had caused the reflection had left her feeling unsettled.

"Janey, hurry up!"

With one last sweep of the road, Jane hurried down to the dock. She immediately saw what had captured Cordelia's attention.

"It's an oversized cooler," said Cordelia.

"They use them for fishing."

"Do fish bleed?"

"Sure."

"Oh."

Cordelia had read nearly every play that had been written in the English language, but when it came to the natural world, she wasn't going to win any contests. She'd once asked Jane if radishes grew on trees.

"Why?"

"Because there's dried blood in here. I'm sure of it."

"And?"

"Well, if Luberman *did* kidnap, murder, and then dump the body, this would be an easy way to do it." She looked up, her eyes traveling over the water. "It's deserted out here. There isn't another dock or cabin in sight. He could do anything he wanted and be completely unobserved."

"He did it once before and it worked. Why not do it again?" said Jane. "But wouldn't you think the cops had already thought of that?"

"Maybe, but if they couldn't get a warrant to search the place, they wouldn't know about the blood. *We* can tell them. Once they know, they talk to a judge, get a search warrant, test the blood for DNA, and while they're waiting for the results, they arrest Luberman on suspicion of murder." She clapped her hands together as if that was the end of the story.

"Doesn't work like that. We're trespassing. I don't think they can use what we found to get a warrant."

"Well, damn. They should just dredge the lake. At least they'd be doing *something*."

"The chest was in plain sight," said Jane, thinking about it a little more. "But you had to take the cover off to see the blood."

"No I didn't. I noticed the blood *on* the cover. That's why I opened it up."

Jane would have to talk to Nolan. He knew the legalities much better than she did.

"Come on, Cordelia. I think we should get out of here."

"Why? We just started."

The queasy feeling in the pit of Jane's stomach was getting worse by the minute. It might not mean anything, but if Luberman felt even the least bit ill at ease about the conversation they'd had at his office, if he had any sense that Jane and Cordelia were part of a tail, then his next move might be to drive around and see if he could find them. Stopping by his house would undoubtedly be part of that search.

"I saw something up on the road. I'm not sure what it was, but if it was Luberman, he could have seen us."

"Oh." Cordelia flew off the boat. "I'm with you, Janey. Let's hit the bricks."

Jane sprinted across the grass to the service road. Cordelia followed, but at a slower pace. When Jane reached the top, she looked around. All was quiet. "You doing okay?" she called, turning around and waiting for Cordelia to catch up.

"I just love rushing up a hill when I'm terrified. Really gets the old juices going." The look on her face suggested she wasn't having any fun at all.

"I'm going to run ahead," said Jane. "But I'll stay within earshot. If I see or hear anything, I'll let you know."

"I'll do the same," said Cordelia, bending over and resting her hands on her knees.

Jane took off at a moderate clip. Half a mile wasn't far. Cordelia had parked around a bend in the road, so she wouldn't be able to see the car until she was right on top of it. She realized now that parking it there had been a mistake. She quickened her pace when she began to smell gasoline. Maybe it was a boat out on the lake, but she doubted it. She should have been able to hear a motor and she couldn't. She stopped for a moment and sniffed the air. The smell was strong now. Knowing in her gut that something was wrong, she took off at a dead run. As she burst around the bend in the road, she saw that her rental car was on fire.

"Mouse!" she screamed, feeling her heart go crazy inside her chest. If she didn't get to him before the gas tank blew, it was all over.

Edging closer, she tried to see him in the backseat, but thick, black smoke was beginning to rise in bitter clouds, obscuring her vision. A gust of wind forced the smoke over her. She tried to wave it away, but it was all around her, inside her, stinging her eyes. She backed off, coughing so hard she thought she'd throw up. She was about ten feet from the car when the gas tank caught. The explosion knocked her flat on her back. Crawling away from the inferno, she screamed, "Mouse! I'm trying!"

She scrambled to her feet, but she couldn't move. She stood at the edge of the road, watching helplessly, hands balled into fists, screaming her dog's name until she had no voice left.

Finally, knowing that it was hopeless, she dropped to her knees, unable to take her eyes off the fiery ball. She felt like someone had taken a razor and sliced her heart in half. Her mind went numb.

As the fire began to burn down, she sat down in the dirt, pulled her knees up to her body, folded her arms around them, and began to rock. It was all her fault. The words "He trusted me" hammered at her. Her fault. Her fault.

"Janey?"

She looked up, saw Cordelia standing over her. At that moment, a feeling of total and absolute hate washed over her. "Luberman torched the car," she said, her voice hoarse.

"God." She stood for a moment, taking in the scene.

Jane pressed her eyes shut. Tears streamed down her cheeks. She wiped them away, seeing that they'd mixed with the soot on her face. Her hand was covered in an oily blackness. Cordelia sat down in the dirt next to her, circled Jane's waist with her arm. That small act of kindness broke something inside her. She rocked forward against her knees, sobs racking her body. "I'll kill him," she said, choking on the words. "I'll kill him."

Neither spoke for several minutes.

Finally, Jane wiped the arm of her jeans jacket across her face and looked up at the sky.

"Do you think," said Cordelia. "I mean, could Luberman still be hiding out there behind a tree somewhere?"

"He's gone. He probably stuck around long enough to watch my reaction. I'm sure that's how he gets his jollies."

Cordelia stared down at the dirt.

Except for the creaking of the white-hot car frame, the road was quiet again. All around them, the normal woodland sounds were returning.

After another couple of minutes, Cordelia said, "It's all my fault, Janey. I shouldn't have used an English accent."

"No, it's not your fault. I made the decision to go in there and talk to him. If anyone's to blame, it's me."

Deep in the woods came the faint sound of a bark.

Jane swiveled around. "Did you hear that?"

"What?"

She moved into a crouch. "There it is again." Rocketing into the woods, she headed toward the sound, jumping over dead logs, side-stepping trees. "Bark again!" she screamed. Her voice seemed to have returned. "Mouse, I'm coming." She knew it could easily be another dog—probably was.

As she ducked under a low-hanging branch, she spied a clearing about a hundred yards ahead. "Mouse? Bark again. Louder!" She ran flat-out. The barking did get louder, more insistent. She felt sure it was him now. If Luberman was holding him captive, she'd deal with it.

Reaching the clearing, the only living being in sight was her dog. He was attached by his leash to a section of clumped birch. When he saw her, he began to jump in the air and yip. He seemed as wild to see her as she was to see him.

"Mouse," she said, sliding to her knees in front of him, grabbing him up in her arms, never wanting to let him go. "Oh, baby, you're alive!" She buried her head in his fur. He licked her face, her hands, her hair, her ears. "You're alive," she repeated again and again, the tears flowing freely down her cheeks.

She heard Cordelia's distant call. "Are you okay?"

"I'm coming," she yelled back. She stood and unhooked Mouse's collar from the leash, then untied the leash from the tree. Hooking Mouse back up, she led him out of the woods, scraping at her face with the cuffs of her jacket.

"Oh, my God," said Cordelia, when she saw them emerge from the woods. Her eyes grew wide watching Mouse trot along beside Jane as if nothing had happened. "What the hell's going on?"

"Luberman has a heart—or the remnants of a conscience. He must have broken into the car and taken him out before he doused it with gasoline."

"Maybe he likes dogs."

Jane had no idea and really didn't give a rip. Except, she didn't want to be beholden to this freak, but like it or not, she was.

Cordelia bent down and gave Mouse a hug. "You're a sight for sore eyes, babe." Glancing up at Jane, she said, "So, now what do we do?"

Jane looked both ways down the dirt road. Nothing seemed impossible now that Mouse was okay. She felt like she could fly home. "I guess we start walking."

"Can't we call a cab?"

Jane laughed, feeling it ease some of the tension in her body. "God, but I love you."

"You do?"

"Only you would suggest calling a cab when we're in the middle of nowhere. Cordelia, there aren't any cab companies out in the boonies."

"A bus, then?"

She shook her head.

"Maybe there's a rental car company around here that picks you up. You know, like Enterprise."

"Try your cell phone. But I figure our best bet is the highway. Maybe somebody will come along and give us a lift back to Eagle Ridge."

"How far away is the highway?"

"About three miles."

"Three miles? *Three* miles!"

"We could jog."

"No, we couldn't."

"Okay, suit yourself." Jane tugged on Mouses's leash and started down the road.

"Hey."

"What."

"I don't suppose I could wait here."

"If you want. But it will likely be dark by the time I get back."

Cordelia rapped the riding crop impatiently against her boot, glared at what was left of the car, then sighed deeply and scurried to catch up.

17

Joanna moved one of the kitchen chairs into the bathroom and placed it next to the sink. She was about to play customer to Faye's professional hairdresser. It was such a large bathroom that it could easily have doubled for a salon stall.

After Joanna sat down, Faye stood back, then pulled both sides of Joanna's hair forward and cupped it around her chin. "I'd take the color down a notch or two. Instead of the light blonde, I'd go to a rich, shimmering gold. And then I'd add both highlights and lowlights. Discreetly done, it could be dazzling."

"You can do that here?"

"You bet I can. And I'd suggest a new cut. We'll look through some of my books, see if anything appeals to you."

Joanna had spent most of yesterday talking to Faye. She had to admit that she thought Faye was a lot of fun. She had a bawdy sense of humor and lots of bad habits. She drank and smoked way the hell too much—her words—and liked cards and casinos. Joanna was just waiting for the first homophobic remark about her brother, but Faye said she thought David seemed like a great guy. The only person Faye didn't like was Freddy Kasimir. She kept bringing the conversation back to him, told Joanna in no uncertain terms to stay way from him.

Faye was very quick with advice—much like Joanna's mother. It actually felt kind of wonderful to have someone take such a personal, motherly interest in her. Yesterday evening, Joanna had given her a tour of her wardrobe. Faye offered her opinions—what she thought was a good color, a good look for Joanna, what she thought wasn't. Their friendship had grown so quickly that Joanna was suspicious of the way Faye made her feel: warm, almost safe. It made no sense, really, except that Joanna needed someone in her life like that right now.

It was approaching three in the afternoon when they finally left the bathroom and returned to the kitchen for coffee. Nolan would be stopping by in a few minutes. Once Joanna listened to his report, she'd have a better sense of how safe she'd feel when she did decide to go outside for the first time.

"What are you thinking about?" asked Faye, getting up to pour herself more coffee.

"Oh, nothing much." Joanna gazed down into her cup.

"You're worried about something. I can tell."

"Don't be silly. You hardly know me."

"I'm a quick study."

Joanna shook her head and laughed. "People always think they know celebrities because we're on TV or they see us up on a big movie screen. We're familiar, but that's a far cry from the real thing."

"Oh, I saw past that crap years ago. You've had a great life, Joanna, one that lots of people would envy."

"I know. Really, I'm grateful."

"Unlucky, too," said Faye, stirring some cream into her cup. "I know you haven't had much success in the love department. All I can say is, welcome to the club."

"Thanks."

"I hope you don't take this the wrong way, but you don't seem like you have many friends."

"I've got lots of friends," said Joanna, knowing she sounded way too defensive.

"Close ones?"

She looked up at the ceiling fan. "Sure. Cordelia, for one."

"But you don't talk to her much. You hardly ever see her. At least, that's the impression I got from her."

"What's your point?" She was starting to get irritated.

"You need people in your life, Joanna. People who care about you."

Lighting up, Joanna said, "Look, everybody wants something from me, okay? They want to manipulate me. Or if they don't, they have a picture of me that's so unrealistic I don't even want to be in the same room with them. I have friends, lots of them. Other actors, actresses. People in the industry. We talk. But I don't trust anyone completely, not anymore. Maybe it's one of the downsides to my profession. I've been burned too many times."

Faye nodded. "Still, it's sad, don't you think?"

"It's the way it is."

"I suppose that means you and me, we'll never be good friends. I'm not in 'the industry.' I'm just an average Joe—or Jane."

"Don't expect anything from me, Faye. That way, you won't be disappointed."

"Okay. Not a problem. You could walk out the door tomorrow and all I'd do is shrug and go back to watching *The Price Is Right*. But here's the deal. I'd miss you—not you the actress, but you the person. I like you, Joanna. You're funny, smart. You've experienced the world from an unusual perspective and that interests me. I've always been the kind of woman who picks up stray animals, tries to find them good homes."

Joanna blinked through the smoke from her cigarette. "You think I'm a *stray*?"

"In a way, yeah, I guess I do. As much as I respect you and what you've accomplished, I think your life is pretty lonely. And yet, in spite of everything that's happened to you, you're still a good person."

"Yeah, right. Sometimes I wonder."

"Well, don't. Give me some credit, lady. I've lived a lot longer than you have and I'm very selective about the people in my life. You may not want to be my friend, but that doesn't stop me from being yours."

The phone rang. Rising from the table, Joanna grabbed the receiver off the wall. She expected it to be Nolan and it was. He was downstairs. She buzzed him in, then turned around and looked at Faye. The question was, should she allow her to stay or ask her to go? "I have a meeting with someone. He'll be up here in a second."

"Want me to skedaddle?"

Joanna glanced at the clock. She wished David were here. On the other hand, after the bizarre way he'd behaved last night, she'd been more than happy to see him leave right after breakfast. "No. Stay."

"Love to. Who's the meeting with?"

"A private investigator I just hired."

Faye's eyes narrowed.

"Long story. Just wait, you'll hear all about it."

Once Nolan arrived, they all sat down in the living room. With his dark skin, stocky frame, gray hair, and mustache, Nolan reminded Joanna of Ossie Davis. She'd worked with Ossie several times. He was a gentle, cultured man. Nolan, on the other hand, was rough. He might not be a cop anymore, but he still gave off cop vibes. Joanna introduced Faye as a friend. She could see a look of pleasure cross Faye's face.

"So," said Joanna, brushing a piece of lint off her gray slacks as she crossed her legs, "what did you find out?" She was trying hard to re-main calm—*look* calm—but inside, she was a mess.

Opening the file folder he'd carried in, Nolan patiently explained everything he'd learned.

The longer he talked, the tighter Joanna held herself. When he was done, she looked down at her hands. "But you don't know for a fact that Gordon was behind those missing women."

"No. There's no proof. That's why the police haven't acted on it."

"So they could be wrong. It might be a coincidence."

Nolan closed the file and set it on a table next to him. "I think, Ms. Kasimir, that we'd be making a big mistake if we treated it that way."

She swallowed, forcing back the bile rushing into her throat. "Sometimes I'm so thick. I actually thought I was rid of him." She knew now that he'd never go away. Gordon had taken her freedom. From the moment he walked into her life, she should have seen him for what he was. That failure had eaten away at her daily for more than fifteen years. "What can we do?"

"We need to find proof that will put him behind bars. Short of that, he's still out there on the street, and that means he's still a danger. I plan to concentrate all my efforts on proving he murdered those two women."

"Does that mean you think he was the one who sent me the pink roses?"

"I do," said Nolan. "I wish I could tell you otherwise."

A wave of fatigue shuddered over her. "It's about what I expected."

"I'm curious," said Nolan, looking at her hard. "During the trial, did you ever talk to a therapist, a counselor, a cop—somebody who knew about the psychology of a stalker?"

She shook her head.

"Actually, in some ways, show folks are a lot like police officers. It's a high-risk profession. You experience too much, see too much. I realize what happened with you and Luberman was a long time ago. Most of the research that's been done on stalkers has been recent. I won't get into details, but in general, one of the biggest mistakes celebrities make is being overly friendly. They let people take their pictures. Send out signed photos to fans. Allow publicity shots of their homes—even their bedrooms."

"I'm not overly friendly," said Joanna. *"Anymore."* Throwing up her hands, she added, "But, I mean, are we supposed to live in a cocoon?" Strange question, she thought, coming from a woman who'd tried to do exactly that. She knew firsthand that being in the public eye wasn't just all about praise. It could also be highly corrosive. For example, she'd been in a bathroom stall once when two women she'd just met— women who had been falling all over her telling her how wonderful she was—came in and started talking about how awful she looked in person. It was enough to drive a sane person stark raving mad.

"I know it's a difficult issue," said Nolan. "Most people look at fame and see only what's positive. The money. The power. Public affection, even adoration. Fame opens doors, provides the famous person with amazing opportunities. But we both know that's only one side of the coin."

"Tell me about it."

"Most people you meet will never be a problem to you. That's a given. But for some, a very few, simple friendliness on your part can trigger a delusional individual into feeling like he has a relationship with you, when in reality, he doesn't. One of the most interesting facts that's come to light in the last few years is, contrary to what we all think, celebrities who attract the biggest number of stalkers—and all celebrities have stalkers, it's just a question of how many—aren't the most glamorous. They're the ones who seem the sweetest, the most wholesome, because *that* makes them approachable."

"But it wasn't like that with Gordon and me," said Joanna. "We had a brief relationship. I invited him into my life. At one point, I thought I loved him. It didn't last long before I saw what he really was, but by then, it was too late."

"Don't be so hard on yourself, Ms. Kasimir. Believe me when I tell you he targeted you. He had you in his sights long before he ever made his first approach."

"You think so?"

"I'm positive."

Joanna felt flattened. "What do I do?"

"Well, first, I'd suggest beefing up the security at the Linden Building. I'd like to put a man on the back door, the one by the parking lot, and by the inside elevator. That way, no one can sneak in. It's just a precaution, but one I'd advise. It will cost some money—"

"Don't worry about that. Can you set it up?"

"I've already arranged for two men to start tonight. They should be here around five."

"What about when I need to leave the building?"

"Have you ever used bodyguards?"

Joanna sighed. "Yes."

"This might be a time when you might want to do it again."

"Can you suggest someone?"

"I do a lot of work with a local company in St. Paul. A lot of the guys they hire are either ex-cops or ex-military, so they know what they're doing." He took a card out of his inner pocket and placed it on the coffee table. "Call this number. Give them an hour's notice."

Joanna nodded, feeling a little better. "But unless you can prove Gordon is guilty of murdering those two women, I'm the one who's going to spend my life in prison."

"Let's hope not," said Nolan, rising. "Jane drove back to Eagle Ridge today. Maybe she found out something that could help us. If not, I'm planning to hire a man to sit on Luberman, follow him everywhere. And tomorrow, I'm heading up to Lake Poygan to research what happened to Mandy Kiskanen. Maybe I can connect some dots."

"Thanks," said Joanna. She walked him to the door.

As they were saying good-bye, her cell phone rang. Joanna looked so startled that Nolan said, "Why don't you answer that while I'm still here."

"If you don't mind, I will."

Faye stood up and handed it to her.

"Hello?" said Joanna, sinking down on the couch.

"Is this Ms. Kasimir?"

It was a man. She didn't recognize the voice. "Who's calling, please?"

"This is Noel Dearborn over at the Allen Grimby. I'm the intern assisting Cordelia Thorn. I'm sorry if I'm catching you at a bad time."

"No, that's okay," said Joanna.

"The reason I'm calling is we got a call from *Milwaukee Magazine*. It's the big glossy monthly that does features on what's new around the city and the region. I'm told they don't usually do stories on events as far away as the Twin Cities, but since you're such a big name, they want to interview you. I'm kind of new around here, so I wasn't sure how to handle it. Cordelia isn't around and nobody else seemed to know what to do, so I took a chance and called. Hope you don't mind. I didn't give out your number because I didn't think you'd want someone calling out of the blue."

"Thanks," said Joanna. "You're right."

"So I took the guy's number, said I'd pass it on to you. If you're interested—and I hope you are—he'd like you to call him back today. It's getting kind of late, so do you think . . ." He paused, allowing Joanna to make the decision.

"Sure. What's the number?" She wrote it on the inside of a *Country Living* magazine.

"Thanks, Ms. Kasimir. I'm looking forward to meeting you next Monday. I'm a huge fan."

"What's your name again?"

"Noel Dearborn."

"I'll call right away. What's the man's name?"

"Victor Allen. He's the features editor."

"Okay. I'm on it."

After saying good-bye, she turned to Nolan. "Everything's fine. Just some publicity stuff I need to deal with."

"Okay," said Nolan. "You take care, then. Call if you have any problems."

After he was gone, Joanna leaned back against the couch cushions. She felt a little better knowing that Nolan was on the case. At least something was being done.

"Boy," said Faye, returning from the kitchen with a fresh cup of coffee for Joanna. "That was an earful I never expected. That's why you look so worried all the time. God, if there's anything I can do—"

"Have dinner with me," said Joanna. "We'll order something from the Greek restaurant downstairs."

"Or I could go get us burgers, or Chinese. Or we've got some great Vietnamese restaurants in town."

"Whatever you want," said Joanna, pressing in Victor Allen's number. She waited through three rings before the phone was picked up.

"Hello?" came a deep voice.

"Mr. Allen?"

There was a long pause. Then, "Joanna, how nice to hear from you again."

She froze. "Gordon?"

"Welcome to the Midwest. Hope you're enjoying your stay." His tone was calm. Mocking. Just the way she remembered.

"You stay the hell away from me!"

"What a way to talk. I tried to get you to clean up your language, Jo. Remember? I guess you never learn."

"If you come near me——"

"What? What are you gonna do? I'm the one who should be angry, Jo. That's why I called. In case you're as brainless as you used to be, let me spell it out for you. Call off the goons."

"Not until you leave me alone!"

He chuckled. "Paranoid as usual. Nothing ever changes. Listen, babe. I'm only going to say this once. If you want to live to see your next birthday, back the hell off. Otherwise, well, I can't be responsible for what happens to you in the big city, can I? Do you know what they call Minneapolis these days?" He voice lowered. "*Murderapolis.* Funny, huh? Well, maybe it is, maybe it isn't. Bye, babe. See you around."

"Joanna, what's wrong?" asked Faye, sitting down next to her.

With all her might, Joanna hurled the phone across the room. It hit the side of a bronze duck sculpture and burst into pieces.

Exactly the way her life just had.

18

Hillary stepped off the elevator on the fourth floor of the Allen Grimby Repertory Theater and approached the reception area with a bright, sunny smile on her face.

"Hey, Hillary," called a male voice.

"Noel." The smile ratcheted up a couple of notches. "I was in the neighborhood. Thought I'd stop by."

Noel was interning at the AGRT through next spring. He was a theater major at the U of M and was lucky enough to land the nine-month job. It didn't pay much, but that didn't matter to Noel. He was the live-in-a-garret-and-exist-on-ramen-noodles type. He was also the one who'd given Hillary the information on when and where Joanna's plane would land. No small leak. Noel was manipulatable. Just the kind of guy Hillary liked.

She sauntered up to his desk and leaned over him, plucking a wrapped peppermint from a clear glass bowl. She was wearing black jeans and a black leather blazer over a red tank top, one that showed an extra inch or two—or three—of cleavage.

"Help yourself," said Noel, speaking directly to her breasts.

"Thanks. What time are you done here?"

"I guess I could leave anytime. It's Friday. Everybody else is gone."

"What are we waiting for?"

"You're in a good mood. What you got in mind?"

Hillary sat down on the edge of the desk, fiddling with Noel's ugly polyester tie. "A drink, maybe?"

"Really?" His eyes finally found hers. "How come I rate?"

"I missed you."

"You did?"

"Sure." She undid the top button of his shirt. "Come on. TGIF, right?"

"What about Cody?"

"What about him?"

"Aren't you two, like, a couple?"

"We date. It's not a serious thing."

"Well, great then. Let me just turn off some lights." He pushed his chair back, ready to get up, but Hillary still held on to his tie. "You gonna let me go?" he asked.

"Maybe. Maybe not."

With a boy-did-I-hit-the-freakin'-jackpot look in his eyes, he pulled her down onto his lap. "My boss has a great couch in her office."

"That right?"

"We could get the drink later."

With a giggle, she brushed a strand of his lanky brown hair away from his forehead. "You're taking this a little fast, don't you think?"

His hand slipped under her jacket. "You tell me."

She closed her eyes, moaning softly. In his ear, she said, "Would you do me one little favor?"

"Anything," he whispered.

"I need Joanna Kasimir's cell phone number."

His hand stopped stroking her breast. Leaning back, he said, "Why?"

"So I can call her about the interview."

"She agreed to one?"

"In principle, yeah. I talked to her at the airport. We really hit it off. She understood totally that this could be my big break. But I'm afraid if I don't follow up on it right away, she may forget about it. She's got a lot on her mind, you know."

He eyed her skeptically.

"Do you have it? The number?"

"Yes."

"She wouldn't mind. I guarantee it. It's all in a good cause."

"I could lose my job if—"

She pressed a finger to his lips. Removing his glasses, she let her hand drift downward. "You won't lose anything, Noel. I promise."

"But—"

She could tell his resolve was weakening. "They could use ancient Chinese water torture on me. I'd never tell where I got it. And I'd be so grateful."

"How grateful?" he whispered, closing his eyes.

They never made it to the couch.

19

An old guy in a beat-up Chevy van rescued Jane and Cordelia as they walked along the highway back to Eagle Ridge. Climbing into the backseat with Mouse, Jane asked if there was a rental car company anywhere close. He drove them straight to Avis. As luck would have it, the only car in the lot that wasn't already spoken for was a Lincoln Town Car, so they rode back to the Twin Cities in a living room with wheels while Cordelia played with the GPS. All the way home, Jane thanked Jesus, the Goddess, Allah, the cosmos, her lucky stars, and anything or anyone else she could think of for saving Mouse's life. The fact that it was actually Luberman she had to thank ate at her until her insides felt raw.

After dropping off Cordelia and Mouse at the loft, Jane returned the rental car, then took a taxi back to the parking lot behind the Linden Building and hopped in her Mini. She wanted to run over to the club and call Nolan, but halfway there, she changed her mind. She had something more important to do. On the drive back from Eagle Ridge, one name kept hammering at her: Brandy Becker. Until Luberman's newest girlfriend was made to listen to the truth, to fully appreciate the danger she was in, she was completely at his mercy.

Jane had no desire to drive another hundred and sixty miles, but she couldn't live with herself if anything happened to Brandy.

The streets of Eagle Ridge were quiet and dark as Jane rolled back into town three hours later. She'd used her cell phone to call the restaurant and find out Brandy's work schedule. Luckily, she was working the late shift tonight, so Jane wouldn't have to try to find her house.

Stopping first at a filling station to get the directions to Reindeer Lake, she finally pulled into the nearly empty IHOP parking lot shortly after one. When she entered the brightly lit restaurant, she saw two women standing behind the counter talking. One was in her early twenties, short and dark haired. The other looked as if she was in her early forties. It struck Jane that if the older woman was indeed Brandy, she and Joanna could have been sisters.

As Jane sat down, the dark-haired waitress came over to take her order. Jane had stopped for a quick burger on the way, so she wasn't hungry. She ordered coffee, then asked the waitress to tell Brandy that she'd like to talk to her.

Brandy walked over a few seconds later, a wary look on her face. "Do I know you?" she asked.

"No," said Jane. She nodded to the chair across from her. "Would you mind sitting down? This won't take long."

"I'm not supposed to," said Brandy. "The night manager doesn't allow it." She glanced back toward the kitchen. " 'Course, he's back there playing cards with the dishwasher."

Jane smiled. "Just for a minute. Please."

"What's this about?"

Jane lowered her voice so that the other two customers in the restaurant couldn't hear. "Gordon Luberman."

Her eyes flickered. "What about him?"

"Look," said Jane. "You can stand if you want to, but this would be easier if you sat down."

Reluctantly, she pulled out a chair.

"I understand you're dating him."

"Yeah? So?"

"There are some things you need to know about Gordon. This may be hard for you to listen to, but hear me out, okay? I've driven all the way from the Twin Cities to talk to you."

Brandy seemed uncomfortable, but she shrugged. "Okay."

"Gordon was arrested for stalking a woman in the early nineties. He served eight years in prison in California. Do you know who Joanna Kasimir is?"

"Sure. Doesn't everyone?"

"She was the one he stalked. It got so bad that Joanna considered suicide. She couldn't even leave her home without fearing for her life. He made threats, threats she knew he would act on sooner or later. Unfortunately, it didn't end with his prison term. After he got out, he dated other women. Two of them are now dead."

Brandy gave a short gasp, pressed a hand to her mouth.

"He has a pattern. Things seem to go along okay until the woman wants out of the relationship. At that point, Gordon plies her with flowers, poems, swears his undying devotion. If she still won't take him back, the threats begin. Has he ever sent you tea roses, Brandy?"

Her big, serious eyes grew even more wary. "Yeah. Red ones. When we first met."

"Have you ever tried to break it off with him?"

"No," she whispered.

She seemed like such a sweet woman, the kind who would be totally unprepared to deal with someone like Gordon Luberman. "That's probably good. The police are doing everything they can to put him back in jail, but it's going to take time. Has he ever mentioned Joanna Kasimir to you?"

"No, but he was looking at a newspaper article about her a few days ago, got real agitated. It was right here in the restaurant. He left without even eating his dinner. But then, the next time I saw him, he never mentioned it."

"And you didn't ask him anything?"

"No. It felt too much like prying."

Jane slipped a business card out and wrote her cell phone number on the back. "My name's Jane Lawless. I own a couple of restaurants in the Twin Cities. I'm also a friend of Joanna's. We believe that he's stalking her again."

Brandy looked down at the card. "I just . . . I mean, this is so sudden, so out of the blue. I have to tell you I have a hard time believing what you're saying. Sure, he's not perfect, but . . . murder?"

Jane leaned back as the young waitress set coffee in front of her. As she walked off, Jane said, "I understand. From what I'm told, Gordon can be very charming. But you've got to believe me. As long as he's in your life, you're in danger."

Brandy seemed flustered. "If that's true, what am I supposed to do? If I break it off, you tell me that he'll come after me."

"Don't break it off," said Jane. "I know this is hard. Do you have someone you could go stay with for a while? Someone Gordon doesn't know about."

"Not really. There's my son, but Gordon knows where he lives. And what about my job? I have to support myself. I can't just take off. Besides, how do I know that what you're telling me is even true?"

"You don't have to trust me," said Jane. "Call the sheriff's office. They'll verify everything I've said."

She looked at the business card again, then put it in her pocket.

Jane watched her closely. "You're scared of him, aren't you."

Brandy slowly shifted her eyes to Jane's face. "A little."

"Call me. If you need a place to stay in Minneapolis, I'll find you one. Just say the word. Do you have a car?"

"Yeah, but I don't drive."

"I'll come pick you up. Or I'll send someone. Day or night. Okay?"

"You think the police will find the evidence to arrest him soon?"

"I hope so."

"You think I'm okay for now?"

"As long as you don't try to break off the relationship, yes. But if you're going to try to wait it out, don't make him mad. And get out if you think something's not right. Even if he doesn't do anything threatening, trust your instincts."

"Okay."

"We can leave right now if you want. Stop by your house and pick up some clothes."

"This . . . this is just too crazy," she said, shaking her head, looking dazed.

"I know it may seem that way. But it's the truth."

"I need some time to process this."

"Just be sure to keep the card. Call me if you need *anything*."

"Why are you doing this? I mean, you don't even know me."

"Honestly, it would kill me to see Gordon hurt another innocent woman. I care what happens to you, Brandy. And I'm not alone."

She nodded with a shy smile. As she got up and walked back to the counter, Jane dropped some cash on the table and left.

Outside, it hit her how exhausted she was. There were a lot of motels in town. Maybe she should find one and spend the night. She opened her car door from several feet away, but before she could get in, she felt a hand grab her arm. When she turned, she saw that it was Luberman.

"What are you doing talking to Brandy?" he demanded.

She panicked, tried to pull her arm away, but he slapped her hard across the face, then slammed her into the side of her car. Furious blood pumped into her veins. "Get the hell away from me!"

He pinned her to the car with the force of his body, pressed a hand over her mouth. "Not until you listen."

She struggled to breathe.

"I don't know what you think you're doing, but if I catch you or that fat friend of yours around here again, I'm gonna do more than burn up your goddamn car. I should have let that dog of yours fry. Nobody messes with me. You hear me?"

She tried to nod.

He removed his hand, eased up a little with the pressure, and brought his mouth close to hers. "I live a quiet life. I'm a model citizen, a guy who doesn't deserve to be treated like a criminal."

"Right," she said with a ragged breath.

He pressed himself against her again. This time, she could feel him getting hard. "You bitch. What did you tell her?"

"Nothing."

"If I find out you're lying, you're dead, you hear me? You think as soon as I let you go that you'll be safe because I don't know who you are? Think again, babe. I've got your license number. I'll know everything about you, including your cunt size, in a matter of hours. Think about that before you decide to come back here again." He backed away from her, walked over to his truck. Before he got in, he turned and said, "I'm a peaceful man. I could've killed you if I'd wanted to. Ponder that on your way home." He sat in his truck and waited for her to go.

It took many hours before the balloon in Jane's chest deflated.

Brandy spent the next couple of hours in a fog of doubt. She had no idea if she should believe this stranger or not. Come morning, she'd be able to call the sheriff's office, but until then she felt like the earth had disappeared beneath her feet. How could she have been that wrong about Gordon? She was so upset that she finally asked to get off early. Her manager huffed around a while, acted like the request was this huge horrible deal, but he finally let her go. She spent a few minutes in the back room putting on her coat and changing her shoes. When she stepped out into the chilly night air, she saw Gordon's truck. It was parked across the lot, but the engine was idling, so she knew he was inside. Sometimes he gave her a lift home, but he hadn't said anything about it tonight. If there'd been any way for her to slip past without him seeing her, she would have taken it, but it was impossible.

Stepping up to the driver's side window, she tapped lightly.

The window rolled down. "Get in," said Gordon.

"Have you been out here waiting for me all this time?" She tried to sound normal, but her voice sounded a little funny. He always told her he could see into her soul. If that was true, he knew she was lying. Tears welled in her eyes. This was too hard. She should have gone with that woman when she'd had the chance. But how could she just pick up and leave? It was all just insane. In the space of a few short minutes, her entire world had come unglued.

"Did you hear me?" said Gordon. "Let's go."

She was scared to get in and scared not to. "Sure. I just didn't expect you to be here."

Once she'd climbed up into the cab, he backed out of the lot and drove toward her house. "Why'd you leave early?"

"They didn't need me," she lied. "Slow night."

He adjusted the heat, played with the volume on the CD he was listening to—a Randy Travis song. "Anything interesting happen?"

"No, not really."

"I saw you talking to a woman. She gave you something. What was it?"

"A woman?"

He pressed the accelerator to the floor, throwing her back against the seat.

"Gordon, stop!" She closed her eyes. "Please!"

"Why are you lying to me? What did she tell you?"

She started to cry.

He eased up on the accelerator. Her house was only two blocks away when he turned the truck onto a road that led to the lake. "Let's start over. This time you tell me the truth. What did that woman tell you?"

"That you'd been in prison."

"Did she say why?"

"She called it stalking."

"And you believed her?"

"I don't know what to believe, Gordon! Is it true?"

He pulled the truck to a stop along the dark road. Without looking at her he said, "Yes, I did serve time in prison. But the stalking part never happened. I got mixed up with a nasty woman, a movie star. I dumped her and she retaliated. It's that simple. She didn't know where I was for years, but now she's found me again. She's trying to ruin me. It's an obsession. That woman who talked to you tonight, it's all part of Joanna's revenge. If she breaks us up, Brandy, she'll have won. Do you see that? Don't let her win, please God, don't believe the crap that woman told you."

She felt more conflicted than she'd ever felt before in her life. "I want to believe you."

"Then *do*," he said, looking up at her, putting his arm around her,

165

pulling her close. "Do you seriously believe I'd ever hurt you—or anyone? I know I have a temper. And I know I'm not perfect, but I love you. You're my life."

He kissed her so tenderly that for a moment, in spite of what she'd just heard, she relaxed.

And then he asked her for the piece of paper the woman had given her.

"It's her business card."

"You don't need it, do you?"

"No," she said, slowly taking it out of her pocket and handing it to him. "I guess not."

Bel Air, California
Spring 1989

*J*oanna was lying in a chaise by the pool when Gordon finally returned, shortly after midnight. The evening breeze was cool and soft, a perfect Southern California night. All the lights were on around the pool, which allowed Gordon to see the look on her face from the entrance gate. He must have seen that something was wrong because he stopped about ten feet away and stared hard. "What?" he said, lowering his arms to his sides.

He was barefoot, jeans rolled up past his ankles, with a yellow cotton shirt open to his waist. He looked good enough to eat, but Joanna refused to be distracted. Not this time.

"What's wrong?" he asked again. "You look . . . funny."

"Do I?" For the first time, all of it came together. She saw what he was, the lies, the charm. He was simply better at it than most. He'd deciphered her vulnerabilities with the skill of a surgeon. He'd played on her insecurities, promised her a love only a pillar of salt wouldn't have grabbed for. And all the while, he'd been laughing at her. What a sucker she was. What a pumped-up Hollywood big shot, a woman who was so pathetically impressed by a man unimpressed with her celebrity that she nearly wet her pants when he talked down to her.

"Joanna, say something. Is it because I wanted to drive up to Sausalito tomorrow and you said you couldn't go? Look, I'm sorry about that. I shouldn't have pushed you."

"No. You shouldn't have."

He hesitated. "Did something else happen while I was gone?"

"Yeah," she said, lifting her legs off the chaise and standing up. "I found my brain."

He frowned, raised his hands to his hips. "What's that supposed to mean?"

"I packed up the clothes you brought over. They're in a box on the patio. Take them and get out."

His face hardened. "Why are you doing this? I love you."

She laughed. "You love a lot of things around here, Gordon, but I'm not one of them."

She could see the flicker of confusion in his eyes. He wasn't sure what had happened and didn't quite know how to arrange his face, what emotional note to play. She'd never seen him in the act of searching for the correct manipulative path. He'd always done it so effortlessly before. She flashed to his comment, that he could see into her soul. She'd believed he could, berated herself for not being able to see into his. Now she understood why it wasn't possible. Gordon didn't have a soul. He had a body, an intellect, and an ego. That was the sum and substance of Gordon Luberman.

Frowning with just a hint of anger, but then thinking better of it and turning the frown to a look of deep sadness, he said, "You owe me an explanation."

"No, I don't. I don't owe you a goddamn thing."

"Someone must have talked to you. Joanna, there are people in this town who don't like me. I didn't think I needed to warn you about them, but maybe I should have. Who was it? Who came over here?"

"No one," she said calmly.

"Then . . . I don't understand."

"I called David."

His face went blank.

"My brother. He's back in Atlanta. We had a long talk."

"You have to understand——"

"No, I don't. I don't need to hear the spin you're about to put on it. You told my brother to leave—that it was what I wanted. You lied to him!"

"I didn't mean——"

"What? What didn't you mean?"

168

"He's a deviant freak, Joanna. He and that Mexican guy he's with. How could you even stand to look at them, knowing what they were doing in that bungalow?"

"They love each other, Gordon. But then I don't expect you to understand that. If you're speaking specifically about the sex part, leave me out of your prehistoric prejudices. You don't speak for me, ever. Got it?" She was so mad, she was shaking.

"They're disgusting."

"You're disgusting. Get the hell out of here and don't come back."

She could see him flailing around, trying to figure out the best tactic. But in the end, he knew better. Say what you would about him, Gordon wasn't a stupid man. He could see he'd lost. What Joanna didn't realize was that he viewed this as one skirmish in a long war, while she thought she'd planted the flag for God and country and that he'd surrendered.

The next morning, Joanna watched from behind the curtains in the living room as a gray delivery truck pulled up in the circular drive in front of her house and a man got out holding a large pink package. When she opened the front door, the man handed it to her, made her sign for it, and then left.

Walking the package over to the dining room table, she ripped off the paper and found a dozen red tea roses inside. And a card.

> Darling, I'm so sorry. I'll make it up to you, I
> swear. I love you more than I have words to tell
> you, but surely you can feel my arms around you,
> even now. I'll call.
>
> > Gordon

"Damn him," she thought. She took the flowers out to the garbage bin by the garage and dropped them in, rubbing her hands together with satisfaction.

Later that afternoon, as she was paging through a bunch of screenplays her agent had sent over, the phone call came.

"Hi, sweetheart. Don't talk. Just give me a minute to explain. First, I love you more than life itself."

Funny how his words seemed so empty, even trite now. Joanna listened for a few minutes as his deep voice crooned its usual blather, then cut him off.

"Gordon, stop. Apparently you didn't get the message last night. Our relationship is over. O-V-E-R. Don't call me again." *She slammed the phone down, assuming that would be the end of it.*

It wasn't.

When she left the house that night, she looked in her rearview mirror and realized he was following her. He must have been outside the house, waiting for her to leave. He tailed her all the way to West Hollywood, where she was meeting a director for dinner. As she was being seated, she saw Gordon enter the restaurant, take off his dark glasses, and stand near the reception desk, waiting to be seated himself.

So this was the way he was going to play it. Joanna decided to ignore him. Eventually he'd get tired and go away. He sat alone at a table not far away and stared at her through the entire meal. And then, on the way home, he followed her again.

After she'd put her car away in the garage, she walked out to his truck. "Leave me alone."

"Not until you let me apologize."

It was dark and beginning to drizzle. "You can apologize all you want, it's not going to change anything."

"Joanna, don't be like that. I was just protecting you."

"From my **brother**?"

"From an influence that I thought was negative. I was wrong, okay? I shouldn't have done it. I overstepped, but God, Joanna, give a guy a break. I told you that if I fell for you, it wouldn't be just a casual thing. Nothing's changed for me. You're still the center of my life. Can't you just give me one more chance? Other than the mess I made with your brother, have I ever hurt you? All I've done is try to love you the best I could. That's all any man can do. I'm not perfect, Jo. I never said I was. But love should count for something."

He was so good at it, but she wasn't buying the line anymore. "It's over, Gordon. I can't produce feelings that aren't there anymore."

"How can you be so cold?"

"I'm not cold, I'm just not in love with you. Maybe I never was." *She backed*

170

away from the truck. "Have a good life, Gordon." She turned and dashed around the side of the house. When she got inside, she rushed to the front windows. His truck hadn't moved.

She made sure all the doors and windows were locked, checked that the security system was on, then went upstairs, got undressed, and took a long hot shower. She wanted the steam and the spray to wash away—to erase—every trace of Gordon. She wished she'd never met him.

Before she turned out the lights that night and went to bed, she crossed over to her second-floor study and looked down on the front drive.

The truck was still there.

20

You really *can* fly this thing, right?" said David, staring out the window of the Cessna, gripping the seat as the ground dropped away under him. He and Jane had just taken off from Flying Cloud field.

"If I can't," said Jane, "you're in big trouble."

"Very funny. FYI, I didn't get in until late last night, so my nerves are already shot. Be nice to me or I might have a nervous breakdown all over you."

"If you're sleepy, go ahead and rest. These seats are amazingly comfortable."

"No, no," he said quickly, sitting forward and looking around. "I'm wide awake. No sleeping for this boy. I close my eyes and I might not wake up."

She thumped his arm. "How's Joanna this morning?"

Jane hadn't told Joanna about her confrontation with Luberman last night. She hadn't told Cordelia either, mainly because Cordelia was asleep when Jane got back from Eagle Ridge, and she was still in bed this morning when Jane left.

Getting out of town right now seemed like the smart thing to do. Jane had placed herself squarely in Luberman's sights last night. She had no expectations that he'd cooled off. On the other hand, even if he got her address from the DMV, he'd have a hard time finding her if she was in Nebraska. When she returned home, she wouldn't be returning to her house, since it was unlivable at the moment. She also had no plans to spend any time at either of her restaurants. If Luberman couldn't find her, she wasn't in any immediate danger. If Brandy told him what they'd talked about, he was probably on his way to Minneapolis right now with a loaded gun. But Jane had the sense that whatever Brandy told him, she'd keep it to a minimum. Brandy had Jane's cell phone number. If things turned ugly, Jane had to trust that she'd call.

"Man, you couldn't give me my sister's life," said David, glancing sideways out the window. "Well, maybe you could at the moment, but being in the public eye—being a celebrity—is hard work. Ever since Joanna broke out with that first film, she's been like a human Rorschach test. People don't see her at all, they just see what they want to see. I read once that Michelle Pfeiffer said she acts for free, but she charges for the inconvenience of being famous. If that doesn't say it all."

"But Joanna never seems to let anybody too close. Cordelia's one of her oldest and best friends, but it's always seemed kind of superficial to me."

"I've got a theory about that," said David. He unzipped his brown suede jacket, fluttered his arms trying to relax them. "I could be wrong, but I think Joanna's always thought that if people truly got to know her—the real her—they'd think, Jeez, she's really nothing at all. She's, like, this adored creature, but she feels like an impostor. Did you know that movie stars are nearly four times more likely to kill themselves than average Americans?"

Jane felt more sorry for Joanna than she'd ever thought possible.

As they moved up through the thermals, David closed his eyes and tightened his seat belt. "Is this normal turbulence? I mean, it's a clear day. Shouldn't it be calm?"

"There's always some turbulence. Don't worry. This plane has lots of power."

"Power," he repeated, as if he didn't quite believe her. "Power is good."

The plane nosed up through the blue morning sky, banking westward, leveling off.

"If you want, I can show you some of the basics," said Jane. "Who knows, you might enjoy becoming a pilot."

"Oh, yes indeedie. Becoming a pilot of a Minnie Mouse planelet is right up there on the list of things I *must* do before I die—directly after I master the basics of marine biology."

"Okay."

"Just get us there safely and *fast* and I'll be a happy man."

"Kenzie is meeting us at the airstrip. She'll drive us back to her place. It's out in the country, really beautiful. You'll love her, David. And she'll love you, I'm sure of it." She covered his hand with hers. "You doing okay?"

"Fine."

They both knew it was an absurd statement. Laughingly meaningless. He wasn't even in the same universe as fine.

"Kenzie a good cook?"

"Ah, no. Can't have everything. But she buys a mean steak."

David nodded to Jane's boots. "She's the one who's influenced your move toward your inner cowboy?"

"Don't be snide." She looked over at him and smiled. She wanted so much for this to be a good trip. It was a touchy thing introducing two people she cared about so deeply, not knowing if they'd even get along, let alone like each other. She felt that David was on the edge of something truly scary. The dark circles under his eyes looked worse every time she saw him. It might be selfish, but she hoped that if he was about to come apart at the seams that he wouldn't do it in Kenzie's living room.

By seven that evening, they were all sitting on the deck behind Kenzie's old farmhouse, drinking mojitos and watching the sun set over the golden fields. Much to Jane's relief, Kenzie and David hit it off immediately. On the way in from the local airfield, they'd begun insulting each other and by late afternoon, they were acting like old friends.

As soon as they reached the ranch, Kenzie insisted that David come out to the barn to meet her horses. She let them out into the field to run around while they all sat on the fence and watched. David seemed to relax for the first time since he'd come back to the Midwest. Jane took it as a good sign.

After a dinner of grilled steak, baked potatoes, and a tossed green salad, David excused himself to go upstairs. He wanted to call Diego and then take a shower. It was going on ten. He told Kenzie that when he came back down, he expected "the women of the house" to have his pipe and slippers ready for him. Kenzie countered by suggesting he might want to get to bed soon because he was scheduled to muck out the barn in the morning.

" 'Muck' isn't in my official Funk and Wagnals Gay Dictionary," said David on his way up the stairs, "so I have no idea what you're talking about. On the other hand, if the barn needs a good interior redesign, you're in luck."

After he'd disappeared upstairs, Kenzie leaned toward Jane and whispered, "He's wonderful. Everything you said he'd be."

They sat for a few minutes, finishing their beers.

Pressing her hand over the cracked surface of the pine table, Jane said, "The problem is, something's bothering him. Something serious. But he won't tell me what it is."

"He *is* wound pretty tight."

"You can tell?"

"In case nobody's mentioned this to you lately, Lawless, so are you."

Jane leaned back in her chair and folded her arms. "Maybe. But he came to Minnesota to see me. He wants my help. I think he would have talked to me the morning after he arrived, but then this thing happened at my house. He was terribly embarrassed, so he just shut down. Whatever it is that's upsetting him, I can tell he's scared. Really scared."

Kenzie got up from the table, carrying the plates and silverware into the kitchen.

Jane followed with the glassware. They set everything on the counter, then moved toward each other. To Jane, Kenzie felt like everything good, everything warm and safe in her life.

"I *know* you're worried about him," said Kenzie, resting her arms on Jane's shoulders. "But you can't make him do what he refuses to do. He'll either tell you what's on his mind, or he won't. I suggest, since he's not in any immediate danger, that until he makes a decision, you concentrate your efforts on other matters."

"For instance?"

"Me."

"You, huh."

"I haven't seen you in three weeks!"

"Feels like years."

"But you've got that plane now, Lawless, except it sure must have lots of *terrible* mechanical problems with it because you never use it."

Kenzie joked a lot, but Jane could always tell when the jokes stopped and the serious comments began. And this was serious. "It's the club, sweetheart. You're right, I get a little . . . overinvolved sometimes."

"Try the word 'workaholic' on for size. See if it fits."

"Okay, okay. But it's up and running now. Doing well. The first year is so important in the life of a restaurant."

"And you're indispensable."

"Well—"

"So let's agree, you *are* indispensable. But you're indispensable in more than one place. You need to spread some of that indispensability around."

"I'll remember that. Actually, after David and I fly home tomorrow, I've got only one other matter I need to deal with and then I'll be back."

"You mean your trashed house."

"Well, yeah. There's that. But David's taking care of it."

"Then what?" She looked at Jane hard. "Tell me it doesn't have anything to do with that PI buddy of yours."

Jane hadn't mentioned anything about Gordon Luberman to

Kenzie because she wasn't sure how long it would take to make progress toward a solution. And she also knew Kenzie wouldn't be thrilled to hear that Jane was working on a case with Nolan. "Well, actually—"

"Be honest with me here, Lawless. Are you putting your life in danger again for some stupid, dumb-ass reason?"

"No, no. Nothing like that. I promise. I'll be back in a few days. By the time I have to leave to go back home, you'll be sick of me."

Kenzie drew Jane against her. "Not much chance of that."

Glancing at the kitchen counter, Jane said, "Let's leave the dishes for David. He can put them in the dishwasher as easily as we can."

"Love the way your mind works, Lawless. When he's done, he can smoke his pipe *and* slippers. They probably taste about the same."

"Besides, he's a night owl," said Jane, caressing the small of Kenzie's back. "And I'm kind of . . . sleepy all of a sudden. Aren't you?"

"Can hardly stand up straight."

"So we should probably hit the sack."

"He'll understand that exhaustion overtook us."

"Exhaustion," said Jane, closing her eyes as Kenzie kissed her, shivered against her. When they were together, it was as if Kenzie could reach inside and pull the one thread that unraveled all the connections that normally held Jane upright. "God, but I've missed you," she whispered.

As they were on their way up the stairs, Jane remembered that David had asked her earlier about getting the keys to Kenzie's truck for him. He said that if he had trouble sleeping, he liked to drive around. It settled him down. But Jane didn't want to break the mood. One night without access to wheels couldn't be that big a deal. Holding hands, Jane and Kenzie entered the bedroom and shut the door behind them.

In the middle of the night, Jane's eyes blinked open. The bedroom was dark except for the tiny red glow from the digital alarm clock on the nightstand and the weak moonlight streaming in through the open window. The red numbers said two forty-three.

Jane wasn't sure why she'd awakened so suddenly. As she lay in Kenzie's arms, listening, getting her bearings, she had a nagging feeling that she should check on David.

It took almost a minute to disengage herself from Kenzie without waking her. Sitting on the edge of the bed, she pulled on her jeans and sweatshirt. She found her boots and socks near the foot of the bed and left the room, closing the door behind her. She stopped by David's room first but found that it was empty. The bed didn't look like it had been slept in.

Tiptoeing down the drafty farmhouse stairway to the first floor, she sat on the piano bench in the living room and yanked on her socks and boots. Glancing to her right, she noticed that there was a dim light flickering in the sunroom at the back of the house. She assumed that David was up watching TV, although he must have the volume pretty low because she couldn't hear a sound.

When she entered the room, she saw that someone had been sleeping on the couch. The side pillows had been propped against one end, and an afghan was bunched up at the other. An empty fifth of rum was lying sideways on the floor next to the couch. The bottle bothered her. David had been drinking too much lately. She felt guilty now for disappearing the way she had. She should have at least said good night. Maybe he felt abandoned when he came down and found that Jane and Kenzie had gone to bed, although he would certainly understand that they hadn't seen each other in weeks. Still, it bothered her.

Opening the double doors to the back deck, she stepped out into the dark country night. A cloud partially obscured the half-moon, but as it sailed away, she could just make out the forms of Ben and Rocket standing outside the fence, their heads down in the grass. A light was on in the barn. Kenzie would never leave the light on and the horses out at night.

Jumping off the side of the deck, Jane sprinted across the grass to the gravel drive. Approaching the horses slowly, she opened the gate to the field and walked them inside, then shut them in. As soon as she entered the barn, she saw that the ladder to the hayloft was lying flat on the ground. It was heavy, made of rough-sawn wood, and would have made a loud noise when it hit. She assumed that's what had spooked the horses. With the barn door open, the noise had no doubt driven them outside—and at the same time, awakened her.

"David?" she called softly, her eyes searching the shadowy interior. Looking up, she saw him standing near the edge of the hayloft, gazing up at the rafters. There was no railing on the loft, which was a good fifteen feet above the ground.

"David?" she said again, more cautious this time. "What are you doing up there?"

He glanced down but didn't reply. In the dimness, she couldn't make out his expression.

"You've got to come down. It's not safe up there. You could fall."

She hefted the ladder back up and propped it against the edge of the loft. Starting up, she wondered if he'd had so much to drink that he wouldn't be able to make it down without falling. If she had to sit up there with him until he sobered up, that's what she'd do.

As she stepped off the ladder onto the hayloft floor, she said, "How drunk are you?" He was about six feet away, his back to her.

When he turned around, his face was screwed into a thick fist of rage. "I knew you'd find me sooner or later."

"David?"

He rushed at her, ramming her into the side wall. She hit with a hard thud, sliding to the floor. "David, it's *me,*" she gasped. But he was at her again, on top of her this time, hands at her throat. She pried a finger free, then a hand, and bit it hard, tasting blood. He yelped and slugged her, grabbed her hair, and slammed her head against the floor.

The world suddenly went hazy.

Feeling his weight lift off her, she tried to focus, to scramble free. She crawled toward the ladder, but he was on her again, this time flipping her on her back. They struggled together, rolled across the hay. He was so much stronger than she was, but he reeked of alcohol. It slowed him down, altered his judgment. "David, it's *me. Jane.*"

"This time, I'm gonna kill you," he bellowed. He rose up over her, both hands clenched together. They were inches from the edge of the loft.

Looking past him, Jane saw Kenzie. She was behind him, a shotgun pointed at his back.

"No," screamed Jane. "Don't!" She bucked, tried to break free.

A blast cracked the air.

Startled, David turned.

Kenzie slammed the butt of the shotgun into his forehead. He fell sideways, moaning in pain, rolling, grasping his head in both hands.

Jane slipped away from the edge. "God," she said, touching a cut near her eye, which was bleeding a thick river down her cheek. "I don't . . . I don't know what happened."

"He was beating the crap out of you, *that's* what happened." Kenzie looked frantic. "Are you okay? Anything broken?" She held the gun on David.

"I don't think so." Jane examined the inside of her mouth with her tongue. With a little time, she hoped the world would rebalance itself.

David was on his hands and knees at the back of the loft, swearing a blue streak.

"Sit down and shut up!" ordered Kenzie.

He turned to look at her.

"Don't make me repeat it!"

He stared at her a moment longer, looking wild, disoriented, then turned and fell backward against the wall.

"What the hell were you doing?" demanded Kenzie. She walked over to him, still keeping the shotgun pointed at his chest. "I fired at the ceiling, asshole, but I should have fired at you."

David stared at her, his mouth slightly open, then fastened his eyes on Jane. "I'm sorry," he said, his voice barely audible.

"Sorry? *Sorry?*"

"I . . . I never meant . . . I mean . . . God, you don't . . . I wouldn't—" It was a sentence that apparently had no end.

Jane was completely bewildered. "Why the hell did you attack me?" she said, moving into a crouch, then standing up. Every inch of her body hurt.

"I . . . I—"

"You said you wanted to kill me."

"No," he said, pressing his fists to his eyes. "Never. God, never."

"Then what's going on, David? Tell me!"

He pulled his knees up to his body and started to cry. "Just shoot me, okay? Get it over with."

"Be careful what you ask for," said Kenzie, her voice cold.

"Do it!"

"David," said Jane, her voice softer this time. "What's *wrong* with you?"

"Everything."

She lowered herself to one knee so she could look him square in the eyes, but she kept her distance. "That's not an answer."

"I'm losing my mind. I'm *insane*. Is that clear enough? Do you *get* it now?"

Jane felt a terrible pressure in the air around her. "David, that's ridiculous. You're as sane as anybody I know."

"Am I? I don't remember anything until I heard that shotgun blast. I don't know what I'm doing anymore, Jane. I'm a danger to everyone around me. I need to be locked up!"

"Just slow down, okay? You said you don't remember fighting with me?"

"No. God, did I hurt you? One minute I'm watching TV on the couch, the next I'm sitting here. Did I really attack you?"

She gave him a questioning look.

"Oh, shit. Shit! Call the police. I'll sit here quietly until they come. Don't take the gun off me."

"Are you telling the truth?" asked Kenzie, her eyes full of suspicion.

He nodded, covering his face with his forearm. "It used to happen less often. Maybe once or twice a year. But it's gotten worse in the last few months. That's why I left Atlanta. I was afraid I'd hurt Diego." He hunched forward, head against his knees. "The night before I left, I woke up out on our front lawn. I had a hammer in my

181

hand. A hammer! Can you understand how much that scared me? I had to get away, figure out what to do. I couldn't explain it to Diego because he would have insisted I stay. But every minute I was there, he was in danger!"

Jane got up and crouched a few feet away from him. He seemed too raw to be touched, but she needed to be closer.

"See," he continued, his entire body slumping with exhaustion, "it usually happens at night, although it happened once during the day. I fall asleep one place and wake up another. That's why I've been sleeping in my car. I use handcuffs, cuff myself to the steering wheel. It's the only way I can make sure I stay put."

Jane remembered the welts under his watchband.

"I've tried ropes, but somehow I manage to untie them. All I can do is hope that I don't figure out how to unlock the handcuffs. I mean, I can go for days and days without an episode, and then it hits like a hurricane. I made the mistake of sleeping in Joanna's loft the other night. I was drunk, not thinking straight. The next morning, I woke up in her bed. She was in the living room on the couch. God knows what I did or said. She gave me a pretty strange look before I left, but I was too embarrassed to ask why."

Jane glanced up at Kenzie.

"I'm tired all the time," he said. "I can't work, can't think straight. I mean . . . I know this is nuts, but I thought if I came to Minnesota, told you what was happening, that you'd help me make a decision. I think . . . I mean, I need to be committed, Jane. I want you to do it."

An involuntary shudder rumbled through her. "Surely there's something we can do short of that."

David scraped tears away from his eyes. "I'm such a mess. I shouldn't have come here. I should have known better."

Jane held out her hand to him, but he pulled his body away.

"Jesus, Jane, don't be nice to me, not after what I just did to you." He broke down, began to sob again.

She moved over next to him, slipped her arms around him. Instead of pushing her away, he gripped her hard. "I feel like I'm falling."

She sat on the floor with him, rocking him in her arms. "We'll figure this out, David. I promise." She looked up at Kenzie, who stared back at her with an expression so swollen with fear that, for a second, Jane wasn't sure she remembered how to breathe.

21

Joanna spent all day Saturday shut up in her loft, reading and rereading the script Freddy had sent her. The more she thought about it, the more desperately she wanted it. She was about to pull a diva-like move that might end a friendship and land her in legal hot water, but she saw no way around it. It not only solved her problems with Gordon, but it also might rejuvenate her waning movie career. She couldn't wait to sign on the dotted line.

Jane had called early on Sunday morning, waking Joanna from a sound sleep. She explained that she and David had changed their plans. They were staying another day in Nebraska. Joanna asked to talk to David, but apparently he was out riding with Jane's new girlfriend, having one hell of a grand time. Well, good for him, thought Joanna. Her life was coming apart, but at least David was enjoying himself.

Joanna spent a good part of the afternoon standing at the windows in the living room, gazing longingly at the windy fall day on the other side of the glass. She wanted to go window-shopping down Hennepin Avenue, but she couldn't bring herself to call the bodyguard service and ask for a man to be sent out to escort her around town. The loft was big and comfortable enough, but after nearly four days cooped up inside, she simply had to get out, even if it was just for a few minutes.

Tomorrow she would need to go to the theater, put up a good show until the details of the film got sorted out, so this afternoon would be a trial run.

After pinning back her hair and donning a hat and a pair of dark glasses, she tossed on a jacket, grabbed her purse and her keys, and headed downstairs. She felt strong in the elevator, as if the act of movement itself was somehow a show of defiance. When she stepped off on the first floor, she nodded to a man standing next to the elevator door. His arms were folded over his chest and he was wearing a uniform—brown slacks, tan shirt, official-looking hat, with a two-way radio pinned on his shoulder. Just the sight of him gave her courage a boost.

She walked through the main floor with her head held high. Nobody seemed to recognize her, or if they did, they let her pass without comment. When she pushed through the front door out into the gray autumn day, she breathed in deeply. She knew it was half car exhaust, but she didn't care. It was the smell of freedom.

Looking both ways down the street, she headed south. There was a deli halfway down on the other side of the street. After her short stroll, a cup of coffee sounded good. She walked along slowly, her eyes darting in every direction. The area around the Linden Building reminded her of SoHo in New York twenty years ago. What had once been a microcosm of inner-city blight was now in the process of being gentrified. The area still had some of the rawness of street life about it, but it was on its way toward respectability.

Entering the deli a few minutes later, she ordered a coffee and waited by the counter as the young man stepped back to the press pot and filled the paper cup. She picked out a lemon bar to go with it and paid cash at the register. Then, turning to survey the room, she decided on a table by the windows. It was an odd sensation, this new-found confidence. She felt like an adult again, something that had evaporated inside her the moment she received that first bouquet in Sandpoint. The short walk had brought her back to herself. She realized that she *did* have power—options.

As she sipped her coffee, she looked out the window, watching the cars, the people, content just to be out of the loft. And that's when she saw him. He was striding along the sidewalk a few hundred feet to the north of the Linden Building. As he approached the front door, he dashed across the street. Joanna couldn't see him now, but she knew he was out there. And she knew why. He was watching her, like he used to. And waiting.

Opening her purse, she removed her cell phone. She searched through the numbers she'd recently called until she found Gordon's. She hit redial and then waited. One ring. Two. Finally, he picked up.

"Out for an afternoon walk?" she asked conversationally. "You're a long way from home."

Silence. Then, "What do you want?"

"You're losing your edge, Gordon. You think you're watching me, but actually, I'm watching you. The prey is hunting the hunter. Ain't it a crazy world?"

"What the hell are you up to?"

"Me? Well, how about a little payback?"

"You fuck with me, Joanna, and it's the last thing you'll ever do."

"You do like to make threats."

"And, if you remember correctly, you can trust me to carry them out."

The comment made a dent in her resolve, but she forged on. She couldn't stop the hate spewing out of her mouth. It had been locked up for too many years. "But you're an old man now, Gordo. You look to me like a heart attack waiting to happen. Couldn't happen to a nicer guy." She laughed. It felt so good. "God, Gordo, you're a tub of lard. What happened to your discipline? Your ideals? I assume you eat most of your *supersized* meals alone now. I mean, who'd date a gross-looking blimp like you? Kind of hard up in the date department, are we, Gordo?"

For some reason, she had the sense that she wasn't succeeding at making him mad, that instead, he was smiling at her.

"You have no idea what my life is like now, Jo. I'm truly a lucky man. I've been blessed with the love of many fine women."

"The ones you murdered? You think I don't know? The police are on to you. It's just a matter of time until they nail you."

"My my, how you do go on."

"I'll bet those women dumped you because you can't get it up anymore. One too many Krispy Kremes?"

"Sounds like you wanna find out, Jo. That can be arranged."

Just the sound of his voice was enough to send a needle through her heart. She needed to end the call before her confidence completely died.

"Joanna, you still there?"

"I'm here, I'm there, I'm all over, Gordon. You never know when I might pop up."

"Shit, woman! What do you *want*?"

Maybe she *had* touched a nerve after all. "What do *you* want? Why the hell don't you leave me alone!"

A long pause. When he finally spoke this time, his voice had taken on a warm, conspiratorial edge. "I want to finish what I started all those years ago. You'll like it, Jo, what I've got planned for you. You may beg me to stop, but I know it's what you want. I can still see into your soul, Jo. It's even blacker than it used to be."

"You . . . you—"

"Think about me tonight when you go to sleep. I'll be there, waiting for you in your dreams."

22

The big morning had arrived. Cordelia was up in her bedroom, going through her clothes closet, trying to figure out what to wear for Joanna's first official day at the theater. She wanted, as always, to make just the right statement.

After dithering over her choices for a few minutes, she settled on something she'd never worn before. She'd been waiting for the right opportunity to present itself, and this morning seemed perfect. She'd purchased it online from her favorite army-navy surplus store. It was a navy blue Basic Issue Ultra Force SWAT Team top and slacks. The ad said it had reinforced elbows, seat, and knees. All important gear for her first rehearsal. She had no interest in the military aspects of it but found the clothing both attractive in an appallingly boring sort of way and comfortable. She completed the ensemble with a red satin scarf draped loosely around her neck with the ends tossed with casual insouciance over each shoulder. She needed *some* color, after all. The scarf gave the SWAT gear attitude.

Once she'd slipped into her black speed-lace jungle boots, she felt ready for anything. She was in the process of doing a final check on her makeup in the bathroom mirror when Hattie skipped up the stairs and rushed toward her.

Cordelia scooped her up in her arms and gave her a big kiss and a hug. Then it dawned on her. "Didn't I say good-bye to you already? It's a baby school day. How come you're still home?"

Hattie shook her head. "Mommy said I should stay home." She patted Cordelia's long auburn curls.

"Mommy?"

"You know her," said Hattie, cocking her head. "That dingbat sister of mine."

Cordelia covered Hattie's mouth. "Honey, don't say that."

"But *you* do."

"Shhh." Cordelia had to think. "How long has she been here?"

The little girl turned her palms faceup and shrugged.

"No, you can't tell time. What am I thinking. Is she alone?"

"Uh-uh."

"Is there a man with her?"

She gave a big nod. "He's nice. He tic-od me."

Peachy, thought Cordelia. Mommy Dearest and the Tickle King arrive unannounced. Just what the day needed. A little nausea.

On her way down the stairs with Hattie tucked safely in her arms, Cordelia was met by a nervous-looking Octavia and a Clive Owen clone. Cecily and Mouse were sitting on the couch, both looking bored. Octavia had that effect.

"Cordelia, hi," said Octavia. She looked flawless, as usual. Willowy and lovely, with an edge of tragedy about her. "Sorry to drop in on you so unexpectedly," she continued, touching her newly dyed brown hair.

"You're not the least bit sorry," said Cordelia, setting Hattie down.

"Come here, sweetheart," said Octavia, motioning for Hattie to join her.

Hattie hid behind Cordelia's legs.

Looking embarrassed, Octavia turned to the man standing next to her. "I'd like you to meet Radley Cunningham."

"Radley?" repeated Cordelia. "Named after Boo Radley?"

"Pardon me?" said the man, using his most cultured British accent.

"Ignore her," said Octavia, her smile tragic.

On further examination, the clone's thinning hair, imperfect teeth, and stomach pushing hard against his belt suggested that this wasn't one of Octavia's usual lust-driven couplings. Oh, no. Cordelia would have bet money that this guy had been admitted to her sister's inner sanctum because she figured he could further her career in some way.

"Radley's a producer," said Octavia, slipping her arm through his.

"Bingo," said Cordelia. She wasn't sure why Octavia seemed so nervous. Normally, she treated Cordelia's loft like her own—and Cordelia like she was part of the staff.

"We were hoping that we might borrow Hattie for the afternoon," said Radley, stroking Octavia's hand. "She seems like a wonderful little girl. We thought we'd take her to this theme park you have here—Camp Snoopy I believe it's called?"

Hattie peeked out from behind Cordelia's legs. "I YUV the Maw of America!"

Cordelia could hardly say no, although she wanted to. The idea that Octavia could just drop in and out of Hattie's life at her whim infuriated her. "She should be in preschool today. She's done with her tortilla work and is supposed to move into pickle work this week. It's *very* important."

"*Pickle* work?" repeated Octavia, a confused look on her face.

"If you were ever around, you'd understand how baby school works."

"I'm sure that's true," said the clone, oozing conviviality. "Octavia would like to rectify that in the future."

It was the last thing Cordelia wanted to hear.

Octavia's tragic expression turned acid. "I don't need your permission to see my own daughter. Hattie, dear, let's find your coat. We're going to have *such* a fun day together. Have you ever been to F.A.O. Schwarz at the Mall of America?"

Hattie's large blue eyes emitted sparks the size of thunderbolts.

"Where are you staying?" demanded Cordelia. "I need phone numbers."

"You have my cell phone," said Octavia.

"Ladies, let's not raise our voices in front of the child," said Radley. "We're at hotel Sofitel in Bloomington, suite six four."

Who the hell did this guy think he was, telling her what to do?

His smile grew amused. "I don't usually argue with women who have the word SWAT written above their shirt pocket."

He was charming. How thrilling. Cordelia crouched down. "Hattie, do you want to go with your mother and this man?"

The little girl looked up at Octavia, then at Cordelia. "Yeah," she said softly. "I miss Mommy Dearest."

"What did she say?" shrieked Octavia.

Radley put his hand on her shoulder. "Just leave it alone, darling. Let's get her things and be on our way."

Cordelia knew it was useless to protest. She had no rights when it came to Hattie, at least none that love didn't bestow. "When will you be back?"

The clone looked at his watch. "We'll have her home by seven. Don't worry, Cordelia. We'll take very good care of her. You have my word on that."

Cordelia had no choice. She helped Hattie get ready and hugged her tight before she left. Hattie might as well have been off to Borneo. Cordelia couldn't have felt more bereft.

By the time she made it out to the parking lot in the back of the building, Cordelia was in the foulest of moods. She was supposed to meet Joanna by the goon-driven black limo parked next to the building. The limo was there. So was the six-foot-five driver with the Beretta. But no Joanna.

"She's on her way down," said the goon, introducing himself as Bonner. She didn't know if it was a first name or a last name, nor did she care. He opened the back door for her, glancing without comment at her clothing. She was about to give him her standard lecture on the importance of costume in social self-expression when Joanna sailed through the back door. She nodded to the security guard, then started down the steps.

A few seconds later, a gray-haired man, one who looked like he was headed for the country club, pushed out of the building. Cordelia found him vaguely familiar, but she couldn't place the face.

As Joanna approached the limo, the older man caught up with her, draping his arm protectively around her shoulders. "You remember Freddy?" she said offhandedly, turning and giving him a peck on his cheek.

"Nice outfit," said Freddy, his eyes dropping to Cordelia's combat boots. "You must have one hell of a problem with your actors," he said, grinning. He was trim and tanned, and still had a fabulous white smile, compliments of his dentist. Cordelia did remember him now. She'd met him only once. His presence this morning filled her with a million questions.

"Bye, Freddy. I'll call you when I'm done," said Joanna, slipping gracefully into the backseat.

"You . . . here on business?" asked Cordelia.

"Something like that."

As they pulled away from the building, Cordelia eyed Joanna suspiciously. "What's going on?"

"Nothing. Unless you're referring to my life exploding all around me."

Cordelia's assignment for the day was to keep Joanna calm and centered. But now that Hattie had fallen into her sister's dastardly clutches, she couldn't even keep herself on task. "How come Freddy's here?"

Joanna leaned her head back and closed her eyes. "Gordon was outside the loft yesterday afternoon."

"Are you serious?"

"I spoke to him on the phone. He's not going to leave me alone, Cordelia. Ever. I knew Freddy was in town, so I called him. Asked him to come over. I couldn't be alone."

"He spent the night?"

Joanna gave her a sideways glance. "We're adults."

"I know that, but he's your *ex*."

"So? We're still friends."

Okay, thought Cordelia. Whatever. "What about Nolan? Did you tell him what happened?"

"Sure. A lot of good he's doing me. He said he had a man surveilling Gordon yesterday. This man apparently watched from the road outside Gordon's cabin all day. He told Nolan the truck never moved. Now, if that's true, then it suggests that Gordon teleports himself through the universe in some new, unique way. I don't buy any of it. And it sure doesn't make me feel very confident about Nolan's services."

Cordelia was at a loss—a rare situation.

"I don't want to talk about it, okay?" Joanna rolled her shoulders and turned her head away.

"Ah, okay. Do you want to talk about anything else?"

"No. I just want to sit here and try not to panic." An instant later, she sat forward. "Driver, turn the car around. Take me back to the loft."

"Excuse me?" said Cordelia. "You're not going to the theater?"

Joanna closed her eyes and deadpanned, "What was your first clue?"

23

The sun was low in the sky over downtown Minneapolis when Jane finally dropped David off in front of the Linden Building. They'd spent an extra day in Nebraska for two reasons—three if you counted the fact that Jane was having a terrible time convincing Kenzie that she'd be safe flying David back to Minneapolis. The main reason they'd stayed was to allow David some time to rest. He was so deeply exhausted that he'd slept nearly all day Sunday. He'd knocked on the locked bedroom door around seven that night. Kenzie had let him out but kept the rifle on him all during dinner. Jane was ready with barbecued chicken, smashed parmesan potatoes, and broccoli au gratin. After apologizing profusely again and again—and promising that he'd see a shrink as soon as he returned to the Twin Cities—he went back to bed and slept peacefully for another sixteen hours.

The other reason that Jane wanted to stay an extra day was because her face looked like she'd gone ten rounds with a rabid moose. Her body felt the same way, but you couldn't see those bruises. She had a bad gash near her left eye, the same eye that had rapidly swollen shut and turned a blackish purple. She also had some scratches on her right cheek and another cut under her chin.

When it came to her appearance, waiting an extra day had been fruitless. David winced when he saw the extent of the damage for the first time on Sunday evening, but there was little he could do except say again how sorry he was. Kenzie had applied some makeup before they left for the airport, not that it helped much. On the way back, Jane and David had talked about a cover story. She'd fallen off a tractor, or been mauled by a cow. It would have been pretty hilarious if it hadn't been so serious. And also, it hurt when Jane laughed. David had his own cuts and bruises, but nothing to match Jane's battered face.

"You going to be okay?" Jane asked as David opened the car door.

"I think so."

"I don't feel entirely comfortable about you sleeping in your car tonight."

"If I don't drink, I've got much better judgment."

"So don't drink. Promise?"

He smiled at her. "Promise."

"You know, we could still rent a motel room. I could stand guard and you could sleep."

"Absolutely not. We've already been through that. I've used my car this long, a few more nights won't kill me."

She gave a grudging nod. "I guess."

"Where are you headed?"

Under normal circumstances, Jane would have gone up to Cordelia's apartment to get Mouse. After nearly losing him, she didn't even like the idea of letting him out of her sight. But she knew he was safe with Cordelia and Cecily. She also had a couple of calls she wanted to make—without Cordelia watering plants or tying a shoelace right next to her. Jane was used to a lot more privacy than Cordelia allowed her.

"I'm not sure." She couldn't go home—Luberman could be lurking. Same with her restaurants. "I may run out to Southdale, try to find some better makeup. Cordelia's going to hit the ceiling when she sees my face."

"What did we settle on?"

"I was thrown from a horse."

"Right. I'm not sure I'd buy it, but hopefully she's more gullible."

"Let's hope," said Jane. "I'll call my old therapist from there. One way or the other, I'll get you in to see someone tomorrow."

"Thanks, Jane. You're my angel."

"Hardly."

"Don't kid yourself. See you in the morning."

As she drove away, she knew without a doubt that David needed to talk to someone and fast—a therapist, or even a plain old doctor, someone who could help him sort out what was happening to him. Until he had a diagnosis, he was a man truly alone in the dark.

Jane drove a few blocks, then pulled into a parking space across from the Butler Building and stopped. She called Nolan on her cell phone.

"Hey, it's me," she said, rolling down the window and resting her elbow on the door. "I'm back from Nebraska."

"Welcome home," said Nolan. "You have a good time?"

"Yes and no."

"Sounds like a story there."

"Where are you?"

"I'm in Winneconne, still working on the Kiskanen murder. So far, it's been a dead end."

All weekend she'd been undecided about whether or not to tell him about the run-in she'd had with Luberman on Friday night. She decided to let it go—for now. "Anything new in Eagle Ridge?"

He explained about Luberman somehow ending up in Minneapolis right outside the Linden Building. "His truck never left his cabin. Far as I know, he doesn't have another car. I don't know *what* happened."

"Joanna must have been terrified."

"And then some. But there is some good news. Just got off the phone with Hitchcock in Eagle Ridge. Seems they're going to start dredging Whitefish Lake in the morning."

"Did you tell him what Cordelia found on Luberman's houseboat?"

"You bet I did. Problem is, they can't get a warrant to search the property without legally obtained evidence." He cleared his throat.

Jane got the point.

"But Hitchcock's been working on a warrant to dredge the lake for

196

weeks. He finally succeeded. If they find the body of that woman, Luberman will be put away for a good long time."

"Have you told Joanna?"

"Not yet. Thought I'd wait, see if they come up with anything. I don't want to get her hopes up. She's kind of, you know . . . emotional."

Jane smiled. That was an understatement.

"Not much more we can do for now. We just gotta show a little patience. My guy in Eagle Ridge said he'd stick to Luberman like glue. If he's got another car somewhere, we'll find it."

They talked for a few more minutes. As soon as they said good-bye, Jane got another call. She checked the caller ID. Cordelia.

"Hi," she said, opening the glove compartment and grabbing a handful of Reese's Pieces. "What's up?"

"You're back?" She sounded breathless.

"Yup."

"Where are you?"

"Ah, the Lyme House. Why?"

"I'm having a nervous breakdown, that's *why*!"

"Joanna?"

"Well there's *that,* yes. But this is about Hattie. Octavia and some new boyfriend of hers stopped by this morning. They're in town for a few days and wanted to take Hatts to the Mall of America. The *Mall of America,* that vile monument to hedonistic consumption!"

"You love the Mall of America."

"Don't change the subject. I didn't want to let her go. I mean, what business does Octavia have waving the name F.A.O. Schwarz in front of Hattie's nose like some . . . some huge lump of bubble gum? It was a bribe. Bribing her own daughter! But that's just like Octavia, oiling around, blinking her fake eyelashes, and looking needy. What could I do? Hattie wanted to go, and Octavia *is* more or less her mother. Anyway, they said they'd have her back by seven, but it's past seven and she's not here! Something bad's happened, Janey, I know it."

Jane checked her watch. It was ten after seven. "They probably got caught in traffic. Give them a little more time, okay?"

"Jane, you have to get back here right away. I need someone to lean on when the phone call comes."

"What phone call?"

"From the police. Or the FBI. Come to think of it, it could even be from the Department of Homeland Security! That new boyfriend of hers is a *foreigner*."

"Where's he from?"

"England!"

There was no point in arguing. Cordelia would worry herself into a frenzy until Hattie was home safe and sound.

"Wait . . . wait," shrieked Cordelia. "That's my cell phone. Just a minute."

Jane could hear Cordelia's voice in the background. A moment later she was back on the line, whispering this time. "It's Octavia."

"And?"

"She wants to keep Hattie overnight."

The problem was the same. Cordelia couldn't really say no. "What does Hattie want?"

"Don't know. Just a sec."

Jane waited for several minutes this time. When Cordelia finally came back, she wasn't whispering anymore. Her voice was flat. "Hattie wants to stay with them. They promised to take her to a movie. More bribes. You know how much Hattie adores modern film. It's all my fault, Jane. I taught her all about the movies, and now it comes back to bite me on the ass."

"Cordelia, she'll be fine. Octavia may not be much of a mother, but she won't let anything happen to Hattie. I'm sure of it."

"Oh, Janey." There was a long pause, during which Cordelia's voice regained some of its normal firmness. "I can't stand this. First thing in the morning I'm contacting a lawyer. I should have done it ages ago. I want full custody of Hattie. And I want it by tomorrow night."

"I, ah, don't think the court system moves that fast."

"Do you think Octavia will contest it?"

"Honestly, Cordelia, I have no idea. For your sake, I hope not."

"Yeah, well, that kid will only be gone one night and I already miss her like . . . like I'd miss my own nose if it fell off."

"Your *nose?*"

"Yeah. You know what I mean."

"Sure."

"Janey, how did this happen to a woman who once viewed all children as sticky, noisy, snot-filled, demanding, malevolent little monsters?"

"Don't know. Guess you actually got to know one."

"Huh." Another pause. "When are you coming back to the loft?"

Jane had pretty much decided that she'd spend the night in a motel. She wanted to give her face a little more time to heal before Cordelia saw it and demanded an explanation. She also had to call her therapist, see if she could get David in first thing tomorrow morning. "Well, I was thinking I'd stay here. Get a little work done."

Jane wasn't sure exactly how, but Cordelia always knew when she wasn't telling the full story.

"What's up?"

"Nothing's up. I just, you know, thought—"

"You never told me how things went with Kenzie."

"You never asked."

"I'm in no mood for *cute,* Jane."

"Kenzie's great. We had a wonderful time."

"But?"

"No buts."

"Janey? It's foolish to try to hide things from Auntie Cordelia."

"If you want me to come back to the loft tonight, I'll come back."

"Excellent. And you'll tell me everything."

"There's nothing to tell."

Big, languorous sigh. "We'll see, dearheart. Gotta go dig out my thumbscrews. Ta."

24

David walked up to the door of the Linden Building with every intention of going through it, but something inside him made him stop. He decided he simply wasn't ready to face Joanna. Instead, he drifted toward First Avenue with his duffel bag slung over his shoulder. He ducked into the first bar he came to, but the nonstop Electroclash mix was booming so loudly from the speakers that it made his brain ache. Hennepin Avenue was no better with its nightly sea of neon. He'd already made his homage visit to the Gay Nineties, so he had no desire to go there, either.

Returning to the warehouse district, he stopped at a small coffee shop on an out-of-the-way street for a sandwich and coffee. Truth was, he was still so ashamed of what he'd done to Jane that he could barely stand up straight. She'd done her best to let him off the hook, but nothing she said made any difference. He could have killed her, and that realization was enough to send him running.

When he finally entered the loft's ground floor an hour later, he noticed immediately that it was much busier than it had been when he left. People were milling around, some with cameras around their necks, some with video equipment, some just rank-and-file curiosity seekers. The Greek restaurant was jammed with diners. David assumed that the Twin Cities had finally wised up to the fact that they had a celebrity in their midst. For a moment, he considered how sweet his anonymity was.

As he threaded his way toward the elevator, a heavyset guy in the restaurant stood up and waved at him. David had never seen the man before. He reminded him of a bird of prey.

Glancing around, David pointed to his chest and mouthed, "Me?"

The bird nodded, motioning for him to come over.

The guy seemed so insistent, David figured he'd see what he wanted.

"David Carlson. That's right, isn't it?" asked the man, extending his hand.

"And you are?"

"Milan Mestrovik. I'm a friend of your sister's. I live upstairs, one floor above her." He motioned for David to sit.

As soon as David pulled up a chair, a waitress appeared to take his order. "A Coke," he said.

"That it?" Her hand remained poised over her pad.

"Yeah, thanks."

As she streaked away, David sat back and looked around. "This place is a freakin' madhouse."

"Has been since last night. Somebody must have spotted Joanna yesterday. I'm told she went out for a short walk. She probably regrets it now that she's been spotted."

"Can't the owners of the building do something?"

Milan shrugged and went back to his meal. "It's a free country."

Leaning into the table, David said, "So what did you call me over for?"

Milan chewed for a second, then said, "The people who love Joanna—and I count myself in that number—should step in and do something about that Luberman character. You with me?"

David's eyes widened slightly. "I don't know. What did you have in mind?"

"Total annihilation."

"Excuse me?"

201

"The man is a menace."

"I agree, but that doesn't give us a license to kill."

"Did I say kill?"

"Well, yeah, I think you did."

He shook his head. "Maybe it won't need to come to that."

"Look—"

"I know, I know. I'm talking last-case scenario here. But I thought of all people in Jo's life, you'd understand how serious this is."

David found Milan Mestrovik beyond creepy. "How well do you know my sister?"

"Very well. Those cases of wine in her loft? They're from me." He winked. "You're gay, right?"

David nodded, not sure what his sexual preference had to do with anything.

"I'm bi. I haven't dated in years. Don't even go to bars anymore. I guess I've been kind of a recluse." He smiled at David. "You like movies?"

"I'm in a committed relationship, Milan." He needed to head off any potential trolling.

"Good for you. You happy?"

"Very."

"You got an open marriage?"

"Nope."

"Too bad." He shoveled the last of the moussaka into his mouth. "I thought we might, you know. I mean, we've got so much in common."

"We do?"

"Sure. Joanna. Far as I'm concerned, we're family."

Milan had mumbled the last few words, and with all the noise in the room, David didn't catch it. "Nice meeting you, but I gotta get going."

"Good to finally meet you, David. I'm sure I'll see you around. Oh, and give my love to your sister. You won't forget, will you? Make sure you say *my love*."

Doing a slow take, David said, "Right."

"Tell her I'm working on the Luberman thing and not to worry. I'll come up with a solution."

"Great. Well." Feeling that he was in the presence of a man with more loose screws than he had in his own head, David backed away. "I'm sure that will put her mind at rest." He walked away as fast as he could without actually breaking and running.

After a bumpy ride up to four on the old freight elevator, David was about to unlock the door to his sister's loft when he heard the door behind him crack open and a voice hiss, "Pssssst. Davey."

He turned around. "Faye?"

"Come 'ere," she whispered.

Hoisting the duffel to his other shoulder, he stepped across the hall.

"How ya doin'?" When Faye opened her door all the way, a gust of cigarette smoke billowed out. She pointed to Joanna's door. "She's not alone."

"No?"

"She's got a man in there with her. He spent the night last night. This is just a guess, you understand, but I think he's gonna stay again tonight." She shook her head. "Bad news."

"Why?"

"It's her ex. Freddy Kasimir. He's no good for her, Davey. He treated her like shit when they were married. I got no idea why she's even giving him the time of day. I mean, I warned her about him."

David nodded. "How do you know so much about Freddy?"

"I read. Men suck."

"Huh. Right. I'll remember that. But actually, he's really not such a bad guy. Neither of them were ready for marriage back then." David wasn't quite sure why he was having this conversation with someone who was, for all practical purposes, a total stranger.

"Don't blame that sister of yours. She's a jewel. Kasimir is an ass-hole, didn't value what he had. In my book, that makes him not only a bastard, but a stupid bastard."

"Joanna's not perfect, you know."

"Wash your mouth out with soap, boy. She's as good as she is beautiful. Take it from me, the only reason she let that jerk into her apartment was because she's scared. It's Gordon Luberman. He's got her so twisted she doesn't know which end is up."

"Yeah, you're probably right."

"Of course I'm right." She sucked in a lungful of smoke, blew it out through her nose.

David was getting a nicotine fix just standing next to her.

"You tell her to get rid of him. She should know better. She needs company, I'm right here."

"Okay."

"Be good to her, Davey."

"I will. I promise."

She looked him full in the face, then nodded and ducked back inside her door.

Surreal, thought David, moving across the hall and fitting his key into the lock. He'd been a resident of the *Twilight Zone* for months, but maybe there were more rooms in it than he'd first thought.

Stepping into the foyer, he deposited his duffel on the floor next to the front closet. He stood for a moment and listened. Soft music drifted out of Joanna's bedroom. Glancing into the kitchen, he saw an empty bottle of champagne and two empty flutes sitting on the counter amid the dregs of a take-out Chinese dinner. He should have called her cell before coming up. That was mistake one.

Mistake two was attempting to creep past Joanna's bedroom door just as she moaned, "Rip my clothes off, Freddy. Rip them off!" He'd almost made it past, when Freddy said, "Jo, we're not alone."

"What?" she said, fear in her voice.

"It's your brother."

Busted, thought David. He was about four feet past the door when Joanna shouted, "David?"

"Hi there."

"Give us a minute, okay?"

"Sure." He cringed-laughed into the cuff of his suede jacket. "You know, I can leave. It's not a problem." He heard more whispers. A few seconds later, Joanna appeared draped in a creamy silk bathrobe.

"You're back."

"Yes, ma'am. I'm back."

She leaned close and said, "Freddy's here."

"Really." He tried to act surprised.

Freddy walked out a few seconds later, sans hairpiece. He had on a striped terry cloth robe. As always, he looked fit.

"Fred," said David, extending his hand.

Freddy shook it. "Great to see you again, David. Your sister and I—"

"No need to explain. We're all adults."

They stood in the hallway, squirming through an awkward pause.

"Let's open a bottle of pinot," said Joanna.

"My pleasure," said Freddy, disappearing into the kitchen.

David followed Joanna into the living room. As they sat down on the couch, he said softly, "May I admit to being a tiny bit dumbfounded."

"If one can *be* a *tiny bit* dumbfounded."

"True. Come on, tell me what's going on."

She rolled her shoulders playfully. Crossing her legs, she sat back. She looked elegant. Thin. Flushed. "We're an item. Again."

"Are you kidding me?"

"It just happened. He's in town . . . on business and we . . . hooked up."

"The old-fashioned way."

"Don't be crude." She leaned forward and plucked a lighter and a package of Djarums off the coffee table.

"Someone's been shopping, I see."

"They're Freddy's. Indonesian clove cigarettes. He's already got me hooked. Try one?"

David shook his head.

"I've always loved him, David," she continued, lighting up. "I think it was inevitable that we'd get back together."

"Kismet." He started to hum the song "Stranger in Paradise."

"Don't be snarky."

"Moi?"

"Only a gay man would be able to remember a song from an ancient Broadway show."

"Now who's being snarky? Show tunes are gay spirituals. They're sacred."

Freddy padded into the living room with the open bottle of pinot and three crystal wineglasses. David felt a sense of ease and comfort in the presence of a man sophisticated enough to understand the importance of the correct glass. Freddy was okay by David. Maybe even better than okay. There was no telling how long this reunion would last, but David silently wished them well. If nothing else, Freddy's sudden reappearance in Joanna's bed seemed to have taken her mind off Luberman. She actually looked radiant tonight.

As they were toasting a rosy future for everyone, Freddy's cell phone began chirping "The Stars and Stripes Forever."

"Sorry," he said, pulling it off the end table and checking the caller ID. "I gotta take that. I'll only be a sec." Moving over to one of the rocking chairs, he said hello.

Since Joanna seemed to want to hear what he was saying, David sat silently and sipped his wine. He'd promised Jane he wouldn't drink until they figured out what was wrong with him, but a few sips of pinot could hardly get him in trouble.

"Good," said Freddy, touching the top of his hairless head and frowning. "That's just what I wanted to hear." He paused. "No, the funding's not a problem. Let me take care of that." He glanced up at Joanna. "Sounds great. I owe you, Kev. Yeah. I'll be in touch." As he slipped the phone back into the pocket of his bathrobe, a smile burst over his face. "It's all set. Now listen, Babycakes, I don't mean to be pushy, but we have a deal, right? We've got to get serious if we're going to make this happen. You promise me you'll call your lawyer tomorrow? See what he can do about . . . you know."

"You know?" repeated David, annoyed that they seemed to be speaking in code.

"To the future," said Joanna, clicking her glass to Freddy's, then turning to David.

"The future," David repeated in a monotone. There was no way he could match their enthusiasm, fearing, as he still did, that he might not have one.

25

The following morning, Jane found Cordelia sitting at the kitchen table, elbows splayed, head bowed, staring at an uneaten Toaster Strudel cooling on a plate in front of her. When Jane pulled back a chair and sat down, Cordelia didn't even look up. All of her usual effervescent irascibility had been replaced by a look of deep gloom. The coffee wasn't even on. Nor were any lights.

"You're up early," said Jane.

Cordelia grunted.

"You miss Hattie."

Another grunt.

"She'll be back tonight, kiddo. And then you'll feel better."

Cordelia lifted her head and eyed Jane's face. "You're still a mess. You might try using some stage makeup."

"I'll think about it."

"Take some advice from a person who knows. Horses and humans don't mix."

"Kenzie would disagree with you."

"Maybe she's not human."

"On that one, I beg to differ."

Cordelia eyed her a moment more. "You're happy with her, aren't you."

"More than I ever thought possible."

"You're happy and I'm miserable. Pardon my lack of graciousness, but I liked it better when I was happy and you were miserable."

Jane laughed. "You'll get this straightened out with Octavia. She's probably just doing the mommy thing to impress her new boyfriend. They'll jet off to somewhere *real* sooner or later."

"You got that right. In Octavia's lexicon of happening places, Minnesota wouldn't even make the top one thousand. For her, visiting the Twin Cities is probably like spending a few days in a village in Tibet."

"She *is* kind of a snob."

"Don't hold your punches on my account." Pushing the Toaster Strudel away, she added, "Don't suppose you'd like to watch *SpongeBob SquarePants* with me. Then we could get out the finger paints afterward and smoosh to our heart's content."

"Boy, you really do miss her. Where's Cecily?"

"With Octavia. Oh, come on, Jane. You don't actually think she'd take Hattie without someone to hand her off to when she feels a slight headache coming on."

Jane groaned. Maybe the idea of having a baby had seemed like a good idea to Octavia once upon a time, but the reality of a child hadn't exactly lit her lamp. "Look, I'm not supposed to tell this to Joanna, but I don't think it's a problem if I tell you, as long as you keep your mouth shut. I spoke to Nolan last night. The police finally got a warrant to dredge Whitefish Lake."

"When?" said Cordelia.

"Today. It's probably already begun. I could be wrong, but I think this may be a very dangerous period for Joanna. She needs to stay in the building, with security men guarding the entrances."

"Believe me, after what happened on Sunday, she's not going anywhere."

"The dredging will be done in full view of everyone who lives on the lake. That means if Luberman dumped a body there, the sight of the search could push him over the edge. In that frame of mind, who knows what he could do."

Cordelia picked up the Toaster Strudel, licked off some of the frosting. "Roger," she said, getting into the mood.

"On the other hand, Luberman might have nothing to fear if he buried the body in the woods or dumped it down a well. We'll just have to wait to find out." Jane checked her watch, then rose from the table. "Mouse," she called, clapping her hands. "Come here, boy." She pulled his leash out of her back pocket.

"Where are you going?" demanded Cordelia.

"I've got an appointment with my therapist this morning."

One of Cordelia's eyebrows arched upward.

"There's nothing wrong, you can retract your eyeballs. Just a standard sixty-thousand-mile checkup." That wasn't exactly true. Jane regretted lying to Cordelia, but David didn't want anyone to know about his problems.

"When will you be back?"

"No idea. But call me if you hear from Octavia."

Cordelia resumed her full-out glum position.

"It's going to work out. You'll see."

"Right."

"Call your lawyer. You might have some rights you don't know about."

"Oh, sure. I have a bunch of them. Like I have the right to remain silent. Anything I say may be used against me in a court of law. I have the right to an attorney. If I can't afford one—"

"That's only if you commit a crime."

"Exactly."

"Go watch *SpongeBob*."

"Good idea."

Jane was sitting in her therapist's waiting room, reading the latest copy of *Newsweek*, when David walked in. She was glad for the interruption. If she read much more about the president and his war in Iraq, she'd need to be put on massive doses of antidepressants. Maybe that's why her therapist's waiting room was stocked with news-magazines. She was drumming up business.

David looked as scared as she'd ever seen him. He was a few minutes early, which was good. Jane wanted a chance to talk to him before they were ushered into the doctor's office.

David winced when he looked at her face. "How are the bruises?"

"Healing."

"Do they hurt?"

"Not much."

Hesitantly, he sat down next to her. He had on a pair of dress slacks and a black silk shirt. He looked great.

"You smell good."

"I'm a gay man. We're supposed to smell good."

That brought a smile. "Are you ready?"

"What did you tell her?"

"What you told Kenzie and me up in the hayloft."

"Did you mention—" He nodded to her face.

"No. I thought I'd let you do that, if you want to."

"Ohmigod," he said, pressing the flats of his hands over his eyes. "What if she says I belong in a looney bin?"

"David, you might try approaching this with a little more—"

"What?"

"Well, respect, for starters. Using a label like 'looney' isn't particularly useful."

"Okay," he said, one leg bouncing nervously. "I've been officially smacked."

She gave him a frustrated stare.

"Don't be upset with me, Janey. This is hard."

"I know. I'm here for you. Anything I can do, I will."

"Anything?" Using a TV announcer voice, he said, "The role of David Carlson is now being played by Jane Lawless."

"I would if I could."

"I wouldn't wish my life on anyone," he mumbled, looking away.

The door to the office opened and Dr. Janice Dowd stepped out. She examined the contents of a folder for a few seconds, then looked up. "Jane?" she said, smiling. "Good to see you again. David? You can both come in now."

They rose in unison and followed her inside.

Dr. Dowd was in her late fifties, a round, motherly looking woman. She was a licensed psychologist with a degree from Brown University. She'd been a practicing therapist for more than thirty years. Her hair had been completely gray when Jane first met her, but somewhere along the line, she'd dyed it back to a shade closer to her original brown.

As the doctor sat down behind her desk, she nodded to Jane's face. "Run into a door?"

"Long story."

"No doubt." She stared at the bruises a moment more, then turned to David. "We're here to talk about you today, Mr. Carlson. May I call you David?"

"Please."

She peered over her glasses, giving him an appraising look. "As you probably know, Jane and I talked at some length last night about your problems, but I'd like you to tell me, in your own words, what you think is happening in your life."

He cleared his throat, looked down, then up, then back down again. For the next ten minutes, he covered the same ground he had with Jane and Kenzie, though in much greater detail.

Dowd sat back and listened. When David slowed his story and finally stopped, she asked him if there was anything else he felt might be important for her to know.

He shrugged, said there wasn't.

"Do you drink?"

"Yes."

"Much?"

"More than I should."

"Every day?"

"Lately, yeah."

She made a couple of notes. "Drugs?"

"Uppers, when I can get them, to stay awake."

"Anything else?"

"I've smoked a little pot, but not recently."

"Cocaine?"

"No."

"Meth?"

"I'm not an idiot."

Her lips turned up in a slight smile. "That's good," she said, leaning forward, giving herself a moment to assemble her thoughts. "After I talked to Jane last night, I did a little research. Nothing you've told me today changes my initial reaction. I called a friend of mine at the University of Minnesota this morning. My recommendation is that you see him. Have you ever heard of parasomnia?"

David shook his head.

She glanced down at the folder in front of her. "It's a sleep-related behavioral disorder. I made a few notes because, frankly, this isn't something I'm qualified to deal with. However, I wanted to be able to give you some information."

"Great," said David, shifting in his seat.

"Parasomnias—and there are lots of different manifestations, with more being discovered all the time—are disorders that intrude into the sleep process and cause disruptive sleep-related events. Like sleepwalking or talking in your sleep. Those are two that we hear about a lot. Most of these disorders are infrequent and mild. What you have, I'm afraid, is neither."

"Tell me about it," said David under his breath.

"I won't get into a lot of detail here because it's not necessary, but the research that's been done tells us that parasomnias are much more common than we ever thought and often have serious consequences."

"What are some examples?" asked Jane.

"Well, for instance, some people, like David, have been known to eat while asleep. That's classified as an eating disorder. Restless leg syndrome and night terrors are two more. If the individual gets out of bed and begins to walk around, sometimes this activity can become frenzied or aggressive. That's another level. People have wielded knives or guns while asleep, which, as you might expect, can cause serious problems within the family. In any event, suppression of the person's normal judgment—leaping out a bedroom window, wandering around outside in the dark—is always part of it. In adults, the duration of the episodes can vary widely. Sometimes, people with parasomnias report that it feels as if they're living inside a dream, acting out some sort of terrifying scenario, though asleep. Sometimes they remember these dreams, sometimes they don't. There's even a sleep disorder that recently made the news, one that had to do with sexual abuse. A man was acquitted of molesting his daughter because it was determined that he was asleep at the time."

"Bizarre," said Jane. "And horrifying."

"It is indeed. I have my own personal doubts about that one, although I have to admit, knowing what we now know about sleep disorders, that it is possible. Parasomnias are classified according to whether the symptoms are primary phenomena of the sleep state itself, or secondary to it, such as some underlying medical or psychiatric disorder."

David closed his eyes, gripped the arms of his chair. "So I *could* still be crazy."

Dowd glanced at Jane, then back at David. "Crazy isn't a very helpful term."

"Right," said David. "Sorry."

"There are too many variables for me to tell you what's actually going on. You need to be evaluated by a specialist."

David nodded, crossed his legs and then uncrossed them. "Does it hurt?"

She smiled. "No. It usually begins with an interview, which covers such things as medical history, sleep-wake patterns, psychiatric history, alcohol and drug use history, family history, and issues of abuse. Then there will be some testing—psychiatric and neurologic examinations. And you'll do an overnight where you'll be monitored."

"It doesn't happen every night," said David.

"Doesn't matter. The overnight exam is still part of the process of determining what's wrong and how to treat it."

"So there is treatment available," said Jane.

"Absolutely. Sometimes it's as simple as a pill."

"When can I do it?" asked David.

"When I talked to my friend at the U this morning—his name is Dr. Terrance Connor—I asked if he had any openings in his schedule. He didn't, but based on my personal request, he agreed to see you. Today is what, Tuesday? He can see you at his office on Thursday morning at eight A.M. You'll be doing tests all day, with a sleepover in their clinic that night." She wrote the address on a slip of paper and handed it to David.

"Thanks," said Jane.

"You may have just saved my life," said David, rising and shaking her hand.

David led the way out of the office, with Jane and the doctor following several paces behind. Before Jane entered the waiting room, Dowd put a hand on her shoulder to stop her. Quickly touching the bruise near Jane's eye, she whispered, "Do us both a favor. Stay away from him when he's asleep. He's dangerous, Jane. Enough said?"

As David got to the door, he turned around to look at them.

"Yes," said Jane, smiling at the doctor. "This has been great. Thanks."

They stopped for lunch at a café along Hennepin. Jane needed to get a sense of what his reaction had been to Dowd.

Over bowls of beef barley soup and slices of French baguette, David seemed upbeat, talked eagerly about what the doctor had said. Jane wasn't entirely sure he felt as positive as he sounded. He could easily have been putting on a happy face just for her benefit.

"Will you tell Diego what Dowd said?" she asked, breaking off another piece of bread.

He shrugged. "I think I may see what this Dr. Connor has to say first. I don't want Diego to get his hopes up if it turns out I'm actually a psychopath after all."

"You're not a *psychopath*."

He grinned. "Okay, let's get this straight. You don't approve of words like 'nuts' or 'crazy.' On the other hand, it *is* my mind that's disintegrating. I should be able to call myself a nutcase if I want to."

She grimaced. Glancing up from her bowl of soup, she caught a fleeting look pass across his face. It might not have been panic, but it was close.

"Will you come with me on Thursday?"

"Absolutely."

"Then you can tell the doc that in the distant mists of prehistory, I used to be a pretty swell guy."

"You still are," she said, her throat tightening.

When David finally left to run over to her house and check on the repairs, Jane returned to her car. She sat in the backseat for a few minutes, cuddling Mouse against her. She needed the feel of another warm body because, inside, she felt deeply, depressingly cold. No matter how hard she tried to put a confident spin on what Dowd had said, an undertow of anxiety still tugged at her.

"Some vacation," she said to Mouse, scratching his belly.

Mouse had an odd habit of looking up at her, then letting his head drop against her. It was an incredibly sweet, intimate gesture that never failed to touch her. He did it now. In response, she kissed the top of his head, resting her mouth next to his ear.

"To think I almost lost you."

Mouse seemed to understand. Very softly, he began to lick her hand.

"I love you too, Mouse."

Finally, removing her cell phone from the pocket of her jeans, she pressed a number. She had Nolan on speed dial. After a couple of rings, he picked up.

"Nolan."

"It's Jane. Any news on the dredging?"

"Nothing yet. I'm standing about a hundred yards down the beach from Luberman's property."

"He there?"

"He was this morning, but he left around noon. Hasn't been back since."

"Did he seem nervous?"

"Not in the least. He stood on his dock with a mug of coffee and watched for about an hour. He even waved at me. Classic, just fucking classic."

"But you've still got a man on him, right?"

"I haven't talked to Irv today, but yeah. He's there."

"You don't think Luberman would run, do you?"

"Anything's possible. Look, let me talk to Irv, see what's going on. I'll call you back."

"Great. Thanks."

After hanging up, Jane sat and stared at the traffic buzzing by outside the car. It didn't take long for the cell to ring.

"Bad news," said Nolan right up front. "Irv's lost him again. His truck is parked outside his business in Chamberlain, but he's gone."

Jane's frustration hit overdrive. "How the hell is that even possible? Is this Irv completely inept?"

"Not usually. He's been working for me for five years and Luberman's the only guy who's ever lost him. Look, I'm as upset about this as you are. Do me a favor. Make sure Joanna stays inside the Linden Building today."

"I don't think she's going anywhere."

"I'll be in touch."

Jane flipped the cell phone closed and was about to get up when she got another call. Checking the caller ID, she saw that it was Cordelia.

"Hi, kiddo. What's up?"

"Janey, God I'm so glad you answered. You've got to get back here right away!"

"Why? What's wrong?"

"It's Hattie. Just come, okay? I'm dying here!" She cut the line.

26

Around three on Tuesday afternoon, Brandy sat on her living room couch, staring at the phone in her hand, trying to make sense of the last few days. After the conversation she'd had with Gordon on Friday night, she was more up in the air about him than ever. He'd been so kind and gentle with her when he'd finally brought her home. He apologized for losing his temper. They'd stayed up until nearly six in the morning, drinking lemonade and talking about their childhoods.

As she'd already begun to suspect, Gordon's childhood had been loveless. His parents had died when he was a small boy and he'd been raised by an aunt, a cold woman who disliked children in general, and him in particular. As an adult, he'd had relationships with several women, but none of them had been happy, not until he'd met her. He emphasized again and again that his relationship with Joanna Kasimir had been completely consensual. He'd been her gardener when she'd seduced him. The relationship hadn't lasted more than a few weeks. But when he cut it off, she not only fired him, she pursued him legally. He never entirely understood her reasoning, but then she had money, power, and privilege on her side, while he'd been basically penniless. And so he'd gone to jail. Sure, it wasn't fair, but he'd put it behind him long ago. But now Joanna was back, pursuing him again. He begged Brandy not to let Joanna destroy what they'd built together.

Brandy wanted desperately to bring peace and love into Gordon's sad life, but she couldn't exactly forget what that woman had told her. She couldn't remember the woman's name, and Gordon had taken her card, so she had no way to contact her. Even if what the woman had told her turned out to be false, it would still take time for her to completely trust Gordon again. She'd been honest with him about her feelings on their way to Minneapolis on Sunday afternoon. He insisted he understood, that he'd do everything in his power to win her trust back. When they'd stopped for lunch, they'd walked hand in hand through a little picnic area along a river. Gordon had taken her in his arms, held her tight. He told her she was the most beautiful woman he'd ever known—far more beautiful than Joanna Kasimir—and also the best thing that ever happened to him. He was a hard man to resist.

But the trip to Minneapolis had left a sour taste in her mouth. He'd appeared at her door early Sunday morning soaking wet, explaining that he'd had to swim over from his cabin. It wasn't that far—the lakes were connected—but he was out of breath, and his face was a deep red. He always bragged about being such a good swimmer, but he was in terrible shape. She couldn't imagine why he'd done it until he told her his truck was in for repairs, so the trip was off—unless they could take the Dodge in her garage. It was a simple enough thing to her—she never used it. But the time in Minneapolis had been a bust. She thought they were driving up to have some fun, go to a movie or an art museum, but instead he'd left her in the car in a dangerous part of town, instructed her not to get out or make eye contact with anyone who walked past. Brandy had been terrified. He wasn't gone long, but when he got back, he was in a foul mood. They had dinner at a crummy little restaurant off I-94 in St. Paul and then drove home.

Brandy had worked the day shift yesterday, hadn't seen Gordon last night. And now, today, as she sat with the phone in her hand, the yellow pages open on the coffee table in front of her, she felt guilty, but she needed to call and talk to a police officer, find out if what that woman told her on Friday night was true. Before she could punch in the number, she heard a knock on the door.

"Brandy?" called Gordon's voice. "It's me. Let me in."

She was seized by a moment of panic. The guilt she felt about calling the police was probably written all over her face.

"Brandy?" He pounded on the door. "Come on!"

When she let him in, he gave her a quick kiss, then crossed into the living room. He looked so sweaty and tired that she glanced outside.

"Where's your truck? I thought you were getting it back today."

"It's still not fixed. I walked over from my office."

"That's five miles!"

"I know. Look, I need to borrow the Dodge again. But I've got great news." He turned around and smiled. "I want you to pack your bags. I've got to get out of this town for good, and I'm taking you with me. Anywhere you want. We could go on a cruise before we settle somewhere. Or maybe Paris." His eyes dropped to the yellow pages.

Oh, Lord, she thought. She'd circled the sheriff's number.

He sat down on the couch, pulled the yellow pages onto his lap. When he looked up at her, he saw the phone in her hand. All expression died on his face. "What are you doing, Brandy?"

"I, ah . . . there were some teenagers going door to door. They were demanding money. I gave them ten dollars because they frightened me. I thought I should call the police, let them know about it."

"I didn't see any teenagers."

"It was a while ago."

"You're lying." Something in his eyes had turned bitterly cold.

She backed up. "Why are you looking at me like that?"

"Because I hate liars. Are you going to turn on me now, too? Just like Joanna and all the other women I've loved?"

"Gordon, please. I'd never turn on you."

"Then why do you need to call the police?" He stood, moved toward her. "This was supposed to be my lucky day. Today would be payback for everything I've suffered. Now you've gone and ruined it."

"I didn't mean to," she said, backing up several more steps.

"What am I going to do with you?"

"Gordon, don't. Please don't hurt me!"

He grabbed her and dragged her into the kitchen. She struggled, but it was like trying to fight off King Kong. Before she knew it, he'd found some duct tape in one of the drawers and bound her hands behind her back. He forced her down on a chair, then wound the tape around her again and again, finishing with her ankles.

"While I'm gone, think about what I should do to you for betraying me." He stood over her, sweat beading on his forehead.

"When are you coming back?"

"You don't deserve an answer. You don't deserve *me*."

The last thing he did before he left was to tape her mouth. She heard the car start up and drive away, heard the clock ticking on the wall, measuring the last moments of her life.

Bel Air, California
Spring–Summer 1989

*O*ver *the next few weeks, wherever Joanna went, Gordon was there. Sometimes he was watching from a balcony, sometimes from a seat at the same restaurant or theater. When she was at the studio, he sat in his truck across the street and waited for her. He never tried to approach her, but his presence was pressure enough.*

One month to the day after Joanna had thrown him out, the phone calls began. They came at all hours of the day or night, entreaties to take him back, to give him another chance, to see for herself that he'd changed. He promised that if she'd just talk to him, have lunch or coffee, she'd realize they were meant to be together. The fact was, what Joanna could see was that Gordon was coming apart mentally.

As the months dragged on, Joanna no longer answered her phone. But that didn't stop Gordon. He'd leave long rambling messages for her, talking about his childhood, his wrestling championships, his ex-girlfriends. Or he'd talk about the future, how he was planning to landscape her place, how they could then sell it for big bucks and move to Texas together. He'd always wanted to live in Texas, on the gulf, and knew Joanna would love it there, too. He begged her to call him back, or have coffee with him. And he continued to send roses every week like clockwork.

Gordon was like a piece of gum Joanna couldn't shake off her shoe. In mid-

July, she talked to a friend of hers, a cop, and made him listen to some of the messages, but he said there was nothing he could do. He suggested that she get a restraining order against Gordon, just in case things turned nasty. So that's what she did. The day he was served, he called and left a message. The words were still beseeching, but the tone was slightly different. She could tell his frustration was at an all-time high. He was growing angry, and that anger made him seem ten times more dangerous. She began to wonder if the restraining order had been a mistake.

Joanna didn't understand it at first, but the restraining order did mark a sea change. Gordon's messages grew more testy, more demanding. When he followed her, he'd move up as close to the back of her car as he could without actually bumping into her. He'd honk his horn, scream at her, make obscene gestures. She could see it all in her rearview mirror. One day, on her way home from a hair appointment in Beverly Hills, he tried to run her off the road.

That was it. She called her cop friend again, but when she explained that there hadn't been any witnesses to Gordon's attempt to kill her—and that's what it was in Joanna's mind—he said there was nothing he could do. He was sorry. She wasn't the first celebrity to have this kind of problem, nor would she be the last. He suggested a bodyguard. She suggested something sexual and highly unpleasant. That was the end of her friendship with the cop.

The phone calls continued, but now they were harassing. Gordon called her filthy, vile names. He blamed her for ruining his life, said she was a closeted lesbian and that's why she could never love him. He said he planned to give an interview to The Pasadena Star, let everyone know what the real Joanna Kasimir was like. But Gordon wasn't stupid. He might slander her on a taped phone message, but he knew enough not to do it in print.

One night she came home and found the word "lesbian" spray-painted in red on her garage door. She quickly had it repainted. Two days later, while she was eating dinner, a brick was hurled through her front window. She moved to a hotel until it was repaired. The phone calls kept coming, as did the roses with pleading messages of love and forgiveness. She felt as if she were living inside a fun house mirror. Everything felt off-kilter, stretched, or compressed. She was starting to limit everything she did, evaluating if the event was worth the risk. Shadows in the house terrified her.

One night she lost electric power. She ran to the front window and looked out at the house across the street to try to determine if the grid in her area had gone down. When she realized it was just her house, she called an ex-boyfriend—a professional stuntman—and told him what had happened, asked him to come over right away. And then she sat in her bed, holding a kitchen knife in both hands, waiting for Gordon to break down the door. He never did. When the stuntman arrived, he found the spot where the lines had been yanked and called to have them repaired. He spent the night. The next day, Gordon's message went on and on about what a slut she was. Feeling unhinged and at her wit's end, she called her security company and asked if they could install an electrified fence around her property.

They couldn't.

Joanna was growing increasingly desperate. She hired a bodyguard to live in her house, but after he walked in on her in the bathroom while she was taking a shower, she fired him. She didn't trust anyone anymore. Her one prayer was that Gordon would eventually grow tired of his game and leave her alone, but if anything, the harassment seemed to be growing worse.

By September, she didn't even want to leave her house for fear of what he might do. Not that she felt safe at home. As far as she could tell, he was watching her almost all the time. In the last few days, he'd started commenting on her clothing, down to the last detail. She assumed he must have bought himself some high-powered binoculars. She pulled her shades and drew her curtains and lived in the dark.

And then the worst phone call came. It was the middle of the night. She listened to the message as he spoke it into the machine. He talked about the gun he'd bought, how he'd been practicing with it at various shooting ranges around L.A. That he was a surprisingly good shot. And he said he'd found a new bookstore that carried some fascinating books. He mentioned a couple of the titles by name, telling her that she might like them, too. She had a girlfriend run down and pick them up the next day. They were all about bondage, about sexual torture. Again, he hadn't threatened her, but the message was clear.

The following night he called and said he planned to see her soon, that she should put a light on in the window for him, that he missed her and still loved her—and that he intended to show her how much the next time they were together.

Joanna freaked. She packed a bag and left the house. It was already dark, so it was easy to tell if someone was following her just by watching for headlights. Nobody was. She made it all the way to West Sunset before she even saw a truck, and this one was red and much smaller than Gordon's white Ford. She checked herself into a bungalow suite at the Beverly Hallmark, exhausted and nauseous with fear. She had no intention of telling anyone except her agent, Marybeth Flagg, where she was until she'd talked to her lawyer. The police could go to hell as far as she was concerned. But there had to be some way to stop this harassment.

She slept until ten the next morning, then took a swim in the pool outside the bungalow. Feeling safe for the first time in months, she ordered lunch from room service, then spent the afternoon on the phone. Her lawyer was out of town, so she was passed along to one of his partners, a man named Stan Hilliker. She had a long conversation with him during which he told her to start documenting Gordon's attempts to harass her. And he insisted that she hire another bodyguard, said he would vouch for the agency he recommended. He offered to arrange it and said he'd call her back later in the day with more specific information.

After hanging up, Joanna felt resigned to the fact that she would have to do the bodyguard thing again. Gordon had left her no other choice. Hilliker echoed her own thoughts that Gordon would eventually get tired of harassing her. But who knew how long that would take? Hilliker said that a bodyguard would ensure that it was sooner rather than later. When Luberman saw she was being protected, he would realize that contact with her was impossible.

From your mouth to God's ears, she thought, closing her eyes and hoping like hell it would happen just that way.

Joanna napped until four, when a phone call from Hilliker woke her. He gave her the name of the agency and the agent to ask for, explained the fees, how the service worked, and said that if she gave him the go-ahead, he could have the man stop by the bungalow in the morning. She agreed to everything he suggested.

After a swim in her private pool, she watched some TV and dozed. As it was getting dark, she flipped through the hotel menu again and ordered dinner. Her agent, Marybeth, called while she was eating, just to make sure everything was okay. Joanna said she felt more confident now that she'd talked to a lawyer. Marybeth said to call her in the morning, and Joanna promised she would.

Around ten, she went out by the pool to have a cigarette. She thought about fixing a drink but didn't feel like going back inside. She was too comfortable. It was such a beautiful fall evening. She realized it had been months since she'd had the guts to sit by her own pool. She watched the light play on the water, let her mind drift.

A click next to her ear startled her. Ducking away, she looked back and saw Gordon standing over her. He was holding a gun. Her world slid sideways.

"Scream and I'll kill you. Get up."

"How . . . how did you find me?"

"Why, Joanna, I never lost you."

"But . . . I never saw your truck."

"I sold it. Move."

She did what he asked. He pushed her back in through the patio doors, told her to sit down on the edge of the bed.

"What are you going to do?" she asked, her voice weak and trembling.

"What would you like?" He pulled a roll of duct tape from behind his back, making quick work of tying her hands and feet. And then he forced her to lie back.

She sucked in her breath when he knelt on the bed next to her and touched her hair.

"Don't, Gordon. Please!"

"Christ, woman, it's been so long. I told you when we were first together that I was nobody's one-night stand."

"I know. I believed you. You were never that."

"No?" He slapped her hard across the face. "That's exactly what you made me. You never understood me. I told you I wanted to be with you forever—for eternity."

"Yes," she said quickly, hoping he wouldn't hit her again.

"Yes what?"

"Yes, I remember you saying that."

"I told you I loved you." He straddled her, put his hands around her waist, and lifted her up. "And what did you do? You spit in my face."

"I'm sorry."

"You are?"

"Yes. Absolutely."

"I don't believe you."

"It's true! But you scare me."

His grip eased. "I don't want to hurt you."

"I know you don't."

He brought his face close to hers, searched her eyes. She could smell the beer on his breath. The fact that he'd been drinking scared her because he never drank.

"Are you worth loving, Jo? Are you?"

"Yes!"

His face softened. "I thought so once."

"Gordon, you have to understand—"

He slapped her again. "Shut up! God," he said, rubbing a hand through his hair, "I'm so tired."

"I know you are."

"You can tell?"

"Sure."

He looked around, saw the minibar. Climbing off her, he yanked the door open and stared at the contents. "Lots of booze. Some peanuts. Chocolate chip cookies. A feast."

She didn't respond. She had to lift her head to see him now.

"You've made me into a drunk, Jo. Are you happy?" He removed several of the small bottles. Dropping down on a chair, he opened them one by one and drank them. "I'm on my last three hundred bucks thanks to you. Had to sell my truck. Bought a junker, which I've been living in for the past few weeks." He looked around at the suite. "This place is much nicer. I told myself when I left home that I'd never live in a dump. I like it here."

"Then you should stay," said Joanna.

"Yeah, think I will, Jo, whether you like it or not." He reached over and removed a bunch more bottles, then eased back in his chair, let his legs fall wide apart. "I'm still thinking we should go to Texas."

"Sure, I'd like that."

"No, you wouldn't."

"I would. It's just . . . like I said . . . you scare me sometimes, Gordon."

He grunted, downed the liquor in a couple more of the tiny bottles.

"That's why I don't want to be around you."

"That's all?"

She couldn't tell if he was drunk, but if he kept removing bottles from the minibar, he would be soon. Maybe she could wait it out. If he drank enough, maybe she could get away.

He sat for a while in silence, drinking and eating peanuts. When he got up to retrieve a few more bottles, he stumbled, nearly fell. "Crap," he said, opening the minibar door and staring inside. He filled his arms this time, looked a second more, and grabbed a package of Ritz crackers.

"Let's talk," he said, dumping it all on the bed next to her. Sitting cross-legged, he ripped open the crackers. "You miss me?"

"I missed you a lot."

He snorted, cracked a bottle of Dewar's. "You can blow shit with the best of them, Jo." As he continued to drink, he talked about his girlfriend in high school, how she fell out of a four-story window and broke her neck. Joanna was waiting for the punch line. About an hour after he'd started the tale of woe, it finally came.

"I pushed her," he said, his words so slurred by then she could hardly understand him. "She was a skank. Total skank. Didn't deserve to live."

All the bottles were empty. Gordon teetered to the right, then to the left. He pushed off the bed but fell back onto it, his body half covering hers. She waited a few minutes until he started to snore, then tried to wiggle free.

He woke with a start, reached his arm around her and pulled her even farther underneath him. "Don't leave me, Jo," he mumbled.

She didn't dare move for the rest of the night.

By seven the next morning, sunlight was streaming in through the partially open curtains. Joanna couldn't believe she'd actually slept, but she must have because time had passed. Gordon had been lying on top of her all night. He'd never moved. She was wide awake now, her mind moving at the speed of light. When he finally opened his eyes, he'd have one hell of a headache, which meant he'd be in a foul mood. He hadn't raped her last night, but that didn't mean he wouldn't.

She lay motionless for the next few hours, listening to his soft snoring. At exactly ten after nine, the phone rang.

Gordon jumped. Turning on his back, he looked up. "God, stop that noise!"

He sat up, glanced at the phone, then back at Joanna. Rubbing his face hard with the flats of his hands, he said, "Answer it. Sound normal." He picked it up and held it next to her ear.

"Hello," said Joanna, clearing her voice.

"It's Marybeth. Did I wake you?"

"No."

"Are you okay?"

"Oh, no," said Joanna, emphasizing the last word but sounding as casual and chipper as she could under the circumstances.

"You're not?"

"Yeah, not at all."

"What's . . . I mean . . . you're not okay?"

"No, dummy. Don't be so dense."

"Is . . . Christ, is Gordon there?"

"Yup. But I can't talk now. If you're around tomorrow, maybe we can connect."

"Holy shit!"

"Yeah. That's nice of you to say. Later, babe."

"Who was it?" asked Gordon, hanging up the phone. He seemed a little dazed, not quite awake. Thank God he wasn't, or he might have listened to the call.

"My agent." Joanna needed to use the bathroom but was afraid to ask.

He stared at the phone a moment, then took it off the hook. "We don't want any interruptions."

She wasn't sure what to say. Staying calm was primary. "Want some breakfast?"

He pressed a hand to his stomach, then got up and rushed around looking for the bathroom. Joanna could hear him throwing up. He came back eventually, a wet towel around his neck.

"Feeling better?"

"Yeah. Thanks."

"Do you think I could use the bathroom?"

He eyed her. "No funny business."

"None. Promise."

He took a knife out of his pocket and cut off the tape, then stood outside the bathroom door until she was finished. She took so long that he told her to hurry up. She assumed Marybeth would call the police. She had to stall until they arrived.

"Think maybe we should have some breakfast," he said, forcing her back down on the bed.

"Don't tie me up again. Please?"

He gave her a grumpy smile. "I never wanted to do that."

"I know. The menu's on the couch."

He stepped over and picked it up. "Hell, let's just order what we want." Pressing the phone back on the hook, he punched in the number for the restaurant. "What do you feel like?"

"Whatever you're having is fine."

He ordered eggs over easy, bacon, toast, American fries, orange juice, and coffee black. He listened a moment, then said thanks. "About half an hour," he added to Joanna. "Hmmm, wonder what we could do to while away half an hour."

Her stomach flipped over. "Gee, don't know." She forced a smile.

"God, but you're beautiful."

His breath stank of vomit, but she kissed him anyway. He came so fast he couldn't even get his pants off. Lying on his back, his breath was labored and raw. "Let's try that again," he said, looking over at her and smiling. "Only this time, let's do it right." He ordered her to get undressed while he watched. As she unsnapped her bra, he opened up the bed and crawled in, staring at her with a grin on his face. "Come here," he said, opening his arms.

Joanna sat down on the edge. She was just about to lie down next to him when the door was rammed open and three cops rushed into the room, guns drawn. Joanna screamed, jumped off the bed, and ran behind them, shouting, "He tried to rape me! Look at my face! He hit me!"

Gordon held up his hands, looking wide-eyed and innocent.

"Arrest him!" demanded Joanna. "He tied me up. He's been harassing me for months!"

The lead cop scratched the back of his head, then looked at Gordon and said, "I think you better come with us."

"This is ridiculous," muttered Gordon. "She's a liar. You can't believe a thing she says."

230

"I need to call my lawyer," said Joanna. "He knows what's been going on."

"You got a weapon?" asked one of the other cops.

"No," said Gordon.

"Yes," said Joanna. "A gun. In his boot, by the foot of the bed."

"Better get dressed, Ms. Kasimir," said the lead cop. As he began to gather things up, he found the snarl of used duct tape.

"She likes it rough," said Gordon, cracking his neck. "Nothing illegal about that."

27

Jane drove back to the Linden Building through rush-hour traffic, an Antigone Rising CD blasting from the speakers in her Mini, feeling like a three-hundred-pound man was standing on her chest. Everywhere she looked there was a crisis.

Parking in the back lot, Jane showed her ID to the guard at the back door, then she and Mouse raced up the stairs to Cordelia's loft.

"What took you so long?" said Cordelia, grabbing Jane by her leather jacket and yanking her inside.

Mouse jumped up on one of the chairs.

"What's wrong?"

"Hattie!"

"What *about* Hattie?"

"Didn't I tell you?"

"No, as usual you left me with one of your dramatic pauses."

Cordelia slumped onto the couch. "Octavia called."

"And?"

"They want to keep her another night."

Jane pressed her lips together and swung her fists in the air, stifling a scream. "I nearly had a heart attack and that's all it is? Hattie's spending another night with Octavia?"

Tears streamed down Cordelia's face. "Yes. That's *all*."

Seeing the tears, Jane felt like a insensitive creep.

"My life is over, but it's nothing."

"Listen, Cordelia, I'm sorry. These past few days have been kind of overwhelming for me."

"Me, too." She rubbed the tears off her cheeks.

"I'm sorry. Really." Jane sat down next to her. As soon as she put her arm around Cordelia's back, Cordelia broke down into full-out wails. "Tell me what your sister said, Cordelia. I want to hear it all."

She cried for another minute, then sniffed, dried her tears on Jane's shirt collar, and looked up. Still sobbing, she hiccuped her response. "She . . . she said that . . . that they were having such a good time—"

"She wanted to keep her another night."

"Yeah. I . . . I already said that." Her eye makeup ran down her cheeks, creating a dark rainbow.

"That's all? Did she say when they'd bring Hattie back?"

"In the morning." She sniffed. "But that's what they've said before and they still have her!"

"Did you get to talk to Hattie?"

"No. Octavia said that Radley had just taken her down to the swimming pool."

It sounded like Octavia was specifically choosing times when Cordelia couldn't talk to Hattie. It might be jealousy or it might be something else. Jane wasn't sure what that something else might be, and not knowing made her feel uneasy. "Have you tried to call Octavia's cell? Tried to talk to Hattie?"

"Octavia won't answer her cell. It's standard procedure. People leave messages for her and if she's in the mood, she calls back. If not, forget it. Oh, and I've called and left at least ten messages for Cecily. I don't know why she hasn't returned any of them. When I've called the suite at the hotel, they're either not there, or Octavia makes up some excuse why Hattie can't come to the phone. Last night she told me I was making a mountain out of a molehill. Me!"

"Well, I mean, maybe you are?"

"Of course I am! It's what I do!"

"Did you call your lawyer?"

"She said I had to talk to an adoption attorney. She gave me a couple of names. I called and left messages but nobody's called me back."

"Look, Cordelia, if they don't return Hattie in the morning, I'll go talk to them."

"You'll never find them."

"I will. Don't worry."

Cordelia took a couple of deep breaths. "I knew you'd make me feel better."

"That's what friends are for. Hey, speaking of friends, do you know if Joanna's here?"

Grabbing the Kleenex box off the coffee table, Cordelia pulled one out and wiped her eyes, then blew her nose with a big honk. "Yes. She refuses to leave the building. I had to call off rehearsals again today. I might as well call them off for the duration. Until you and Nolan figure out some way to put Luberman behind bars."

Jane didn't want to tell her that they weren't doing so great with that. "I think we should stay in for the evening, too."

"It's my poker club night. People will be arriving around eight. You can sit in if you want."

"I'll see."

"Or you could make us sandwiches if you had the time."

"I'd be happy to do that."

"Little tea sandwiches like you do. With the crusts cut off. Cream cheese and nuts and olives. I've got everything."

"Doesn't sound very pokerlike."

"Or you could do that Austrian omelet with the jam inside. That's yummy. People never think of eggs as a dessert. Or, hey, I've got some fresh salmon. You could do a salmon mouse. With little toast points. I don't have any fresh dill, but I have dried."

"Okay."

"Maybe we should get out the deep fryer—do those little balls of dough you fry and then roll in cinnamon and sugar. They're incredible."

"We could do that."

Jane let her talk. A little food porn always calmed Cordelia down.

David cupped the phone between his shoulder and ear as he lay on his bed in Joanna's loft, talking to Diego. It was just after eight. He'd shared a pizza with Joanna and Freddy, and then Freddy had taken off for the airport. He was flying back to L.A. for a few days but planned to return to Minnesota—and to Joanna—by the end of the week.

"She was a total basket case, and then Freddy appeared," said David, scratching his chest through his shirt. "Poof. I mean, Luberman's still out there, but she's like a different person today. Almost happy. Talking about the future."

"I can't believe they're together again after all these years," said Diego. "But anything that brings you home sooner is great by me."

"Exactly." There was so much David wanted to say but couldn't. Not yet. He'd given Dr. Dowd's words a lot of thought this afternoon as he stood in Jane's house watching the last coat of poly being applied to the new oak floor. The icy truth was, Dowd had said what was happening to him *could* be a treatable sleep disturbance, but, and it was a big but, it might also be a symptom of a deeper psychiatric disorder. David felt as if he were perched at the edge of a precipice watching the ground weaken and drop away beneath his feet. There was no firm purchase anywhere he looked.

"David? You still there?"

"I'm here."

"I haven't talked to you since you got back from Nebraska. You said you liked Jane's new girlfriend."

"Yeah, she's nice." *Even though she almost blew my brains out.* "She's attractive but not as good-looking as Jane."

"I miss you, babe. Come home soon."

"I will."

"Promise?"

"I won't stay away a second more than necessary."

They spoke for a few more minutes and then said good-bye.

David didn't feel like turning in for the night just yet. He passed

Joanna's closed bedroom door on the way to the kitchen. The pizza box still sat on the center of the table. Removing the last slice, he sat down and pulled the final contractor's bill out of his back pocket. He studied it while he finished the pizza.

Jane hadn't seen the basement redo yet. Maybe he'd swing her by there late in the day tomorrow. By then, the floors would be safe to walk on in their stocking feet. He'd gone a little wild with some of the new furniture and electronics in the rec room, but he was pretty sure she'd like it.

As David was watching a rerun of *Law & Order* in the study, Joanna emerged from her bedroom to join him. She sat down on an overstuffed leather armchair, rearranging her peach satin bathrobe over her legs.

"You look, I don't know, sort of wired," said David, surprised to see her so wide awake. He glanced at his watch and saw that it was quarter of eleven. "Couldn't get to sleep?"

"I need a cigarette."

"Sorry, I'm all out. You can always go next door and get one from Faye."

She made a sour face. "Faye's mad at me."

"Why?"

"She thinks I'm making a big mistake getting back together with Freddy."

"It's none of her business."

"I know. But it really seems to bug the hell out of her, and you know Faye, she's not shy about giving advice. I think I'll just stay away from her for a while."

David shrugged. "I can go out and buy you a pack."

"No. Stay put. I don't want to be alone."

"Okay. Whatever."

They watched TV in silence for a few minutes.

"I ate the last piece of pizza," said David during one of the commercial breaks, forcing a little-boy guilty look. "Sorry. If you're hungry, I could fix you something."

She shook her head. When the program resumed, she began tapping her fingernails on the arms of the chair.

"What's wrong, Joanna?"

"Everything. I wish Freddy hadn't left."

"I'll protect you," said David, beating on his chest with his fists.

"Great." But then her expression softened. "Thanks."

"No problem. Look, Luberman can't get in here. You're safe."

"Safe," she repeated. "I don't even know what that means anymore." She rose and drifted out of the room.

David followed. He was worried. All her confidence seemed to have walked out the door with Freddy.

Standing at the bank of windows, she stared up at the night sky. "I wish he was dead."

"Me too. Hey, did I tell you Milan Mestrovik wants to take Gordon out. He actually talked to me about it. Asked if I wanted to help."

Joanna turned around. "He actually said that?"

"He thinks everyone who loves you—and that includes him—should band together and take care of Luberman."

"Murder?"

"He didn't use that exact word, but his meaning was pretty clear."

She pulled her robe more closely around her. "To be honest, that guy makes my skin crawl."

"No argument there."

A cell phone trilled.

"That's mine," said Joanna with a sigh. "It's over there on the end table. But I can't talk to anyone, unless it's Freddy. Will you answer it?"

David scooped it off the table and flipped it open. "Hello?"

"Ah . . . hi . . . is this . . . Joanna's cell phone?"

It was a woman's voice, not one he recognized. "Who's calling?"

"My name's Hillary Schinn. I'm a journalist. I met Joanna at Flying Cloud airport the day she flew in. She agreed to do an interview with me. I'm sorry I'm calling so late."

"Just a sec." He muted the phone by pressing it to his chest. In a whisper, he said, "Hillary Schinn?"

"Who?"

"Says she's a journalist. Met you at Flying Cloud field."

Joanna looked down, repeating the name to herself. The light finally dawned. "Get rid of her. No, wait. Tell her to call me tomorrow."

David repeated the message.

"Great," said Hillary. "Fabulous. Fantastic! What time?"

"Afternoon is probably best."

"Thanks so much!"

"Boy," said David, snapping the cell phone shut, "you sure made her night."

Joanna eventually drifted back to her bedroom. David watched TV until around midnight, then listened outside her door, hoping she'd finally fallen asleep. He stood next to the front closet and slipped on his jacket, feeling in the pockets for his car keys and handcuffs, and then left the loft for the night. He waved to the peephole in Faye's door before he headed to the back stairs, assuming that she was, as usual, performing her role as resident busybody.

Just before two, David's eyes snapped open. Looking around to get his bearings, he saw that he was in his car in the parking lot. "Am I awake or asleep?" he whispered. He truly didn't know. He tried pinching himself.

"Ouch," he said, staring up at the roof of the car. His seat was re-clined. Reaching around, he pushed a button and the seat came up.

"I think I'm awake," he said to himself. He squinted at the bright light above the door to the back of the building. And then it hit him. The guard was gone.

Feeling for the keys in his pocket, he unlocked the handcuffs. "Maybe I'm dreaming," he whispered, rubbing his eyes. "Christ, how do I *know*?"

He got out and scanned the lot. The Linden Building was blocks from the main part of downtown Minneapolis. Behind him was the Mississippi River. As far as he could tell, he was alone.

Walking slowly at first, David edged his way through the parked cars, keeping his eyes peeled for any movement. As he got closer, he could see that the guard was slumped down against the brick wall next to the door. A line of blood ran from a hole in the guard's right temple down to his chin, where it bled into his uniform. "Shit!" he groaned, bending down, trying to get a pulse. There wasn't one.

David closed his eyes, then opened them. He did it over and over. "Wake up," he said. "Wake up! Wake up! Wake up!" He slapped his face, did a couple of deep-knee bends.

The back door was open. Large drops of blood covered the cement. The blood didn't appear to have come from the guard. Following the trail inside, David started up the metal stairs. The raw light from the bare bulbs hurt his eyes. As he made it to the landing on the third level, he came to an abrupt halt. Luberman was lying there in front of him, legs splayed, the upper part of his body twisted over, face against the cold metal railing.

David froze. Underneath Luberman was a large, sticky pool of blood. His blue polo shirt was soaked. The air all around him smelled foul, sweaty. "Fuck," he rasped. He watched Luberman for any sign of movement. He wasn't sure how long he stood there, but eventually he touched the body with his foot. When nothing happened, he held his breath, bent down, felt for a pulse. He sensed a little something under his fingertips but wasn't sure if it was Luberman's or his own blood he was feeling.

A sudden anger surged through him. He grabbed what was left of Luberman's hair and yanked his head around, looking hard into lifeless, staring eyes.

Standing up, David kicked him. It felt so good, he kicked him again, harder this time. He couldn't seem to stop. He stomped on his groin, slammed his shoe on top of his right thigh and felt a bone crack.

"You fucking psycho piece of garbage," he barked. He kept kicking him until he was exhausted.

Finally, turning away, he dragged himself up to the landing on the fourth floor and sat down on the steps to catch his breath. It was darker there, the light was burned out. He dropped his head in his hands. He still wasn't sure if he was awake or asleep. The horror of it made him think he might be dreaming. If he was, what had he just done?

"God," he cried, covering his mouth with the back of his hand. He dug in his pocket for his cell phone and punched in Jane's number. He waited, feeling light-headed, like he was coming apart inside and there was nothing to stop him this time.

Jane answered. She sounded a long way off. She was. She was back on earth.

"Come get me, please?" he pleaded. "I'm in the stairway. I think . . . I think I just did something really bad."

28

Jane shot off the chaise. She ran her hands through her hair for a few seconds, getting her bearings, then yanked on her jeans and boots, pulled off her T-shirt and replaced it with a clean sweatshirt. She'd never heard David's voice sound so weak and just plain weird before. With Mouse hot on her heels, she dashed to the front door.

Cordelia was still up, lying on the couch in the living room, reading a book. One of her cats was perched on her stomach, one was draped around her neck, while the third and largest, Lucifer, was on top of the card table grazing through the remnants of the poker game food. "Who just called?" she asked, lowering the book.

"David."

"Something wrong?"

"Will you take care of Mouse? I'll be right back." She grabbed her wallet and shoved it in her back pocket, then shut the door and rushed for the stairs.

She found David huddled near the railing on the fourth-floor landing. Something dark was smeared all over his clothing. Glancing down at his white Nikes, she saw that they were soaked with the same dark-colored liquid. "Is that blood?"

He gazed up at her with a strange expression. "Am I awake, Jane? Tell me!"

"I don't know."

"Are you real or part of a dream?"

"I'm real," she said, bending down and staring deep into his eyes.

"Jesus," he said, turning his face away. "This is total crap! I can't live like this! I can't even tell what's real anymore." He plucked his shirt away from his chest, stared at it, started to cry.

"David, listen to me. Look at me."

He lifted his eyes.

"What happened?"

"Luberman. He's dead. I think. No, he *has* to be dead. He's down one floor, on the landing."

"Did you—"

"No. I mean . . . I don't know. No!"

"Then how did your clothes get so covered in blood?"

"I . . . I kicked him."

"That's it? That's all?"

"It's not my fault. He deserved to die!"

Jane wasn't sure what to do. "Okay, let's think this through. I'll run down and see what's what. You stay put."

He nodded. But he seemed far away, disconnected.

"David?" she repeated.

"What!"

"Stay here."

"Where the hell am I gonna go?"

She gripped his arm to steady him, then headed down.

On the third floor she found Luberman lying in a pool of his own blood, his head tilted to one side, his eyes lifeless. She didn't want to get too close, but from what she could see, his T-shirt was soaked in blood on both the front and the back. One leg looked like it might be broken. Noticing that a trail of blood led down to the next level, she followed it all the way down to the locked security door. As she pushed through out into the chill night air, she discovered the answer to her next question—how Luberman had gotten into the building.

Leaning down, Jane pressed her fingers to the guard's neck, but from the moment she saw him, she knew he was dead.

Luberman had most likely shot the guard and entered the stairwell. He was bleeding, so maybe the guard had managed to get off a round before Luberman killed him. But the guard's gun was still in its holster, so that didn't work. And where did David come in?

Jane flipped open her cell and punched in 911. She reported the murders, then stood for a moment on the dock outside the building to get her bearings. Finally, she called Nolan.

"Christ, Jane. It's the middle of the night." His voice was a deep rumble in her ear.

"I think you better get over to the Linden Building."

"Why? What happened?"

"Luberman. He's dead. And so is one of the security guards."

"On my way," said Nolan without a moment's hesitation. "Are you okay?"

"I've been better."

"You're not hurt?"

"No."

"Did you call the police?"

"Right before I called you."

"Good. Just hold on."

She stood for a moment more under the bright security light, staring out at the dark parking lot. She felt dazed, unable to make sense of anything. Going back inside, she rushed up the steps. When she swung around to the landing on four, she found the stairwell empty.

David was gone.

The police arrived with sirens blaring within two minutes of her 911 call. Two squads. Three men and one woman. Under other circumstances, Jane might have gone looking for David, but she had to talk to the police first.

The lead cop, a ropy, athletic-looking black guy who introduced himself as Sergeant Dreashon Johnson, took her aside and asked her a bunch of questions while the rest of the officers fanned out.

"What happened to your face?"

"I fell off a horse."

"Sure you did." He checked out her bruises for another few seconds, then went on with his interrogation. While they were talking, he stopped several times to confer with the other officers. They were almost finished with the interview when Nolan roared up in his SUV. He killed the motor and slid out.

"Why, *Mr.* Nolan," said Johnson, hands rising to his hips. "What a surprise."

Trotting up the steps, Nolan put a hand on Jane's shoulder but removed it when he saw her face. "What the hell happened?" He tipped her face up to the light.

"Fell off a horse when I was in Nebraska."

"She must figure we're pretty stupid," said Johnson with a smirk.

Nolan turned to him. "It's been a while, Drea."

"That it has."

Nolan was almost a foot taller than Johnson and probably had a good fifty pounds on him. Johnson didn't seem comfortable with Nolan standing so close. He moved back a few steps. "Got a couple of dead men on the premises, though I expect you already know that. This lady here says she's a friend of yours, that you been handling a case involving the guy inside. Privately."

"That's right." Nolan's gaze shifted to the dead guard.

"Well, it's public now. In a big way. Since you did me the favor of showing up at the scene, I'm gonna need you to answer some questions."

"Am I done?" asked Jane.

"For now," said the sergeant. "We need to talk with your friend, Mr. Carlson. Have any idea where we might find him?"

"None," said Jane.

"Well, I guess we'll just have to look under every rock until he crawls out."

She didn't like the sound of that.

"Mind if I take a look inside?" asked Nolan. "And I need to check on my client, Joanna Kasimir. She lives in the building up on four."

244

The sergeant didn't answer right away. One of his officers had pulled him aside.

From the moment Nolan got out of his car, Jane got the impression that there was a certain friction between Nolan and Johnson. Most of Nolan's friends called him simply that—Nolan. The *Mr.* Nolan thing was done for a reason. She figured these two weren't old buddies.

As Johnson continued to confer with one of the officers, Nolan bent down to get a closer look at the dead guard. "Looks like a twenty-two. Close range."

"That'd be my guess," said Johnson, returning to the conversation. "Notice the blood trail. You can't see it very well in the dark, but it begins way on the other end of the building. I'll wager it starts even before that."

"You think Luberman was injured before he got to the Linden Building?" asked Jane.

"Shot, yeah. That's exactly what I think. But we'll have to wait for confirmation." He frowned at Nolan a moment, then led the way inside.

As soon as they made it to the third level, Nolan crouched down to view the bloody scene at close range. Jane stood back and watched.

"Look at this," said Johnson. He took a pen out of his pocket, crouched down and pressed it against Luberman's right thigh. A piece of metal was wedged underneath.

"What is it?" asked Nolan.

"A knife. A damn odd one."

Jane bent over to take a look. "It's a Global."

"A what?" asked the cop.

"I own a couple of restaurants in town, so I'm pretty familiar with cutlery. It's an Asian vegetable knife manufactured by a company called Yoshikin, sort of on the order of a small chef's knife. They're marketed under the name Global."

"Do you use them in your restaurants?"

"No."

"How about this building? Know anyone who has a set of them?"

"Afraid not."

"What are you thinking?" asked Nolan, glancing over at the cop. "Somebody used the knife on Luberman, or maybe he had it as a backup and somebody took it away from him and cut him?"

"Not clear yet," said Johnson, removing the pen but remaining in his crouch. "Lots of unanswered questions about these two murders."

"If I'm free to go," said Jane, "I'd like to get back upstairs. I'm feeling a little . . . sick to my stomach." The sight of the knife had startled her, though she wasn't about to let on to either man about her concerns. Not until she had a chance to check it out.

"Sure," said Johnson. "But we may need to talk to you again."

"I'll be around."

"And if you see your friend, Mr. Carlson, tell him the police want to talk to him. No big deal. Nothing to be frightened of. We just need to know what he saw."

No big deal, my ass, thought Jane. "I will." Turning away, she nearly bumped into Joanna, who was rushing down the stairway in her satin bathrobe. She looked wild-eyed.

"What's going on?" she all but screamed. Seeing Luberman lying on the floor, she turned around and doubled back up the stairs. Halfway up she slowed, then stopped. Looking over her shoulder, she said, "Is he—" She started back down, her eyes full of horror—and something else. To Jane, it looked like elation.

"Ma'am, you can't be in here," said Johnson, standing up to block her from coming any closer.

"He is!" she cried.

"He's dead," said Nolan, moving over to the stairway, looking up at her. "Sergeant Johnson, this is my client, Joanna Kasimir."

"But . . . how did he get in?" she demanded.

"It's all over now," said Nolan, moving up a couple of steps. "Let's get you back to your loft. I'll explain everything, as much as I know."

"Have you seen David?" asked Jane.

"David?" Her eyes edged sideways, as if the wall had just spoken. "Yes, we talked for a while around midnight and then I went to bed. But he must have gone out."

"Come on, Joanna," said Nolan, pressing a hand to the small of her back, leading her up the stairway. "This is no place for you."

As they moved away, Jane struggled to put it all together. David had most likely gone out to sleep in his car. That meant it was possible, even likely, he'd seen Luberman shoot the guard and enter the building. And then what? Had David gone inside himself? Had he stabbed Luberman with the vegetable knife in an effort to protect his sister?

Jane had too many questions and not enough answers. Instead of returning to Cordelia's loft, she raced back down the stairs and jumped in her car. The scary fact was, she was the only person she knew who owned a set of Global knives. Since David had access to her kitchen, she had to check if that particular knife was missing. She prayed it was there safe in her kitchen drawer, that the murder knife had come from somewhere else. But praying wouldn't make it so.

Jane parked her car a couple of doors down from her house. A dim light burned in one of the bedrooms upstairs, but otherwise the place was dark. Thank God she had nothing to fear from Gordon anymore, not that it mattered much at the moment.

Unlocking the front door, she stepped into the foyer and felt along the wall until she found the light switch. The smell of polyurethane nearly knocked her over. Retreating back outside, she removed her boots and then entered again, this time in her stocking feet. Thankfully, the floor seemed to be dry enough to walk on. She glanced into the living room, thinking how strange it was to see it without furniture. The new floor looked beautiful. She wanted to turn on all the lights, get a better look at it, but that would have to wait.

Flipping on the overhead light in the kitchen, she walked hesitantly over to the drawer where she kept her knives.

"Please," she whispered. She opened it slowly, staring down at the empty slot where the vegetable knife should have been. Her throat tightened. She closed her eyes.

Above her, she heard the floor creak.

"David?" she called. A hit of adrenaline burst inside her like a bomb. "David, is that you?" She dashed back to the foyer and bolted up the steps to the second floor. "David, it's me!"

She glanced down the hall toward the bathroom, noticing that the door to the third floor was open. She rushed for the stairway and took the steps two at a time. For many years she'd rented out her third floor. But it was empty now.

"David! Stop! We have to talk!"

When she reached the top, she saw that the door to the outside stairway was open. "David, wait!" She plunged through the screen door, out onto the landing just in time to see him leap from the stairway into the backyard.

"David! Please!"

But it was too late. He'd already rushed across the backyard, jumped the fence, and disappeared into the alley. As she stood looking down into the yard, an electric chill ran through her. Why wouldn't he talk to her?

She stood there for a few seconds more, her mind racing in too many directions, and then closed the door and went back downstairs to the second level. He'd probably come here because it was the only safe place he could think of—until her presence chased him out. She glanced into the guest bedroom, then walked down the hall to the bathroom.

"Good God," she said, sucking in her breath, seeing David's bloody clothing in a heap on the floor. There was blood in the sink and blood on several of her towels. Checking behind the shower curtain, she saw that the showerhead was still dripping water. He must have just finished when she'd come in. He'd taken a shower, cleaned himself up. But he hadn't had enough time to get rid of his clothes— or, put another way, the evidence.

Rushing back to her bedroom, Jane could tell by the disordered look of her closet that he'd rummaged through it until he'd found something to wear. Sweats, most likely, since they weren't anywhere near the same size.

And that left her with another difficult question. What did she do with his clothes? By all rights, she should turn them over to the police. She sat down on her bed and dropped her head in her hands. Luberman deserved to die. Isn't that what David had said? She didn't disagree, but she couldn't protect a murderer.

Could she?

If she did, she was pretty sure it would make her an accomplice. If—and it was a big if—he *had* murdered Luberman. She couldn't bring herself to believe that the David she used to know could kill a man. He might have beaten Luberman to a bloody pulp, and enjoyed every minute of it, but murder? No. And yet, David wasn't the same man she used to know.

The longer Jane sat on her bed, the clearer the moral question became: Could she live with herself if she turned his bloody clothes over to the police without first making sure he was guilty? She knew what the law required, but her own sense of loyalty required, in this instance, something different.

Jane ran downstairs and retrieved a large plastic garbage bag from a box under the sink. After stuffing David's clothing inside, she spent the next couple of hours cleaning the bathroom. She doubted she got all the blood evidence, but then the police would have no reason to examine her house. She hoped. She took the garbage bag out to her garage and hid it in a box with a bunch of gardening tools.

The sun was coming up when she finally drove away.

29

Where have you been!" demanded Cordelia. "Do you know what happened here last night?"

"I know," said Jane, dumping herself on the couch next to Mouse. She hugged him, kissed his neck.

Cordelia bent over and sniffed Jane's clothes. "You smell like bleach."

"I do? Must be that new laundry detergent I'm using."

One eyebrow shot upward. "Didn't you leave wearing a red sweatshirt and jeans?"

Jane shrugged. "Can't remember."

"Well, I do. And now you have on a black shirt and gray cords. What's the deal? You're hiding something."

"Me? No way. I know better than to hide things from you. I've learned my lesson."

"Well, I should hope so." She eyed Jane a moment more, then flopped down on a chair with a tired sigh. "Where were you?" she said, lifting her legs onto an ottoman.

"Out trying to find David."

"I heard he took off. Not very smart." She looked frazzled, like she hadn't slept all night. Which she probably hadn't. And as luck would have it, her tiredness no doubt saved Jane a whole lot of explaining.

"Have you talked to Joanna?" she asked.

"Are you kidding me? I was down in her loft until about fifteen minutes ago. She's ecstatic."

Jane nodded and looked away.

"Well, ecstatic and——" She cleared her throat. "Death is a sad circumstance, I realize, but . . . oh, hell, she's thrilled. So am I. That man deserved what he got."

"I suppose."

"Joanna called Freddy. Instead of staying in L.A., he's flying back. He's already on the plane. Joanna wants us to come down to her loft when he gets back so we can celebrate her freedom."

Sure, Jane understood how Joanna must feel with Luberman out of her life for good, but with all the questions surrounding David and his potential involvement in the murder, celebrating sounded a little premature.

"Come on, Janey. Don't look so dour. Joanna's free! She can come and go as she wants. The show must go on and all that crap. I told her that I'd give her a couple of days to rest and recuperate, and then we'd start rehearsals."

"Great," said Jane, knowing she hadn't put quite the sense of joy in the word that Cordelia might have liked. "Did Nolan talk to her?"

"Yes, at great length."

"The police come to any conclusions while I was gone?"

She shook her head. "Nolan said he'll call you if he hears anything."

Jane was pretty sure that even though Nolan wasn't bosom buddies with Sergeant Dreashon Johnson, he'd still find a way to get information about the ongoing investigation. Glancing at her watch, she saw that it was ten after six. "You know, Cordelia, I've got to catch some shut-eye. Otherwise, I'll be walking into walls by afternoon."

"You can *sleep* at a time like this?"

"I can give it the old college try."

"Hattie should be home by ten. That's another reason *I'm* wide awake."

"Good for you." Jane gave Cordelia a congratulatory chuck on her arm. "See how nice it is to be up during the early morning hours?"

On her way back to her makeshift bedroom, she called over her shoulder, "Hey, why don't you take this once-in-a-lifetime chance to go outside and examine the morning dew."

Shortly before noon, Jane was awakened by the sound of a shriek. She cracked an eye just in time to duck as Cordelia leaped through the curtains and landed next to her on the chaise.

"Hey!" she shouted. After making sure she had no broken bones, she sat up.

"Octavia just called."

"Oh, goodie."

"She heard what happened here last night on the morning news. She said she and Radley had talked about it and decided they couldn't bring Hattie back to a place where two men had just been murdered."

Jane groaned. It had never occurred to her Octavia would use that. Not that she didn't have a legitimate point. "What did you tell her?"

"That *I* hadn't done the murders, so what was her problem?"

"I'm sure she loved that. How long did she say she's keeping Hattie for?"

"She was dialed up to high witch, let me tell you. She wouldn't commit to anything, but they're extending their stay. All I can say is just freakin' *faboo*. As if no murders ever happen in L.A. or London. This world is seriously depraved, Jane. *I'm* not responsible for it!"

"Did you get a chance to talk to Hattie?"

"Octavia said she was taking a bubble bath, couldn't be disturbed."

"That is *so* bogus," said Jane.

"Tell me about it. She's separating me from her, little by little, day by day. But it won't work. Unlike my sister, Hattie has a heart."

Jane's cell phone rang. It was on the table next to the chaise. "God, I need a vacation."

"You're on vacation."

"Then I need a vacation from my vacation." Flipping it open, she said hello.

"It's Nolan. How you doing?"

"Better, thanks."

"We need to talk about your face."

"But not now."

"Okay, not now. But we *are* talkin'. Have you heard from David?"

"Afraid not." The fact that she'd seen him—that he'd left his bloody clothes in her house—was a fine distinction she decided to ignore. The idea that the murder weapon probably belonged to her wasn't so fine a point, but then Nolan hadn't directly asked her about it. When it came to David, so many things had piled up so fast, she hadn't had a chance to talk to him about any of them. Now she was glad she hadn't. If he ever found out what she was keeping from him, it might be the end of their friendship. She hated all this sinning by omission stuff, but she didn't see that she had a choice.

"You've got to find him, Jane. You must have some idea where he's gone."

"I'm working on it."

"At the very least he's a material witness." He paused. "The cops like him for Luberman's murder, you know."

"I figured as much."

"He had motive and opportunity. I'm inclined to agree. But you think he's innocent?"

"To be honest, I don't know."

"Well, here's what I just found out from a friend in the ME's office. They put a priority on the autopsy. Looks like before Luberman made it to the Linden Building, he'd been shot at close range in the chest. The police traced the blood trail back to an alley outside the Singapore Bar. It's a dive not far from the lofts."

Jane sat up straight. "What do you suppose all that was about?"

"The cops aren't sure. They stopped by the bar this morning, talked to the owner, who also happened to be there last night. They showed him a photo of Luberman and he said he recognized him, that he'd come in around one A.M., sat alone at a table in the back until sometime around one-thirty, when another guy showed up and joined him."

"What did the other guy look like?" asked Jane.

"Not much of a description. White. Baseball cap. Dark clothes. The bartender said he never really looked at him. They must have left fairly soon after the second guy showed up."

"Together?"

"He couldn't say because he didn't see them leave, but the cops are pretty sure they went outside to the alley, got into some kind of scuffle, and two shots were fired. One from Luberman's twenty-two and the other from the second guy's thirty-eight. They know it was a thirty-eight because that's what hit Luberman in the chest. They also found two different blood types in the alley."

"But—" It didn't make any sense. "Luberman gets shot and the first thing he does is head over to the Linden Building?"

"Exactly. He picks off the guard and uses the guard's keys to let himself in."

"And then what?"

"Again, the cops aren't sure. But it seems like he must have met someone in the stairwell who had a knife. Get this. He had thirty-two knife wounds in his chest, his back, several on his arms, a couple to his neck. He'd already lost a lot of blood, so when he got knifed, he bled out pretty fast."

"Minutes?"

"Yeah. Minutes. And then, and I know this sounds crazy, but it looks like someone kicked him, broke some ribs, one of his legs, crushed part of the back of his skull. I mean, the guy was already dead and his killer was still waling on him."

"David told me he kicked Luberman."

Silence. "Did you tell that to the police?"

"I didn't . . . I mean . . . no."

"Jane? What were you thinking? Withholding evidence is a crime."

"But if David kicked him after he was dead, that means he didn't kill him."

"You don't know that. He could have knifed him, then maybe he went to wash his hands, or have a smoke. People do crazy stuff at times like that. Maybe, when he came back to see if Luberman was dead, he started kicking him. Whoever killed Luberman was in a state of pure rage. This murder was personal. The killer knew Luberman and wanted to annihilate him."

Jane felt like she'd been rolled over by a steam shovel. But what Nolan said made sense. The therapist had already told Jane that David was dangerous. How much more proof did she need?

"Did he say anything else to you?" asked Nolan.

"He said that when he found Luberman, he was pretty sure he wasn't breathing."

More silence. "Why was David in the stairwell?"

"He didn't say."

"Seems kind of fishy, don't you think?"

"Maybe he was just coming in. He could have been out on the town."

"And just happened to find Luberman right after he died? You believe that?"

"I don't know. It's possible."

"Look, Jane, when you find him, I suggest you call me before you try to talk to him. I know you consider him a friend—"

She lowered her head. "I hear you."

"I'm sorry, but with what you just told me, I'd say it's not only probable but likely David's our guy."

She felt a heaviness in her chest, that same sense of dread that had been dogging her ever since David had left the water on in her house all night. She knew it wasn't the act of a man who was in control of all his faculties. She'd wanted to believe he was okay, just tired, or distracted, in the midst of relationship problems, business or personal problems, so she'd made excuses. She'd excused the destruction to her house, the heavy drinking, the attack in the barn. Was this new parasomnia diagnosis just one more in a long line of excuses? Was she refusing to see what was right in front of her face?

"Thanks for calling," she said. "Will you let me know if you hear anything more?"

"Yeah. But you've got to promise me something, too, Jane. No more withholding evidence from the police—or me."

"Right. Should I call and tell them what I didn't tell them last night?"

Nolan sighed. "No, just leave it for now. If we're lucky, it won't ever be an issue."

"Okay. Keep in touch."

As soon as she closed the phone, Cordelia was all over her for a replay of what Nolan had said.

"I'll tell you, but I have to eat something first."

"Fine," said Cordelia, leaping up.

Jane saw now that she was wearing a black halter-top dress with a sequined belt and a shredded handkerchief hem. It looked like the perfect evening wear for after that unexpected shipwreck. Totally inappropriate attire for the middle of an autumn day in chilly Minnesota. And of course, that's what made it so Cordelia.

"Tuck in your shirt and follow me down to Joanna's apartment. The official celebration starts at noon. Not that I'm exactly up for it. I thought Hattie would be with us. But we can't let Joanna down."

"Oh, Cordelia," said Jane, lying back against the pillows. "I don't feel like celebrating."

"But you feel like eating, right? She's having it catered. It's just a small affair. You and me and Joanna and Freddy. Oh, and Faye, too. It is a *must do*. Come on." She tugged on Jane's arm. Since she had the strength to flip Jane into the air, catch her, and carry her downstairs if she wanted to, the tug was a sop to Jane's reticence.

"Okay." Jane figured she'd eat something and then take off. She planned to spend the rest of the day looking for David.

"Let me pour you a glass," said Freddy. He was standing in the kitchen, opening a bottle of Roederer Cristal Rose Limited. Jane couldn't even imagine what it had cost. If it was under a thousand bucks she would have been surprised.

On the table in the dining room was a feast of hors d'oeuvres: a one-kilo tin of Beluga caviar surrounded by Russian-style blinis and crème fraîche; smoked salmon and dill timbales; fresh pears, green grapes and Roquefort cheese; and a plate of mango slices, foie gras, strips of rare roasted duck breast that had been drizzled with white truffle oil and chestnut honey. Jane knew what it all was because Joanna was standing next to it, martini in hand, explaining everything in great detail.

When her cell phone rang, Joanna's mood grew strained. "I'm going to break every goddamn phone I own. It's never anything but bad news."

Jane commiserated. "I know what you mean."

"Will you be a lamb and get that, Freddy?"

"Will do, Babycakes." He brought Cordelia and Jane each a filled champagne flute, then picked up the cell off the coffee table in the living room. "Yeah?" said Freddy. He listened a moment. Glancing back over his shoulder, he said, "Joanna, it's somebody named Hillary. She says she has an appointment with you. *Right now.*" He shot her an is-this-for-real look.

"Tell her I've changed my mind," said Joanna.

Freddy made quick work of brushing the woman off, then returned to the dining room. "I don't know about you folks, but this boy is starving."

"Have you heard from David?" asked Jane, sipping the champagne. It tasted like vinegar in her mouth.

"Not a word," said Joanna. "I told the police what I think. David couldn't have murdered Gordon. It's impossible. If he'd just come back here, I'm sure we could straighten everything out. Besides, the real murderer will be caught eventually."

"Or maybe not," said Freddy. "Be fine with me if he got away with it."

"If David does come back to the loft, will you call me?" asked Jane.

"Of course," said Joanna. "I know how much he means to you, too."

They all took their plates into the living room and sat down.

Faye brought up the rear. Jane had met her only once before—at Cordelia's card game last night. She'd sat in for about an hour, been very talkative at the table, but today, she seemed subdued. She glowered at Freddy as she sat down on one of the chairs. Jane wondered what the look was all about.

For the next half hour, Joanna talked about how relieved she was. Jane tried to follow the conversation, but it was impossible. All she could think about was David. She stayed long enough to have a slice of linzertorte, then excused herself. As she was heading out the front door, she saw a delivery man speeding toward her down the hallway. "What's that?" she asked, nodding to the package in his hand.

"Flowers," he said. "Are you—" He looked at the delivery slip. "Joanna Kasimir?"

"No," said Jane, feeling instantly wary. Drawing her eyes away from the package, she stepped back inside and said, "Joanna, there's a flower delivery for you."

All conversation stopped.

Joanna's eyes, sparkling from several drinks, registered shock.

"Flowers?" repeated Freddy. Rising from his chair, he said, "I'm sure it's nothing, babe. Let me take care of it." He signed the slip, then carried the package over to the dining room table and tore off the paper. Underneath was a bouquet of pink tea roses.

Jane closed the door and came back inside. She locked eyes with Cordelia.

"This . . . this has got to be a joke," said Joanna, giving a high, nervous laugh. "Freddy, is there a message?" She tried to sound light, but there was an unmistakable quiver in her voice.

A small white envelope was attached to a plastic card holder. Freddy opened it and read it silently.

"What does it say?" asked Joanna.

He looked up. "It's just what we thought. A joke. Let's toss the whole thing in the trash."

"No," said Joanna, standing up this time. "Read it."

"Babycakes—"

"Read it !"

Clearing his throat, he read,

> " *'See how much I love you?*
> *Maybe* now *you'll understand.'* "

30

Hillary stood just outside the Greek restaurant on the first floor of the Linden Building and stared at the open cell phone in her hand. Had she heard the man right? Joanna wasn't interested in giving an interview? She'd promised!

Hillary backed away from a pillar, then turned and rushed for the door.

Charging out into the gray afternoon light, she pressed her hands to the sides of her head, trying to stop her brain from spinning out of control. Somehow, she found her car, climbed in, and drove home, barely registering the other cars, the traffic lights, the people out walking or riding their bikes. Before she knew it, she was in the driveway of her father's house.

"Fuck," she screamed, glancing over at the new briefcase she'd brought. She'd gone out yesterday to look for one. Two hundred and seventy-nine dollars. All leather. She wanted to impress Joanna with her professionalism. She'd bought a Waterman fountain pen with a gold tip. Another hundred bucks. A digital camera so she could take pictures. Three hundred and change. A wool, rayon, and silk suit jacket and slacks. Anne Klein. Nordstrom. Even on sale it was over three hundred. But it fit like a glove, made her feel important. Stylish. So what was she supposed to do now? Go inside and impress her fat-assed father with how cool she looked?

Entering through the back door, she felt as if sharp claws were digging at her shoulder blades.

"Hill, that you?" Her father was in the living room, as usual. Watching something inane on the tube.

"Yeah," she yelled back. She opened the fridge and grabbed a Coke.

"Hill, would you get me a Sprite?"

"No. I'm busy," she said, adding, "you damn pervert," under her breath as she dashed up the stairs.

Flinging the briefcase on the bed, she cracked the top of the can, then stomped around the bedroom. She had to figure out what to do next. She'd signed a contract with the editor at *Mill City Magazine* that she'd have a feature article to him by tomorrow morning. They wanted it ASAP, mostly because they didn't want anyone else scooping them. The money she would earn would not only cover everything she'd bought but also put some cash in the bank. Joanna Kasimir's name was like catnip to an editor. Hillary had talked it up, said they were friends, that she'd picked Joanna up at Flying Cloud the day her private jet had landed. That she'd never used her journalism degree before, but now she felt it was time. The guy wanted a résumé, samples of what she'd written, but Hillary said to take the deal or leave it. If he didn't want it, somebody else would.

She liked playing hardball with the big guys, felt that she was born to do it. This was her big break. How could Joanna have shafted her? They were kindred spirits. Sisters.

Sitting down on the bed, Hillary pulled off her jacket and unbuttoned her blouse. She moved slowly, deliberately. Once she'd undressed, she hung up the new suit in the closet and then picked up her Coke and walked into the bathroom.

She stood next to the toilet and examined herself in the mirror. "You're a loser," she said, a disgusted sneer on her face. "I hate you. You're a worm. You deserve nothing and that's what you get. You're fat. Ugly. Useless!" A rushing noise filled her ears. She was repulsed, sickened by the sight of her breasts, her hair, her face. Everything about her was just gross.

She opened the medicine cabinet and took out a razor. She felt like a spectator watching someone else. Staring at her image in the mirror, she cut herself, sliced her upper thigh right next to the other cuts that had healed into scars. Blood trickled down her leg. It wasn't real. But then the pain hit. She closed hear eyes, breathed in deeply, felt a sense of release.

It wasn't enough. Easing down against the shower door, she cut herself again. Her upper arm, where nobody could see but Cody. He didn't understand. He never would. Each time she cut again, the tension in her body eased a little more. A few more drops of blood dripped onto the bathroom floor. She set the razor on her knee.

"I hate you," she said, staring up at the ceiling. "I hate you, Joanna Kasimir. You ruined everything. You'll pay for treating me like I'm nothing. That's a promise—and I *keep* my promises."

31

With Mouse in tow, Jane began her search for David by covering the bars closest to the Linden Building and then fanning out. It was slow, tedious work. She had a photo of him in her wallet, a close-up, one he'd sent her several years ago. He and Diego had taken a cruise to the eastern Caribbean. He was standing on a beach in St. Maarten, looking windblown and happy. Examining his face, she had a hard time believing it was the same ravaged-looking man she'd seen last night in the stairwell.

At the Gay Nineties on Hennepin, one of the best-known gay bars in the Twin Cities, she talked to lots of people who hesitated over the snapshot. One man, a dark-haired preppy type in his early thirties, hesitated the longest, but in the end, said David looked like a man he'd talked to last night, but he couldn't be sure.

At the Brass Rail, Jane spoke with anyone who would talk to her. She must have handed out thirty cards. Before she left, she ran into a real lowlife character—a seedy-looking guy with tin-colored hair. He smelled bad and looked dirty. His face lit up when he saw the picture, but he turned back to his drink without comment. When she pressed him on it, he said he'd never seen the man before and to leave him alone. Jane pulled one of her cards out of her pocket and set it down next to his beer.

Around seven, feeling tired and dispirited, she took Mouse for a walk down by the Mississippi River. They both needed some fresh air. She'd been racking her brain all afternoon trying to think of where David might have gone. She had a headache from all the thinking.

As she sat down on the bench, she gazed at the water. It was a gray, dreary evening. The river looked hard, like it was made of liquid slate. If David wanted to drink and be invisible, he'd probably pick someplace dark and divey, someplace out of the way. Considering all the dark, out-of-the-way dives in the Twin Cities, Jane figured she could be at this for years.

"Okay, Mouse. Just listen. If David thinks he's losing his mind, and if you add to that the knowledge—real or imagined—that he may have killed someone, I think it's possible he took off. He ran away from Atlanta. I think there's a better than even chance that he's done the same now—left Minneapolis. You agree?"

Mouse liked to listen, but he wasn't quick with opinions.

"It's a hard call." Looking down at the phone in her hand, she pushed in the number for Nolan. When he picked up, she said, "It's Jane. Where are you?"

"Working at home."

"Did you hear about the roses Joanna received today?"

"Got an earful from both her and her boyfriend."

"What do you think?"

"I think," he said, releasing a breath, "that we've been spinning our wheels. All this time we thought Luberman was sending the flowers. Now it turns out it was someone else."

Jane had come to the same conclusion.

"Hitchcock called me a few minutes ago. Get this. Around one this afternoon, they pulled a woman's body out of Whitefish Lake."

Her eyes fastened on the river. "Is it—"

"They found a ring on one of the fingers. The father ID'd it. The

264

body's pretty badly decomposed, so they'll have to do tests to make sure, but Hitchcock sounded pretty positive."

Jane's thoughts started to ricochet like pinballs. "That means whoever killed Luberman thinking he was doing Joanna a favor, if he'd just waited, if he'd just given it a little more time, none of it would have been necessary."

"The police would have done their job and Luberman would be behind bars by now."

Jane shook her head, trying to absorb what it all meant. "So if Joanna hadn't hired you and sent us chasing after him, none of this would have happened. It was her fear that drew him back into her life. Talk about a tragedy of errors."

"That about covers it. But we've got to move on because there's someone out there who may still present a danger to Joanna."

"I wondered about that, too." She looked down at Mouse, pulled his ear.

"I had Joanna's people in L.A. send me the current files on the crazies in her life. It's all on a CD. I never looked at it because I thought Luberman was our man."

"Do the police have a copy of the CD?"

"I burned two copies. Sent one over to Drea. That's what I've been looking at for the last half hour. What fries me is the bizarre stuff people do. Get this. One fan in Florida sends her his hair clippings— every time he gets a haircut. You wouldn't believe the kind of crap people mail her. 'Course, I shouldn't be surprised after what I've seen in my lifetime, but I have to admit, I am. Hey, I don't suppose I could get you to take a look at this file."

"Is the file divided by areas of the country?"

"No, by levels of potential danger. You got anything on your agenda for the rest of the night?"

"I've been out looking for David."

"Any luck?"

"Nope."

"Then stop by. I'll give you the disk and you can take it home. If you find something, let me know."

Jane figured she might as well keep busy. She had no desire to spend any more time running around the city, looking for the proverbial needle in a haystack.

As she hung up, a runner came past. Mouse tugged at the leash. And that's when Jane remembered Brandy. At least she was safe now that Gordon was dead. But she probably hadn't heard the news.

Using her cell phone again, she called directory assistance and was put through to the IHOP in Eagle Ridge. The man who answered said that Brandy wasn't there. She was supposed to be working the evening shift but hadn't come in and hadn't called. He sounded frustrated, said he'd called her house about an hour ago, but there was no answer.

Panic squeezed Jane hard. She disconnected and tapped in 411 right away, asked to be connected to the sheriff's office in Eagle Ridge.

"Hi, my name's Jane Lawless. I live in Minneapolis. There's a woman in your town you need to check on—something might have happened to her. Her name is Brandy Becker. She was dating Gordon Luberman. You know who he is?"

The officer said he did.

"Brandy didn't show up for work tonight, and she doesn't answer her home phone. Can you send someone over to her house to see if she's okay? It's urgent. She could be hurt—or worse."

Once Jane was assured an officer would be sent immediately, she asked if someone could call her back, let her know that Brandy was safe. She gave the man her cell number, thanked him, then hung up.

32

Cordelia was so bone weary from worrying about Hattie and from general lack of sleep that even the tips of her fingers were deeply, profoundly enervated. She could barely type in her Web mail address as she sat at the computer in her study. Without Hattie playing in the living room, the loft felt lifeless. Cordelia had wasted an entire afternoon tap dancing as fast as she could, trying to prevent Joanna from having a complete meltdown. It had taken her mind off her own problems, so maybe it hadn't been a complete waste of time. She'd lit incense. Chanted her own—secret—mantra. Made gallons of soothing chamomile tea.

When none of that worked, she'd run upstairs to her loft and brought back a do-it-yourself feng shui space-cleaning kit. She'd draped a healing stone necklace around Joanna's neck, run around the loft with a lit organic juniper space-cleaning wand, especially useful for quick tune-ups. She'd used special rock salt, excellent for removing negative energy, or "sha chi" from interior space. She sprinkled it across the doorways, dumped little piles in the corners of rooms, thus preventing the "sha chi" from escaping into the atmosphere. And finally, she'd held a singing bowl next to Joanna's ear and banged it over and over again with a rosewood wand. When Joanna screamed, "Feng shui is shit!" Cordelia decided to try something else.

She got out her tarot cards and did a special reading, lying through her teeth, telling Joanna all would be well when, in reality, the cards spoke of nothing but doom!

"That woman is cursed," muttered Cordelia, finally bringing up her Web mail. Dropping her chin on her hand, she looked down at Blanche, the matriarch of her cat colony, who was sitting next to the computer. "You know, maybe I should have tried my Tibetan tingsha bells." Thinking about it a moment more, she said, "Nah."

Checking through her e-mail, she found a bunch of messages for enlarging her penis, pharmacy addresses where she could get cheap Viagra. A woman named "Hot Mamma" offered to perform wild illegal acts on her if she'd just click on her site.

"And all this wonderful news," muttered Cordelia, "even with my spam blocker set on 'stun.' "

But there, in the midst of all this junk, was a note from RCunningham. Cordelia clicked on the words, "From Cecily." Up came the e-mail.

> Cordelia, it's me. I'm using Radley's computer. He and your sister are downstairs with Hattie, but they should be back any minute. I feel like I'm in prison!
>
> I wanted you to know that Hattie is okay. Well, she was actually really having fun for the first few days, but today she seems kind of sullen. Keeps saying she misses you. Keeps asking why she can't talk to you. I'm not sure what Octavia is up to, but I want you to know that the only reason I'm here is to provide Hattie with some continuity.
>
> Octavia needs to leave for L.A. on Friday so I assume she'll drop us back at the loft before that. I think she really enjoys making you sweat. So nasty! I can tell she's already sick of having

Hattie around all the time. But she's putting up a good show for Radley's sake. He seems like a nice enuf guy and I feel sorry for him, getting mixed up with a piece of work like Octavia.

Boy, am sick to death of her big, fake innocent eyes. Oh, somehow or other, I've managed to lose my cell phone. Can't imagine what I did with it because I'm always so careful to put it back in my purse. Octavia checks the hotel bill every morning. She told me if I called you that she'd not only fire me, but she'd take me to court. I'm not sure what that means, but she's not somebody I want to mess with. So that's why I haven't called.

Oh, Jeez, here they come. Later.

As sick as the note made Cordelia feel, it also gave her hope for the first time in days that she'd see Hattie again soon. If all Octavia wanted was to stick it to her, fine. Stick away. As long as Hattie came home at the end of Octavia's martial arts event.

The ring of Cordelia's phone startled her. As soon as she picked up, she heard, "I can't stay in this loft another minute! If I don't get out, I'll lose my mind completely!"

"Hi, Joanna. Long time no see."

"And since Nolan tells me I still can't go outside without risking my life, Freddy and I are coming up to your loft for dinner. We don't care what we eat. Anything you prepare is fine."

"Prepare?" said Cordelia.

"Don't go to any trouble. We're just folks."

Just folks. Right.

The last thing Cordelia wanted was to spend even one more minute with those two. But, of course, she would. Because she was nothing if not a stellar friend. However. Cooking was another matter entirely. "I have about twenty-five take-out menus I'd be happy to share with you. Unless you'd like PediaSure and Toaster Strudel for dinner. *That's* what I've got to eat."

"Takeout sounds fine," said Joanna. "We'll be up in a sec."

Cordelia took that second to change into something more comfortable. A bright pink-and-yellow caftan. She stabbed chopsticks through her hair to get it off her neck, then met the happy couple at the door.

"It's really nice of you to invite us up," said Freddy.

Like she had a choice.

Freddy had changed into jeans with a crease down the front of the legs and a red flannel cowboy shirt. Hiho, Silver. Joanna was still in her blue gown, but she'd redone her makeup, so she no longer looked like Vampira.

They settled on an extra-large Pizza Margarita, which the restaurant said would arrive within the hour.

Cordelia brought out three diet Pepsis.

"Cordelia," said Joanna, crossing her legs and clearing her throat. "There was another reason I wanted to come up here. I have some bad news, I'm afraid, but I hope you'll take it like the friend you've always been."

Cordelia couldn't take *any* more news—good or bad. She sank down on the ottoman.

"I simply can't go on with the play. Freddy and I are leaving, flying to South America on Saturday."

"What!" Cordelia felt as if an anvil had dropped out of the sky and landed on her head. "Are you serious? You're backing out!"

"She has to," said Freddy. "Surely you see why she can't stay here. There's a wack job out there breathing down her neck."

"But—"

"I've found a replacement for you, if you'll give me a chance to explain," said Freddy.

"Replacement?"

"Eugenia Benet. I know she's not in Joanna's league—"

Cordelia sniffed the air. "Really? Eugenia!"

"Don't sound so eager, dear," said Joanna, sipping her Pepsi. "I can always change my mind."

"No. I mean, yes! That works for me."

"Good," said Freddy. "I'll call her in the morning. She'll be here by next Monday. Same deal as Joanna's. Oh, and by the way, if I were you, I'd find her a different place to live while she's in town."

"Sure. Anything. I mean, I'll be sorry to see you go," said Cordelia, trying to project sadness with just the right amount of nostalgic regret.

"Cut the crap," said Joanna. "You'll be happy to see me go. I've been nothing but trouble."

"Not you," said Cordelia. "It wasn't your fault."

The pizza arrived early. They talked companionably for another hour or so while they ate, and then Joanna and Freddy bid Cordelia a good night.

Cordelia felt sure she would be sad to see them go. At least a little.

As soon as Freddy and Joanna were back in their loft, Joanna went to open a bottle of wine. "Someone's been in here," she said, turning to Freddy, a frightened look on her face.

"How could you possibly know that?"

Diving behind a chair, she whispered, "Look around."

"Maybe we should call the police?"

"Please! Just check it out."

Freddy seemed flustered. His face turned crimson and he appeared to dither as he stood next to the chain-saw bear sculpture. Finally, picking up an empty champagne bottle by the neck, he crouched. "I'll take care of it. If I don't find anything, I'll call an all clear."

Joanna watched him enter the kitchen, then disappear into the back of the loft, where the bedrooms were located. She could hear him opening and closing closet doors. Next, one of the shower doors. The seconds ticked by.

"Oh, Christ," he said after nearly a minute. "What the hell?"

"What is it?" called Joanna.

"You better come look."

She found him in the bathroom standing in front of the mirror.

Cracks spread out from a central impact point like a spiderweb. Underneath, someone had written in lipstick:

> You don't play fair!
> I demand respect.
> And don't forget,
> I OWN YOU! ! ! ! ! ! ! ! !

33

Jane was sitting at Cordelia's computer, examining the CD Nolan had given her, when her cell phone rang. She hoped it would be a cop from Eagle Ridge with good news.

"Is this Jane?" came a tentative voice.

"Yes? Who's calling?"

"This is Brandy Becker. You saved my life."

Jane felt a wave of relief wash over her. "Are you okay?"

Brandy explained that Gordon had tied her up in the kitchen of her house yesterday afternoon. When she heard the police outside her back door a few minutes ago, she'd tried to make as much noise as possible so they'd break down the door. She'd been sitting in the dark all night, waiting for Gordon to come back. She was sure he was going to kill her.

"That won't happen," said Jane. "He's dead."

Silence. "Dead?"

"He was shot and killed last night here in Minneapolis."

"Lord, why?"

"We're not sure. Did the police tell you about the body they dredged from Whitefish Lake?"

"Yes. That's why I had to call—to thank you. I don't know what I would have done if you hadn't warned me about him. You're a very special woman."

"I'm just glad you're safe."

"Someday I'll find a way to thank you properly."

They talked for a few more seconds and then said good-bye. As Jane set the cell phone down next to the computer, Cordelia dragged through the front door.

"Another crisis," she said, sinking down on a chair, narrowly missing one of her cats.

Jane looked over at her. "I don't even want to ask."

Cordelia explained about dinner, about Joanna backing out of the production.

"That's it? That's the crisis?"

"No, no. Give me a chance, will you? I have to do this in a linear fashion. I'm too tired to explain it any other way."

Cordelia finally got to the point—the shattered mirror and the message. "This is way too weird for me. Makes me feel like moving to Iowa."

"No, it doesn't."

"You're right. It doesn't. What are you reading?"

Jane explained about the files, then told her about the body found in Whitefish Lake—about how ironic it had been that Joanna had essentially caused Luberman to come back into her life. She'd jumped to a wrong conclusion about the flowers, and that had become the first domino in a long chain that eventually led to Luberman and the guard's murder.

"I hate irony," said Cordelia. "It so ironic."

"Why don't you get out your reading glasses and help me look through this file?"

"No, no. We've got to talk about the mirror thing! That file is a waste of time. Reading about people in South Carolina or Arizona, I mean, who cares? Whoever got into Joanna's apartment while we were all having dinner must've had a key. It's got to be someone in this building. We need action, Jane! Instinct, and pure, hard, cold logic."

"I think you're right about the key. But with the amount of sleep we've both missed, I doubt we have the brainpower between us to open a can of soup."

"Piffle." Cordelia got up and, as usual, began to pace. "Let's think this through. How could someone get a key to that loft?"

"You go first."

"Well, I have one. Tammi Bonifay, the woman who owns the loft, gave me two sets when she agreed to sublet. I gave both to Joanna, made myself an extra set—it's on my key ring in my desk drawer, right in front of where you're sitting there. And, of course, there's a master key down in the Tenants' Association office. But that's kept locked, and the keys themselves are in a safe."

"Cross that off, then," said Jane.

"Unless we've got a stalker psychic."

Cordelia always came up with such useful ideas. "Who would have access to your set of keys?"

"You. Hattie. Cecily."

"What about while you're at work?"

"Who'd be interested in my keys at the theater?"

Jane shrugged. "Just a thought."

Cordelia stood in front of the windows and looked down at the city. "Think, Jane!"

"I am!"

"Think harder. Whoever got into Joanna's apartment had a key."

"Where's Bonifay?"

"Madrid. I wonder if she ever gave a key to anyone. You know, like someone to water her plants if she happened to be gone."

"What if she gave it to another tenant in the building?" Jane felt as if a light switch had just burst on inside her. "That's it, Cordelia. Whoever knifed Luberman met him on the stairs. I didn't see it before, but you're right. It had to be someone who lived *in* the building.

The police thought it was David, but what if it was one of the other tenants? This person knifes Luberman, then slips back to his apartment and nobody's any the wiser." Except, thought Jane, there was one big hole in that theory. How did this person get his hands on her Global knife? Unless it *was* David. "Do you have a number for Bonifay in Madrid?"

"In the Tenants' Association office in the basement."

"What are we waiting for?" asked Jane. "Let's give her a call."

Downstairs in Joanna's loft, the phone rang. Joanna was lying on the couch, a cool washcloth draped over her forehead. Freddy rushed in from the kitchen, where he'd been heating them mugs of cocoa in the microwave. Answering the phone, he said, "Yeah, what?" He wasn't in a good mood.

"This is Abbott Northwestern Hospital calling for Joanna Kasimir." The woman's voice had an Indian accent.

"Hospital?" repeated Freddy. "What's this about?"

Joanna sat up.

"I'm an emergency room nurse. Indrani Azim. We just admitted a woman who is asking for Ms. Kasimir. The woman is in serious condition. We were hoping Ms. Kasimir might be able to come down to the hospital."

"What's the woman's name?" asked Freddy.

"Cordelia. That's all we know."

"My God! What happened?"

"We believe it was a suicide attempt. Do you need directions to the hospital?"

Freddy glanced down at Joanna. "Do you know where Abbott Northwestern Hospital is?"

"Sure? Why?"

"We'll be right there."

"What?" said Joanna.

"The nurse said they just brought Cordelia in. She tried to commit suicide?"

"Not possible. We just saw her."

"But that was over an hour ago."

Joanna's instincts told her it was a ruse to get her out of the building. She grabbed the phone out of Freddy's hand and punched in Cordelia's number. She let it ring and ring. When the voice mail picked up, she cut the line. "I still don't believe it. Did the nurse give you her name?"

"Indrani Azim."

"I'll bet you Abbott Northwestern's never heard of a Indrani Azim." She called directory assistance and then waited while she was connected. "Emergency room, please," she said, looking up at Freddy.

Two rings. Three. "Emergency," said a male voice.

"Do you have a nurse named Indrani Azim working tonight?"

"Let me check." A moment later, the man came back. "Yes, but she's with a patient at the moment. Can I take a message?"

Joanna couldn't believe it. "Did you just admit a woman named Thorn?"

"Sorry, we can't give out that information. If you'd like, I could have Indrani call you back."

"No," said Joanna. "It's okay. Thanks." Her eyes rose to Freddy's. "The nurse is for real."

"If something really did happen to Cordelia and she's asking for you—"

"I know," said Joanna. "I know." She looked down at her nightclothes, unsure what to do.

"The nurse said she was in serious condition."

That did it. "Call Nolan. See how fast he can have a car and driver for us."

Rushing back to her bedroom, she threw off her nightclothes and changed into jeans and a sweater. She was scared to death to leave the building, but if Cordelia was asking for her, she had to go.

Down in the basement of the Linden Building, Cordelia and Jane searched through Bonifay's file until they found a piece of paper with a number for her in Madrid.

"What time is it there?" asked Cordelia, sitting down behind the desk.

Jane looked up at the clock on the cement wall, did a quick calculation. "It's just after ten here, so that means it would be just after five in the morning in Spain."

"So even though Tammi likes to party, she should be home by now." Cordelia punched in the number using the phone on the desktop, then hit speakerphone so they could both hear.

Jane sat on the edge of the desk. It was the first time she'd ever been in the tenants' office. It was a depressing room, made even more depressing by the fact that it was tiny and windowless. Cordelia always made being president of the tenants' association sound as if it was just one rung lower than being president of Microsoft. So much for Cordelia's ability to hype what was essentially unhypable.

After several odd-sounding rings, a voice answered. "Hello?"

"Tammi?" shouted Cordelia, as if she had to yell across the pond to be heard. "It's Cordelia Thorn."

"Who?"

"Cordelia Thorn. Back in Minnesota."

"Wait. Let me turn on the light." After a few seconds she was back. "Do you know what time it is?"

"Late here. Early there. I suppose I should say good morning."

"What's wrong? Why are you calling me?"

"I need to know if you've ever given your key to one of the other tenants."

"Why? Did something happen to my loft?" Now she sounded upset.

"No, Tammi, your loft is fine."

"Stop yelling," whispered Jane.

"Hey, is someone else there with you?" asked Tammi. "Is it the police? What the hell's going on?"

"Nothing. Your . . . loft . . . is . . . fine. How many ways can I say it?"

"Then why did you call?"

Cordelia huffed. "Have you ever given your key to one of the other tenants?"

"Yeah," she said finally. "I gave it to Milan Mestrovik once so he could deliver some wine while I was out. But he gave me the key back. No big deal."

"Anyone else?"

"You know, like, to water my plants, pick up my mail downstairs? It's not illegal. I know you think that ever since you were elected president of the tenants' council that you're the fucking Gestapo, but you're not."

Cordelia stiffened. "Who did you give the key to?" she demanded.

"Don't take that high-minded tone with me. I gave it to Faye, okay? She's right across the hall. I mean, she offered. It's not like I twisted her arm or anything. And for your information, if a woman wants to do a little coke in the privacy of her own home, it's none of your damn business. Is that what this is all about? Kasimir found some of my stash?"

"Thanks, Tammi. Go back to sleep now."

"Yeah, like I can sleep after you got me all riled up."

"How's the coke in Madrid?"

The conversation ended with a dial tone.

"Actually, I always suspected she was a doper," said Cordelia with a satisfied sigh. "With the hideous decorating in that loft, you have to be medicated or you couldn't survive."

"We got our answer," said Jane.

"Two of them," said Cordelia. "Now what?"

Across town, Joanna and Freddy walked into the bright lights of the emergency room.

"I can't believe this is happening," said Joanna.

Freddy gave their names at the desk, explained that Indrani Azim had called them, that they were waiting to see Cordelia Thorn. A young dark-haired nurse in blue scrubs finally came out, introducing herself as Indrani.

"How's Cordelia doing?" asked Freddy.

"Can we see her?" asked Joanna.

The nurse gazed at them sympathetically. "She's lost a lot of blood. I'm afraid she's very weak. She cut her wrists. The police brought her in. I'm not sure where they found her exactly, but I was told it was in an alley somewhere in Richfield. She didn't have any identification on her, but she gave the name 'Cordelia' to one of the paramedics. Wouldn't give us any other information, except to call you. She kept repeating your number."

"Richfield?" said Joanna, giving Freddy a confused look. "What on earth was Cordelia doing there?" For a brief moment, she wondered if the fact that she'd pulled out of the production at the theater had prompted this moment of insanity, but then she remembered Cordelia's reaction to Eugenia's name. Maybe it was the problems over Hattie that had caused a mental break. "I need to see her."

"As I said, she's very weak. I can only let one of you in at a time."

"You go," said Freddy.

Joanna followed the nurse back through a locked door. The patient cubicles circled the main emergency desk. When she finally entered the room, she saw that a curtain had been drawn around the bed. The lights were low.

Pulling the curtain back, the nurse said, "I'll be right outside. Anything you need, just ask."

Joanna was about to say thanks when she realized the woman lying in the bed wasn't Cordelia. "Who——" She turned to the nurse, but she'd already gone.

"Don't go," came a tiny voice.

The woman was hooked up to all sorts of monitors. She was being given blood through a tube taped to her hand. Her skin looked deathly pale.

"Who are you?" asked Joanna, keeping her distance. She hated hospitals. Her first reaction on seeing that it wasn't Cordelia was to bolt.

She couldn't be sure this wasn't a setup, a way to draw her out of the loft into the open. And yet, staring at the strange woman, it hardly seemed possible.

"You don't remember me," said a tiny, flat voice. "Why would you?"

Joanna could hardly hear her. She took a couple of steps closer. "Have we met?"

"Hillary. The journalist. Remember? Flying Cloud? We talked. You were nice to me. I thought . . . we were friends."

Joanna looked down, shook her head. And then she remembered. "Of course." As her eyes met Hillary's, she realized she had absolutely no idea why she was here. "Why did you have the hospital call *me*?"

Gazing up at Joanna with a strangely satisfied smile on her face, Hillary whispered, "You came. I knew you would."

Joanna might be a little slow on the uptake, but she got it now. "You gave the nurse Cordelia's name because you knew if I thought she was in the emergency room, I'd come."

"I'm so glad you're here."

Joanna was at a complete loss. The summons *was* a ruse. Was the suicide attempt a ruse too? "Why did you . . . do it?"

Hillary closed her eyes. After a long moment, she said, "I couldn't stop."

"You couldn't stop what?"

"Cutting."

"You *wanted* to end your life?"

A nod.

"Is it that awful, that hopeless?"

"*I'm* hopeless," she whispered. "Worthless. Nothing I want ever comes true."

"What do you want?"

"Nothing very much." Looking up at Joanna, she bit her lip. "A small thing, really. I want you to love me."

"What?" Joanna felt like someone had just hit her with a brick. "We're strangers."

"No, we're not. You listened when I talked about my dreams. You understood. Tell me I'm wrong."

"Well—"

"Will you hold my hand? Just for a minute. I won't ask for anything else. Please?" Her eyes pleaded.

"Hillary, I don't—"

"Yes, you do. You know me. You *are* me. We're sisters."

Before Joanna could stop herself, she'd moved up to the bed and covered Hillary's hand with her own. "How's that?"

"Good," she whispered. Looking up at Joanna with tears in her eyes, she said, "It's really you, right? I'm not dreaming this?"

"It's really me," said Joanna, a bewildered look on her face. "I'm sorry you felt you had no other choice but to . . . I mean . . . the cuts . . . you didn't do it just to—" No, thought Joanna, that was way the hell too far beyond the pale.

"Yes," whispered Hillary. "That was part of it." Turning her head away, she withdrew her hand. "You better go. You're important. You've got important things to do."

"I can stay a few more minutes."

"No, I want you to go."

"Why?"

"Because . . . because I'm *pathetic,* that's why. You think this is the first time I've tried it?"

"Isn't it?"

"I told you, I'm worthless. I bought all these clothes so that when I interviewed you, you'd think I was cool. But then you nixed it because you knew I'm not any of that. I'm an impostor. I hate myself. I'm not like you at all. I just pretend. It works for a while, but then . . . I know inside what I really am and I want to puke my guts out!"

"Hillary—"

"Do you have any idea how much I love you? I'd do anything for you. *Anything.*"

Joanna felt crushed by the weight of the comment. How could

something so empty feel so heavy? "But don't you have other relationships—a boyfriend? A family?"

"All my boyfriend wants from me is sex. As for my dad, I'd be happier if he were six feet under."

"How can you say that?"

"Because of what he did—what he *is*."

Joanna felt she knew what was coming next. But she had the sense that Hillary wanted her to ask. "Did he molest you when you were a child?"

"What? Christ, no," she rasped. "If he'd ever touched me I would have killed him. It's what he did to my girlfriend. We were thirteen. He raped her. She said it was all her idea, but I knew she was just lying to make it all go away."

"How do you know he raped her?"

"I heard her crying, walked in on them. I never told anyone. Just like my friend. I took the easy way out. But I told you now. I trust you, Joanna. You're the only one who knows my secret. Doesn't that mean something?"

"Where was your mother when it happened?"

"At work. I hated her, too. She's dead now and that's just fine with me. My job sucks. I don't have a single friend I care about. All I care about is *you,* and you're too goddamn important to give me the time of day."

"Hillary, you can't actually expect me to . . . I mean, if all the people who consider themselves fans of mine expected me to love them . . . it's impossible."

"So go. Get out."

"You have to be reasonable, think about this rationally."

"No, I don't. I think with my heart. That's who I am. I thought we were soul mates, but I see now that we're not. You're cold, Joanna. You don't care about anyone but yourself."

"That's not true." She didn't know why, but she felt like she was pleading for her life. "All I am is an actor. I'm not the parts I play in movies. I'm not heroic. I can't be expected to take care of people I don't even know." She felt like she was in a cage with a herd of wild animals all trying to rip chunks out of her flesh.

The nurse burst back into the cubicle. "I'm sorry, but you've got to keep your voice down." She gave Joanna a stern look.

"I can't do this," said Joanna, feeling as if every fuse in her brain was about to blow. Turning, she rushed out of the room.

34

You be the good cop and I'll be the bad cop," said Cordelia.

"Not a good idea," said Jane, striding down the hall toward Faye's loft. They'd already tried Milan's place, but he was either out or refusing to talk to them. "We want answers. That means we need her cooperation."

Jane knocked on the door, glad Cordelia didn't own an Uzi.

"She's in there," whispered Cordelia. "I can smell the smoke. Carcinogen city. We should get hazard pay for going in there."

Jane knocked again. The door finally cracked open, revealing a thin slice of Faye's face.

"Cordelia?" she said, a question mark in her voice. "I thought . . . I mean, how are you feeling?"

"Me? Fine."

"Are you sure? 'Cause I thought . . ." Her voice trailed off.

"Thought what?"

"Oh, nothing. I guess . . . I guess I'm confused." A cigarette dangled from her mouth. She took a drag, then blew smoke out her nose. "Kind of late for a social call."

"Can we come in?" asked Jane.

Faye regarded Cordelia a moment more, then said, "'Spose so.

You're in luck, ladies. Just took some chocolate chip cookies out of the oven. I always bake when I can't sleep."

"Cookies," said Cordelia, sniffing the air, then coughing as the Chesterfields clogged her airways.

On her way to the kitchen, Faye said, "Did you know Joanna and that piss bag ex-husband of hers left the building 'bout half an hour ago?"

Cordelia did a double take. "Are you kidding me?"

"Nope," said Faye, piling some of the warm cookies onto a plate. "Here, I got milk."

"No thanks," said Jane. "Did Joanna tell you why she was leaving?"

"Since the piss bag arrived, she hasn't had much time for me."

"I wonder where they went?" said Cordelia, helping herself to the biggest cookie on the plate.

"I saw them get into a limo together," said Faye, staring hard at Cordelia for a long moment, then shaking her head. "Watched out my back window, I did. Wouldn't think she'd leave the safety of the building since she got another flower delivery this afternoon."

"Look, Faye," said Jane. "We know you have a key to Joanna's loft."

"Who told you that?"

"Tammi Bonifay."

"Oh. Well, yeah. I got one. So what?"

"You ever go in there when Joanna wasn't around?"

"What are you insinuating?"

"Someone broke the mirror in Joanna's bathroom earlier this evening, and then wrote a message in lipstick on what was left of it."

"Yeah? So?"

"You don't act very surprised," said Cordelia, her right hand hovering next to the plate, waiting for Faye to look away so she could snatch another cookie.

"I'm not surprised by anything that happens to that woman."

"Whoever wrote the message didn't break in," said Jane. "The person had a key."

"Tammi probably gave keys to other folks."

"Just one," said Jane. "But the man gave it back."

"What did you mean when you wrote, 'I own you'?" Cordelia asked.

Go right for the jugular, thought Jane.

"Don't know what you're talking about," said Faye.

"And the flowers. You sent all of them, right?"

"No law against sending flowers—if I did, which I didn't. Most people'd look upon it as a kindness."

They tried a few more questions, but Jane realized they were getting nowhere, so she yanked Cordelia away from the cookies and said good night.

"We could have pressed her harder," said Cordelia on the way to the elevator. "She knows more than she's telling."

"I get that same feeling, but we can't beat it out of her."

Cordelia grunted. "I could have *leaned* on her a little."

"Cordelia!"

They returned to her loft. As Jane sat down at the computer and Cordelia retreated to the bathroom to soak in the tub, her cell phone rang again. She checked the caller ID but didn't recognize the number. "Hello," she said, checking the e-mail at her office.

"Is this Jane Lawless?"

It was a man. She didn't recognize the voice. "Yes?"

"We met yesterday at the Brass Rail. You showed me a picture of a guy. David Carlson. I know where he is."

A gust of hope blew into her chest. "Where?"

"I want two hundred bucks, okay?"

"No problem. Just tell me where to come."

He repeated the address. It was a hotel on Hennepin, one she'd never heard of. Most of the downtown hotels on Hennepin were flophouses. "I'll be there in ten minutes."

"Room two oh four. Knock twice."

"Is David okay?"

"You'll see when you come." The line disconnected.

Jane shot off her chair and grabbed her car keys and her jeans jacket. "Cordelia, I'm leaving. Take care of Mouse, okay?"

She didn't wait for a response. She charged down the back steps and jumped into her Mini. She found a parking place in a lot half a block from the hotel and rushed up the steps to the second floor. The smell of stale smoke, sour sweet, ancient dirt, and urine hung in the air. She tried to swallow back her revulsion, but with all the emotions swirling around inside her, she felt like she had a basset hound stuck in her chest. She knocked twice on the door and waited.

The man with the tin-colored hair opened the door a crack, then slipped out into the hall. "You got the money?" He was excruciatingly thin, with the kind of yellowish skin that came from spending every waking moment indoors, probably sitting at a bar. He'd rolled up the sleeves of his T-shirt, as if he had biceps he wanted to show off.

Jane pulled her wallet out of her back pocket.

The man chewed his lips as she counted out ten twenty-dollar bills. She was glad he hadn't asked for more because the two hundred pretty much cleaned her out.

"Found him in an alley," he said, pocketing the money. "He'd passed out. He doesn't belong here. But if you don't help him, this is where he'll end up—or under a bridge sleeping on a piece of cardboard. I like him. Figure, with a friend like you, he's got a chance. I don't want him here when I get back. Understood?"

Jane nodded.

"Tell him . . . tell him I said good-bye, okay?"

Jane watched him disappear down the stairs, then turned and entered the room. There was only one light on inside, on the nightstand next to the bed, and it was pretty dim. She glanced around for another one to turn on, but there weren't any. The bed was made. Two empty gin bottles sat on the window ledge next to it. Squinting into the semi-darkness, she saw David sitting in a chair next to a beat-up love seat. His face was turned away from her, but he was awake, smoking.

She let the stillness settle in between them for a few seconds. "David?" she said finally. "I came to take you home." Moving a few steps closer, she saw that one side of his face was scraped and raw. She felt a sudden sadness expand inside her chest.

She wasn't sure what he'd say or do. She remembered Nolan's warning, asking her to contact him before she met with David. But all that faded away. It was just the two of them. The way it should be. "Did you hear me?"

A rocky moment followed as her words hung in the air.

Finally, he cleared his throat. "Remember when we first met?"

He'd given her an opening. It was something she could work with. "Sure I do. Like it was yesterday."

"It was at a dance. I'd seen you running track, thought you were pretty hot. So I cut in. We danced four more songs together. I charmed you with the wonderfulness of me, then we went outside. It was fall. We walked over to the football field and sat on the bleachers."

"You tried to kiss me."

"I *did* kiss you. Do you remember what you said?"

Jane struggled to recall. "That—"

"You said it was *nice*. Nice! So I asked you if you wanted me to kiss you again."

"How did I respond?"

He smiled. "*Not really,* you said. That's a quote. I was shattered."

"I doubt that."

"And then, just to push a little more, I said, hell, don't you like guys? For Christ's sake, I was a football jock. Prime pickings."

"And I said I liked them well enough."

"Precisely. Not a glowing recommendation. So, as a joke, I asked if you liked girls better. And there was *that long pause.* If you hadn't paused, Jane, our lives would never have connected. We told each other the truth that night. It was one of the most important nights of my life. It's amazing, really. One minute you're alone in the universe and then circuits connect."

When he looked up at her, she knew with total certainty that those blue eyes of his were still wired to her soul. "Let's tell the truth again. Right now, Davey."

With a straight face, he said, "Okay. I finally figured it out. I've got a vitamin deficiency, Jane. That's all. Low on my B complex."

"Don't start joking around. Not now. Be serious."

"That's all I ever am these days. And I'm sick of it."

"Let me take you home."

"You don't like this place?" He spread his arms wide.

"No, I don't."

"Whose home are we talking about? Your home? Aren't you afraid I'll burn it down? Blow it up?"

"No. I'm not afraid. Are you?"

"Yes!" he screamed. "I'm terrified! You want the truth, that's it!"

Jane felt a heavy ache behind her eyes.

"And I'll give you one more piece of truth if you're interested. I didn't kill Luberman." He took a hit off the cigarette. "That's the one thing I figured out sitting here in this dump. I was awake when I found him in the staircase. Awake when I stomped on him. He was already dead. But I totally lost it when I called you. I couldn't seem to get my bearings. And then I took off, trashed your bathroom, left you to clean it up. I'm sorry, Jane. Might as well make 'I'm sorry' my mantra."

"What about the knife?" she said, squeezing her hands to fists inside her jacket pockets.

"What knife?"

"The one you took from my kitchen drawer."

He frowned, looked confused.

"It's molded stainless steel, all one piece, with a dimpled handle."

Light came into his eyes. "Oh, that. I wondered where it came from. It was in my duffel when I opened it at Joanna's apartment. I didn't want it, so I put it in one of her kitchen drawers. Why? What's so important about the knife?"

David had never been a good liar. She didn't think he was lying now, yet her own intuition wasn't enough. She had to prove he was innocent. "Come on. Let's go. I'll explain everything that's happened on the way back to my house."

"Wait a minute, wait a minute. We go to your house and then what? You adopt me? You hire me on as your wine steward? I don't have a life anymore, Jane. Did we forget that little detail?"

"Come on," she said, tugging on his hand. "Tomorrow, I'll drive you over to the university for your appointment. Remember? You're being tested. And then, we'll just have to wait to see what the doctors say."

He looked up at her. "That simple, huh."

"Yeah. I know what I'm doing. I'll keep you safe, and I'll keep me safe at the same time."

After snuffing out his cigarette, David stood. "What did I ever do to deserve you?" he said, crushing her in his arms.

35

Jane returned to Cordelia's loft the next morning around eleven-thirty. She used her key to let herself in. An energetic Mouse greeted her at the door with a wagging tale and breath that smelled like spaghetti sauce. "Jeez, Mouse. I can't turn my back on Cordelia for five minutes without her feeding you some crap." From the other side of the screen that separated the living room from the den, Jane could hear Cordelia's voice.

"Woowie wow! That must have been *really* fun."

Jane peeked around the screen. Cordelia was standing next to the desk, wearing a dark green football jacket with white leather sleeves over a loose gray cotton shirt that hung untucked over black leggings. She raised her eyebrows and mouthed, "Hattie."

"Finally," whispered Jane, lowering herself into a chair to listen.

"I yuv . . . I mean love you too, sweetheart," said Cordelia. She listened a moment more. "I know. I miss you tons and tons. But I'll see you tomorrow, okay? Can you wait just a little while longer?" She sat down, pinched the bridge of her nose with her free hand. "I know, Hatts. But it won't be long. And then, when you get home, we can make hot chocolate. I'll even make Fluffernutter sandwiches for us. What? Yes, we can watch *Mildred* again. I promise." She put her hand over the mouthpiece and whispered, "The kid loves the movie *Mildred Pierce*. Begs to watch it. Isn't she amazing?"

Back to the conversation with Hattie, Cordelia said, "I miss you, too. Listen, Hatts, we've only got a minute before Octavia comes back to your room, so give the phone to Cecily, okay? Oh, give me a kiss before you go." She listened, then smooched back. "Did you catch my kiss? What? No, Hatts, I can't see your new stuffed dog through the phone. Well, because you can't *see* through the phone, that's why. Can you see me? You can? Well, I guess my eyes aren't as good as yours. Now hurry, sweet pie. Give the phone to Cecily." She mimicked a scream, flung herself back against her chair, and closed her eyes. "Yes, I'm sure the doggie has pretty eyes. But I can't see them, okay. No, Hattie, even if you hold the doggie real close to the phone. Hattie, listen to me. I need to talk to Cecily. This is very important. No, honey, there are no monsters in your room, I promise." Except for your mother, she said under her breath.

Cordelia was at her wit's end when she finally breathed, "Cecily. Okay, what's the plan?" She looked down, chewed her lower lip. "Right, I'll be there. Eleven on the dot. Give Hattie a hug from me, okay? Tell her I miss her like crazy. I'll see you both tomorrow. Now hang up quick before the witch finds out you called."

Cordelia clicked off the phone and slumped in her chair. "I feel like I've been through a war."

"But a war you're winning," said Jane. "Sounds like Hattie is going to be dropped off tomorrow?"

"Radley's bringing her to the theater. Cecily told him that's where I'd be. Octavia has a morning massage." She rolled her eyes. "So she won't be coming along. Boo-hoo. I won't get to say good-bye in person. I know this sounds paranoid, Janey, but I won't relax until Hattie's home where she belongs."

"Apparently Octavia must've changed her mind. She thinks your loft is a safe place for Hattie to come home to after all."

Cordelia snorted. "What a crock. Cecily said she could tell that Octavia was about to go tilt. Being around a kid for so many days in a row was taking a definite toll. She wants to assert her mommy power, make me sweat, but in the end, she can't hold out forever. That's my one ace in the hole."

"I'm so glad you finally got a chance to talk to Hattie."

"What about you? How's David?"

Jane had called Cordelia last night after she and David got back to her house. She didn't want Cordelia to worry. "I just dropped him off at the U. He'll stay overnight so they can assess his sleep pattern. God, I hope, whatever it is that's wrong with him, that they find a way to help."

"What about the police? They want to talk to him, right?"

"I know," said Jane, playing with one of the snaps on her jeans jacket. "But I have no intention of telling the police where he is. It would only put off the meeting with this doctor, maybe indefinitely. The cops can wait. David can't." She glanced down at Mouse, who was sitting at her feet, his head resting on her knee. "Did you feed him spaghetti?"

"Me?" said Cordelia, innocence incarnate. "Certainly not. I know you have rules about what he can eat."

"Then he must have opened the can all by himself."

"Bad Mouse," said Cordelia, glaring down at him. "Hey, changing the subject, we've got to talk, girlfriend. I spent some time last night looking through the CD Nolan gave you. Guess what?"

"What?"

"There are two names on the list that we know. Personally."

"Who?"

"Well, Faye for one. Doesn't surprise me. Apparently, she's been writing Joanna for over twenty years, giving her advice on her love life. She wasn't in the supercrazy category, but she was definitely someone whose mail Joanna's gatekeepers continued to read."

"She kept writing even when Joanna didn't answer her?"

"They all did. Thousands of them. It's insane."

"What was the other name?"

Cordelia picked up a pencil and tapped it against her coffee mug. "Noel Dearborn, my intern at the Allen Grimby. He wrote her several times in the past few months. His name was only on the list because his last letter was nasty. He was mad that she didn't answer his first letter personally."

"You think *he* could've been the one who sent her flowers?"

Cordelia shook her head. "I don't know what to believe anymore. But here's the other piece of news. Joanna and Freddy have flown the coop."

"Meaning what?"

"You weren't the only one who didn't come home last night."

"Where are they?"

Cordelia tried to suppress a grin. "You'll never guess. They checked into a hotel down in Bloomington. They're getting married today! In their hotel room. It's all arranged."

"It is? They are?"

"And we're invited. Actually, they need us to be witnesses. It's all very hush-hush. Freddy went down to get the license yesterday. Didn't even pop the question until last night."

"So that's where they were," said Jane, recalling that Faye had said they'd left the building. "Freddy took her somewhere romantic and proposed to her?"

"Well, no," said Cordelia, picking up a pencil and tapping it against her coffee mug. "There's more to the story. Remember that woman we met at Flying Cloud last week? The one who wanted to interview Joanna?"

"Vaguely."

"Seems she tried to commit suicide last night. Slashed her wrists. When she was brought into the emergency room, she used the name 'Cordelia' and gave them Joanna's cell phone number as her next of kin. It was all a ruse. Joanna smelled a rat because they'd just seen me, but when she couldn't get me on the line—we must have been down in the basement talking to Bonifay in Madrid—she and Freddy called the goon squad and had a limo take them to the hospital. To hear Joanna talk about it, it was all pretty grim."

"Huh," said Jane. "I guess it makes sense then that Faye—" She stared at Cordelia, cocked her head. "No it doesn't."

"What doesn't?"

She thought it through for another couple of seconds. "When we knocked on Faye's door last night, she was surprised to see you. She gave the impression that she thought you were sick."

"Yeah, now that you mention it, I remember."

"But if she didn't talk to Joanna or Freddy before they left, then how did she know about that call? She must've thought you were at the emergency room. And if you were in the hospital, how could you be standing outside her door?"

Cordelia nodded, thinking it over. "She kept looking at me funny. I didn't understand why."

"Cordelia, think about it. There's no way she could have known about it unless she knew Hillary and Hillary told her. Or—"

"Or she'd bugged the loft?"

"Bugging equipment is easy to get your hands on and it doesn't take a rocket scientist to use. If she had access to the loft, and we know she did, she could have planted a bug before Joanna arrived."

"That's sick."

"She obviously feels deeply connected to Joanna if she's been writing her all these years."

"And she sure as hell doesn't like Freddy."

Jane stood and reached for the phone. Tapping in the numbers for the security detail downstairs, she waited through three rings until the line was picked up.

"Melby."

"This is Jane Lawless. I'm up in Cordelia Thorn's loft. I wonder if you could give me a call if you see Faye O'Halleron leave the building. She owns the loft next to Joanna Kasimir's up on four. She's in her seventies, about five-nine, dyed red hair—"

"I know her," said Melby. "You're in luck. She left about an hour ago. She goes out most days around ten, comes back in the early afternoon, sometimes with groceries."

"Great, thanks." As she clicked off the phone, she looked over at Cordelia. "Come on. I want you to search Joanna's loft for a bug, and while you're doing that, I'm going in to take a good long look at Faye's place. You got keys, right?"

"We've got to hurry, Janey. I promised Joanna that we'd be at the hotel by twelve-thirty. That's when the minister arrives. We don't want to keep them waiting."

Jane stood just inside Faye's front door, deciding what to look at first. The loft was essentially open, with bookcases and curio cabinets separating different sections. The living room was off to her right, a study off to the left. Nothing high-tech or electronic jumped out at her. She pulled back a long, mirrored folding door in Faye's bedroom and glanced into the closet. The apartment might smell like an ancient ashtray, but everything was neat and organized. And that's why a plastic sack stuffed haphazardly in the far corner behind a metal shoe rack caught her attention.

Crouching down, Jane pulled it free. Whatever was inside didn't weigh much. As she worked on the knot at the top, a whiff of something foul leaked out. She drew her head back and waved the stink away. When she finally got it open, she nearly gagged. Inside was a women's raincoat and gloves soaked in blood. "Jesus," she whispered, moving it aside with the tips of her fingers. Beneath the coat were Joanna's white jeans and blue silk shirt, the clothes she'd changed into after her flight to Minneapolis last week. The coat was by far the bloodiest—stiff near the collar, the sleeves still damp—but the jeans and shirt were also covered. The stench discouraged her from examining them any closer.

It was pretty clear what they meant. Joanna was the one who'd attacked Luberman with the knife. But why did Faye have them hidden in her closet? And how had Joanna known Luberman was coming to the lofts? He'd already been shot by an unknown assailant behind a downtown bar, so he was hurt, undoubtedly weakened. Had she seen him approach the building from her back window? Had she panicked? However she ended up in the stairwell, she must have done the deed, then rushed back to her loft to change out of her bloody clothes and try to hide the fact that she'd just committed a murder. She'd even come down to talk to the police, looking terrified, acting like she didn't know what had happened. Jane felt like a fool. It had never occurred to her that Joanna had been acting. Maybe the terror was real, but everything else was a lie, calculated to throw the police off the track. Worst of all, she'd allowed the police to think David might be the killer. She'd left her brother to swing in the wind while she'd gone off with Freddy to get married.

Jane glanced back down at the bloody clothes, then closed and tied the sack. She carried it out to the living room, then continued her search for anything electronic that Faye might have used as a monitoring device. It seemed more clear than ever that she knew what was going on inside Joanna's loft.

After a quick check of what appeared to be a guest bedroom, Jane entered the study. On the desk she found an old computer. Next to it was a personal address book. Behind and to the right of the computer was a lump covered by a flowered silk scarf. Jane pulled the scarf off the top.

"What have we got here?" she whispered. Easing back the desk chair, she sat down and stared at two tiny video monitors. She switched one on. Up flickered a black-and-white shot of Joanna's kitchen. She switched on the second one and found herself gazing at Joanna's bedroom. "This is sick," she said out loud. Playing with the dials on the front of the little monitor, she brought up the living room and the dining room. She heard some humming. Then a familiar voice burst into song: "And I . . . e . . I . . . e . . I will always love . . . *chocolate* . . . e . . I . . . e . . I . . . e . . I . . ."

Cordelia twirled through the living room, arms spread wide, searching high and low for a bug. She didn't look at all like Whitney Houston, but she had all the right moves.

Jane played with the sound. It was a little tinny but not bad. She turned it up to high as Cordelia continued to enumerate what she loved. Pistachios. Natalie Portman. Drambuie. Juliette Binoche. Ted Kooser. Silk underwear. It was getting a little repetitive and she was about to turn the sound down when a voice boomed, "What the hell?"

Jane whirled around to find Faye standing a few yards away, a grocery sack in each arm.

"You have no right—" Her voice shook with anger.

"I know about the bloody clothes." Jane stood and turned to face her. "And obviously you've been bugging Joanna's loft."

"Get out of here!"

"Not until you tell me what I want to know."

They stared each other down.

Turning on her heel, Faye headed into the kitchen, set the groceries on the counter, and out of habit, put the teakettle on to boil. "Who let you in here?" she demanded. "Was it Cordelia? I'll call the police, have them arrest her! Get out of here! You're invading my privacy!"

"I'm not the only one who's been invading privacy around here. Where did you find those clothes?"

"I'm not telling you a thing."

"Joanna killed a man."

"He deserved it."

"Did you see her do it?"

"I'd rather go to prison than say a word against her."

"Faye, that's just crazy. Do you really want to spend the rest of your life behind bars just to protect her?"

"Won't happen. Never. Not in a million years."

Jane heard the front door open and Cordelia call, "Janey, I didn't find a thing. But we gotta get going, otherwise Freddy and Joanna will have to find someone else to be witnesses at their wedding."

A tremor passed across Faye's face. "They're getting married?" she said, her voice full of disbelief. "Is that your idea of a joke?"

Cordelia sauntered into the kitchen. "Ooops," she said, glancing at Jane. "Busted. No, Faye. No joke. They're tying the knot this afternoon. You know what they say. It's better the second time around."

Faye looked down, her wiry eyebrows knit together. "She wouldn't do that. We talked about it. She agreed with me."

"Well, apparently she's changed her mind," said Cordelia, stuffing her hands into the pockets of her football jacket. "Jane?" She tilted her head toward the door. "Shall we go?"

But Jane kept her eyes on Faye. By the look on the old woman's face, she could tell that a fierce internal battle was being waged between her sense of loyalty and her feelings of betrayal.

Faye stood next to the stove, her hand massaging her temple. Suddenly, without warning, she swept the teapot off the burner.

Jane and Cordelia jumped back as it crashed to the floor in front of them, belching water all over the floor.

"No," she roared, shaking her hand, trying to wave away the pain. "After everything I've done for her!" cried Faye. "All these years, all my love and concern. And what does she do? She goes against everything I've tried to teach her! She might as well spit in my face! *Me! Me.*" Glaring at Jane, she said, "I've had it. I'm done. You want to know why I did what I did? I'll tell you."

36

Is that woman's brain made of cement or *what?*" demanded Faye, rubbing some antiseptic into her burn.

They were all seated at the kitchen table, Cordelia eating one of Faye's cookies.

"How could she do this to me? I had such plans for her, for our future together."

"Plans?" Jane repeated.

Faye's head snapped up. "You know, missy, you're on my shit list. And so are you, Cordelia. I assume you gave her the key so she could get in here."

"We're sorry," said Jane, hoping an apology might head off a rant.

"Yeah, well. I could call the police if I wanted to, you know, have you both arrested. But I won't." She lifted a pack of Chesterfields out of the pocket of her orange cardigan. "You both love Joanna, so I figure I can talk to you. The only thing I ask is, unless I decide different, whatever I say goes no farther than this room. You promise?"

Cordelia snorted. "Are you kidding—"

Jane kicked her under the table.

"Hey," she said, "what did I tell you about kicking—"

"We promise," said Jane, slapping Cordelia's back. "Right?"

"Right," said Cordelia, moving some fake sincerity through her vocal cords. "Yeah, mum's the word, Faye. *No problemo.*"

"Will you start at the beginning?" asked Jane. "So that everything's clear for us."

She tapped a cigarette out of the pack, grabbed a Bic lighter off the table, and lit up. "Okay. You're probably right. All this goes way back. I was still living in my old apartment in Bloomington when I read that interview you did with *The Rake,* Cordelia. It was a couple of years ago. I remember you said you were working on a deal to get Joanna to come to town to do a play. Well, I thought, hell, if I could just find out where you lived, I might get to meet her in person if I waited around outside your house long enough. When I found out you lived here, I told my real estate agent to get me in. It took him nearly fourteen months, but he did it. And then I wheedled my way into your poker game, got to know you. I never expected that Joanna would stay here when she came to town. You don't get lucky all that often in your life, but I was due for a break.

"Before Joanna arrived, I checked out what was available in surveillance equipment. It was all too complicated and expensive for me. I settled for two upscale but relatively cheap baby monitors. Amazing what you can do with technology these days. I know, I know. You're thinking, how could I do something like that? It's probably immoral. But when it comes to Joanna . . . I don't know how else to say this except, she's like my daughter. We have a real, important relationship. You don't know this, but I've been writing her for years. The letters are never returned, so that's proof she reads them. I hope I've helped her. I believe, in my heart, that I have. I've seen her take my advice more than once, so again, even though we'd never actually met, we had—through my letters. I thought maybe, when I introduced myself, that she'd recognize my name. When she didn't, I guess I was a little sad." Faye frowned. She seemed to get lost in her thoughts.

"Did you send her the flowers?" asked Jane.

"Huh? Oh, sure I did. I didn't know this Luberman fellow had sent her flowers, I just thought it was a sweet thing to do. I wanted her to know she was welcome here, loved, you know. That I was happy to see her."

"But you kept sending them even *after* you knew it was Luberman's calling card."

She lifted her head. "Well, but he was dead when I sent the last bouquet. Joanna must have known they couldn't be from him, so I didn't think it would be a problem. Actually, that was my way of telling her that they never *were* from him in the first place—they were from someone who truly loved her."

"Why didn't you sign your name?" asked Jane.

"Actually, I was about to tell her they were from me, her beloved letter-writing friend, when she went and agreed to marry Freddy. I mean, sleeping with that piss bag was bad enough, but marriage? I had to put the kibosh on that, and I mean fast."

"So you broke the mirror in her bathroom?" said Cordelia, tapping her fingers impatiently on the tabletop. "Left her that message saying not to cross you because you *owned* her."

"I was so mad. Can you blame me?"

In Faye's world, thought Jane, this twisted thinking must have a certain logic. "You owned her because you knew she'd killed Luberman."

Faye looked down at her sweater, began picking off some lint. "It wasn't very nice of me, I agree, but I was desperate. We'd talked about Freddy a lot last week. I thought I'd made myself clear—he was no good for her. She needed to listen to me! All that new movie script crap was just stardust he was blowing at her as a way to get her in bed. I told her she'd get down to South America and it would all fall through. No Kevin Spacey. No Tim Robbins. No Chris Cooper. Nothing. Just Freddy, his toupee, and his lecherous grin. *But,*" she said, holding up one finger, "she had nothing to fear from me. I would never have hurt a hair on her head. How could I? She's like my own daughter. Except, after what you just told me about her getting married today, I've come to the conclusion that she has some hard lessons to learn. Who am I to stand in the way of that? Sometimes, we *need* hard lessons so we can grow. That's what my mother always told me, and I believe it's true. I was just . . . I mean, I was hoping I could help

303

spare her more trouble. She's had enough in her life for twelve people. But if she's going to be hardheaded—"

"Did Joanna know you had her bloody clothes?" asked Jane.

Cordelia turned to Jane, a startled look on her face. "What bloody clothes?"

"I'll explain in a minute. Just let her talk."

"No," said Faye, tapping some ash on a saucer. "Unless she guessed. I suppose I should have been more direct. I should have told her I had them, blackmailed her into tossing Freddy out of her life. I blame myself for what's happening today."

"You were heading toward blackmail when you wrote that you owned her," said Jane.

"Yeah, I suppose, but she just never got the point. Again, my fault. If she'd just dumped Freddy, she could have gone on with her life as if nothing had happened."

"How did you get your hands on the clothes?" asked Jane, angry that in all her feelings of protectiveness, she'd never once considered David.

"Well, truth be told, Joanna isn't much of a criminal. After she knifed Luberman in the stairwell, she came back to her loft, stripped, then took a half-filled garbage bag from her kitchen and stuffed the clothes down inside. She showered, dressed, and then went out into the hallway and tossed the bag down the garbage chute. I ran down to the basement and retrieved it, just in case the police decided to check the Dumpster. I had to protect her, didn't I?"

"You watched all this on one of those video monitors I found in your study?" asked Jane.

"*Video?*" repeated Cordelia, locking eyes with Jane. "I leave you alone for ten minutes and you hit the friggin' jackpot."

"Sure, I watched it." Faye lifted her chin in defiance. "I taped my game shows, so I didn't miss anything while I was watching the monitors."

"But . . . how did Joanna know that Luberman would be in the stairwell?" asked Jane.

"Oh, that. It's kind of a long story."

"We've got time," said Jane.

"No we don't," whispered Cordelia out of the side of her mouth. She pointed at her watch.

"Faye," said Jane. "Would you excuse us a moment?"

Faye shrugged, reaching for a pack of cigarettes and firing another one up.

Jane walked Cordelia back to the front door. "Listen," she said, keeping her voice low, "I'll tell her you left to go to the wedding. Where the hell is it, anyway?"

"Flying Cloud Inn. It's close to the airport."

"Okay. Here's what you do. As soon as you're out of here, call the police. Tell them about Faye, the clothes, the baby monitors, everything. I can't leave until the police have her in custody. And also tell them about Joanna, about knifing Luberman. They need to get a squad car down to that hotel right away. Where were she and Freddy headed after the wedding?"

Cordelia bit a fingernail. "Switzerland. It's Freddy's wedding present. A private jet will be waiting for them at Flying Cloud field—they planned to leave directly after the ceremony."

"Hurry," said Jane. "Oh, and call Nolan. Tell him what's happened and that we'll meet him at the hotel as soon as we can. Wait for me outside in the parking lot."

"I feel like such a traitor," said Cordelia, her eyes rising to the ceiling.

"Feel any way you want," said Jane, opening the door and shoving her out, "but make those calls."

When she returned to the kitchen, Faye was putting away the groceries.

"Cordelia seemed pretty antsy about getting to that wedding," said Faye, cigarette dangling from the corner of her mouth. "I can't understand how a friend of Joanna's could approve of that vile man."

"Me, too," said Jane. "That's why I told her to go without me. I'd rather stay here and talk to you."

The comment seemed to please Faye. "You know, Jane, I'd call the police on them, but . . . I still can't bring myself to hurt Joanna. Do you think I'm being a bad mother?"

"Not at all." She gave it a few seconds, then said, "You were about to explain how Joanna knew Luberman was in the stairwell."

"Oh, right." She folded up the two empty sacks, then sat down on a kitchen stool. "Well, see, Freddy organized the whole thing. He told Joanna that he knew a guy who knew a guy, who . . . et cetera, et cetera. You get what I'm saying? He was friends with thugs who could get anything done for the right price. He hired a man to call Luberman and tell him that Joanna would pay him off if he'd just leave her alone. Half a million dollars. In cash. All he had to do was show up at this bar last Tuesday night, promise he'd never contact Joanna again, and the money was his. Joanna didn't think he'd bite, that he'd figure it was a setup, but he apparently showed up.

"The thug was supposed to put a bullet in Luberman and then get rid of the body. But something must have gone wrong. Luberman was shot, all right, but so was the other guy. The thug called Joanna around one forty-five in the morning. I couldn't hear his side of the conversation, but he must have told her to get out of the building fast. As soon as she hung up, she started to get dressed. I could tell she was in a panic, so I knew something had gone wrong. When she left her loft, I padded down the hall after her in my stocking feet. I didn't want to make any noise that would tip her off that I was following. I stayed back a ways, hid in the shadows, so she didn't see me. She must have met Luberman on the stairs as he was coming up. By the time I'd crept down the steps, she was kneeling next to his body, stabbing him over and over. It was like she couldn't stop. He wasn't moving. It made me so sick to my stomach that I came back to my loft and lost my cookies in the toilet." She waved away the memory.

"True to form, Freddy was out in L.A. that night. I never heard him say it, but I think he wanted an alibi. I assume a locked security building was supposed to be Joanna's. If only she'd never let him talk her into it, none of this would have happened. It's *all* Freddy's fault!"

"It must have been awful for you," said Jane, stalling for time.

"Yeah, it was. Nobody understands how much a mother worries. It's not a job for sissies, that's for sure." She crushed out her cigarette and immediately lit another. "I mean, there aren't any books on parenting that cover a situation like this. I've been thinking, maybe I should get rid of those bloody clothes. If it were up to you, what would you do?"

"I don't know," said Jane. "I'd have to think about it."

"I have half a mind to crash that wedding." She glanced at her watch. "Do you know where they're holding it?"

"Flying Cloud Inn."

"In Bloomington. I know the place." She thought a minute more. "Would you be up for it? I don't have a car, but you do. I'd have to change my clothes. Wouldn't take but a few minutes for me to get ready."

"Sure," said Jane. "I suppose."

"You wait right here." She got down off the stool, stubbed out the cigarette, and went back to her bedroom.

Instead of staying put, Jane returned to the living room. If the police didn't arrive before Faye got dressed, she'd simply have to think of another way to stall. But just as she stuffed the bloody clothes sack behind a chair, out of Faye's direct line of sight, she heard a key slip into the lock. A moment later, three policemen filled the doorway. She pointed them to the sack, told them about the monitors in the study, then explained that Faye was in the bedroom changing her clothes. Satisfied now that three armed cops were on the scene, Jane headed out the door.

37

She won't come out of the room," said Nolan, pulling Jane and Cordelia aside as they entered the lobby of the hotel. "She's got a gun, says she'll use it on herself if the police try to break in."

On the way to Bloomington, Jane had called Nolan to tell him that Freddy was involved, too. She gave him all the details. Nolan said he'd pass it on.

"Where's Freddy?" asked Jane, glancing down a hallway and seeing a bunch of uniforms milling around.

"He broke a window and climbed out when he heard the sirens, but two officers caught him as he was making a run for it across a field just west of the building. Good thing the cops got here when they did. All thanks to you two."

"How come Joanna didn't go with him?" asked Cordelia, unbuttoning her football jacket.

Nolan shook his head. "No idea."

"Where's the room?"

"It's a suite. Down the hall, across from the pool."

"Are they married?" asked Jane.

Nolan nodded to a young man sitting in the hotel's deserted coffee shop. He was talking to another, older man, probably a detective in plain clothes. "That's the guy who performed the service. They used two cleaning women for their witnesses. Now that they're legal, they can't be forced to testify against each other."

"Is *that* why they did it?" asked Cordelia, her jaw dropping.

"You'll have to ask Joanna. Freddy's out in one of the squad cars. He refuses to talk until he has a lawyer present."

"But what about Joanna?" said Cordelia. "Maybe I can talk to her, get her to listen to reason." She turned and rushed for the hallway. A cop who was standing guard near the entrance stopped her. "Sorry, ma'am. Off limits. You shouldn't even be in the building."

"I'm the one who friggin' called you! You wouldn't even *be* here if it wasn't for me. *Joanna!*" she shouted. "It's me. Cordelia. I'm here for you, babe! Tell them to let me in and we'll talk."

The response was loud and clear. Through the wall, everyone heard Joanna scream, "If you let her in here, I'll not only shoot myself, I'll shoot her, too!"

Cordelia blinked. "I . . . I don't understand. She must not be in her right mind."

The cop pushed her back into the lobby.

"A uniformed neanderthal isn't going to kick me out of here!" she sputtered.

"It's okay, Cordelia," said Nolan, holding up his hand and nodding to the cop that he'd take care of it. "We're all cleared to be in here. We just can't go back to the room."

Two hours later, they were seated at one of the tables in the empty coffee shop when Dreashon Johnson walked up, pulled out a chair, and sat down.

He crossed his hands on the table, eyed each one of them briefly, then said, "We've been talking to Ms. Kasimir on the hotel phone, trying to get her to agree to let one of our people in. Unfortunately, she refuses." He glanced at Nolan, then looked directly at Jane. "She asked if you were here, Ms. Lawless. Said she'd be willing to talk to you."

Cordelia nearly erupted out of her chair. "Why Jane? Why not me?"

Johnson shifted his gaze to Cordelia, said nothing, then turned back to Jane. "Ordinarily, I wouldn't even consider it, except that we spoke to Mr. Kasimir. He said he didn't have a gun with him, and he's almost positive Joanna didn't either. I talked to him for quite a while. I could be wrong, but I feel like he cares about her, that he wants her out of there safely." Fingering a sticky spot on the table, he continued, "We could fit you with a protective vest. Other than that, you'd be on your own. But we'd be right outside. What do you say? It might be the only way to get her out of there."

Jane had worn body armor before, so it wasn't something new. "Okay," she said, feeling her palms begin to sweat.

As she started to get up, Johnson stopped her. "Even if she doesn't have a gun, she could have some other kind of weapon. A fork or a knife from a dinner tray. Scissors. You'll have to play it very carefully."

"I intend to," said Jane.

After being fitted with the vest, she slipped her jacket back on. As she was led back through the front lobby, she saw Cordelia sitting morosely in one of the chairs. There wasn't much she could say to make her feel better.

Johnson accompanied her down the hall to Room 122. He knocked, then called, "Ms. Kasimir? Jane's here. Open up."

A few seconds later, the bolt was thrown from inside and the door eased back a crack. "Don't try anything or we'll all be sorry," came Joanna's voice.

Jane glanced at Johnson, feeling the blood pump hard in her chest. Nolan had taught her that in tense situations, she needed to slow everything down, stay focused. And that's what she did. She breathed in slowly, let it out slowly. She did that a couple of times and then said, "It's me, Joanna. I'm coming in."

The room was pitch-dark. Jane could sense a body standing next to her.

"Walk away from the door," said Joanna. Her voice held no warmth.

As she moved a few steps farther into the room, the bolt snapped back into place behind her.

"Sit down on the floor," said Joanna.

It took a few seconds for Jane's eyes to adjust. When they did, she noticed that a crack in the curtains let in a thin sliver of light. It wasn't much, but it was enough. Joanna was still wearing her wedding dress. She rustled over to a chair across the room. "Where's the gun?" asked Jane. She sat down on the floor by the bed, leaned her back against the frame.

"Don't worry, I don't plan to use it on you."

If that was supposed to make her feel better, it didn't. "How come you asked for me?"

"Because I wanted to talk to someone other than the police."

"Why not Cordelia?"

Joanna laughed. "She having a fit about that?"

"Yeah, pretty much."

"I'm sorry. I didn't mean to hurt her. But, like I said, I wanted a conversation, not an argument. Now that you're here, I need you to do me a favor."

Jane waited.

"Do you have your cell phone with you?"

"Yes."

"Mine's dead. And they won't let me call out on the hotel phone. I want you to call Abbott Northwestern Hospital. Give them my name and tell them you were there last night to see Hillary Schinn or no, 'Cordelia.' She was in the emergency room. I need to know how she's doing."

Jane held up both hands. "The cell's in the pocket of my jacket."

"Go ahead," said Joanna. "Get it out."

Jane pulled it free and flipped it open. "Hillary. She's the woman we met at Flying Cloud the day you arrived. The one who'd tried to commit suicide last night."

"I see the real Cordelia's filled you in. Make the call." She switched on the light next to her.

Jane punched in the number for directory assistance and had them connect her.

Joanna watched steadily, her hands busily kneading the fabric of her skirt. She looked like a wreck of a human being, her eyes too bright, her skin impossibly pale.

It took a few minutes, but Jane finally got the information Joanna wanted. "Looks like she's doing much better. The nurse expects her to make a full recovery."

Joanna exhaled, bowed her head. After nearly a minute of silence, she looked up and said, "This may sound strange to you, Jane, but I don't know what I would have done if she'd died."

"But you hardly knew her."

"Doesn't make any sense to me, either. After I saw her last night, I couldn't get her face out of my mind. There's no logic to it. If Gordon were here, he'd put it in some larger philosophical context."

"Gordon?"

Her head fell back against the chair. "Yeah. He was always good at throwing around big words like he understood them. 'Redemption.' 'Freedom.' 'Meaning.' 'Love.' Sometimes I think he did understand them—at least, better than I did."

Jane prayed that Joanna would leave the light on. It was easier to track her mood if she could see her face, watch her eyes.

As if reading her mind, Joanna switched the light back off. "I like the dark. Gordon said we all lived in the dark. That's why we needed to find a star to navigate by. Gordon said he'd be that star for me. I wanted so badly for that to be true."

"Are you saying that you actually loved him?"

Her voice had softened. "Ever since I was a kid, I've felt like something huge and vital was missing inside me. Like I had only one lung. Or half a heart. I thought if I just pursued my dreams, when I achieved them, *they* would fill the void. It never happened. Maybe religion fills that need in some people. Maybe what I craved was a sense of safety— or certainty. Whatever it was, those first few days I spent with Gordon, that feeling went away. I was happy in a way I'd never been before or since. I don't understand it. I don't like it. How can the man who ruined my life also be the only one I ever loved? Because I think that's what it was, Jane. Love. What's worse, *what* I loved wasn't even real."

In the darkness, Jane could just make out Joanna's body huddled in the chair, hands in her lap. She was a crumbling soul trying to understand her past.

"Freddy's a good man. He says he loves me, that he never stopped. It's funny, but I believe him. The only problem is, I never loved him. I still don't. But he's a good man. More than that, he's funny, smart—everything I'm not. He doesn't see that I'm really a very average person. I just happen to have an attractive façade, one that others have used to project images on." She paused, then said, "Do you think I'm shallow, Jane?"

"Of course not."

"No, I want your real opinion."

"I'm not sure I want to play this game with someone holding a gun."

Joanna laughed. "I see your point. But I'm serious. I respect you. I always have. And I promise I won't hurt you. I'd just like an honest answer."

Jane didn't like being put on the spot. There was something she wanted to say, but she wasn't sure this was the time.

"Come on, Jane. Do you think I'm shallow?"

"I'm not sure I'd use that word."

"What word would you use?"

"Well." She drew her legs up to her chest. "It seems kind of strange to me that I've been in here for over ten minutes and you haven't asked once about David. You knew he'd run away. You killed Luberman, but you let the police think David had. How could you do that?"

The words seemed to startle her. "But they know the truth now."

"Yes, but couldn't you see that David's in terrible shape? Have you got any idea what it's been like for him these last few days? He thought he might go to jail, Joanna. Do you know what that can do to a guy who's already living on the edge?"

"I never would have allowed it."

"*He* didn't know that. He's sick. Has been for months. If you weren't so fixated on yourself, you might have noticed it."

"I . . . I did," she countered. "He and Diego are having problems. Diego's been sleeping around."

313

"No he hasn't. You don't have a clue what's going on with your brother. And I think that speaks volumes."

Joanna sat up straighter. "I'm selfish? Uncaring?"

Jane didn't answer. She prayed that Johnson was right, that Joanna didn't have a gun.

The quiet that replaced their conversation felt thick and corroded.

Finally, Joanna stood. "You're right, Jane. I'm a selfish bitch. Incapable of love."

"I didn't say that."

"Sure you did. I'm not sure I disagree." She stepped away from the chair. As she passed Jane, she paused and dropped the gun in her lap. "Will you do me one last favor?"

"Anything."

"Tell Cordelia how glad I am that she has Hattie in her life now. For a long time, I thought she might be suffering from the same malady as me—that she had lots of lovers but didn't know how to love in return. Gordon was right about one thing. You do need a guiding star in this dark, dark world." With that, she turned and, head held high, crossed to the door and walked out into the arms of the waiting police.

38

The next morning, Jane carried two cups of coffee and one cup of hot chocolate into Cordelia's office at the theater.

"Zero minus five minutes and counting," said Cordelia, looking at her watch. She was sitting behind her desk, two large pink stuffed bunnies on either side of her, gifts for the returning Hattie.

"You need some of this," said Jane, setting one of the coffees down in front of her.

"Cream and sugar?"

"The requisite amount."

"Good woman." She rubbed her hands together. "And the hot chocolate?"

"In the small cup."

"Excellent. Now, what should we talk about? You have to take my mind off my anxiety, Jane. I'm close to total meltdown."

"You don't think Radley will show up on time?"

"Or that they'll be in a car wreck, or that Radley will slip into a fugue state and forget where he is. Or that—"

"I get it," said Jane, lowering herself into a chair on the other side of the desk. "You're catastrophizing."

"And I do it so well. Speaking of that, I called my new lawyer this

315

morning. No more living on borrowed time. I'm about to sue my sister for legal and physical custody of Hattie. The papers should be drawn up by early next week."

"Wonderful," said Jane. "You've got a good lawyer?"

"My personal attorney says she's the best. Now, entertain me, Jane. Sing something. Recite a poem. Tell me something I don't know."

"Okay, I talked to David before I drove over here."

"Ah, yes. David. I'm glad you finally decided to tell me what was really going on with him."

"Well, I had to distract you last night, *too,* remember? You were pretty upset about Joanna and Freddy when we got back to the loft."

"Magnanimous diva that I am, I've forgiven her for talking to you instead of to me. I see now that she didn't want to put my life in danger."

"That's right," said Jane, coughing into her fist. "I'm more disposable."

"Not to me, you're not. So tell me about David." She laced her fingers together over her ample bosom.

"He's spending another night at the sleep lab. But he did have an episode last night, which was good. They think they might have a handle on what's wrong with him. And it's treatable. They've put him on something called Klonopin. They want him to stay in town for a week or so, so they can adjust the dosage. But if all goes well, he can fly back to Atlanta next weekend."

"The police let him completely off the hook?"

"Well, technically, they could charge him. Mutilation of a dead body, or something like that. But Nolan didn't think it was very likely."

"All good news." She looked at her watch, shook it, then lifted it to her ear to make sure it was still ticking.

"Nolan called me on my cell as I was pulling into the parking lot downstairs. I asked him if he'd heard anything about Joanna and Freddy. He said they'd lawyered up—separate lawyers, which he said was smart. He thought both of them would be out by late this afternoon."

"It's all so awful. They're looking at a long trial, major prison time."

"Actually, Nolan said he'd be surprised if Joanna even served a day. She's got a great case for self-defense. And she's a celebrity. The public adores her, so jurors will instinctively want to believe the best about her. And as for Freddy and the thug he hired to murder Luberman, Nolan thinks they'll have a hard time proving it. Faye may testify—or she may not. If the DA cuts her a deal over the concealing evidence and unlawful surveillance charges, maybe she'll talk. But if she doesn't, who knows? They don't even have a lead on who the thug might be. He called Joanna from a cell the night he botched the murder, but it was one of those throwaway cell phones. Can't be traced. Nolan figured a good defense lawyer could make it all go away. All except for the death of the security guard. Freddy would still be on the hook for that."

"Time will tell, I guess," said Cordelia. She looked at her watch again. "Two minutes."

"You know, he might not be here right on the dot."

"He better be," she said, a snarl in her voice. She turned and patted one of the stuffed rabbits. "Say, how's your house coming along?"

"The rugs and the furniture will be moved back in today. I can sleep in my own home again tonight."

"I'll miss you," said Cordelia. "It was fun having you around."

"Excuse me," said Cordelia's secretary, knocking softly on the door. "There's a man out here to see you. He says his name is Cunningham, that you were expecting him."

"It's *just* him? Isn't Hattie with him?"

"Um, no, Cordelia. It's just the man."

"I'll kill him!" She exploded out of her chair. But before she could get to the door, Radley appeared.

Cordelia was right. He did look a little like Clive Owen. Dark hair, dark stubble, intense eyes, almost a Roman face. But heavier, older.

"Where's Hattie!"

He was wearing a long trench coat and held a brown fedora in his hands. He looked rumpled, the way Englishmen often looked to Jane. Like they needed tending, as her English grandmother used to say.

"She's not with me," said Radley.

"I can see that! Where *is* she?"

"Can we talk privately for a second?" He glanced at Jane.

"Anything you have to say to me can be said in front of her. Now talk!"

He closed the door. "You see, Hattie's with Octavia and Cecily," he said, leaving Cordelia standing by the door. He sat down on a chair next to Jane. "They flew back to London this morning."

Cordelia turned to look at him. "Say that again?"

"I have a home there, and one in Northumberland. Don't worry, she's being well cared for."

"You promised you bring her here, back to *me*."

"I know," he said, looking down at his hat. "That's what I wanted to talk to you about."

Holding her body rigid, Cordelia returned to her chair and sat. "Speak. Make it fast, unless you want to see a middle-aged woman have a heart attack right in front of you."

A smile tugged at his mouth. "You're really a lot like your sister."

"No, I'm not!"

Pressing his lips together, he said, "What Octavia didn't tell you the other day was that she and I are married, have been for almost seven months. It was a private ceremony at my home in London."

"Well, that must make you feel really special to be one of a dozen."

Again he looked down. "You're quite a lot like your sister, actually."

"Get to the point."

"Octavia has been wanting to make some changes in her life. Part of that has to do with Hattie. I've always wanted a child, and Octavia has been hoping to spend more time with her. She's an amazing little girl. I know a great deal of that has to do with you. She's very well adjusted, knows she's loved, feels at ease in the world."

"You're right. She sure as hell didn't get that from Octavia."

He gave a slow nod. "But the great thing about life is that sometimes we get second chances. That's what Octavia craves. Neither one of us wants to shut you out of her life. You can come visit whenever you want. Call, or write. As far as her coming to visit you here in Minneapolis, we'd like to keep her with us for the next year or two, but after that, I'm sure we can work out something that will be good for all of us. Sensible. Maybe she could spend the summer. Or Easter vacation."

Jane could see that Cordelia was about to come apart at the seams. Her face was ashen, but her eyes glittered. "Easter vacation? You think that's a *sensible* solution, do you?"

"I knew you'd be upset. And I'm very, very sorry. But Octavia *is* her mother. That trumps everything."

"Even Hattie's welfare?"

"Motherhood is an unbreakable bond."

"You silly man," she said, her voice quivering with suppressed fury. "That bond is broken all the time. You think there's something sacred about biology? A mother is as a mother *does*. What's sacred in this world is love—real down deep and dirty love. The kind that changes diapers and cleans up vomit. The kind that sits up all night with a kid because she's sick or scared. The kind that helps a little girl learn to love Brie, or introduces her to noir movie classics! Has Octavia *ever* done *any* of those things?"

Radley stared at her. After a long moment, he said, "Honestly, I don't know."

"Well I do. The answer is no."

"I'm sorry this is so hard for you."

"Did you think it would be easy?"

"No," he said, his voice grown soft. "It wouldn't be easy for anyone to leave Hattie."

Slowly, like a volcano spewing in slow motion, Cordelia stood and pointed at the door. "Get out of here."

"I wish we could have come to a better understanding."

"I understand perfectly. Octavia's finally found herself a guy who likes kids. You're not her usual type, but then, at her age, I expect she's getting desperate. You're the one who wants Hattie, not Octavia. If you don't see that, you're a bigger fool than even *I* think you are. So you better be prepared to be a single parent, Radley. On the other hand, don't get too comfortable in that position. You can tell Octavia from me that I'm suing for custody of Hattie— both legal and physical. And maybe, just maybe, I'll let you see her for Easter vacation in a couple of years. That seem fair to you?"

Radley stood. He seemed to hesitate. There was clearly something more he wanted to say, but in the end, he put on his hat and left.

Jane was there to catch Cordelia when she fell backward, almost missing her chair. Jane guided her down safely.

Looking up with desperate eyes, Cordelia said, "What am I going to do, Jane?"

"Just what you said."

"What did I say?"

Jane crouched down next to her. "You're going to be Cordelia M. Thorn. You're going to be strong. And you're going to be smart. You've got a good lawyer, and you've got a chance."

"And you'll be there to help me, right?"

Taking Cordelia's hands in hers, Jane said, "Always."